"Auchincloss, who is probably the foremost novelist of manners in the country and who is also a partner [in a law firm] . . . is one of the few major American writers to take business as his subject. . . . For nearly 40 years, Auchincloss has been chronicling the changes in the world of finance and law. There is *The Great World and Timothy Colt*, with its fiduciary fraud . . . Wills and estates is Auchincloss's field, and on the surface, it seems rather quiet. But, as Auchincloss has written in *The Great World and Timothy Colt*, this branch of the law offers 'the drama of family struggles, of veiled lady clients interviewed mysteriously behind closed doors.' Many of Auchincloss's novels draw on his practice, and he's one of the few authors who can make the complicated differences between a charitable trust and a foundation sound interesting. . . .

"These days, as society becomes more interested in business and in manners, Auchincloss is coming into his own as a kind of latter-day Saint-Simon, a man who has defined his age."

—*New York Magazine*

"People who have followed the writing career of Louis Auchincloss have been waiting for him to tackle the downtown legal world head-on in a novel. . . . Now, with *The Great World and Timothy Colt*, he has done it, and has done it well, bringing to this task the qualities that were to be found in almost all of his earlier work: a limpid style, an easy skill at letting his characters come alive through dialogue, a willingness to deal with important issues and an ability to dramatize them in human terms."

—*New York Times*

"Mr. Auchincloss is proving himself an authority on the kind of people whose grandparents were so ably dissected by Edith Wharton and Henry James."

—*Christian Science Monitor*

"An absorbing adult novel."

—*Best Sellers*

ALSO BY LOUIS AUCHINCLOSS

FICTION

The Indifferent Children
The Injustice Collectors
Sybil
A Law for the Lion
The Romantic Egoists
Venus in Sparta
Pursuit of the Prodigal
The House of Five Talents
Portrait in Brownstone
Powers of Attorney
The Rector of Justin
The Embezzler
Tales of Manhattan
A World of Profit
Second Chance
I Come as a Thief
The Partners
The Winthrop Covenant
The Dark Lady
The Country Cousin
The House of the Prophet
The Cat and the King
Watchfires
Narcissa and Other Fables
Exit Lady Masham
The Book Class
Honorable Men
Diary of a Yuppie

NONFICTION

Reflections of a Jacobite
Pioneers and Caretakers
Motiveless Malignity
Edith Wharton
Richelieu
A Writer's Capital
Reading Henry James
Life, Law and Letters
Persons of Consequence: Queen Victoria
and Her Circle
False Dawn: Women in the
Age of the Sun King

THE
GREAT WORLD
AND
TIMOTHY COLT

Louis Auchincloss

McGRAW-HILL BOOK COMPANY

New York   St. Louis   San Francisco
Toronto   Hamburg   Mexico

Reprinted by arrangement with Houghton Mifflin Co.

First McGraw-Hill Paperback edition, 1987

1 2 3 4 5 6 7 8 9 A R G A R G 8 7

ISBN 0-07-002445-6

LIBRARY OF CONGRESS CATALOGING-IN-PUBLICATION DATA

Auchincloss, Louis.
  The great world and Timothy Colt.
  I. Title.
PS3501.U25G7 1987   813'.54   87-4197
  ISBN 0-07-002445-6 (pbk.)

For Parky and Elizabeth Shaw

PART ONE

TIMOTHY

1

ANN COLT enjoyed breakfast with her family more than any other part of her day. Well, perhaps not more than the part in the late evening when Timmy came home from the office and they drank two old-fashioneds before she even thought of supper. But at breakfast Timmy could linger over the paper and his coffee without feeling guilty about it; even he realized that the office didn't mind a man's being late who worked as many nights as he did. And George and Walter would drink their milk in the slightly doped way of children who have slept too long and ask questions that even they did not expect to be answered. Ann, going to the kitchen for more coffee, would look out the window and catch a glimpse, between the two red multilateral apartment houses across the way, of sunlight on the grey surface of the East River. In a few minutes Timmy would be off and the boys to school; she would have their images if not their presence; she could turn from the window and the great new apartment development that she so oddly loved, all red brick and grass, treeless, the tall buildings lonely for not being shoulder to shoulder, and know that happiness for a whole day could be contained in a single moment.

"Daddy, do you ever see criminals downtown?" George was asking. "Do you, Daddy?" He stuck his round chin forward, his eyes challenging Timmy.

"Not ones I recognize as such." Timmy did not even look up.

"What would you do if you did?" George persisted. "Would you defend one? Would you be a mouthpiece?"

"George, you know perfectly well I'm not that kind of a lawyer. I don't argue in court."

"What do you do then? Shuffle papers?"

"Yes," Timmy agreed, still reading the newspaper. "I shuffle papers. As you do in school."

"But we *speak* in our class," Walter protested, looking to his older brother for confirmation. "We have public speaking. And next year we have debates. George debates now, don't you, George?"

"It just goes to show," Timmy said placidly, "how much better it is to be in school than downtown."

Ann resumed her place at the table with the coffee. "You know your father's only joking," she told George. "He does lots more than shuffle papers downtown. He gives advice to all sorts of important men, and that's why we can have the things we do have and can go to Ketauset in the summer."

Both boys looked at her in disgust. She had broken into a mood of masculine unity. Timmy they might regard with superiority, but it was a friendly superiority. Basically, he was one of them. Given half a chance, he might measure up. But she, the warner, the fusser, whose female literalism prohibited important communication, was, like the majority of mothers, impossible.

"Time for school," she warned them. "Get your hats and coats, boys."

They left the table in a sudden joint rush, and she wondered, with a touch of complacency, if two such self-centered and aggressive beings could ever brood as mistily as she had in her own childhood.

"You shouldn't run yourself down before them," she said to Timmy. "George can't conceive that anyone could say he did nothing but shuffle papers if it wasn't so. And Walter believes George."

"It's lucky he has someone to look up to."

It was always this way about the boys. He treated them as adults not so much from any deference to seven- and six-year-olds as from an inner attitude of: Who am *I* to treat them otherwise? They loved him for it, and in time, perhaps, would admire him. If they ever took after him. George was dark like his father and had something of the same steady, faintly curious look in his eyes, but he was plump and quick and loud, and Walter, though a tough child and muscular for his years, had a certain undeniable coarseness of feature under his curly blond hair that she uneasily felt must have come from her family. Neither, so far at least, had anything of Timmy's charm.

"One of the best things about this apartment is having a

school in the same block," she observed. "It at least gives us some time to be alone together."

"We were lucky to get it," he grunted without looking up.

"We were lucky to get it seven years ago," she corrected him. "We were lucky not to have to go on living with your mother. We're not lucky to be in it still."

He looked up now and gazed at her. "Why? Don't you like it?"

"It's not that I don't like it. That's not the point." She paused. "Timmy, can I ask you something?"

"Why, sure." She saw his eyes just glance at the clock on the mantel.

"Where are we going this summer?"

"Why, wherever you want, I guess," he answered, surprised. "What about Ketauset again? The boys seemed to like it. Maybe we could get that same house."

"When are you going to take your vacation?"

"You know how Knox is." He shrugged. "August, I suppose."

"Which is just what I want to talk about," she said, determined to be firm. "Darling, I don't want to do what we do every summer, wait till the last minute and then grab some ramshackle beach house that no one else wants and have you leave me and the boys after a week when Mr. Knox calls you back to town." She paused to swallow, suddenly tense; she had his attention now. "I want to plan ahead and get a proper house near someone we know who has children the same age as ours. And I want to take the boys there for two months and have you come on weekends when you're not on vacation." She paused for breath. "There!"

"Well!" He was smiling at her. "How long have you been storing this up?"

"For a long time, Timmy!" she cried, afraid suddenly that he would laugh her out of it. "For months!"

"Well, honey, of course, we can do it," he said soothingly. "I think it's a fine idea. Why don't you see what sort of house you can get?"

"Not unless you promise me you'll be there a full month!"

He looked across the table and smiled. "I promise."

"Oh, Timmy," she said bitterly. "You're only joking with me, and you shouldn't. Because I *care* so!"

"Well, really, Ann," he said with a slight frown, "are you being quite fair? You don't suppose I *like* to stay in New York in the heat, do you?"

"I sometimes wonder what you like, Timmy. Honestly, I do."

"What's got into you, anyway? You know what working for Knox is." He folded his paper brusquely. "You know that I can't control my hours and vacations. And you've always been a great sport about it. Why cut up now?"

"Because the children are getting older. Because you and I are getting older, that's why!"

"Darling, if you're going to get philosophical, let's save it for tonight, shall we?" He stood up. "I must get to the office."

"Timmy," she protested, jumping up after him, "please! This is important. It's taken me weeks to get up the courage to say it. If we put it off now, I never will!"

He saw the earnestness in her eyes and, after a pause, nodded. "The floor is yours, Ann," he said, sitting down again. "Shoot."

"You say that I know about your work," she began tensely, "and that I've always been a sport about it. I don't know if that is true. I used to think that *nobody* could practice law in Sheffield, Knox and have anything left of a private life. I used to think the wives just had to make the best of it. But that isn't quite the case, Timmy. Larry Duane always takes August off. So does Austin Cochran. I know what they say about you."

"What?" His tone was sharper.

"That if the work wasn't there, you'd make it."

"That's perfectly ridiculous!" he exploded. "I may work harder than they do, but that's my way of getting things done. And done right, damn it!"

"Even if it kills you? Even if it keeps your family from leading a normal, sensible life?"

His eyes were suddenly suspicious. "What do you mean by that?"

"Just what I say." She sat down suddenly, feeling weak. "Timmy, I should have said this long ago. I've been putting it off and off. The whole thing has been as much my fault as yours. More, really. Because I love our life. Too much."

"Are you crazy?" he demanded, staring at her. "Why shouldn't you?"

"I've loved the things I haven't had to do," she continued, shaking her head. "Not having to live in the suburbs and cope with women's groups. Not having to be social or keep up with the Joneses or even be a good cook. Seeing only office people and their wives on Saturday night drinking parties. Being able to read all day while the boys are at school. Oh, Timmy, I've indulged myself!"

"And what's wrong with that, I'd like to know!" he protested. "You've been a good wife and a good mother and *I* think, a good cook. Why shouldn't you read all day? And why shouldn't I work the way I like? If we're happy, what the hell?"

"Because we're getting older," she explained patiently. "You're going to be made a partner one of these days. Oh, I know you're superstitious about mentioning it, but you are. And some day you're going to be—I don't know. Rich, maybe." She shrugged almost angrily at the idea of such a thing mattering. "And some day, too, you and I have got to stop living in an apartment that's too small for us because we're too preoccupied to leave it. And we ought to start seeing *some* people outside the office. And go away sensibly in the summer and make plans in advance and even sometimes go to a play or an opera. Oh, I don't mean that we have to change much, Timmy!" she exclaimed, unable to bear his hurt look. "Only a little. We have to grow up, darling. Now the boys are growing up. We have to be like other people. Now and then."

"I don't know if I see what you mean," he said in a dryer tone, staring down at the surface of the table, "but I know one thing. If you don't like things the way they are—"

"But I do, darling, that's the point!"

"If you don't think it's right for us, then," he continued firmly, "you must draw up a plan, that's all. We'll change it any way you like. Only you'll have to do the changing."

"But will you *admit* that we live rather differently from most people?" she begged.

"Not fundamentally, no."

"Oh, not fundamentally, of course," she agreed quickly. "Everything fundamental's all right. That's not what I'm worried about."

"Well, think it out, dear," he said in a gentler tone, getting up, "and we'll talk about it. As I say, we'll do it your way. I guess we have been rather stodgy, at that." He leaned down to kiss her on the cheek. "And I really *must* get to the office."

When he had gone she did not take up a book as usual, but sat on, rather dismally, with the empty coffee cups. She was not assured by his promise; she had learned from experience, not to distrust his sincerity, but to comprehend his inertia. He would be quite capable of barely recalling their discussion when he came home that evening. And had she the right to make him? Looking about the living room in which she had spent so many of her waking hours, at the large green rug, the one expensive thing they had ever bought, that went so badly with the red overstuffed sofa on permanent loan from Mrs. Colt, at George's electric train from last Christmas, still holding down a whole corner of the room although the boys had lost interest in it, at the photograph of Timmy's destroyer entering Golden Gate, at the built-in bookcases, waist level, containing her secondhand sets of Victorian novelists, her paperbacks, her accumulated magazines, she wondered if it didn't suit her, the unromantic, far better than it could ever suit him. Didn't it go, fundamentally, with sandy hair that was too prim when set and too messy a day later, with brown eyes that had a tendency to be too reproachful, with her rather colorless skin that would never tan in summer, her small, slightly hooked nose and the oval chin raised in stubbornness rather than determination? She hated her quality of mild desperation, of hoping that her hair was brushed and her dress straight, of trying too hard and working at cross purposes to her own wishes, so that the very tug that was meant to straighten the skirt was the one that revealed the slip to anyone standing behind. Should she not be down on her hands and knees thanking God for the miracle of Timmy's acceptance of their way of life instead of trying to change it? And leaving the dishes, she wandered about the room, looking for something that she could read even as preoccupied as she was, until, giving it up, she turned up the radio in the kitchen and listened, as she cleared the table, to the overamplified strains of a Brandenburg Concerto.

2

COMING OUT of the office elevator, Timmy passed the sober bronze plaque that bore the legend "Sheffield, Knox, Stevens

& Dale." As when these names appeared after the "Very truly yours" at the end of a terse legal opinion, giving no hint of the complex research that had preceded it, so the simple label failed to herald the size of the two great floors that lay beyond. One might have anticipated a handful of brief-littered offices with roll-top desks, never the regular outline of long, wide corridors, lined with grey walls and glazed interior windows, ballooning at intervals into vast rooms, two stories high, with balconies running about the middle of their walls: the library, the file room, the accounting department, so that a visitor had an impression of wandering through the bright, clean avenues of an ordered city from park to park. Along the passageways were the offices of the associate lawyers, or clerks, identical except for the size and number of occupants, with cream-colored walls, cabinet bookcases and lithographs of English judges and cartoons of barristers from *Vanity Fair.* In the center was the reception room, again a two-storied space with a circular Georgian stairway and life-size portraits by Sargent of Mr. Sheffield and the late Judge Livermore. The stairway led up to the offices of the senior partners, decorated according to the individual taste of each, varying from the mahogany gleam of Mr. Knox's old-fashioned room to the smooth grey quarters of Mr. Stevens with aluminum models of airplanes and signed photographs of young generals emerging from jet machines. The whole great hushed interior, with its hum of muted typewriters, its discreet scurrying of office boys and the distant, silvery bong of the endlessly repeated autocall, summoning the absent to their telephones, gave an impression of efficiency but not, as in some firms, of an efficiency that was ruthless, or even harsh. There was a distinct air of gentility about Sheffield, Knox, conveyed not so much by the Georgian stairway or the Sargent portraits as by one's sense that if things were neat and ordered, they were still not overregimented. The library, for example, had expanded like a great trailing plant over the rest of the office, leaving reassuring piles of reporters and advance sheets in odd corners. There was the hospitality of the open doors to every office through one of which, on summer days, even the great Mr. Knox could be seen working in his shirt sleeves. There was, too, the rather imposing informality of the older female members of the staff, the librarian, the chief cashier, the file clerk, grey and round and tough, as superbly self-assured and as occasionally kind as naval chief petty officers, whose loud maternal injunctions rose above the murmuring stillness of the atmosphere. Oh, we can be grand, if it's grandness you want, the long corridors seemed carelessly to echo, but who are *you* to want it?

Larry Duane was sitting in Timmy's office reading his law journal when the latter came in. He was an amiable, sandy-haired, square-faced, lanky young man, rather better dressed than his type, who might not have rated a job in the firm had he not married one of the Knox girls. If Larry surprised with his clothes, however, he surprised even more with his worrying. He clung to Timmy like a younger brother, making of him a reluctant confidant, flattering him with his trust even as he irritated him with his self-absorption.

"Nothing to do, I suppose," said Timmy, picking up the first of his letters. "What's wrong with your own office? Must I be the lounge?"

"I'm reading the surrogate's decisions," Larry explained airily. "In my department we do have to keep up on the law, you know."

"I'm glad you're so well occupied. Maybe you'll stop pestering me to get you into litigation." Larry worked in estates, a section in Mr. Dale's department. It was rather looked down upon by the corporate men, but then, as Larry complained, they looked down on everything.

"Oh, Timmy, please," he pleaded. "Get me out of estates, will you? I might as well be an undertaker. And that Dale. What a fishy eye!"

"I thought you said he never criticized you."

"But he never praises me!"

"Has he had the occasion?"

"Well, where's the occasion with what I do?" Larry protested. "Timmy, will you speak to my father-in-law? He'll do anything you say; everyone knows that. But as for me, gosh, he never pays *any* attention. It's all he can do to nod when we meet in the elevator. And to think I was afraid of pull when I took this job!"

"He doesn't play favorites, that's all."

"Except with you!"

"Anything I get around here, I work for," Timmy said more sharply. "And I advise you to do the same. You're too old to be thinking of yourself as Clarence Darrow."

"And I'm too young to be ordering tombstones!" Larry exclaimed. "Look, Timmy, suppose anything happened to my father-in-law. Then I'd be stuck good. Dale would run the show, and I'd never get out of estates!"

"And just what do you think is going to happen to your father-in-law?"

"He's pushing sixty. He might want to retire, mightn't he?"

"I don't see how he can retire while he has you on his hands," Timmy retorted, getting up. "And if you'll excuse me, I'm due in his office right now."

Mr. Sheffield's office was the largest of the partners', but Mr. Sheffield was in his upper eighties and rarely came downtown now. Henry Knox, as acting senior, occupied the adjoining office, only slightly smaller, but very distant in spirit from the tawdry grandeur of the Paris hotel sitting room which Mr. Sheffield emulated. The son of a New England headmaster, Knox had copied the simplicity of his late father's study at Milford Academy. A huge square mahogany desk took up the center of the room, with two long tables jutting off it as wings for associates to work at in drafting conferences. The walls and the tops of the cabinet bookcases were covered with framed photographs, not of graduates, but of lawyers who had once been with the firm. When Timmy came in he found Mr. Knox at his desk bent over a galley proof, with Austin Cochran seated opposite. Austin, an associate and law school classmate of Timmy's, was a small, spare, bespectacled man with long hair parted in the middle and rising over his forehead like a sailor's cap. He worked as hard as Timmy, but the still smile in his gravely questioning eyes seemed to betray a faint indifference, an unexpected apathy. It was as if his attitude was: What else? What do *you* offer? He looked up now to nod to Timmy, but their senior made no acknowledgement of his entrance. Knox was a tall, bony man with worn, mobile, rather hardened features and thick, tousled grey hair. When not absolutely still and concentrated as he was at the moment, he was inclined to quiver with nervous activity, to pull at his face, to rub his chin and eyelids, to nod his head up and down and suddenly to swing around in his swivel chair and throw his feet up on the radiator or hit at its pipes with his ruler until they rang. Repose became him, as did gauntness; it was out of key that his girth had increased with his restlessness.

"You've certainly taken your own sweet time this morning, Tim," he muttered finally. "Austin and I have finished two riders already."

Timmy, without answering, took his seat at one of the long tables and picked up his typed copies of the riders, reading them quickly. The three had worked until the previous midnight on the terms of a trust indenture.

17

"It won't do."

"Won't do?" Knox raised his head and glared at him. "Why won't it do?"

"You can't put those funds in reserve maintenance. If you had second-issue bonds under the twenty per cent earnings test, half would go to insurance and half to debt service reserve. It's spelled right out in Section 37."

There was a pause while Knox and Austin turned their pages to this section. After a moment Knox glanced up at Austin who simply nodded.

"That's it, sir. He's right."

"I must have had a brainstorm," Knox answered with a grunt, tearing his riders in two. "These damn things! I keep thinking that *some* day I'll run into one that's the same as one I've done before. But never. There's always a twist."

Timmy no more noticed the absence of comment on his criticism than he had noted Knox's failure to greet him. They had worked too closely, too long, for either to observe the amenities.

"Excuse me, Mr. Knox, but you wanted to know when Mr. Shaughnessy was here. On the Lockwood Estate." It was Mr. Springs, from the trust department, peering in a crack of the barely opened door. "They have an appointment with Mr. Stevens, but he told me to take them to you first."

The senior partner had too many responsibilities not to interrupt his hours of draftsmanship with interviews. On such occasions Timmy and Austin were not even introduced to callers; they continued their work uninterrupted.

"Yes, yes. Yes indeed." Mr. Knox assumed his most benevolent smile as a little group gathered at the door. "Come in, gentlemen. I understand you're on your way to see Mr. Stevens and to work out an arrangement of this tangled matter. If such is possible, and I'm sure it is."

Timmy glanced up as a mottle-faced, suspicious old lawyer slowly entered the room followed by two diffident-looking, angular clerks carrying briefcases. Glancing at Springs, who closed the door behind them, he winked. Both knew that the visitors represented the next-of-kin of an old woman who had left her fortune to Mr. Knox's favorite divinity school; both knew also that Knox would have only the haziest concept of the issues at stake. It was a game that the senior partner played with himself in matters too small for his personal attention, to see how far he could conceal his ignorance under a grandiloquent manner. It was not, however, a game to which he ever confessed, even to Timmy.

"We all know the unfortunate reputation of charitable institutions," Knox continued with his bland smile. "How they are supposed to take the nickel out of the beggar's cup to swell the coffers of their own wards. How they recognize no poverty or distress outside the categories of their own charters. I pride myself that I have checked this tendency in the charity boards on which I have sat. I am sure, gentlemen, that you want to do business with us and that we want to do business with you."

"It's not a question of your *wanting* to do business with us, Mr. Knox," the old man retorted with unexpected tartness. "You've got to. You've got to unless you want to go to court!"

Timmy almost laughed aloud as he watched the benevolence drain out of Knox's face. Seeing the divinity school file on the table, he took out a copy of the old lady's will and placed it silently on Knox's desk. The latter immediately started flipping the carbon pages with a snap, snap. "Whom do you represent, Mr. Shaughnessy?" he demanded in a sharper tone.

"Who indeed? Who but the shorn next-of-kin!"

"The nephews and nieces?" Knox resumed his study of the will. "It seems to me that they're handsomely provided for. What are all these thousand-dollar bequests?"

"A stinking thousand dollars for each of her own flesh and blood!" Mr. Shaughnessy exploded. "And the rest to a school for parsons! Is it decent, I ask you? Was it the school that cared for her in her old age? Was it the school that sat up with her at night when she was spitting her old lungs out? Oh, no, Mr. Knox, it's a crime. A crime against nature!"

Knox had recovered now from his first surprise. He was even smiling, benign again. "Tell me, Mr. Shaughnessy. Are you a married man?"

"I am that."

"And you have a family?"

"I have no children, if that's what you mean."

"But you have brothers and sisters?"

"That I have. Seven in all."

"And do they have children?"

"They do."

"And as a careful lawyer, I needn't ask whether or not you have a duly executed will?" Mr. Shaughnessy remained silent at this, suspicious again, and Knox pressed on: "I can presume, then, that you have not 'shorn' your next of kin? That after due allowance for your good wife you have

19

divided your residuary estate—which I have no doubt is a substantial one—among your siblings and their issue in equal shares, *per stirpes?*"

Timmy had a brief picture, in the shocked glimmer that he caught in the old lawyer's eye, of how little the collateral Shaughnessys might have to profit by their uncle's demise.

"There can be different factors in different families, Mr. Knox," Mr. Shaughnessy protested.

"But I thought we were dealing with absolutes!" Knox exclaimed. "I thought you spoke of a natural rule!"

"Come now, Mr. Knox, we're all lawyers here. Our clients aren't listening."

"I would never have guessed it," Knox retorted, "from your impassioned plea. Do you tell me now it was only window dressing? Save it for the jury, Mr. Shaughnessy!"

"I thought we were going to avoid a jury," the old man said, taken aback.

"So did I! So did I, indeed! Until you started treating *me* as one!"

"Do you mean, Mr. Knox, that you've changed your mind? That you won't negotiate?"

Knox looked at him quizzically for a moment and then elaborately shrugged. "See Mike Stevens, Mr. Shaughnessy," he said in a bored tone, as if the whole matter were now out of his hands. "See what you get out of him. I'm sure you'll present the best case that you can. I have no doubt he will find your oratory persuasive. But I can tell you right now, he's going to have a hard time persuading me, as chairman of Trinity's board, to forego one jot or one tittle of the legacy that—" here his eyes dropped for a second to the will; "that Mrs. Lockwood so generously left us."

"*Miss* Lockwood," the old lawyer contemptuously corrected him and turned to his associates. "Come on, boys. We may as well see what this fellow Stevens has to say."

They left without further word, Mr. Springs ushering them hurriedly out. Austin and Timmy exchanged smiles as Knox rose to stand by the window.

"I know," he grumbled, his back to them. "You think I'm an old ham. But I'm not, basically. I may not have read all the papers, but I'll still bet you both the old man hasn't any case. I scared him. He ought to be easier to settle with now." He turned around, irritated by their continuing impassivity. "The trouble with you two is that you think because you're good securities lawyers, you know everything worth knowing. That's what's wrong with all this overspecialization today. I

20

started out trying negligence cases for an insurance company in the city court. It was an experience I wouldn't trade for all the registration statements in the world!"

"I'm glad to hear you say that, sir," Austin said, getting up and going over to Knox's "in" basket. "Because I have a memo here for you. I assume you haven't read it yet." Reaching down through piles of folders he pulled out a single sheet of typed paper and dropped it lightly in the middle of the desk. "You'll find it's my request to be assigned to Legal Aid for a month. The firm's been loaning out the boys in litigation. Why not us?"

"Because we only give litigators!" Knox exclaimed, disconcerted. "And only the ones just out of law school. For heaven's sake, Austin, you don't think I'm going to give them a man of your experience to defend loiterers in subway washrooms?"

"Even in this age of overspecialization?" Austin masked his impertinence under an air of assumed gravity. "Even for me to achieve an experience that I won't trade for all the—"

"All right, all right," Knox cut in irritably. "Why can't I keep my big mouth shut? Go on, get out of here."

"You mean I can, sir? Really?"

"If you go right now. Let's start that damn month rolling as soon as we can. Timmy and I can finish this up. It's about done, anyway."

"Thank you, sir," Austin said, smiling broadly. "Thanks very much."

When Austin had gone, Knox remained by the window, looking moodily out at the East River, while Timmy continued to mark up the proof. "Why do we work the way we do, Tim?" he demanded suddenly, without turning from his view. Timmy looked up for a moment at the broad, tweeded back and sighed. It was going to be one of *those* days. "When I look out at the boats on the river," Knox continued, "I wonder if we're not damn fools."

"I suppose someone is working on them, too."

"What do *you* want out of life, Tim?" Knox demanded, still without turning. "Do you want a small expensive house in an exclusive suburb that it will kill you to commute from? And private boarding schools to make your boys grow up with the idea that their boys will have to go, too?"

"I don't know. I don't think much about it."

"You're like me. And what have I got, after all?"

21

"Only the reputation of the best securities lawyer in the Street."

"And what's that?"

"What's anything?" Timmy came back at him.

"But do you ever stop to think how much there is in first-class legal work that isn't any better than second? That extra touch, that smoother language, that remote contingency so neatly provided for? That clever tax angle that so often boomerangs?" He turned now and looked reproachfully at Timmy. "There it is. I see it in your eyes. 'He's getting old,' you're thinking. No, don't deny it. I don't care whether you think so or not. Because it's true. And what I should try to understand is that even if you believe the things that I believe, they're irrelevant to you. Because you're young." He sat down, but turned his chair away. "Even if you knew now that when you were my age the game wouldn't be worth the candle, you wouldn't care. Why should you? As long as it seems worth it now? 'Seems' is as good as 'is' to youth. And why not? So there we are. I with my disillusionment and you with the reassurance that yours is still twenty years away."

"I don't know why you should be disillusioned," Timmy said stubbornly. "I don't know anyone who's accomplished more in his profession."

Knox threw back his head and laughed. "That's what I wanted you to say, my boy. You see what an old phony I am. But it's only my little way of leading up to a personal subject."

"Oh?"

"I want you to take a real vacation this summer," Knox continued, now in his business tone, switching his chair around suddenly to face Timmy. "My wife's been after me. She says I'm running you into the ground."

Timmy passed a hand over his brow. What a day! "Well, you won't find any kick on my part," he said dryly. "If that's what you're worried about. I'd love a decent vacation."

"Won't I? Hear me out." Knox picked up his ruler and started slapping it into the palm of his hand. "I want you to take six weeks beginning with the Fourth of July. I want you to get the hell out of the city and not take a single paper from this office with you. And furthermore, I'm going to promise you something. You won't get a single call from here. Not if the roof falls in."

Timmy stared at him. "Well, that sounds swell," he murmured. "I appreciate it. But could we start it in the middle of

August? There's the Milbank issue coming up. I have to do that first."

The ruler slapped again into Knox's hand. "You're not going to be on the Milbank issue," he said sharply. "My wife has been talking to Ann."

Timmy, as he took this in, flushed with irritation. It was intolerable that such things should be arranged in the conferences of nervous women. "Give me to the end of July," he said abruptly, "and then I'll go."

"Timmy, you know that Milbank deal will run right through October," Knox said with a shake of his head. "It's no use."

"Who will you get?"

"I don't know. Bill Hazlitt. Or Congdon. Or maybe Austin." He took in the stubbornness of Timmy's expression. "Well, what the hell do you think we have eighty lawyers in the firm for?"

"But I did the last Milbank issue," Timmy protested. "I could do this one in half the time it would take anyone else. Besides, I have a lot of ideas on this deal."

Knox shrugged and looked away. "I won't have it," he said. "I've told you so twice now, and that's final."

Timmy stood up. "I think if you don't mind, sir, I can handle my own private life."

Knox shook his head several times rapidly. "If I thought that, I wouldn't interfere."

"What about *your* health?" Timmy demanded. "What about *your* vacation?"

"I was away this winter."

"That didn't count. You were sick."

"Well, maybe I'll go away in July." Knox, irritated now, swung his chair around to present his back to Timmy. "Maybe I'll take the whole damn summer off. Who the hell do you think is senior partner, you or me? Now get out of here and do as you're told."

Timmy stared at the grey head and broad, bent shoulders. "Don't you want to finish this proof?"

"No, you do it," Knox snapped. "You're Mr. Know-it-all."

Timmy gathered up his papers in silence and left, smarting with irritation. In the corridor he almost collided with Miss Schulze.

"Why, Mr. Colt, just the man I was looking for!"

Mr. Dale's secretary came from that other world of estates and trusts. If Larry Duane saw it as a morgue, she saw it as

23

the drama of wills and family struggles, of veiled lady clients interviewed mysteriously behind closed doors. The secretaries of her department were as opposite to those of corporate as the king's musketeers to the cardinal's guards; they wore their colors in jauntiness, a hint of beads and tassels, a suggestion of intimacy behind the high-pitched overpoliteness of their laughs.

"Mr. Dale has been looking for you," she continued brightly. "Could you see him now, please?"

"Can it wait, Miss Schulze? I'm awfully busy."

The surprise on her face was admonitory, half sympathetic. "Oh, I think it's quite urgent. He told me twice to get you."

Timmy turned away without answering and marched across the corridor to Mr. Dale's office. The latter was talking on the telephone, and waved him to a seat. Timmy slumped in a chair and watched him critically. He disliked Mr. Dale, because Knox disliked him. He disliked his heavy, bulldog appearance and his air of false heartiness. He disliked the show-off of the great bare office with its simple silver-framed photograph of Mr. Sheffield on the wall; he disliked its occupant's attitude, as he slowly bit his pipe, of seeming to offer clients the clean bare pad of his total attention. The manners were a little too good, the figure too stout, the crinkly smile too crinkly. Timmy fancied he could see behind them the sort of lawyer Dale might have been had he never come to Sheffield, Knox; the portly political advocate in the light blue suit, too light, with a suggestion of dandruff about the shoulders, a gold ring with a diamond and the habit of describing ladies as "gracious," homes as "charming." It was a type that could only now peep out, with just a touch of unctuousness, behind the somber dark of the banker's grey, the dull rich claret of the shoe shine, the impeccable propriety of the signet ring. But if Dale's manners, particularly in contrast to Knox's, seemed to verge on the greasy, it was nonetheless, as even Timmy had to concede, the grease of confidence rather than of false humility, a grease essential to the easy meshing of the massive gears of his self-assertion.

"Well, that's it," Dale was saying into the telephone, "the terms are final. I mean that. When we get the deed to the house and the assignment of the insurance policies, he can see the children for a month in the summer. Tough? Of course, it's tough. But if a man wants to make a fool of himself at his age, he has to pay for the privilege." Hanging up, he turned immediately to Timmy with a welcoming smile,

24

perfunctory but pleasant. "Sorry to keep you waiting, Timmy. I wondered if I might do a little raiding in the corporate department. Could you help me?"

"Well, if it won't take all my time," Timmy said dubiously.

"It won't, it won't," Dale said blandly. "Let me explain. I'd like you to help me on what may turn out to be a rather complicated business deal that my wife's nephew has got himself into. His name is George Emlen, and he's an extremely smart young man. A wealthy one, too, I might add. George has a sharp enough nose for a quick profit, but he sometimes doesn't stop to think things through. By the way, would you mind closing the door?"

Timmy rose, reflecting rather sourly as he did so that Knox would have closed it himself. George Emlen. Wealthy. He remembered that Dale had married a wealthy woman. *And* a client.

"He and a bunch of other young fellows of some means have got together to buy a textile business," Dale continued as Timmy sat down. "They've found one controlled by an estate that wants to sell. As far as George is concerned, the deal's closed. The 'grubby details' can be left to the lawyers. You and I know this is just the beginning. Particularly in a deal like this one—"

Timmy listened as Dale explained the complications with increased uneasiness. It was obvious that he was talking about a real job, not a "do this when you find a minute" affair such as partners, half guiltily, were apt to throw their juniors on Friday afternoons. "Excuse me, sir," he said at a point where Dale paused. "Have you cleared this with Mr. Knox?"

Dale's eyes narrowed. "Cleared what?"

"Putting me on this deal," he explained. "He usually assigns my time."

"I've never been much on these little office games," Dale said, scowling. "A works for B, and C for D. Like cops and robbers. Too damn overspecialized. You'd better not get too far from Henry Knox's apron strings, my boy. You might even find yourself practicing law." There was a heavy, rather gravelly humor in his tone, but the words were hostile.

"I didn't invent the system, sir."

"No, but you think it's a dandy, don't you?"

Just then, from the corridor behind the closed door Timmy faintly made out the bong of his autocall. He jumped up.

"I think that's my call," he said. "It's probably Collins at Marston, Carter about my proofs. Could I take it in here, sir?" Dale shrugged, and Timmy, picking up his telephone, dialed the operator. He made it as brief as possible, but looking down as he talked, over the heavy, oval, turned-away jaw of the obviously disgruntled man behind the desk, he realized his tactical error. It was one thing to take an outside call in Knox's office where it was usually from one of his own clients and where in any event the rule was fixed that business took precedence over protocol. It was quite another to do so with a man as prickly as Dale.

"Tell me, Colt," Dale said in a dry tone, when he had finished. "Would you have done that in Knox's office?"

"Done what, sir?"

"Taken a call like that."

"From a client? Certainly."

"Well maybe you would and maybe you wouldn't," Dale said slowly, turning back to stare at him with a rejecting blankness. "But it's not what I expect. When I invite a younger man to my office I expect his attention. As he may expect mine. You boys in the corporate department are getting too big for your boots. You think you're the only people who do any work around here."

Timmy stood up. "May I go now, sir?"

Dale looked up for a moment half quizzically at his sullen, flushed face. Then he shrugged. "Go ahead," he said, turning to a paper on his desk. "I'll speak to Knox about getting you on my nephew's deal."

Timmy, in the corridor, wondered if he would have believed anyone that morning who should have told him that before the lunch hour he would have quarreled with each of the two most senior partners of the firm.

3

GENEVIEVE, Timmy's mother, had married Philemon Colt when the latter was well over sixty. She herself had been thirty and a trained nurse. As soon as he had proposed to her, with his funny little bow, on leaving the sanatorium where she had met him professionally, she had promptly accepted. She knew that he was not rich, but she had been more hopeful about his social position. This was particularly important to her, the daughter of a Richmond dentist who had been a Carter but not the right kind. Genevieve had always indulged in secret fantasies of distinction; she had prided herself that her oval face and high-braided blond hair had more than a touch of aristocratic Edwardian beauty. And Mr. Colt, an affable, rather bouncing bachelor whose life was encased in a hard glaze of bright salutations and cheerful anecdotes (he only crumpled into the little sanatorium on the rare occasions when the glaze broke), was indisputably a member of an old Manhattan family and a grandson of the Reverend Timothy Colt, once rector of Trinity Church. What Genevieve failed to take into consideration was how little all this meant in a city as big as New York. Families disappeared as fast as the houses which they had occupied, and there was nothing in the great old shabby West Side hotel where Philemon took her to live to bespeak a grander past, nothing, for that matter, in their daily life or round but a couple of darkened portraits, a collection of miniatures, several volumes of genealogy and privately printed memorials (*Abram S. Colt, his story for his descendants*) and Philemon's way of saying "poil" for "pearl" which most people took for modern Brooklyn rather than old New York. There were, it was true, more prosperous second cousins across the Park, but even first cousins in New York, after childhood, are considered rather distant relations, and Philemon, to make things worse, was thought to have made a fool of himself in marriage. When he died, only seven years after the event, Genevieve discovered that half his small income had been derived from an annuity and that a few securities of uncertain yield and such talents as she might have as a bridge teacher, a reader or a paid companion (for she would *never* go back to nursing) were the only assets with which she was expected to rear the great-grandson of the Reverend Timothy.

But Timmy, fortunately for himself, grew up the very opposite of his mother. Where she was flighty, he was grave; where she was snobbish, he was totally without pretension; where she lived amid fantasies, he was soberly realistic. He was a good and conscientious boy, if a bit on the quiet side, who was never any trouble to anyone. He saw his mother with unclouded eye from the beginning, saw the drinking, the wishful thinking, the false pride, the oddness of their way of life. He never believed for a moment that the hotel was a real home or ever suggested that he ask another child for a meal.

27

He seemed to quite understand that if Genevieve's remnant of income was inadequate for herself, it was totally unavailable to him. All his youth he worked, at night, during summers, in laundries and restaurants, in banks and garages; he put himself through Columbia with only a minimum of unexpected aid from a Colt cousin. And he never reproached Genevieve. He and she were allies by necessity in their gilded hotel world, fated to stand together before the suspicious eyes of an infinity of clerks and doormen. If Genevieve was apt to stumble, to protest too much, to talk overloudly, unconscious of the eyes that scorned, the ears that maliciously listened, then he had to be more circumspect, more silent, more industrious. It was as if she were an actual part of him, the looser, lighter side of his own nature, the one that he had to make up for before the great round golden eye of a demanding God glaring down through the faded curlicues and candelabra of endless lobbies and vestibules. Only in the spare neatness of his own small room, under the green lamp with his law books, was there rest from the pressure of his imagined overseer, as in childhood at the same desk he had sought the solace of the solved equation, the translated stanza. What Genevieve threatened to upset with her fictional past and far from fictional bottle had to be righted by remorseless application of himself.

The only thing that was in any way aristocratic about Timmy was his looks, and Genevieve made as much of these as she could. Sitting over the family miniatures on the small top-floor room to which she had removed and where she did her more serious drinking, she had selected, from amidst the whiskered bankers, the long-cheeked, raven-haired, high-browed wives of an earlier New York, two miniatures of a beautiful young man who had, it seemed, died young. In one, pale, wide-eyed, with long wavy black hair, he was carrying a gun, an alert spaniel at his heels. The other, in more Gothic mood, showed him bent over an opened book of stanzas on a garden bench. These pictures, bathed in the romantic aura of the early nineteenth century, fascinated Genevieve with their fancied resemblance to Timmy. It was not, of course, that Timmy was quite the young man of the artist's conception; his hair, if long and dark, was combed back straight until he had messed it by a nervous habit of tugging at it; his face was squarer, healthier than the young hunter's, and if his large, gazing grey eyes had some of the stillness, the momentarily caught serenity of the reader of poems, that stillness could nonetheless be broken by a certain moody irritability.

But there it was, nonetheless, when it *was* there, that air of unruffled, of romantic detachment, and his own unawareness that he looked anything but the most ordinary law student, the most run-of-the-mill clerk, could never quite destroy her illusion that he, like his mother, yearned for a different world.

His looks, of course, were not of interest alone to Genevieve. Timmy, who was more reserved than shy, had a particular appeal for older and more sophisticated women. It was the appeal of an Armand for a Marguerite, the appeal of the pale face and a seemingly virginal male intensity. When on more intimate acquaintance they found him more experienced and matter-of-fact than they had anticipated, his charm tended somewhat to fade. Timmy was not hurt by this. He was even dryly amused. He knew that he was less interesting than the man they first took him to be, but more so than the one who ultimately bored them. The particular charm of Ann was that from the very beginning she took him for just what he was.

They met in the winter of 1941 when he was in his second year at Columbia Law and she a junior at Barnard. One of his campus jobs was tutoring in economics, but he found himself quite unable to get even the first principles across to her. Yet it was not that she did not try. She sat very still, staring at him with rather desperate eyes. He had the impression that every word he uttered was promptly rejected by some mental process beyond her control.

"Why do you take economics?" he asked her finally. "Obviously, you have some sort of block against it."

"Well, I can't take *just* English courses. It's all I've done all my life. And read novels."

"It sounds delightful."

"You don't really think so."

He looked at her with surprise. "As a matter of fact, I don't. All right, why not take a course in history of art? Something like that?"

"Because of just that. The way you put it."

"The way *I* put it?"

"It's your attitude. The attitude of people like you. You think if someone can't understand a *real* subject, like economics, they may as well fool around with art."

He sighed. "But at least you could pass art."

"Oh, don't say that!" Her face was vivid now with alarm. "I've got to pass! Oh, Mr. Colt, if you *knew* the trouble I had getting my family to send me here. I'll simply die if I don't pass!"

29

He studied her for a moment in perplexity. "Well, we'll have to find some way around that block. We might go out and have a beer. Got any money?"

In the bar she listened, carefully attentive, while he talked about the *Law Review*. She did not seem to find it in the least odd that her tutor should take her to a bar and talk about his own work while she paid for his beer.

"Thanks *so* much, Mr. Colt," she said afterwards, giving his hand a vigorous shake. "It's been a *most* interesting evening."

He got her through the examination. It was close, but he got her through, and her gratitude was boundless. They continued to see each other. He had never been attracted to a girl in quite this way. She was a bit too tall and inclined, when flustered, to be ungainly in her movements; her hair had a dull, sandy coloring and the effect of high cheekbones and a slightly recessive chin was to give an impression of rather breathless expectancy. Yet her skin was clear, even beautiful, and her large worried eyes had a compelling intensity. She was *good*, he felt, whatever the word meant, remarkably, even pathetically good. He felt it in her sentiment for small, undistinguished things, a charm bracelet, a Venetian scarf, a turquoise brooch, and at the same time in her faculty for losing them. She meant well—no one, he was sure, had ever meant better—but her plans and resolutions were apt to encounter the most curious snags. He found himself irritated at the sentimentality in himself that caused him to pity her. For she did not need his pity. If she needed anything, it was obviously his love, and it was half out of guilt that he kissed her one night.

"You didn't have to do that, you know," she said, flushing. "We can be just friends."

"But I wanted to."

"Well, that's very nice. But I mean you don't have to feel involved."

"I don't feel in the least involved."

"Oh, I don't mean involved in the sense that you have to marry me or anything like that," she said, flustered, sensing that the matter was out of control. "I mean involved in the sense that you have to kiss me every time we go out."

"Really, Ann!"

"It's terrible, isn't it!" she exclaimed with a nervous giggle. "I guess I'd better shut up!"

Yet she was by no means always compliant. She could be very severe with him when she was sure that she was in the right. They had a brisk argument one night after she had taken him to a party given by two female graduate students. Timmy had sat sullenly on the floor, radiating disapproval of what to him was an atmosphere of long hair, spectacles and violent opinions on aesthetic trivia.

"Thank God!" he exclaimed as they came out. "Really, Ann, have you *no* discrimination?"

"But, Timmy, they're friends of mine. I *like* them!"

"Well, that doesn't mean I have to."

"Of course not. But you might at least be polite to them."

"I *was* polite."

"I distinctly heard you use the word 'quack.' When you were talking to that medical student."

"I was only referring to psychiatrists. Not doctors in general."

"But he's going to *be* a psychiatrist!"

"Then he's going to be a quack."

She stopped and pulled him around to face her. "I won't have you talk that way!"

"Look, Ann," he protested. "You don't understand people like that. Half of them were commies. Sounding off about the war like a bunch of hysterics!"

"Being against Hitler does not happen to be synonymous with being a communist," she said with icy dignity.

"No? Well, I bet there wasn't a peep out of one of them till he walked into Russia."

"My friends are not communists," she retorted. "Except maybe for Angela, and that's Angela's affair. But that's not the important thing. The important thing is that *you* think anyone who likes abstract painting or non-rhyming poetry is a red."

"Well, it's a good way to start."

"Oh, Timmy, you're terrible. You really are!" He had to smile at the earnestness of her expression. It was so easy to bait her. "You think because you're on the *Law Review,* you're entitled to look down on people. Well, suppose you *are* brilliant. Brilliance isn't everything!"

"It's not a question of brilliance. It's a question of clear thinking. I can't bear people who think sloppily."

"And who are you to judge what's sloppy? You think anyone's sloppy who's not as cut and dried as you are. You're intolerant, Timmy!"

"It must be the old New York in me."

"So that's it. You're a snob, too." She suddenly laughed. "I think it's actually presumptuous to be as right wing as you are. Anyone would think you had a million dollars in the bank!"

He went out to Orange one Sunday to meet her parents, but only once. They had little enough interest in Ann. Her father was a real estate broker, volatile, anecdotal, touchy about his lack of success, impossible to please; her greying, placid mother was phlegmatic, platitudinous, impossible to make a dent in. There were two older brothers who worked for their father and whose only effort at lunch was to make Timmy feel that it was no such great thing to be a lawyer. They evidently regarded Ann as a scatterbrain and thought the less of him for being with her.

On the other hand, he took her quite often to see Genevieve at her hotel, despite his mother's obvious feeling of Ann's social inadequacy. For Genevieve, at best, was not unfriendly. She was only too glad to have someone to whom she could boast about the past. She would contemplate Ann mistily, following the direction of her eyes until they alighted on some object that could be seized upon to open the floodgates of her reminiscence.

"You're looking at that little picture on the cabinet, I see," she would say. "Nice, isn't it? I mean nice, of course, in an utterly unpretentious way. What is it? Oh, just an old beach house on the dunes at East Hampton. I used to go there with Mr. Colt. It belonged to a cousin of his. My, did we used to be packed in! Think of it, nine cousins and two uncles and aunts, not to speak of five maids! Maids were cheap as dirt, you know, in those days. Might as well have them as not. And how we used to laugh at the dressed up people, the stuffy crowd! We found them kind of common. It was a smaller world in those days. Everyone *knew* if you were a lady, so why pretend? But in the city, of course, it was different. *There* one behaved. Not like these days when you see girls smoking on Fifth Avenue! Why, do you know, Ann, when I was a girl in Richmond, a lady couldn't even button her glove in the street!"

"They must have been less sure of themselves," Timmy remarked. "Scared that some guy would think they were trying to pick him up!"

"Oh, Timmy, you're disgusting!" his mother wailed. "But there you are, Ann, what can I do with him? Brought up in the city, poor child, with public schools and all that. I suppose I should be glad he's not worse."

One night, after Genevieve had been rambling on with a particular aimlessness on the subject of East Hampton, repeating herself about the happy standards of the dear, dead past, her eyes suddenly closed and her head slid forward, and she appeared to be sleeping, open-mouthed.

"Oh, Timmy, do you suppose she's ill?" Ann watched him nervously as he moved to prop his mother's head against a pillow, to take off her shoes and raise her feet to the sofa. He did these things with a silent and rather matter-of-fact efficiency, like a nurse dealing with a patient of long standing.

"Is she asleep?"

"She's passed out." He looked at her calmly. "Can't you tell when someone's drunk, Ann?"

"Oh, but not someone like her!" Ann looked horrified. "Shouldn't we be quiet? Won't she hear?"

"She won't hear anything for a couple of hours," he said with a faint shrug. "Don't worry. She's used to it. We'll go out and have something to eat and drop in later to check up."

Ann immediately sprang into action, straightening the cushions, putting away the cocktail things, making coffee and pouring it in the thermos to leave by the sofa. She seemed disturbed, however, and later, at the cafeteria, suddenly put her hand on his.

"Poor Timmy," she said softly. "I knew there was something that worried you. I didn't realize it was that."

"It doesn't really worry me," he insisted, half irritated, half touched by her sympathy. "You don't see it, Ann. Genevieve's all the family I've got. Besides the Colt cousins whom she dreams about. She may be an odd root, but she's still a root. One doesn't worry about roots. They're there, that's all."

"You pretend you're so down to earth and matter-of-fact. But fundamentally you're not. Fundamentally you're an old softy."

He changed the subject abruptly, but she was not in the least put out, and when he took her back to the dormitory he knew that she would not object again to his kissing her.

That summer turned out to be the turning point in his career. He was offered a job for July and August in the Wall Street firm of Sheffield, Knox, Stevens & Dale on the strength of a note in the *Law Review* that had come to the attention of Mr. Henry Knox himself. When June came, however, and Genevieve was obliged to make one of her habitual retreats to a sanatorium, he found it imperative to make more money than summer law clerks were paid. He wrote his excuse to Mr. Knox and was surprised by return mail to be offered better pay as a summer tutor to the latter's four daughters. It was not an offer that he could afford to turn down, but he told Ann, rather gloomily, that he expected to spend the summer reading aloud from *The Mill on the Floss*.

"I'll bet your mother's pleased, anyway," she retorted with a touch of bitterness. "She's pinned all her hopes on your marrying a debutante. This should be your big chance!"

But the Knox girls were not debutantes. They were all between the ages of twelve and sixteen, all round and insignificantly pretty, all gushingly enthusiastic and healthily unintelligent, all very much awed by parents whom they didn't in the least resemble. It was as if Mr. and Mrs. Knox had discovered four orphaned sisters and adopted them. Mrs. Knox was quiet, grave and serene, elaborate only in her devotion to her tall, rangy husband whose rugged features, shaggy grey hair and huge, cerebral brow utterly dominated the household. The girls might have squealed with terror at his sarcasms, but they were almost compulsively anxious to confide in him. He was their god, and like all gods could be feared but not fooled. Timmy was an object of envy because he was allowed to sit alone with him after dinner and discuss law over a brandy.

"You young fellows today know nothing about the philosophy of law," Mr. Knox would tell him irritably. Knox, he found, was inclined to be irritable. Yet it was the irritability of a man who was impatient with his own limitations and torn between the simultaneous pain and pleasure given him by what he saw as the absurd admiration of others. "You read a few hundred decisions in law school, top it all off by a reverent perusal of Cardozo's *Nature of the Judicial Process* and call yourselves lawyers. Not a word of Whitehead. Not a paragraph of Morris Cohen. Not a backward glance at Roman law. With Brandeis your idol, you burrow into facts. Facts from fact-finding boards. Social facts. Economic facts. Facts! Like Holmes, I hate them! How can you *think*, man, if you're obsessed with facts?"

He gave Timmy books to read, some by the authors that he had mentioned and others by Maitland, Pollock, Maine. He blandly assumed that anyone could proceed at his own pace, but Timmy soon floundered. Where Mr. Knox's mind soared to the general, Timmy's clung to the particular; he had to isolate his problem, large or small, and work it meticulously out. He could be interested in land tenure in the reign of William Rufus or rent control in New York; he had no inclination, like Knox, to speculate on what the latter might have derived from the former. His employer would probably have lost patience with him had a project not turned up where Timmy was able to render him a real assistance.

Knox had decided to spend his vacation that summer on Long Island rather than to go away. Vacations were not to him what they were to others. He would sit by the swimming pool in the morning and work on a memorandum to the Securities and Exchange Commission, proposing changes in the law and regulations. This was duly discussed with Timmy, and at last their minds met on common ground. Timmy went to work in the library, reading and digesting cases, reports and articles, and came up with a draft of a memorandum that took Knox aback. Abruptly he told his wife to get a new tutor for the girls. "I'm putting Tim on this memo full time," he snapped when she protested at the interruption of their schedule. "And I'm going to raise his pay, too. He's too damn good to be helping Sally with *The Swiss Family Robinson*."

Timmy and Knox worked diligently together through the hot, damp Long Island days. Timmy, his feet at last squarely on the ground, lost all his shyness. He would defend his draft of the memorandum stubbornly against Knox's tendency to weigh it down with historical and philosophical dissertations on the interrelation between business and government, arguing firmly that these could be kept for a *Law Review* article. The paper itself was sacred to him; it had a purpose to accomplish, and anything not bearing directly on that purpose was to be ruthlessly eliminated. He appreciated that he was working with a great authority, but he knew that great authorities had occasionally to be kept to the point. Knox would get testy with him, but even this was a compliment. It was the testiness one meted out to an equal.

"You know something, Tim?" Knox asked him as he finished reading the final draft. "I think I've done you an injustice. I said you weren't a philosopher. Well, you're not. But I didn't realize *why* you weren't. Now I see it. You're an artist. The two rarely go together."

Timmy relayed this in a long letter to Ann. He had reached the point where nothing of any significance could happen to him without his wanting immediately to tell her about it. She was spending a rather dreary summer in Orange, working as a typist in her father's office.

Your friends may think me a Philistine because I don't like poems that are made by writing a page of prose and tearing it in two. It's some consolation that a man like Knox (whom, of course, they'd despise) has a better estimate of my talents. Maybe one doesn't have to wear black-rimmed glasses and let one's hair grow to be an artist. And maybe if one of our children tears off to the Left Bank in Paris with a paintbrush, it'll be a joint responsibility.

The last sentence he wrote without a thought. The thought came a moment later. But after staring at his own handwriting for a sober minute, he simply smiled and finished the letter. All that day he pictured how her face would be when she read it, imagining her sudden gasp when she came upon that sentence.

Yet when her answer came, as it always did two days later, for Ann had no coyness, it was barren of any reference to his remark. He even wondered if at the last moment he might not have crossed it out. She wrote, instead, in her rather bouncy style:

I never expected to hear as much from you as I have this summer. I pictured you sitting in shirt sleeves by a long blue pool, solving algebra equations, while four bronzed adolescents in meager bathing suits, absorbed in their own incipient sex appeal, sunbathed around you. But I gather from your letters that I have misconceived my rival. Obviously it is Mr. Knox. Whoever said that America was a matriarchy? Wait till I tell them about Mrs. Knox losing her tutor!

When they met again in the fall, however, he could tell immediately that she had understood him. She was very nervous and would not look him in the eye. She chatted on apprehensively about her coming graduation and the sort of job that she might get.

"Job?" he asked, looking at her gravely. "I thought we were going to get married."

"Oh, Timmy." She turned away and shook her head several times rapidly. "I don't know how to say it, but—well, I have a feeling you've been pushed into this."

"I haven't been pushed into anything."

"Then ... maybe we both have."

"Ann." He put his hands on her shoulders and turned her around. "Tell me just one thing. Do you love me?"

"But that's not the point!"

"Do you or don't you?"

"Well, you know I do!" she cried at last in a tone that was almost petulant. "I have from the beginning. That's the thing about me. I'm a clinger. But you shouldn't marry a clinger. It's a mistake!"

"That's my decision," he said firmly. "Things are going to be a lot easier for you when you learn there are certain decisions that have to be left to me." The intensity of hope in her eyes had removed his last doubt. For doubts there had been. In his earlier fantasies he had always been married to a beautiful girl. But those were fantasies. What was real now was the conviction of how he needed her. That was the thing about Ann. She was simply indispensable.

"Even decisions like marriage?" she asked.

"Especially decisions like marriage."

"And what sort of decisions will be left for me?"

"I'll decide that later."

"But *you* will decide it?"

"Look, Ann. You don't have to worry about it. Because I promise you this. Whenever there's something you want me to do, *really* want me to do, I'll do it. And that's not just a romantic promise. I mean it."

When she gave in, he knew that she had given in for good. The question of their marriage, however little referred to, was settled. Pearl Harbor only accelerated the date. Timmy had already applied for midshipmen's school and was to go immediately after his graduation; he told her they would get married in the spring. Only Genevieve objected, putting on one last desperate scene.

"Aside from everything else, it isn't fair to Ann," she argued, throwing her a long sad look of unfelt concern. "Suppose the worst happens and you don't come back. We have to face these things, darling. It's what war is."

"*I* have to face them, Ma," Timmy said dryly. "I don't see that you do."

"But for Ann to be left a widow, so young? With her life before her? Is it *fair*, Timmy?"

"War widows always marry well," he retorted. "There's something appealing about them. As a matter of fact, I shouldn't be surprised if it improved Ann's chances."

His mother's lips puckered in disgust. "Oh, Timmy, you're

37

so callous. Really and truly you are. It's characteristic of your whole generation."

"What do you think, Ann?" he demanded, turning to her. "Do *you* think I'm callous? Would it be callous of me to come back with no arms and legs and make you nurse me for the rest of your life?"

"We take our chances," she said, looking evenly at the woman who was now to be her mother-in-law. "It doesn't make sense any other way. If you came back like that, I'd marry you just the same. And then people would say it was pity."

"You see, Ma!"

"But if there's a baby, Timmy!" his mother cried, playing her final card. "Who's going to support it?"

"Babies can wait," he said shortly. "I'm talking about marriage. Anyway, Ann could bring it up. I could count on her."

In the four years of the war Timmy and Ann were almost constantly separated. She followed him about the country from base to base in the first year, but when his destroyer went out to the Pacific for the rest of the war, she worked for the Red Cross in New York and tried to keep Genevieve from drinking herself to death. Timmy was not one of those who were stirred even briefly by the emotionalism of conflict, by the sense of sharing in a cosmic tragedy. To him, from beginning to end, it was a bore and an interruption. He was a good gunnery officer and moderately popular with the other officers and men, and if he seemed, despite his patience and equanimity, a somewhat dim figure who was apt, off duty, to be found reading books or writing letters in his cabin, it was because they in turn were dim to him. The ship and even the fighting had never half the reality of the job which Henry Knox had promised him after the war.

It may be that I lack imagination [*he wrote Ann shortly before V-J Day*]. *So many of the men I meet at officers' clubs say they're not going back to their old jobs when peace comes. Maybe it's just talk, though it makes me feel rather a poke not to want to take advantage of the great second chance that the end of the war apparently means to some. But if you've known what you wanted all along, the war isn't anything but four years hacked out of a career. Oh, you can say it's been a valuable and broadening experience, as most lawyers in*

the service do (they're incurable wishful thinkers) but
when you get right down to it, the only thing that really
makes a good lawyer is hard, digging work. I can't see
the war in any but negative terms. The Japs had to be
stopped, and they've been stopped. The cancer's out, or
some of it, anyway, but you don't expect the patient to
feel better than before he was sick.

And when he came back only three months later, tired
and slightly yellowish from a bout of malaria, he took only
two weeks of terminal leave before going to work in
Sheffield, Knox. This was now eight years ago, a period
double the length of the war, but to Timmy it seemed only
half as long. His and Ann's life had quickly assumed its
present pace of occupied monotony, interrupted only by the
births of George and Walter and their own removal, after a
desperate, long-smothered appeal by Ann, from an apartment
shared with Genevieve to one for themselves in the East River
development. It was a monotony, however, that he had taken
for granted. The bulk of his energy went into work; it was
routine for him to stay at the office three or four nights a
week, frequently into the small hours of the morning. Satur-
days, even Sundays, were apt to be workdays. But when the
task was once accomplished, at no matter what toll of hours,
and the remorseless deity for a time placated, he wanted
nothing better than to stay at home with his wife and
children and a little whiskey. If Ann came second, she was a
constant second; he was a one-man dog. She had seen it this
way, he knew, from the beginning and had seen that it was
what she wanted. He had never promised her anything else.
And it had worked, he insisted; he had no patience with her
new argument that it had worked too well. She had her
books, Lord knew, enough to satisfy every conceivable taste.
Kant, Spinoza, Thackeray, George Eliot, Mickey Spillane,
Screen Romances. It would have been easy for her to call
herself a neglected wife, abandoned for her husband's office,
but she was too fair to do this. She *wasn't* neglected, and she
knew it. It was the way, fundamentally, that they both
wanted to live.

39

4

SHERIDAN DALE had always been jealous of Henry Knox. It
went back to the beginning of their association in the firm of
Hale & Sheffield thirty-five years before, when Knox, the
young, snotty, bright-eyed New Englander of colonial antece-
dents and of a high, tense, enthusiastic pitch of voice, fresh
from the glories of the *Harvard Law Review*, had been
employed by a benevolent Mr. Sheffield as the kind of
associate who would surely one day be a partner. Dale,
already working in the managing clerk's office, a rough,
blocky young man from Fordham Law, could look forward
to years of answering calendars and serving papers and
possibly to the ultimate position of managing clerk itself, no
more. He could not expect to be a partner or to be on the
same social level as the other clerks or even be asked to the
Christmas parties. Yet Dale had learned the dangerous futility
of jealousy; he remembered from the long dark years of a
poor Brooklyn childhood how quickly it could turn one's life
into the ashes of angry fantasy. He tried successfully not to be
envious of his elegant superiors in Hale & Sheffield. But
Henry Knox was different. Knox sought him out when he
did not have to, took him to lunch, asked him to his
apartment, attempted to make him a part of a legal discussion
group. And when Dale, thinking that his one point of
superiority was his knowledge of the courts, the clerks, the
city itself, when he tried to temper lofty arguments of munici-
pal reform with a reminder of the lower kind of political
facts, when he ventured to hint that Knox might be living in
the clouds of an unrealistic idealism, he found that instead of
the deference to the practical that practical men expect, Knox
drew away from him. What Dale passionately resented ever
afterwards was that Knox had dropped him, not because he
wasn't a gentlemen, but because he wasn't, in the New

40

Englander's complicated moral categories, quite straight. For such hypocrisy there could be no forgiveness.

And it *was* hypocrisy. It had to be. How else could he explain the phenomenal success of the New Englander in a world of tough, unyielding facts? For it was Knox, indubitably, who had checked, almost single-handed, the rot that had set into the organization with the death of Mr. Hale. Cyrus Sheffield might have looked the leader—no distinguished old gentleman, in fact, had ever looked it more—but everyone on the inside knew that his major contribution had been to spot in the energy and brilliance of Knox the catalytic agents that would pull together and rejuvenate his firm. It was just this that Dale, a good predictor, had not predicted. He had seen the rot all right; he had watched with the closest attention its gradual development: the desire to fight a case sliding into the desire to settle it, the pride in staff efficiency turning into a reverence for routine, the habit of overbilling for unique and imaginative services degenerating into the habit of over-billing. He had foreseen the break-up of the old guard and that changes were bound to come, but he had dared to think that it might be *he* who would make them, that a different phoenix might rise from the ashes of Hale & Sheffield.

Yet rationally he could not complain. He had done dazzlingly well. If Mr. Sheffield had been shrewd enough to see in Knox the future adviser of his great corporations, he had also seen in the unprepossessing young man from Fordham the future confidant of his rich widows and old maids. Such work had been too contemptuously relegated in the past to attenuated young men of better family than brains. What Sheffield had the wits to perceive was that affluent ladies from east of Central Park, distrustful of anyone from their own world as for that very reason too soft, would eagerly embrace, in their business affairs, a champion from the great murky outside city which they felt to threaten them—that they would prefer to fight, like ancient Romans, barbarians with barbarians. There was plenty in this, of course, for Dale to resent, but Dale had learned to treat resentment not as a sore to be cauterized but as a yearning to be satisfied. As an ear it could be deafened with the klaxon of admiration, as a nose filled with the heady aroma of incense, as a hand crammed with gold, until the whole body was occupied with receiving and had no emptiness for the small, persistent throb of anxiety.

Even Knox could no longer ignore him when, at Mr. Sheffield's insistence, Dale was made the partner in charge of estates and trusts. There was no underestimating the increasing number of important persons in varied fields who came to seek the advice of the plain, heavy-set, rather ordinary looking man in expensive tweeds who viewed them with a silent, almost staring concentration and settled their problems with a sudden rumble of words that were no less efficacious for being commonplace. His vision might have been occasionally short-sighted, his solutions even provoked new problems or cut too short corners or not been in accordance with what the client more deeply, more basically required, but solutions of some sort they invariably were, and clients liked solutions. To "get things done" was the be-all and end-all of his creed, expressed with a fervor that suggested something un-American in the dissenter and posed at least the possibility that to get things done crudely was better than not getting them done at all.

But for all his success, Sheridan Dale was still no Henry Knox. The firm was still spoken of in the Street as Knox's firm. The major earnings were still from Knox's clients. And it was to Knox that the venerable, now almost senile Cyrus Sheffield, however much flattered and cultivated by Dale, primarily turned his deafening ear. Yet all this could have been borne, could have been explained away, even, by Knox's early head start. What could not easily be explained and what bit in more deeply as time went by was that Knox commanded a dedication and loyalty among the younger men who worked for him that Dale never received from his. Like acolytes at an altar, the corporation experts moved silently to and fro with absorbed, preoccupied faces, conscious only of their high priest and his ministrations. To get one of them even temporarily into his own department, Dale had to exert every kind of pressure, and then he had the constant sense of their being like faithful dogs who, at the first glimpse of Knox, would break their leash and go bounding after him. Timothy Colt was easily the worst; he had a sublime unawareness of any other department that hit Dale harder than contempt. It was true that he was polite—or that he had been until their last interview—but his attitude that everyone in the firm, including Dale himself, had to concede that Knox was a leader almost divinely appointed was intolerable. It was as if Knox had been reborn to condescend to him all over again in a new cycle of time, and Dale had a violent need to seek his own reflection, even momentarily, in the unseeing grey of those younger eyes.

It was for this that he left his office in the morning of his talk with Timmy and ambled down the corridor to Knox's door.

"Can I see you a moment, Henry?"

Knox looked up quickly at the familiar rumble and made an effort to smile. It was a poor enough joke between them that they only met when there was a problem. "Of course, Sheridan. What seems to be the trouble now?"

"I've come to rob your larder," Dale said with a humorless smile. "I want some help from a corporate man on a deal my nephew, George Emlen, has dreamed up. It's a pretty big deal. Six million bucks. I spoke to Timmy Colt just now, but he seemed to feel it wasn't big enough for him."

The statement was casual, but Knox was quite aware of its challenge. All of his partners knew that Timmy Colt worked exclusively for him. "I keep Timmy pretty busy," he said guardedly. "Rather too busy, I'm afraid. I've just ordered him to take six weeks off this summer. He's been killing himself, that boy."

"Six weeks?" Dale lifted his eyebrows as if to indicate that he would never come to an end of the eccentricities of the corporate department. "I wish I could do that for some of my boys."

"Well, if any of them worked like Timmy," Knox said a bit snappishly, "you'd find you had to."

Dale looked at him a moment with a hard little twinkle. "Oh, we work, Henry," he said softly. "We work."

"I know that," Knox retorted, irked to have made the slip. "But Timmy's an exception in any department."

"Perhaps he overdoes it. Perhaps it accounts for his manners."

Knox looked up. "His manners? What's wrong with his manners?"

"He practically bit my head off when I suggested he do the job for me. He seemed to think I'd been impertinent. Who are you letting him think he is, Henry?" This last was delivered more pointedly, the chin thrust forward, like the sudden charge to the open of a heavy hoofed animal skulking in the brush. "And while I'm on the subject, there's something else I'd like to bring up. The distribution of associates in general. You've got all the smartest boys in corporate. It just doesn't correspond to the business that's coming into my bailiwick. You know that, don't you, Henry?"

Knox sighed. He did know it. "Whom do you want,

43

Sheridan?" he asked with the attempt of a brisk smile. "Name your men."

"I told you. I'd like Colt."

Knox's jaw dropped. "Just because he was rude to you?" he exclaimed. "You want a chance to get back at him?"

Dale shook his head placidly several times in succession. "You've never understood how I operate, Henry," he said patiently. "You've never been able to take in the fact that I'm not petty. If I were, there are plenty of things that I'd have resented years ago. I think you can imagine the kind of things I mean." There was an awkward pause while Knox played with his paper cutter, jabbing it into the blotter. "I want Colt because, in the first place, he's smart. And in the second place, it's obvious that you're grooming him for a partnership. I'd like this deal to be sort of a test for him. I'd like to observe him at work. I'd like to see how he gets on with people like George. I may be all wet, but I have a suspicion you've made him feel he's too good to deal with ordinary businessmen."

Knox nodded, breathing hard. There was something in what Dale said. He had allowed Timmy to grow up in the vacuum of imperial favor, to develop his talent in competition only with the most talented. He had done this selfishly, too; he had wanted to lean like an aging emperor on that youthful shoulder. And Timmy had suffered. He had developed the unworldliness of the perfectionist, the maker of mosaics; preoccupied, he brooded over his work with poised hammer. Now he would have to look up.

"I'll see what I can do for you, Sheridan," Knox said heavily. "I really will. Don't worry."

"Thanks, Henry. I'll hear from you, then?"

Knox stared fixedly down at his desk until he knew that he was alone. For once again he felt the tearing in his chest, the dizziness; once again he had seen the hard bright throbbing lines before his eyes. It passed now, and he rubbed his fingers gently against his eyelids. Everybody died, he told himself for the thousandth time; there was really nothing to it. Oh, if he retired, if he took it easy, if he went south, maybe it was ten years off or more, as the sad, friendly doctor had told him when he was sitting in the office after the examination, dressed again for the verdict, the tubes and cords and the ugly white cot on wheels thrust behind green curtains. Mrs. Knox, of course, must be told immediately, didn't he agree? But no. Not right away anyhow. Gazing now at the papers on his desk, the unsigned letters in his basket, he had no sense of futility or disillusionment or least of all fear. He had only a wry bitterness. He would not be a judge or even the president of a small university; it was doubtful if he would write a book, and it was manifestly impossible for him to make the African tour of missions, so long a cherished project. He would be remembered a few years as a lawyer; then he would be identified only as a photograph in the hallway to the files as a name, recently removed, in the title of the firm. And he was only fifty-eight. Mr. Sheffield, whose complacency seemed immune to time, was thirty years older; Dale, whose rugged frame might defy decomposition itself, a year younger. Together they seemed to touch hands over the tumble of his romantic ideas. When he had gone things would be as they always had been. He would simply have taken his place on the wall of the long corridor by the reception hall with the peculiar deadness that attaches to the photographs of deceased partners.

And yet as a boy he had drunk deep of the cold, bright insistent spring of his clerical father's idealism. He had never been able to tolerate that the lares and penates of his adult years should be more gilded than those of his youth. In contraposition to his parent he had set up the ideal, incarnate in Mr. Sheffield, of the philosopher-advocate whose duty was to handle the little cases equally with the big, the wise counselor who could turn with the same tolerance and sympathy from an issue of tens of millions to a mother who distrusted a prospective son-in-law. If he tended now in his own mind to exaggerate the time that he actually spent with unhappy mothers, it was only because of his dismay that these periods had so dwindled. His corporations had formed a tight little circle around him, and the most important had elbowed their way roughly to the front row. He had the reputation of a tough and exacting lawyer for a tough and exacting clientele; "if you can pay, go to Knox," people said; "it's cheap in the end." It was only to be expected that mothers with family problems, unless they owned controlling shares in his corporations, should seek their counsel at a lower level. He was trapped in his own success; even in the desperate gratification of his biggest deals, even in those clear, high moments when the drudgery was over and the pieces fell suddenly together, he would wonder if he should not have taken over the New Hampshire school that his father had founded, or been a professor or minister or missionary, and given out the words of God and medicaments on a small and torrid island in a distant sea. It was all quite sincere. There was nothing of the Pharisee in his religious observance, his Sunday passing of the plate, his position on the Protestant council of churches. Such things only helped to alleviate the constant small anxiety, however logically rebutted, that he had "sold out," that he had betrayed, in some degree or other, the faith that his parent had placed in him. He had been considered quixotic, half out of his mind, when once, nearing the climax of his legal career, he had taken a year's leave of absence to handle a drive for funds for a divinity school. It had been said that it was a nervous breakdown, that he would never come back. Yet he had come back and come back to be acting senior partner of the firm.

But he had come back also to a firm that already courted the rising star of Dale. And Knox detested the man; there was no other word for it. In the beginning he had felt guilty about it, wondering uneasily if his feeling might not stem from a New England prejudice against all that was indigenous to New York, that arrogant assumption that with the exception of a handful of men in the financial district who had largely come from outside the city, one could expect to be met with a slick urban chicanery, hardened by the cynicism of Old World religions. Later, when Dale began to bring in clients from the social world, when he started to give his great, mixed, sprawling cocktail parties, when he took advantage of a professional relationship to walk into the addled affections of Mrs. Polhemus, Knox had felt less guilty. The man was a toady, and that was that. Yet his dislike had become almost an obsession with him. It was more than the mounting list of Dale's clients, real estate manipulators, postwar bright boys with collapsible corporations and ballooning deductions, divorcing actresses and café socialites, rich refugees with tax nationalities; it was more than the increasing and unwelcome publicity of the firm, more than Dale's own continuously expanding girth, calm and general geniality. What irked Knox far more than any of these things was his sense of Dale's conviction, never articulated but vividly expressed in the clear cynicism of his wide eyes, the faint shrug of his big shoulders, that what was all the shouting about, weren't they engaged, all of them, in heartily rowing the same boat? And Knox knew, too, he exasperatedly knew, that no amount of persuasion, however patient or labored, could ever convince a man like Dale that there was any difference between his type of practice and that of his senior partner's. And was there? Was either he or Dale anything more than a clenched fist jabbed in the direction of a client's antagonist?

Was any lawyer? In such moments of desperate solitude, of agonized self-appraisal, it seemed to Knox that Dale's round, half-smiling face had risen over him like a pale moon to cast its mocking light not only over the years of his own professional life but over the whole distinguished history of the firm.

5

THE NIGHT after Dale's interview with Knox, Timmy was to meet Ann at the Larry Duanes' for dinner, and he went straight from the office to their apartment. It was in the same development, across the street and with the same floor plan as the Colts', but its atmosphere was as different as if it were uptown east of the park. For it was obvious that the Duanes were only there on a temporary basis; the gleaming break front with the wedding china, the large new sofa from Sloane's, the low, lung-shaped coffee table and the sporting prints, even the expectant crib, gaily painted, in the guest room, were manifestly destined to be moved, after only a brief interlude of self-support, to larger quarters jointly subsidized by senior Duanes and Knoxes. Sally Knox Duane presided prettily over her small quarters while the older generation exclaimed at her competence as a housekeeper, leaning over, with upraised hands, amazed, as with a doll's house, at how real the tiny chairs and saucers seemed. Sally herself was small, with short, curly, dark hair; her currently pregnant state gave a foretaste of the plump busy matron that she would so soon become.

Ann had already arrived and was drinking cocktails with Sally and Larry when Timmy came in. She was sitting up very straight in her chair as she always did in the early part of any party, even a supper for just four friends, talking with the rather strained politeness in which she tried to disguise her shyness. There was a suppressed excitability behind her "social manner," as Timmy used jokingly to call it, that always made him smile; she felt so strongly about things that her dammed up feeling was apt to leak out in even the most trivial discussion. From the hall he could hear her holding forth about the house which they had taken the summer before in Ketauset and which they had been planning to rent again.

"It's really adorable," she was exclaiming. "I do hope you'll come down, Sally. You can see the water from the second floor, and there used to be a sweet little lawn until the owner burnt it out because she was afraid of ticks. Timmy finds it a bit noisy on Saturday nights with the clubhouse so near, but—oh, darling, there you are. I was just telling them about Ketauset."

Timmy greeted the Duanes, walking slowly over to each and shaking hands to gain time before telling her.

"It sounds divine," Sally said politely. "I hope we can come and visit after the baby comes."

"Oh, it's nothing much," Timmy said deprecatingly. "You know Ann. She always makes the best of things."

"Timmy makes me sound like a Pollyanna! But I'm not. It *is* a nice house."

"It's really just an old dump, Sally," he continued. "Don't let Ann take you in. Damp, with sand in everything. Hot water only when you least expect it."

"Why, Timothy Colt!" Ann was staring at him with indignant eyes. Even a single cocktail was apt to make her rather belligerent. "Does all of life have to depend on a few drops of hot water coming out of a pipe?"

"It does there."

"You've changed your attitude since this morning," she continued, suddenly suspicious. "What happened? Oh, Timmy, you telephoned the agent." She clasped her hands. "You couldn't get the house!"

"I could get it, but you've always said you wouldn't go down there alone." The disappointment in her eyes was too vivid; he hurried, brutally, to finish with it. "Look, darling, it's happened again. I'm on a deal that'll take two months. I just can't get away. That's all there is to it."

"Oh, Timmy," she wailed. "You *promised* me!"

"I know, sweetheart, but I'm not the boss."

"But Mr. Knox was going to *make* you take a vacation. I *know* that, Timmy. Mrs. Knox told me so."

"It was he who gave me the job."

"Really, Sally, your *father!*" Ann had turned explosively to

48

her hostess. "What's he trying to do? Kill my Timmy?"

"But Daddy adores Timmy," Sally assured her, shocked. "Everyone knows that. It must be something really important."

"It's always important. Everything about your father *always* has to be important."

"Now, Ann," Timmy cautioned her.

Larry intervened. "What's the job, Tim?"

"Buying a business from an estate. Textiles. Big deal. And it's all mine, that's the beauty of it. A completely free hand."

"You see what I'm up against, Sally!" Ann protested. "He's actually *glad* about it!"

"Of course he's glad about it," Larry retorted. "You know what it means, don't you? A free hand on a deal like that?"

"I know it means a hot summer in town for my boys."

"It means this is his big chance! This is the test, Ann!"

"For what? The least-vacation-since-the-war prize?"

"For a partnership!" Larry exclaimed.

But Ann only shrugged. "I wonder if it isn't the same thing."

"You can take the boys down to the Knoxes whenever you want," Timmy pointed out to her. "Mr. Knox told me to tell you that. He said the pool was theirs. Which, by the way, Sally, was terrific of him." He turned back to Ann. "The moment I'm through, we'll take off somewhere. Just you and I. I promise."

"I wish I had a dollar for every time I've heard that."

"You will, Ann!" Larry exclaimed, laughing. "You will!"

Timmy, watching her, could see that she had already accepted it. She would protest and grumble just a bit more, and then, with apparent ease, she would adapt herself to the new situation as if they had never planned anything else. Yet he hated to do it to her; she had made such a point of this particular summer and she asked for so little. "Larry," he said loudly, to change the subject, "do you still want to get out of estates? This is your chance. I can pick my number two man."

Larry looked at him in consternation. "Gosh, Tim."

"It'll be a big job. You'll have to cut down your night life. Rather drastically, I'm afraid."

"I don't know much about corporate work."

"You'll pick it up."

"Larry, don't!" Ann warned him earnestly. "He just wants to ruin your summer because your father-in-law has ruined his. Timmy's a puritan, you know. He doesn't really believe in vacations. Particularly if *he's* not going to get one!"

Timmy could tell by Larry's puckered brow and set chin that he was undergoing a severe test. There was something almost comical about the way he overdignified the importance of things, not only the importance of parties and weekends that he might be giving up, but the importance in his career of taking on this particular job. Larry saw the most minor steps in life in immediate relation to his own ultimate partnership. "Tim, I'll do it!" he cried.

"I really should apologize for Timmy," Ann said dryly to Sally. "Now he's spoiled your summer, too. You know, I sometimes think I really could take it all better if there was a purpose in it. Even a worldly purpose. But that's what's so funny. Timmy's not even ambitious."

"Timmy?" Larry interjected. "Oh, he's ambitious, all right."

"You think so," Ann retorted, "because you are yourself!"

"Suppose we all talk about something else," Timmy suggested uneasily. "I think we've spent more than enough time on me. With or without my ambition." To his relief, they all dropped the subject, even Ann, nor did she revert to it after they got home. When she came up behind him, as he was listening to the late news on their radio, and silently kissed him on the cheek, he knew that it was her way of apologizing for making even the little fuss that she had.

The next morning he and Larry met George Emlen in Knox's office. George, of course, was Dale's client, and Timmy was to be working now in Dale's department, but Sheffield, Knox was not so tightly compartmented that a corporate deal as big as the Emlen contract would not be referred, at least for general supervision, to the primary corporate expert of the firm. Timmy was not impressed with the client's appearance which contained some curious contradictions. His hairless, oval face with small dark eyes and thick curly blond hair seemed young enough, but the dry, pouting arrogance of his big lips, the wrinkles under his eyes, the low, deliberate tone of his speaking voice seemed that of a man who had been born middle-aged. Timmy calculated, if he was Mrs. Dale's nephew, that he couldn't be much over forty. When Emlen got up restlessly to walk about the room, as he several times did while Knox was talking, he appeared at least five and a half feet, but his stocky build and wide rear end made him seem much shorter. It was clear that if he was

50

impressed at being received by the senior partner, he was not going to let anyone know it.

"It's quite a deal," Knox was saying. "From a legal point of view, anyway. You've got just about every problem in the books, Tim. If you pull this one off, you can write a text. Title clouds in the real estate, questions about the executors' powers, capital-gains snarl, problem of registration on the ultimate sale. Boy, it's a beaut! Well, there we are, Mr. Emlen. I'm putting you in competent hands."

Emlen turned from the window. "I beg your pardon, Mr. Knox. But am I to understand that you won't be handling the matter yourself?"

"Not directly, no. Mr. Colt will be handling it."

"I don't wish to cast any reflection on Mr. Colt, but is he a member of the firm?"

"Actually not." Knox's eyes glittered slightly over his smile. "Mr. Colt is one of our ablest and most trusted associates."

"Quite so. But I had thought a deal where I and *my* partners were going to have to raise and pay over something in the nature of six million dollars might have been considered big enough for one of *your* partners."

"I don't think you quite understand how we work, Mr. Emlen," Knox responded, speaking slowly and maintaining his now rather fixed smile. "The law is a profession, and every lawyer in this office is a professional man. The distinction between partner and associate is purely an intra-firm matter, a feature of management necessary in any large organization. When you get Timmy Colt, you're getting someone who's as good as we've got. Believe me."

"Then where does the responsibility lie?"

"With me, of course," Knox said dryly. "I will be entirely responsible for the caliber of the work done."

"Very well, if that's the way you feel," Emlen said with a shrug. "I suppose it's all right. But you don't think it looks a bit condescending to the sellers' lawyers?"

"I don't care in the least how it looks to the sellers' lawyers."

Timmy felt that it was a bad beginning indeed, and he was not encouraged by the explanation that Knox gave him later.

"Don't worry about Emlen," Knox told him with a wave of his hand. "He feels he has to act that way. His father was a real tycoon. Chairman of the board of Holcombe Textiles. Young George is always afraid people are going to take him for granted. He's determined to be as big a man as his father."

"In textiles?"

"In anything. What I really mean is as rich a man as his father. No, richer. George is rich now, by any reasonable standards, and he'll have more when his mother dies. But that's nothing to him. He's got the real money bug." Knox shook his head, changing to his philosophic mood. "You see a lot of it around these days. Money for money's sake. None of the false piety of the old robber barons. No interest in art treasures. None even in grand living and social climbing. Just the bare desire to accumulate. Maybe the miser is coming back. I understand Emlen lives as a bachelor with his mother and makes her pay his laundry bills."

"What's the best way to handle him?"

"That's up to you," Knox said with a shrug. "But just remember one thing. He'll never fire us. He knows damn well he won't find another firm with an uncle like Dale to give him a break on bills. So there you are, my boy. And don't forget I'm right here to help."

Which, of course, was just what Timmy was most careful to forget. He knew that after the initial briefing Knox would hate to be disturbed unless the question was really important. When George Emlen came next to the office, he arranged to have him shown to his own room. Emlen slouched easily in the armchair and glanced appraisingly about the small space.

"What do they pay you here?" he asked. "Pretty small cheese, I guess." It was his first personal remark, and Timmy wondered if it might not be his peculiar method of making friends.

"I'm afraid we'll have to regard that as my affair."

"Well, I bet it's not more than ten," George retorted.

"You could be right."

"Hell's bells, man, there are men in this town not much older than you and with probably half your brains who've already made their first million!"

"Well, I'm still a virgin, then," Timmy replied briskly, clipping some papers. "Unless you'd prefer to call me an old maid."

"Are you satisfied?"

"We can't all have the same goals."

"Can't we?" George's laugh was frankly unbelieving. "Do you mean to tell me that you're happy pushing papers around this word shop and listening to that damn autocall going bong-bong? Don't try to kid me."

Timmy looked up at him. "I'm not trying to kid you, Mr.

Emlen," he said. "I wouldn't expect you to understand the satisfactions of my profession."

"All right, all right." George raised his hands in a careless gesture of apology. "Don't take it personally. I'm only asking. And you'd better start calling me George. I guess you and I are going to be seeing a lot of each other in the next weeks. I'm not one of these clients who comes to the closing and says 'Where do I sign?' By the time you're through with this deal, Timothy, you're going to feel that you and I are twins."

Timmy nodded and turned his attention to the bulging briefcase that George proceeded to deposit on his desk. It was that, he hoped, rather than its owner which he would try to make his twin.

6

HE WAS DETERMINED that George Emlen's ungraciousness was not going to destroy his satisfaction at being in charge. The deal itself was too beautiful. In the early days of piecing it together, he would arrive at the office a good hour before anyone else and sit in silence before a huge sheet of paper which he called the "problem chart" and on which he had drawn lines with arrows under which, in neat, small, rounded handwriting he had inscribed labels and questions. One border of the paper represented the mills and holdings of the sellers; the other the group of purchasers organized by George Emlen. Arrows, some with short, stubby tails and others several inches or even feet in length, indicated the ultimate coming together of the two, and as the arrows turned upwards in the center in a noble, full fanning out, they were joined by red ones standing for tax warnings and green ones for securities regulations. Timmy, hunched over his chart, would occasionally add a line, but more often jot his thought down on a small pad. There was always an answer; *something* could be devised. He loved the abstractness of the practice of law; he found it actually exciting that on the signing of the final paper, the passing of the final check, after the hurly-burly of the conference tables and all the talk, there would have been no change in anything physical, no alteration in the appearance of a mill smoking by a sleepy river, no shift in the vast, ordered weight of bales in a soot-stained warehouse. If this was sterility to a vulgar mind, it was beauty to him, the approach to the essence of things without disarrangement. It sometimes made him too exacting a taskmaster, as Larry Duane had early occasion to discover.

"But, Tim, what does it matter?" he demanded wearily one night late when they were revising a letter on covenants for the seventh time. "Everyone knows what it means. Does it have to be deathless prose?"

"Of course it has to be. And if everyone *really* understood it, it would be. But go home, Larry. I'll finish it."

Larry, in fact, had done better than Timmy had thought he would. It was too much to expect him to be an artist, too. He had been a valuable leg man, trotting between the mill owners and the Emlen accountants, and if his demands on legal language were only those of a cement dealer, namely that it should stick for a certain time, he was no different from the majority of lawyers. And he was willing to work. After somewhat dramatically announcing that he and Sally had canceled all social engagements until the deal was finished, a fact not impressive to Timmy who never made any, he had placed his days and nights at Timmy's disposal with the determined enthusiasm but grave demeanor of a new ensign reporting on the bridge. On as many nights as he could, Timmy contrived to send him home early. Larry would linger guiltily, not wanting to seem to walk out on him, but as he turned to go, Timmy, amused, could tell by his suddenly quickened step in the corridor that he was hurrying to make the party that he had previously declined.

He could dismiss Larry when he wanted to be alone, but there was no dismissing George. The latter, as he had warned Timmy, had evidently nothing in the world to do but follow, step by step, the legal negotiations of the deal that he had inspired. He would drop into Timmy's office, unannounced, having come in on the floor above the reception hall, and sit, casually helping himself to documents from the desk while Timmy telephoned or dictated. He interrupted whenever he liked, putting his questions with the air of blunt suspicion that he never bothered to keep out of his voice and simply grunting when he got his invariably polite and painstaking reply. That George did not trust so junior a lawyer was bad enough, but what made it worse was that he seemed to resent the very existence of the legal profession and what he chose to regard as its unwarranted intrusion into fields that were peculiarly the capitalist's own. "I can thank my lucky stars if all this quibbling doesn't cost me my deal," he would mutter a dozen times a day, and when he left, Timmy knew it was only to check up on his answers at his own office, at the bar of his club, at a dinner party, with any second-guesser whom he chanced to meet. For George lived the deal, in his own way, as completely as Timmy did; he could have been a good client had he had the generosity to recognize competence in any area but his chosen one of preserving and making money. Timmy's only defense was that of inflexible courtesy and unvarying patience, and if these sometimes formed the grey panes and lattices behind which an equally inflexible dislike could be just detected, he did not care. The client was entitled to the job done and the job done well. Beyond that they met as equals. If George wanted a friend, George would have to be more friendly; if he wanted an admirer, he would have to be admirable.

For all his politeness, however, Timmy never yielded an inch where he felt that George was wrong. They had their first serious row over delivery of a draft of the final contract of sale. George wanted it before Timmy was ready.

"You'll just fuss over it all night and take out a couple of commas," he said. "Or else put them in. In the meantime I could be going over it with my partners. Hell's bells, man, I could buy and sell twenty companies while you're fiddling with one contract."

"Maybe. You don't pay me to buy and sell companies. You pay me to get the sale right. And it's *going* to be right."

"Well, what's holding it up now?"

"I've told you," Timmy said evenly, as he lined up the pencils on his desk in the shape of a pipe organ. "I'm waiting for Larry to make a final check on the powers of ancillary executors in New Jersey."

"Powers to do what? To sell?"

"To sell without a court order."

"Well, I'll be damned!" George turned on the disconcerted Larry who was standing behind him. "If executors can't sell, what the hell *can* they do?"

"Well, they can, Mr. Emlen, under ordinary circumstances," Larry was beginning, "but here we're faced with—"

"We're faced with red tape!" George interrupted roughly, turning back to Timmy. "I think I'd like that draft, thank you, Colt."

Timmy's lips became very tight. "I'm sorry. As Larry was about to say, we're faced with a situation for which we have no exact precedent. Presumably you mean us to do the research, not guess. I can't take the responsibility otherwise."

George crossed his arms and glared balefully at him. "Is there really any reason why you *should* take the responsibility?"

"What do you mean?"

"Well, isn't that the job of a member of the firm? Of Mr. Knox, for example? Or even my uncle?"

"You can see Mr. Knox whenever you wish," Timmy said, flushing. "Would you like me to make an appointment?"

"I can make my own appointments, thank you," George said angrily, getting up. "And you don't have to sneer at me, either." Timmy remained immobile, his eyes fixed on his desk. "After all, Knox is my lawyer. All I want to know is whether *you* don't wish to see him." He stared down coldly at Timmy. "Whether you don't think you could use a little of his advice. Are you so sure you have *all* the answers, Colt?"

"I'm sure that I'm getting them."

"All right, then," George grunted as he turned to the door. "We'll see it your way. But it better be right, boy. That's all I can tell you. It sure as hell better be right."

As he sauntered out of the room Timmy looked silently up to encounter Larry's outraged stare.

"Are you going to let him get away with that?" Larry exploded as soon as they were alone. "Will *you* tell Mr. Knox or shall I?"

"Please, Larry." Timmy closed his eyes for a moment while he got hold of himself. "This is my affair. We'll play it my way."

"But he has no business to speak to you that way! My God, we're not dirt, are we?"

"Of course he has no business to. And maybe I have no business to take it. But I choose to. Is that clear?"

"You're the boss," Larry said, shrugging. "But he'd better not take that tone with me, that's all I can say. I might forget I was a slave, you know. I might just poke him one."

"He won't bother you. It's me he has it in for. Only me. You must remember, Larry, he's responsible for a lot of money."

"Which entitles him to be a son of a bitch?"

"No. But which explains his being one."

"You know something? I think you actually *like* the guy!"

Timmy simply shrugged as he turned back to his work. What he would not bother to explain was that what made it endurable to work with George was that the latter was not so much a master as a fellow servant. Timmy remembered from his own experience how the Japanese had preserved their dignity by regarding the American military as bound equally with themselves to the job of carrying out a plan of occupation imposed by authorities superior to each. George, being intensely egotistical, naturally resented Timmy's elevation of his own deal above himself, but it was not an elevation that he could openly criticize or one that he even rationally wanted to. George, after all, knew how small a percentage of the purchase price he personally was putting up and how ill it befitted him, a quasi trustee for others, to throw his weight around for personal reasons. However galling, he would see things in the end Timmy's way. Had he not tacitly conceded this in leaving his office without demanding an interview with Mr. Knox?

George's supervision, however, continued as steadily as before. He even began to call Timmy at home during the few hours that he was to be found there. Ann came to hate the very sound of his voice. "If he has you for fifteen hours a day, isn't that enough!" she exploded one night after George had called at midnight. "You might as well be married to him!"

"I don't think he'd make a very good mother for George and Walter."

"Timmy Colt, will you never be serious about anything but your work?" She was sitting up in bed, glaring at him as he sat in his pajamas by the telephone, abstractedly smoking a cigarette. "You've been walking in and out of this apartment like a sleepwalker for three weeks now. Does that man think he owns you?"

"He does. For the time being, anyway."

"Don't think I haven't heard about him! Sally Duane has told me all about his manners. He's a horror, that's what he is!"

"Darling," he said wearily, "it'll only be a few more weeks. Then we'll go off somewhere."

"I've heard that before."

"Please, Ann." He came over and sat down beside her, resting his head suddenly on her shoulder. "You've been an angel. Don't spoil it now. I promise we'll go off. Really."

"Oh, poor sweetheart." She supported his head to the

pillow. His eyes were already closed. "Don't think I'm impatient." She leaned over and tucked him in. "But this deal really worries me. You hardly even speak about it. What is he doing to you, that man? I wish I could get my hands on him. Just once!" But Timmy was asleep. When the telephone rang again she stole over to it quickly and answered in a whisper. "My husband is asleep, Mr. Emlen," she hissed into the telephone when she heard the despised voice. "And I have no intention of waking him! Whatever it is will have to wait till the morning!"

The deal became more and more involved. The accountants reported the inventory at less than it had been represented; tax difficulties bristled, and two of George's partners began to seek excuses to renege. George's temper became even shorter, his tone shriller; he suspected everyone about him now and brought all his complaints to Timmy. The latter stepped up his hours, ate sandwich meals and even took to spending some of his nights on a cot in the office. Yet between his moments of obsessive toil, as he disappeared, like a mountain climber, upwards into the mist, he would catch himself wondering if Ann wasn't perhaps right, if living cheek by jowl with George's unvarying distrust wasn't doing something strange to him. He had read during the Nazi war trials of prisoners in concentration camps, thoroughly brutalized, who had developed a cringing, almost canine affection for the very guards who beat them. It seemed to him at times, as he walked home from the subway late at night, that with George he must have run into the incarnation of the spirit that had ruled his old hotel world, the one that from his earliest years he had tried to placate with work. For had he ever really fooled that spirit, with all his application, his concentration; had he ever, at school or even at law school, done anything but cast a few small specks of dust into that stern and watching eye? Which, after a moment's blinking, had only focused on him again, holding him paralyzed in the chilly glare of its knowledge that he could do better, work harder, that *he*, in fact, had to, because—well, because he was himself, Timothy Colt, that was all.

Just at the point when he had decided that his relations with George had deteriorated to a point where improvement was the only possible further change, the floor dropped away, and they took a sudden, deeper plunge. This occurred at a large conference with the executors and their counsel and most of George's partners in the venture. Certain minor deposits made by the purchasers were being returned under the terms of the contract, and the checks, because of the illness of one of the executors whose signature had been required, were actually three days late. Nobody had seen fit to comment on this until George, after making the nervous clucking noise in his throat that always preceded one of his controversial statements, called across the table to one of the sellers' lawyers:

"What about interest? The checks are late, aren't they? What about interest on my money?" He turned to Timmy. "You're meant to be looking after me, aren't you? Why don't you think of these things?" He smiled around at the table in a sudden pale beam of what was evidently meant to be a businessman's jocularity. "I always thought it was the lawyer's role to be the son of a bitch while the client played the nice guy. In this case it seems to be just the reverse."

"I assumed the interest would be waived," Timmy said tersely.

"Oh, you did? Well, it may be easy enough for you to waive it, but it's not quite so simple a matter for me." George again glanced around the table with a wink to comply with the rigid custom that requires the rich, in speaking of their own, to depreciate its quantity, to protest that they, too, must watch their pennies. "It happens to be my money, Mr. Colt."

Timmy, without answering, made a rapid calculation on the pad before him. "Will you make out an extra check for Mr. Emlen, please?" he said in a dry, distant tone to the executor's accountant. "I calculate the interest on three days allocable to his share at $17.16."

George's face slowly reddened in the silence that followed. "Now just a minute, Colt, just a minute," he said, raising his hand. "I didn't say anything about anyone drawing me a check. All I heard was that the checks were late. I asked about interest. That's natural, isn't it? If my counsel had been on his toes and calculated the interest before hand, the matter would never have come up. Now I see it's only a few bucks, and of course I waive it." He nodded as graciously as he could to the accountant. "I only like to know, that's all. I only like to know what's going on. Seems I need a Ouija board."

When the conference was over, George followed Timmy out of the room and down the hall to the latter's office.

"You did that on purpose," he hissed. "You did it on purpose to humiliate me!"

"You brought it up." Timmy's eyes were fixed ahead

down the corridor. "It was your idea to ask about the interest."

"You did it on purpose," George repeated angrily. "You wanted to make a fool of me. Because you think I *am* a fool. You've looked down your nose at me from the beginning! Well, let me tell you something, Colt. I can make plenty of trouble for you around here if I want to. *Plenty* of trouble!"

"That, of course, is your privilege," Timmy said coldly. "It doesn't happen to interest me. I'm trying to do a job, that's all."

And the job was approaching its end. The pieces were beginning to fit. He could hold out a little longer, if only for the pleasure of telling Knox afterwards, as they contemplated the smooth, resilient, completed bridge between buyer and seller, the circumstances under which it had been built. And he had not complained, he reminded himself with a grim satisfaction. He had not complained once.

Two days later he and Larry were summoned to Knox's office by a call from his secretary, Miss Glenn.

"It's trouble," he told Larry gloomily as they walked down the corridor. "It always means trouble when he doesn't call me himself."

But Knox, it seemed at first, only wanted a progress report on the deal. He listened perfunctorily as Timmy outlined what was happening, nodding his head steadily and hitting with his ruler the thin silk-socked ankle crossed over his knee. "Good, good," he said. "It looks as if we are going to be able to close on schedule. How about you, Larry?" he added, turning suddenly to his son-in-law. "Are you surviving? Or has Timmy worked you to death?"

"Oh, I'm fine, sir."

"Larry's really got the hang of it now," Timmy volunteered. "He's been a great help."

"Excellent. There's just one thing I don't quite understand." Knox paused, as if considering how he was to phrase it. "George Emlen dropped in to see me yesterday. He seemed not to be quite satisfied at the service he was getting. What's happened, Timmy? Are you doping off?"

Timmy stared at him, incredulous, his anger a sudden ripping tide, for the moment in suspense. "Was that *his* term?"

"As a matter of fact, it was."

"I don't think I've left the office before midnight in four weeks," Timmy said in the same repressed, distant tone.

"Last night I was here till three. Does he call *that* doping off?"

"He's been having your real estate descriptions checked." Here Knox spread out a blueprint on his desk, carefully smoothing down the corners. "Look here. He says this sliver two hundred feet by thirty is missing from the proposed deed." Knox tapped the area on the chart with his ruler. Timmy stepped forward immediately to examine it and then, without a word to Knox, picked up the copy of the deed on the desk and handed it to Larry.

"Read the description," he said abruptly. With eyes intent on the white lines of the blueprint he remained absolutely still while Larry read and for several seconds afterwards. Then his shoulders sagged. "Emlen's right, sir. It's not in there."

"How do you explain it?"

"It's a hack, that's all." Timmy's voice was strained. "A common or garden hack. Emlen's right. He's not getting the service he's entitled to."

Knox looked at him gravely for a moment and then suddenly broke into a laugh. "Do you know what I told that psychopathic bastard, Timmy?" he said loudly. "I told him if he'd complained about any other associate in the whole damn office, I'd have checked up. But Timmy Colt, I said, no. Never. That deed's only a draft. The error would have been picked up ten times over before it was done in final form."

Timmy, looking into the friendly eyes, the broad smile of his employer, slowly shook his head. It was as if he had been sitting in a windowless bathhouse by the sea, and the door had suddenly blown open to reveal in a glare of light the broad white sand and sparkling ocean of unquestionable facts, glittering facts, the facts of Knox's warmth and approval and unwavering loyalty, of his own clear competence and success. But he was too tired, and there was that within him that made him want to shade his eyes and swing the door closed and sit back in the damp darkness rather than join the others in the bright outside. "I don't see any reason to assume it," he said sullenly. "A hack's a hack."

"Oh, come, Timmy." Knox's smile slightly faded. "You don't care what a guy like Emlen says, do you? *I* know you're doing a bang-up job."

"Maybe you ought to put someone on the job who can satisfy him," Timmy continued in a more surly tone. "Someone who doesn't make mistakes in real estate descriptions. Someone who's up to the Emlen standards!"

Knox's smile had entirely disappeared by now. "Larry, we

won't need you any more. Thanks." When they were alone he continued: "I know you've been under a strain, Timmy. Don't think I don't know what's going on in the office. I know the hours you've been keeping. But that's no reason for letting Emlen get you down. He's not worth it. He's not worth a moment's worry."

The full enormity of Emlen's complaint, of his singling out a single error from weeks of grinding work, suddenly flooded Timmy's mind. "But I hate him!" he shouted. "Don't you see? I hate him!"

Knox's expression became very grave. "Timmy, I'm afraid you're behaving like a child. What you feel about George Emlen is a matter of no consequence. However out of scale. What's a good deal more important is what he thinks of you. Have you let him feel that you dislike him?"

"*He* started it! The very first day! He even sneered at my salary!"

"He's the client," Knox shouted back at him, suddenly striking the table. "You have no business being snotty to clients! You have no business looking down your nose at them! Or at least you have no business letting them *see* it when you do!"

"I didn't know you wanted me to be an ass kisser!"

Knox swung around in his chair at this, placing his back to Timmy. "I think you'd better run along now," he said icily. "And I advise you to have a long quiet think about what happens to young men who take themselves too seriously."

When Timmy arrived in Larry's office his shoulders and arms were still shaking with anger. "I want every one of those God damn real estate descriptions!" he cried. "I'm going to check and recheck every one of them tonight. He's got me this time, just this once, but I'll see him in hell before he catches me again!"

"Oh, Timmy." Larry's face was long with discouragement. "We've been over and *over* them!"

"And we're going over them again," Timmy retorted grimly. "Or rather I am. You can go home. I'll get one of the girls to stay down and read them to me."

The fact that Larry immediately took him up on this, that he did not make even a gesture toward remaining, did a good deal to make him realize, in the long hours while he pored over the printed proofs, how far he had left behind even his own standards of what was rational caution. All right, he thought furiously, so he *was* cracking up. So *what?*

7

THE KNOXES' country home was a plain white farmhouse in Cold Spring Harbor which they had bought in their youngish days and had expensively but not always successfully embellished and added to in the years of their waxing prosperity. There was a long wing in the back now, unexpectedly French, to house the new living room; there were bay windows in odd places, or in places that looked odd from the outside, and a swimming pool, too close to the front door, that occupied almost all of the rather needed lawn space. The family, however, adored it, and Ann, who had come down for the weekend to get the boys out of the city heat, admired their reluctance to sacrifice it for anything grander. Sitting on Sunday morning by the pool with Sally Dunne, they talked about their husbands.

"What do you suppose they're doing now?"

"Well, I can tell you what they're *not* doing," Sally said as she threaded a needle. She was sewing for the child that was to be born the following month. "They're not at church. Not Larry, anyway. I suppose they're working."

"Poor things. I guess we're lucky to be women."

"Oh, but they *like* it, Ann."

"Do they? All the time?"

"Well, maybe not *all* the time. But fundamentally."

Ann let it drop. One could never argue such matters with Sally. It was rather wonderful, the number of things that she took for granted in her neat, contented way: that her father was the greatest man in the world, except maybe for old Mr. Sheffield, that Larry was the kindest husband, that men liked their work, women their homes and that getting ahead was fun. Yet there was a sweetness about her that checked any gloating anticipation of what might happen if she ever gave the world a long, hard look. Ann sighed. She was in no position not to envy the complacent. She did not even know

63

if Timmy liked his work. Or if he simply liked getting it done. "I sometimes can't help wondering what there is in it for you," she remarked. "Larry will work for years and years and finally be able to buy you a swimming pool. And here you have one already."

"Oh, but not our *own*."

"It's just as wet as if it were." But when she saw Sally's perplexed expression, she was ashamed. "Oh, don't pay any attention to me. I'm just jealous, that's all. Not of your swimming pool, but of your wanting one. It gives our kind of life so much more point if you want things. I'm as jaded as an oil heiress. I don't want anything."

"Oh, but it's not just a swimming pool," Sally protested, shocked at a mistake so fundamental. "I don't care about a swimming pool, either. Not really. It's the other things. The things for the children. Schools and camps and subscription dances."

"But you see, I never had those things," Ann said gloomily. "Timmy and I went to public school. Maybe that's what's wrong with us. We're not afraid enough of being poor."

"But it was different in your case," Sally reassured her quickly. "You weren't brought up in New York, were you? I wouldn't mind a public school in the suburbs, but in New York with Puerto Ricans and juvenile delinquents . . ."

"Timmy went to school in New York," Ann interrupted tersely and left poor Sally to find her own way out of it. Mr. Knox had made his appearance at the other end of the pool in a great baggy pair of blue bathing trunks, and she watched him carefully as he walked slowly around the flagstone border to join them. She had come down with the resolution that she was going to complain about what was happening to Timmy. So far she had not dared.

"My two law widows," Knox said blandly, waving an arm at them. "How are you bearing up? Sally, my dear, your mother is asking for you." He did not occupy the chair that she now vacated, but sat at the edge of the pool, his long legs dangling in the water. Ann, looking at his broad white back and slumped shoulders, thought with a rather unnerving pity how old and tired he suddenly seemed.

"I've been showing George and Walter the barn," he told her. "They think I'm a terrible fraud because there are no cows or pigs. Not even a horse. Nothing but one old station wagon. They made me feel like Marie Antoinette dressing up as a shepherdess."

"But she had real sheep."

"Did she?" He turned around to smile at her. "Think of it. I'm a greater phony than Marie Antoinette. But they're nice boys, Ann. You and Timmy have brought them up well."

"I'm afraid I'll have to take all the credit. You keep poor Timmy too busy to do much bringing up."

Knox turned back to the pool with a shrug, as if to emphasize his helplessness in such matters. There had always been a slight strain in their relations, but she suspected that he appreciated her honesty in not concealing it.

"Keep the boys out of the law, Ann," he said gruffly. "It's a rat race. Make brokers out of them. Or insurance salesmen."

"Don't think I wouldn't it I could. But Timmy would never let me. He's worse than you about the law."

"Worse than me? Oh, come, Ann. I'm no admirer of lawyers."

"Your façade is admirable."

"You do me a grave injustice," he protested. "I only became a lawyer because my father hated the profession. It's not every day that a man gets such a beautiful opportunity to disoblige."

"Why didn't he like lawyers?"

"He said they were immoral."

"All of them?"

"All of them." He threw his arms up in emphasis. "It was as simple as that."

"And you agree with him? Is that what you're trying to tell me?"

"I've often wondered," he mused. "Your client wants to do something grasping and selfish. But quite within the law. As a lawyer you're not his conscience, are you? You advise him that he can do it. So he does it and tells his victim: 'My lawyer made me!' You're satisfied, and so is he, and the moral question falls gently between two schools."

"You don't believe a word of it!" she exclaimed, provoked by a detachment that she knew was not genuine. "You know you believe the law is a great profession!"

"Do I, my dear? What makes you so sure?"

"Because you've created a world that believes it," she replied, thinking suddenly that it was Timmy's world, this world that he now affected to despise. "Could you have done that if you hadn't believed it yourself?"

"I wonder. I wonder indeed."

"You believe in the tradition of old Mr. Sheffield. Timmy's always said that!"

"The tradition of old Mr. Sheffield," he repeated slowly, rubbing his cheeks with his thumb and fingers. "But might I not have created that, too? As well as the world that believes it?"

"Oh," she murmured and realized with a shock that he was serious. *"Did* you?"

"Imagine, Ann," he continued, with a sudden rather reckless note in his tone, "a large unwieldy firm with a reputation based on long deceased partners, mighty men. Imagine Sheffield, a lone survivor from that age of titans, yet not himself a true titan. But with all the bearings of one. Oh, yes. The smooth, silky white hair streaked with yellow. The long, lean, unwrinkled cheeks. The thin, flawlessly garbed frame. Imagine me, a younger man, called to take over the firm, bewildered, passionately in need of a unifying symbol. Wasn't he made to order?"

"But Mr. Sheffield already had a great reputation!"

"You mean the legend had already been started? True. The old man had started it himself. Few were alive to remember how small his earlier role had been. There was a triumph in his mere survival that won everyone's admiration. He had become 'wonderful,' and that word is half the battle of the legend makers. Yes, my dear. You're right. My work had largely been done for me. I had only to complete it."

"But there's something you've left out!" she cried, forgetting everything in her sudden excitement.

"And what is that?"

"The reason you wanted the legend. It wasn't for the firm. It was for yourself. So you *could* believe!"

His face for a moment was blank with surprise, and then he suddenly chuckled. "You're perceptive, Ann! My God, I had no idea you were so perceptive." He paused to reflect. "Perhaps I had an idea of it, though," he continued after a few moments. "Perhaps it's why I told you about Mr. Sheffield. Something I've never even told my wife. I had thought it was because you didn't like me. I'm always more at ease with people who don't like me. There's no legend to maintain."

"But I *do* like you, Mr. Knox!"

"Nonsense, my dear. Why should you? You must feel I've taken up an undue amount of Timmy's life. And I have. I'm not pleading my defense. I'm simply asking forgiveness. As any parent does. Not now, of course. But when you're my age, and I'm dead." He pulled out a few blades of grass and tossed them impatiently on the surface of the pool. "Oh, very long dead. Then I want you to remember that I, too, was a product as well as a cause. Of the whole bloody system."

"Mr. Knox," she begged him. "I don't need to forgive you. I have nothing to forgive. But if you *really* feel that way, maybe there is something you can do for me. Or for Timmy, rather." She saw in the sudden weariness of his eyes that the last thing he wanted was to be pulled from the abstract world of speculation in which he had been playing. But she didn't care; it was her only moment to speak. "Could you take him off this Emlen deal? Couldn't someone else finish it?" Her old nervousness came back as he turned his head away from her. "Please, Mr. Knox. It's killing him. Really, it is!"

"Would he want you to ask me?"

"Him? My God, he'd kill me!"

"Stick it out a bit longer, Ann. It's almost over."

"But you don't know what it's doing to him!" she insisted tensely. "I *know*. George Emlen must be some kind of fiend!"

"Really, my dear. George Emlen is an unusually egocentric man. He has the peculiar ungraciousness that is only found in the best society. But he's hardly a fiend. He's not that important."

"Not to you, maybe. Not to anyone else, perhaps. But to Timmy, yes. He's a fiend to Timmy!"

"Why?"

She looked unhappily across the pool into the tired, hot foliage and wondered if there was any use in explaining. "Because he sees Timmy as Timmy sees himself."

"And how is that?"

"As lazy. Shiftless." She shrugged, looking away, irritated at having to say it and at the prospect of the immediate, the automatic denial. "Incompetent." She knew he was staring at her now.

"Those aren't exactly words that one usually associates with Timmy," he said softly.

"What does that matter?" she said impatiently. "If they're the words that he associates with himself?"

"Consciously?"

"Oh, consciously enough. Whatever consciously is."

"If that is true, then George *is* a fiend." Knox nodded gravely now. "His fiend, anyway. Or one of his furies." He shook his head reflectively. "What an awful thought, to meet a man who gives you your own grade of yourself. Your secret grade."

"Then you'll do something about it?" she begged, afraid

that he would lose sight of Timmy in another of his speculations. "You'll put someone else on the deal?"

"I'll put someone else on it, yes," he said as he rose
laboriously to his feet. "I'll put Austin Cochran on it. He's
finished his month with Legal Aid now. He can take some of
the pressure off Timmy."

She jumped up, her face contracted with disappointment.
"*Some* of it?"

"Oh, I can't take Timmy off the deal, my dear," he said,
turning to walk up to the house. "You wouldn't want me to
do that yourself. If you knew what depended on it."

"What depends on it?" she called boldly after him. He
paused, but did not turn.

"A partnership, maybe."

"But I don't *care* about a partnership!"

"I'm sure you don't, my dear. But that, you will agree, is
another matter."

Watching his broad back as he slowly crossed the grass,
she reflected ruefully on the small impact of her first conscious interference in Timmy's life. She even wondered if her
peculiar feeling of emptiness might not be relief.

8

AS THE EMLEN PURCHASE approached completion, Timmy
developed a new worry. He was actually afraid now that
George might ruin the whole deal by the closeness of his
bargaining, by his stubbornness on minor points, by his
sudden irascibility. George was far too anxious to prove at all
times that he was a tougher businessman than the sellers; his
reputation in this respect was probably the only thing in the
world for which he would have sacrificed not only his own
profit but the profit of his partners. To Timmy, breathlessly
watching the two ends of his laboriously constructed bridge
about to meet to form an arch over the churning legal rapids,
it was the purest agony to see George running senselessly up

and down the unfinished structure and stamping like an angry child on its tenderest parts. He suspected that George knew the pain he was causing him and that this knowledge made him even more reckless, taking revenge for Timmy's failure to appreciate his own business merits by threatening destruction of his masterpiece. For could he not by doing so prove at an easy stroke the basic superiority of the client? What was the virtue of being a lawyer if a lawyer's advice was not taken? "Look," he told Timmy once, "I may not even *want* to go through with this deal. You get so wrapped up in your commas and semicolons that you forget it's only a matter of dollars and cents to me." He could trumpet the profit motive with the sure knowledge that no one, not even Timmy, could question it. Why, after all, were any of them, businessmen or lawyers, congregated in high buildings at the southern tip of a skinny island if it was not for profit? What other motive did not make fools of them? And Timmy, nodding briefly, speeded the work to save his creation, huddled away in his office with the door now closed, jealous of all interference, within the office or without. He jumped, one Monday morning, to hear a voice exclaim:

"Now *that's* what I call concentration."

He looked up to see Mr. Knox in the doorway. "I'm sorry, sir."

"I've had a very nice weekend with your family," Knox continued, moving slowly into the room, his hands in his pockets. "They're good boys, George and Walter."

"You were good to have them, sir. I'm afraid I haven't been much of a father recently."

"That's what I wanted to speak to you about. I'm afraid you're overdoing it. I want Austin to help you—now don't *look* at me like that, Timmy! Nobody's going to rob you. You're clinging to those papers like an old cat with kittens. Relax."

"But I've got the thing licked now," Timmy protested strongly. "I don't *need* help. It would take more time to explain it to Austin than to do it myself."

"That's never true," Knox retorted. "That's the statement of a man who can't delegate. And a man who can't delegate never gets anywhere."

"Then I'll never get anywhere. But would you *mind* letting me finish my own way?"

"Yes, Timmy, I would mind. I'm going to send Austin up, and I'll expect you to keep him busy."

Timmy simply looked down at the papers on his desk without answering.

"Well?" Knox demanded in a crisper tone.

"Well, *what*, sir?"

"Will you give him some work or won't you?"

"You're the boss," Timmy said sullenly. "What do you expect me to do?"

"Good," Knox grunted, shrugging, as he turned to the door. "But why the hell do you have to throw the soup back in the Saint Bernard's face? Oh, it's fun, I suppose. It's fun!"

When Austin came up, he had obviously been briefed by Knox. He was positively jaunty in his effort not to seem oversolicitous. "I hear you need help. That things are out of control. Am I too late? Is the deal completely hacked?"

"Things are fine, just fine," Timmy said testily. "I'll have to find time to dream up something for you to do. Something to make you look busy."

"Let's not be like that, shall we?" Austin retorted brightly. "Let's be *such* a help to each other. Suppose I do the closing papers?"

Which, of course, he did to perfection. And it was, after all, a help to have him. Larry, for all his earnestness, lacked the experience to do closing papers, and Timmy, even in his present state, was able to appreciate Austin's tact in seeking to help in a part of the work that could not possibly interfere with his own monopoly of the credit. But that was like Austin, a small, sober, rather owlish young man of predetermined good spirits who managed to retain his cynicism about clients despite his own constantly increasing investment of time and skill in the unraveling of their affairs. Austin and his wife, who lived in Riverdale and had a joint hobby of raising money for a settlement house when they were not raising children, seemed peculiarly adjusted to every vicissitude of modern life. Ann used to say it was because they were the only people she knew who had religion.

Everybody liked Austin, and George proved no exception. Austin treated him with a mixture of deference and rather impertinent familiarity that he seemed to find actually agreeable. It was impossible to tell whether Austin would answer one of his questions with meticulous good manners or would reach over instead to tap a paragraph under his very nose and exclaim with a chuckle: "There, man, there! If it was any larger, it would bite you!" George, suspicious at first, was gradually mollified. For there was nothing, after all, really personal in Austin's quality of dry bounciness, and he was another person whose opinion George could use to check against Timmy's. Larry had been too lowly to use as a foil, but now George could turn airily after listening to Timmy and say: "What's your thought on that, Austin?" or "Let's see what the bright boy has to say. How about it, Austin?" The worst of these times was when George requested that Austin attend the actual closing.

"It's not necessary at all, George," Austin said immediately. "The papers are done, and that was my job. You've got Timmy, and Timmy doesn't need a side-kick. I'd just be window-dressing. Besides, there's my time to consider. It would probably cost you an extra fifty bucks."

But George, missing the dig in this, thought it was his moment for the sweeping gesture. "When I think what I'm going to have to pay for all this paper shuffling," he said grandly, "I'm not going to quibble about a few extra bucks. Not when it's a question of the closing, anyway. I think we could use Austin, don't you, Timmy?"

"I'm always glad to have Austin."

"You see!" George exclaimed. "That settles it."

When he had gone, Timmy was careful not to look at Austin. They both read papers for several minutes until Timmy muttered between his teeth: "It doesn't look as if I'm needed at all."

"How's that?"

"At the closing. I'm sure you'll handle it beautifully. I'm sure George would much prefer you to handle it without me. I'm sure everybody would."

Austin stood up. "Just what the hell do you mean, Timmy?"

"Well, wouldn't you?"

"Have you gone completely crazy? Do you really think I'm trying to cut you out?"

Timmy covered his eyes with his finger tips, his elbows resting on the desk. "I don't know what I think any more."

"Man, you're in a bad way." Austin moved over quietly behind the desk and put a hand on Timmy's shoulder. "You've let that guy get you down. You've got to pull yourself together. Try to see it his way."

"*His* way!"

"Stop making him feel what a louse you think he is." Austin shook his head. "I wouldn't like to work with you, Timmy, if you thought I was a louse. Poor George, I'm sure it's not a pleasant experience."

"Thanks, Austin." Timmy looked up and managed to smile. "You're a friend. Thanks."

And in three more days the deal was closed. Timmy presided in the firm's paneled conference room under yet another portrait of Mr. Sheffield, at the head of a long mahogany table about which were grouped twenty men, each with a portfolio containing the previously signed documents. It went off without a hitch. As the expected final calls from the title companies came in, the various closing papers, the checks, bonds, mortgages, assignments, guarantees, affidavits, letters of indemnity and deeds were transferred, back and forth across the long table, with the labored solemnity of a Japanese dance. When the last check had passed Timmy looked up to see George Emlen standing over him with hand outstretched saying: "Well, congratulations, fella. It's been a long haul."

George gave a "smoker" that night at his club for all the men on both sides who had worked on the deal. As Austin pointed out to Timmy, it was really the cheapest kind of party he could get away with. When Timmy arrived with Ann, for wives were invited, at nine o'clock, he found some forty persons gathered in a private room drinking whiskey and water and murmuring in the subdued fashion of a business group where only the husbands were acquainted. From the high blue walls between the scarlet curtains former presidents and officers of George's club looked down on them, Schermerhorns, Livingstons, Jays, removed from the dusty actuality of commerce by the dignification of the painter's process. But to Timmy, standing alone by the white cloth-covered table with its neat triangular army of glasses, sipping a dark drink while Ann went to greet Austin, these figures of the past had small luster. He could move them down into the room that night as easily as he could relate George, officiously, arrogantly hospitable, to their painted height; he saw all the figures, in canvas or in flesh, as dry with the dryness of practical business. For he seemed to have lost his faith in the form, the equation, the contract; the "realities" of George's deal, the Emlenization of everything, the exchanged deed and dollar, had reduced his own role to less than nothing. Larry came over and made him a little bow.

"Well, Maestro, we made it."

"Yes, we made it."

"You know something? I bet even George is pleased. I bet he asks for you on every one of his jobs from now on."

"The Lord preserve me."

"Oh, come, Tim, it's over now. Don't be such an old gloom."

"Larry, be a good boy and leave me be."

"All right. All right." Larry's eyes suddenly dilated and he grabbed Timmy's arm. "Well, for Pete's sake, look! You're made, kid! Mr. Sheffield himself!"

And sure enough, there was the old gentleman, tall, gaunt, bent over now, but with magnificent white hair and a long dry brown face, in a black suit with a high stiff collar, being led slowly about among the guests by Sheridan Dale, the latter showing an unwonted, an almost bouncing enthusiasm, yet conveying, with his large hand tightly on Mr. Sheffield's elbow, a sense of proprietorship that clashed with his obsequious role of steward. When he saw Timmy watching him he beckoned him over abruptly with his free hand.

"We're certainly honored tonight," he said as Timmy came up. "I ran into Mr. Sheffield coming out of the dining room, and I induced him to look in on the party. This is Timothy Colt, Mr. Sheffield," he continued to the impassive old man. "He worked on this deal for my nephew, George. One of our brightest young men, sir."

"I'd like to sit down, Dale," Mr. Sheffield said testily. "And I'd like a glass of soda water." Timmy was about to go for it when Dale caught him.

"Sit down with Mr. Sheffield," he whispered quickly. "I'll get the soda water. He likes to meet the younger men."

Timmy sat down awkwardly on a sofa by Mr. Sheffield and looked at the grim, placid features. "I've had the pleasure of meeting you once before, sir," he began. "At Mr. Knox's."

"Where?"

"At Henry Knox's."

"Oh, Knox." The old man nodded curtly. "He's a good man, Knox. Very good on detail. Not a man for clients, though. I had the slot for Knox, and I put him in it. It's a question of knowing where to place people. That's half the battle. Half the battle. Do you agree, young man?"

"I think I'd be willing to put Mr. Knox in almost any slot."

"Would you? Would you, indeed? Now that's interesting." The old man nodded vigorously. "I would never have put him where I put Dale, for example. With lady clients. Not everyone would have seen that, you know. There were those who called Dale a rough diamond."

"Oh?"

"Certainly. Certainly. But that's what we need from time to time. A rough diamond. A good man on the market, too."

"The market, sir?"

"The stock market. I don't mind telling you I've made a very good thing on a couple of tips he's handed me."

Timmy remembered the time that he had listened to the old man a year before, in the Knoxes' library after dinner. Then he had construed the mood of lofty vanity in which Mr. Sheffield had purported to have created single-handed the various partners of his firm as the understandable, the even rather endearing egocentricity of an infinitely distinguished octogenarian. He had always secretly believed that Mr. Sheffield owed more to Knox than Knox to Sheffield, but it was part of this very belief that Knox, at least, had once been the old man's disciple. Now he wondered. Was it Dale's and Emlen's firm, after all, and was Sheffield, instead of the giant of an earlier and purer world, more truly the living proof of how long it *had* been Dale's? Was Dale, in other words, not Sheffield's continuation rather than his decadence, and were he himself and Henry Knox anything more than men of good will who had deluded themselves? He and Knox? Or was it he alone?

Ann, talking with Austin, was keeping an eye on her husband. "I don't like his mood. I don't like it at all. He seems so deflated. As if he had some horrid little inward wound that was festering."

"Timmy's an artist, Ann. As Mr. Knox has always said. It's only natural that he should feel deflated when he's finished a job. He puts so much of himself into it."

"But I don't see that at all," she protested. "I thought artists had tremendous satisfactions. The composer who's finished a symphony. Isn't he elated?"

"Maybe that's it. Maybe Timmy should have been a composer. A creator, anyway. A real artist."

"Tell me, Austin." She hesitated. "Is he really good? All *that* good, I mean?"

"Knox told me he doubted if there was another man in the firm who could have worked that deal out," he said gravely. "I've worked with a lot of legal draftsmen myself, Ann. And I've never seen a better. That's all I can say. You can't describe it to anyone who hasn't seen all the problems. You have to see them to know why his finished product is such a—well, such a poem."

Ann looked over at Timmy as Mr. Sheffield rose to be

taken off by Dale. With a wrench at her heart she took in the renewed somberness of his eyes. "I love to hear that, Austin. I really do. But what does it mean to *me* if it doesn't mean more to him? If *he* got a thrill out of it—ah, well, then everything would be worth it."

She went over to where Timmy was sitting now alone. "Austin's wife has sense," she said, sitting down beside him. "She doesn't come to these things. Do you mind if I talk to you? I know it's a crime to be seen talking to one's husband. But if he's the only person one *wants* to talk to?"

"You ought to be mingling," Timmy told her. "You ought to be scintillating. You ought to be moving gaily from group to group so that everyone says 'Gosh! Did you meet that Mrs. Colt? Isn't *she* something?' And tomorrow my office would be jammed with clients."

She loved the gravity of his teasing; it was the way he always was when a deal was over. She laughed, but a trifle desperately, to hide from herself the suspicion that this time it was different. That the spirit was out of it. Oh, no, she told herself quickly, it was only that he was tired. And why not, in God's name? Why *not?* "Would you like me better that way?"

"I like you the way you are," he said, giving her a pinch above the elbow. "Just the way you are."

"Oh, Timmy, I have a confession to make!"

"A confession? You, Ann?"

"Darling, I'm serious." She watched the corners of his lips carefully. "I asked Mr. Knox to take you off the Emlen deal. When I was down in Cold Spring Harbor." She threw her chin out defiantly. "So there!"

"Is that all?"

"You mean you don't mind!"

He leaned forward, his elbows on his knees, and stared at the floor. "You poor kid. What a bastard I've been. Of course I don't mind. I don't blame you in the least."

"But you would have if you'd known!"

"Oh, 'would have.'" He shrugged. "What difference does 'would have' make? I've neglected you rottenly. But I'll make up for it now. You see if I don't."

"You're always so sweet to me when a job's over."

"Oh, darling," he said reproachfully. "Is it *that* bad?"

"And now they'll make you a partner? And we'll live happily ever after?"

"Stranger things have happened."

She looked away quickly to fight her tears. "Then why do

I feel like bawling like a baby? Oh, it's nothing really." She ran a finger gingerly over her eyelids. "It's only that I've felt so far away from you in the last weeks. It must be that dreadful man. Ugh! I can hardly bring myself to speak to him. Look at him, the pig."

"*You* look at him. I've been doing nothing else for weeks."

But everyone was now looking at George for he was rapping a spoon sharply against the side of an empty glass and calling out: "Ladies and gentlemen, your attention please!" Ann stared, fascinated, at the sudden assertiveness in that oval, hairless face. Whatever else he was, George Emlen was not a weak man. His strength might have been a barnacle growth, the accumulation of years of inner resentments and irritations, but it was nonetheless there, and it was prickly. "It would certainly never do for us not to drink the health of *all* the guys who have worked to make this deal the success it has been. I don't mean just the principals. I don't mean just myself and my partners in the enterprise on whom the responsibility primarily lay. I mean the butchers and bakers and candlestick makers, the lawyers and accountants and title searchers, each of whom has certainly contributed his bit. And in deals like this the little guy can be as vital as the big one. We all know that a chain is no stronger than its weakest link. And that is why I want to propose a toast tonight to each and every one of you."

George paused here for a moment, and there were cries of "Hear! Hear!" and a general raising of glasses. "Just a minute. Just a minute." He shook his head testily. "I want to tell you a little something about each of the principal assistants on the deal. What's the point of your drinking when you don't know who the hell you're drinking to?" There was silence and a few nervous laughs. "I want to start by telling you about Timmy Colt of Sheffield, Knox." Ann felt Timmy immediately stiffen beside her and dared not look at him. Please, God, *please*, she begged silently, as George turned a bland expression in their direction. "Timmy and I have got to know each other pretty well in the past few weeks. I hope he doesn't regard me as too much of a slave driver. I think most of you know by now that when I want a thing done I just can't rest till it's done. Poor old Timmy. He really hit the books, that boy." If you don't stop him, God, Ann prayed desperately, I'll never believe in you again! I *mean* it! "Now as the lawyers here probably all know, Timmy has a first-class legal ticker." George tapped his own high forehead significantly. "He can distinguish a covenant running with the land from a covenant that's too lazy even to hitchhike before you can say 'Felix Frankfurter.' He can bail you out of a bailment before you even know you're in." A small ripple of perfunctory laughter eddied through the smoky air. "But when it comes to the practicalities of business, the *real* world, if I'm permitted to call it that," George continued in a more pompous tone, "I think even our brilliant Timmy can pick up a couple of pointers from poor old plodding George. For if there's one thing I keep my mind on, it's the facts. I told Uncle Sherry Dale once that my only value at a conference with his legal eagles was that every now and then I could act as a sort of weight around their legs to keep them from flying off altogether into the wild blue yonder. Not that there's anything wrong with the wild blue yonder. A man's reach must exceed his grasp, and all that. But whenever we take off there, we ought to know that our landing gear is in good condition. Because we *do* eventually have to come back to earth. Isn't that so, Timmy?"

Ann, still not daring to turn, knew without doing so that Timmy was not going to answer him. She felt the surprise and then the quick embarrassment in the hushed room, and George, with a shrug, went on: "Well, I guess we can take silence for assent. Timmy is a great man for silences. Anyway, he's done such a good job on the whole deal that I'm sure he won't mind if I give him just a bit of ribbing on one small point. It was one of his wild-blue-yonder moments, and it illustrates the value of the old client watchdog who, while he may be incapable of great flights of fancy, nonetheless has his eye peeled on that bone. Well, you'll all remember about the Jersey mill and how the tract of land on which it stands is shaped like a rhomboid—"

Ann, immobile, stared fixedly at George as he picked his condescending way through the tired little tale of the error in the real estate description. In the vague stirrings about her she could sense the room's uneasy reaction to the inappropriateness of such an anecdote at such a time. Even George must have sensed it, for there was defiance in the fixed staleness of his smile, a seeming attitude of: "This is a *funny* story. A friendly story. Is there one of you with guts enough to stand up and tell me it's not? Let's just see!" She felt her hatred cold and compact, an icy cloud over his head; she felt detached, as if she could view this hatred and George together as two parts of the same thing. It was as if she had finally entered into Timmy's actual fantasy, breaking in with the sheer force of her agonized sympathy, but when she reached for his hand on the couch beside her she clutched on space, and she realized that he was standing up and that George, still smiling, had finished.

"Why drink to me?" Timmy shouted in a high, tense voice. "Why drink to the candlestick maker? The dreamer in the wild blue yonder? Oh, no! Let's drink to George, the man of substance! Ladies and gentlemen, I give you George Emlen!" He raised his glass like a beacon as he stared around the room. "His own financier, his own lawyer, his own accountant, and if there's any justice in the afterlife, which I very much doubt, his own hell!" He turned in the horrified silence and said: "Come on, Ann. Let's get out of here."

She almost ran as she followed him out of the door past a blur of startled faces and down the long corridor and empty stairway. He grabbed their coats from the doorman and went out to the street to hail a taxi without even giving her a chance to put hers on. Once in the cab, however, he seemed to crumple; he dropped his head suddenly on her shoulder and moaned: "Ann, Ann, what have I done to you?"

"It's all right, darling," she said firmly. "It's perfectly all right. I'm glad you did it. I'm glad you got it off your chest." She put her hand on his head and stroked his hair and felt the simplification of known catastrophe. But he was silent and later at home, when he made love to her, there was a clutching, almost desperate quality in his embrace, as if he were trying to escape with her into a black void of shared intimacy where everything that had occurred at George's club was obliterated. And lying awake beside him afterwards, when he had fallen into a dead sleep, she looked up into the darkness and knew that the time had finally come when she would have to take the lead.

9

WHEN SHERIDAN DALE, standing in the back of the room, witnessed Timmy's shocking outburst, his first impulse was to step quickly on him, to cover the offending creature with the broad sole of his anger and blot him out once and for all.

Not vindictively, but efficiently. For Dale was not a man to minimize the danger to which Timmy had exposed him. George was an invaluable asset, not only in himself, but as his mother's son. Florence Emlen owned far too much textile stock to be subjected, even indirectly, to an insult from any associate in Dale's firm. But as he thought it over the following morning, he wondered if it might not be solved another way. He hated to jettison Timmy. Would it not only emphasize the galling distinction between him and Knox that this young man, with a blameless record after eight years of working for the latter, should crack up on his first job with him? Besides, he had handled the job to perfection, and everyone, even Florence, knew how exasperating George could be. Leaving his office, he ambled down the corridor and stuck his head in Knox's door.

"Got a minute, Henry?"

Knox looked up slowly from an advance sheet and blinked at him for a moment. "Sure."

"Mind if I close the door?"

Knox shifted uncomfortably. All his worst conversations with Dale had been behind that closed door.

"Go ahead."

"It's about Colt," Dale started on a tone that was serious but not overly concerned. "He doesn't seem to like George Emlen."

"I don't like him myself," Knox snapped. "Even if he is Clarissa's nephew. I'm sorry, Sheridan, but that's the way I feel. He actually had the gall to walk into this office and complain that Timmy was lazy. Lazy, mind you! No, I'm afraid I don't like him any more than Timmy does."

"Ah, but that's different," Dale conceded easily. "You're not working for George. Not directly, at least. You can dislike him as much as you please. But Timmy was supposed to be doing a job for him."

"Does that mean he has to like him?" Knox looked down at his desk and warned himself to take it easy. Otherwise it would be like the other times; he would lose his temper, and Dale would win.

"Did I say he did?" Dale paused for a moment, as if waiting for an answer. "You know as well as I do, Henry, that a lawyer's first job is to give at least the impression of sympathy."

Knox grunted. "And Timmy hasn't?"

"No, Timmy certainly hasn't," Dale continued with a nod. "Obviously you haven't heard about last night. It was quite a little drama. If I hadn't been so involved, I might even have rather enjoyed it." He proceeded, at his own labored, deliberate pace, to tell in meticulous detail the story of Timmy's outburst. "I suppose," he concluded, "that even as staunch a supporter of Timmy's as yourself would concede that this fell something short of creating an impression of sympathy?"

Knox turned his chair away roughly, breathing hard again. It was far worse than he could have imagined. How in the name of heaven could Timmy be such an ass? In his sudden exasperation he turned on Dale.

"Isn't this the kind of thing you've got to expect?" he demanded harshly. "Isn't this what your George Emlens lead to? Sitting over a bright, hard-working boy like Timmy and playing Simon Legree! All right! So Timmy's got guts. So he objects. Well, God, so do I!"

Dale nodded his head several times in silence. Then he tapped on the table with his pencil. He seemed only to be taking in, without grudge, what Knox had said. "Perhaps if it was your nephew who had been insulted by one of the boys in my department, you would feel differently," he suggested in a reasonable tone. "I am confident you would. But these are not points that I came to argue with you. I fear it would simply be a waste of your time and mine. The only thing I want to find out from you is whether we must now consult the personal views of each of the associates before assigning them to clients? Is that your position?"

"No, no," Knox answered impatiently, "of course, that isn't my position. I simply point out that here's a young man who has been in the office for years without getting into hot water with a single client. Until he runs into your George. I wonder if the trouble isn't with George."

"Undoubtedly," Dale replied smoothly. "Undoubtedly with George and myself and I daresay my wife's whole family. And undoubtedly, too, with Mr. Sheffield."

Knox looked up sharply. "With Mr. Sheffield? How does he come into it?"

"Only because he was there. Only because Colt's conduct was an insult to him, too. I talked to him afterwards. I've never seen the old boy so upset."

Knox got up and stood facing the window, his hands clasped behind his back. "I suppose you'll want me to get rid of Timmy now," he said with heavy bitterness. "Well, I won't do it. You can keep him from becoming a partner, I suppose, but you can't fire him, Sheridan. I won't let you."

He stood looking out over the bay until he heard Dale's voice again. It was still unruffled.

"Have I said anything about firing, Henry?"

Knox turned back from the window with a sigh, knowing again that he had been outplayed. "What is it that you want me to do, Sheridan?" he asked wearily.

"I want you to use your good offices with this young man to induce him to come to his senses. I want you to persuade him that future partners of yours and mine do not behave like small, spoiled children."

Knox, deflated, settled. once more in his chair. "Oh," he said. "You still think of him as a future partner?"

"Of course, I do!" Dale answered cheerfully. "Timmy's far too valuable a man to lose over a fit of temper. Anyone can see that. That's why I want you to drum a little sense into his head. You say he never gave you any trouble with clients before. Quite true. But hasn't he been operating entirely with investment bankers? And aren't they all tin gods to him? Be frank, Henry. Wasn't it because you thought he needed broadening that you loaned him to me?"

This was a thrust. "Maybe."

"And isn't this just the kind of thing you expected to come up?" Dale pursued. "Just the sort of client relationship you wanted him to learn to handle?"

Knox smiled candidly, as he always did when he was beaten. "All right, Sheridan," he said, "what do you think I should tell him?"

"I think you should first make him apologize to George," Dale answered promptly. "It seems to me that's indispensable. Timmy was there last night in a dual capacity: as George's lawyer and as his guest. From two points of view he owed him the duty of common civility. And I think he should also apologize to me. For the embarrassment that he caused me. You can tell him from me, when he's done this, that I will bear him no grudge. You can even tell him that I will do my best to restore him to George's good graces. He's a good man, your Timmy. I, for one, have no wish to lose him."

Knox looked at him and nodded slowly. "Very well, Sheridan. It's fair enough. Except it may not be easy. He's stubborn, you know."

"Oh, I think you'll manage it, Henry," Dale said, getting up. "Those fellows in the corporate department will do anything you say."

When he had gone, Henry Knox settled heavily back in his chair and remained motionless. He had felt the giddiness

81

again, had seen again the crisscross of lines and flashes before his eyes. Now as he blinked and focused on the bronze bust of Mr. Sheffield on the cabinet, he faced again the conviction that he would die and that death in removing him would restore the eternal equality of things that he and the other self-deluded had tried to upset. Then the bust of his senior partner would be equal to the bronze out of which it was made and to the ashtray on his desk or even the ash at the end of his extinguished cigar. And the brief would be the equal of the words that made it up, the prayer of its syllables. And who could preside more appropriately over the restoration to normal than Sheridan Dale? He pulled himself to his feet and trudged down the corridor to Timmy's room.

Larry Duane was talking to Timmy; he murmured something respectful and left immediately when his father-in-law came in. Knox noticed Timmy's sullen expression; he walked past his desk with only a nod and took his stand by the window, his hands clasped behind his back.

"Dale has told me about last night," he said tersely, without looking around. "I'd like your explanation."

"I simply told George Emlen what I ought to have told him two months ago!" Timmy exploded immediately. "If I'd only had the guts!"

"All right, Tim, all right. Just tell me about it, will you?"

Knox stood silently at the window as the explanation poured forth, the long, bitter account of George's petty persecution. From time to time he shook his head sadly. The story would have been more appropriate to a boys' boarding school than to a law firm. And yet there was passion in Timmy's voice, unmistakable passion.

"What does all this have to do with last night?" he interrupted irritably. "What has it to do with your childish behavior to Emlen while you were a guest at his party?"

"What does it have to do with it? I despise him, that's what it has to do with it!"

"And what right do you have to despise clients?" Knox demanded angrily, turning around now to face him. "What do your feelings have to do with your job? You're taking the world on your shoulders, young man, and no one, to the best of my knowledge, has asked you to!"

Timmy's lips became a thin line. "I'm sorry, sir. I must be guided by my conscience."

Knox, staring at him, felt the dizziness again. He sat down in a chair by the desk and looked away. He couldn't bear Timmy's eyes; they seemed suddenly, with their violence and sincerity, to make a grotesque parody of his own life. Feeling, too much feeling, masses of feeling, and about *what?* How could Timmy ever live in a Dale world with such feeling? The hopelessness of explaining it, the biting sense of his own responsibility for it, the prospect, whatever happened, of the firm becoming so soon Dale's firm, combined to make him suddenly peevish and short.

"You'll apologize to Emlen," he snapped. "At least you will if you know what's good for you. And you'll apologize to Dale, too. He said that if you do this, nothing will be held against you. He even offered to make things right again between you and George. Which, under the circumstances, I think is handsome of him."

"All right between me and George!" Timmy's voice was high and excited now. "Are you serious, sir? Do you honestly and truly expect me to work for that bastard again? Is that what you think of me? Have we misunderstood each other all these years?"

Knox felt a sharp pain in his side. "You're being absurd, Timmy."

"You mean that, sir? Truly?"

He looked away from Timmy and managed to get to his feet. "I mean what I say," he said in as dry a tone as he could manage, getting up and turning to the door. "Think it over. I'm sure that after a little sober reflection you'll conclude I'm right." He stepped out into the corridor.

"Never!" he heard from behind him. "Never!" Timmy repeated. Knox became aware of two stenographers passing in the corridor and reflected vaguely how odd it would seem to them to hear an associate speaking this way to him.

"It's your own funeral, my boy," he muttered and hurried on back to his office. "Yours and mine," he repeated softly to himself.

10

It took Ann most of that evening to extract from Timmy just what had happened between him and Mr. Knox. She had never before seen him so drawn into himself. She sympathized about the apology, but could not understand why quite such an issue had to be made of it. When she ventured, however, to suggest this, he answered her so bitterly that she dropped the subject immediately. She was, in fact, frightened. There had always been a side of Timmy that she had never quite plumbed, a side as mysterious to her as the constancy of his loyalty, a side suggested by his occasional moodiness, his unexpected remotenesses, his capacity, beneath a benign and friendly surface, of suddenly remembering slights, of flaring up over small issues. Such moments gave her an uneasy sense of wells of resentment that he might have accumulated within, yet she had, at the same time, an odd feeling that it might be folly to inquire, that her role might be that of a latterday Elsa whose happiness had been granted at the price of not asking her husband's name. Now, however, she had a confused sense that a crisis, long dreaded even if unidentified, had arrived, and that unlike Elsa she did not know of what her test consisted.

The only person with whom she could really discuss it was Mrs. Knox. Timmy's mother had no understanding of such things, and most of her friends, like Sally Duane, were not true intimates. Mrs. Knox had been consistently kind to her, almost as if she were trying to balance her husband's semi-adoption of Timmy, to make Ann feel that she, too, could be the object of a particular sympathy. With her high grey hair, parted in the middle, her plain, Roman, long-nosed, high-foreheaded face, she was a symbol of matronly serenity, a Cornelia behind brownstone. She appeared to accept the world of Sheffield, Knox as the world over which she had been destined to preside, with no seeming desire to go in any way beyond it save in the volumes of Greek poetry and early Christian theology in which she so frequently immersed herself. Ann, of course, did not know the friends of her younger days, of the outside world, or of their speculations that Marian Knox was a cold, diffident woman, driven by duty, hiding behind the elaboration of her plans and schedules. To Ann she was only the great lady of Timmy's firm whose sympathy, however seemingly spontaneous, was still in the nature of bounty. She summoned up her courage and called the following day and found herself alone that afternoon with Mrs. Knox by a silver tea tray in the dark, leathery library.

"It's about Timmy and Mr. Knox," she began nervously. "I don't know whether or not you've heard, but—"

"Of course, I've heard, my dear," Mrs. Knox interrupted her easily, leaning forward to pour their tea. "What sort of people do you suppose Harry and I are? Do you think for a minute that caring about Timmy the way he does, he wouldn't have told me about it?"

"Oh." Ann was slightly taken aback. It was warming, it was encouraging, but at the same time it made what Timmy proposed to do, or rather not to do, seem even more crude. "Then you know how much is at stake."

Mrs. Knox nodded. "I think I do."

"I don't know what to do," Ann said desperately. "It seems as if everything was all of a sudden out of control."

"And perhaps just a touch out of proportion?" Mrs. Knox suggested gently.

"How do you mean?"

"Only that I wonder, when everyone starts talking in loud voices, if we don't tend to lose our balance. To forget how small this all will seem in a few months' time."

"I see." After a pause Ann went on in a duller tone. "You think he should apologize."

"Well, my dear, don't you? Deep down?"

"No," Ann shook her head. "Or anyway I don't know. Any more than I know what my own role should be. When Mr. Knox left the firm to raise money for that divinity school, did you object?"

"Heavens, no!" Mrs. Knox exclaimed in surprise. "But that was a great project. I wouldn't have objected if he'd left the firm permanently for *that*."

"But how can you tell what is and what's not a great project?"

"Surely, my dear," Mrs. Knox replied, again in that gentler tone that she used for suggestion, "apologizing to George Emlen is not one."

"Couldn't it be?"

"Is there anything but pride on one side and pique on the other?"

"There couldn't be integrity?" Ann pursued. "On ours?"

"Of course, you can read integrity into anything. But if you stick to the facts, the simple facts, my dear, I wonder if you won't see where the exaggeration lies. Timmy was rude to a client at a client's party. Doesn't it follow that Timmy should apologize?"

Ann felt dreary and deflated, as if she and Timmy had been two little children, playing in the sand, building a castle to surprise their mother, only to be told by the latter, shrinking back from their dirty hands, that it was nothing but a mud hut and that besides, it was time to go home. She wondered sadly if the abandonment of her and Timmy's mud hut might not involve the abandonment of something basic to their intimacy. Yet she could not sacrifice his future to this. Would Mrs. Knox have?

"Your Timmy has a great career in the firm," Mrs. Knox continued. "You mustn't let him spoil it."

"But there can be greater careers!" Ann protested with a last touch of defiance. "What did you just say about the divinity school?"

"Well, of course, if Timmy had something like *that*," Mrs. Knox conceded. She couldn't quite restrain her shrug.

Ann saw it now. Unless it was a divinity school, there was nothing finer, to Mrs. Knox's mind, than her husband's firm. Being of noble thoughts, she had ennobled the world in which she lived, creating around herself, with a wishful imagination that amounted almost to genius, the austerity and idealism of that Roman republic that her appearance evoked.

"And what about Mr. Dale?" Ann demanded. "Is it right for Timmy to apologize to him, too?"

Mrs. Knox's lips tightened as she looked down at the tray, and Ann had the gloomy satisfaction of feeling that here at least was one figure who defied her efforts to clothe him in a senator's toga. "I'm afraid you're going to find a Mr. Dale in every large firm," she murmured, conscious, no doubt, of the questionable propriety of criticizing a partner of her husband's to one in Ann's position. "I daresay he's not as bad as you think. We can't expect perfection, can we? Why don't you tell Timmy to do it right away and get it over with? Then Harry will have him back where he belongs, and everything will be as it was."

"Yes," Ann said dubiously. "If it ever can be."

"Of course it can be!" Mrs. Knox leaned forward to give her hand a small, encouraging pat. "You know, I have a very special feeling about you, my dear. A feeling that you're a good deal the way I was at your age. One gives up a lot for the firm, I know. But if Timmy gets what he wants in the end, it'll be all right. He'll be grateful to you. Mark my words. Very grateful."

When she left, Ann took a taxi directly to her mother-in-law's apartment where she and Timmy were to meet that night. She was glad, she decided grimly, that she had gone to Mrs. Knox's. The latter, however unrealistic in her own life, had still the power to destroy illusions in others. Ann was beginning to suspect that she and Timmy had simply been on a spree. It might have been fun, even exhilarating, but like the children with the mud hut, it was time to go home.

Her feelings were strengthened by the scene that she encountered in her mother-in-law's dark, faintly Turkish interior. Genevieve, her long white fingers on the handle of a pitcher of martinis, had been listening with evident sympathy to her indignant son.

"Ann, Ann," she wailed as the latter came in, "what things he's been telling me! That vulgar, terrible Mr. Emlen. The idea of Timmy having to apologize to *him!* Have a drink, dear?" There was always a contrast between Genevieve's languorous air and her sudden efficiency about the ingredients of a cocktail. She poured straight from the bottle like a bartender, leaving no balance over to waste itself in ice. "Of course, the Colts wouldn't have even known the Emlens two generations ago! And this Mr. Emlen's mother, she was a Bertrand, wasn't she? Why, she got her money out of a jewelry store!"

Ann saw Timmy's filial, almost fatuous smile, noted his empty glass and thought with a sinking heart of the power of mothers. How, in spite of all the hundred ways that Genevieve had failed him, he still cared for her approval. Oh, her disapproval he ignored, yes, as when he had married, but it was Genevieve's rare enthusiasm that still brought that complacent smile to his lips. As she looked about the room with its tawdry evocation of a past that had never existed, its photographs of possible cousins on horses, the water-color copy of what might have been a grandmother's portrait, she felt that the alliance of its occupant was the ultimate proof, if proof was still needed, that she and Timmy had lost their heads.

"I was wondering," she said finally. "Is there anything actually wrong about apologizing for bad manners?"

Timmy looked up at her sharply. "What's got into you?"

"Well, is there?"

"It's not a question of manners," he retorted. "It's a simple question of honesty."

"It's even more than that," Genevieve intervened, waving her cigarette holder at Ann in languid reproach. "It's a question of survival. Of not being trampled underfoot by a crew of vulgarians who think they can buy even a Colt with their filthy money!"

"Oh, Genevieve, don't be dramatic," Ann snapped at her. "We won't get anywhere that way."

"Sure," Timmy snorted as his mother lapsed into hurt silence. "Decency can always be laughed out of court. Who dares be called dramatic?"

"Timmy!" Ann straightened up. "Surely you think I'm decent?"

"Oh, you are where you're concerned," he conceded impatiently. "Like most women you're entirely moral where your own home is involved. But what the breadwinner does in his office—ah, well, that's another matter, isn't it? Not so important, of course. Not quite real, I suspect?"

Ann drew back before the glitter in his eyes. "Timmy, what do you mean?"

"What do I mean?" he exclaimed, taking a step towards her. "I won't go on with it, that's what I mean. I'm going to quit the firm, that's what I mean."

Ann, gazing down at the rug to conceal her sudden tears, thought dully of the years that had gone into getting where they were. The endless nights of the telephone calls to say he wouldn't be home for supper, until midnight, at all. The short vacations interrupted by Mr. Knox's apologetic but inevitable remands. The long gossips with office couples, so radiant with the future implicit in them, about the partners, the cases, the ultimate goal. And this was to have been for nothing. For *nothing*. She shook her head, as if to wake up.

"You're crazy, Timmy," she said quietly. "You're simply crazy, that's all."

"Then I'm crazy. So be it."

She closed her lips tightly. It was out of the question to appeal on the grounds of his own career. The more he gave up, the higher would leap the flames of his martyrdom.

"I can't see why you're taking on so, Ann," Genevieve intervened, this time in a sulky tone. "It isn't as if Sheffield, Knox was the only firm in town. Do you suppose for a minute Timmy couldn't get a job at twice what he's paid now?"

"Of course, I know that!" Ann turned abruptly away from her. Genevieve's mournful face was too dangerously provoking. "But other firms aren't the same thing. We know what this one means to Timmy."

"You'll see what it means to me," he said grimly. "Just exactly what it means!"

She raised her hands suddenly to her eyes. She didn't dare look at him. "Timmy," she said in a low voice, "if I ever had any credit with you, I want to draw on it now. Please do this for me. Please apologize to George."

He was staring at her, hard and straight. "Have you gone crazy?"

"Timmy, I mean it. You told me once that if there was ever anything I really wanted you to do, that mattered to me more than anything in the world, to ask you and you'd do it for me. I'm asking you now."

"Ann, you're not making sense!" Genevieve exclaimed. "That's not the sort of thing one asks a husband!"

But Ann and Timmy alike ignored her, their eyes fixed on each other. "It's true I told you that, Ann," he said quietly. "And I meant it. We'll play things your way. I've always been willing to do that. But I also told you something else. I told you there were certain things you'd much better leave to me. Do you remember that?"

She nodded without speaking.

"I say this is one of them," he continued. "Do you still want me to apologize?"

"I do," She was barely audible now.

"Very well." He nodded gravely. "I will do what you want. There'll be no question about that. I'll do what you want, and I'll do it handsomely. But *you* will have assumed responsibility for what happens afterwards. You will have altered the direction of our lives."

Again she nodded.

"Then I think we're ready to go out for dinner," he said, turning to his mother. "We won't mention this tiresome subject again."

For the rest of the evening, at the restaurant, Timmy and his mother chatted with nervous animation while Ann sat despondently silent. She had never heard him be more amusing or more informative, but unlike him or Genevieve she was incapable of acting. When they got home she supposed that he would go to bed without speaking to her. Instead he sat up over another drink and talked about general topics with a sustained artificiality that made her wonder, in the long wakeful hours that followed, how insignificant this day would appear, according to Mrs. Knox's prediction, in any number of months or years to come.

11

TIMMY sat alone in his office the next morning with his door inhospitably shut. Such was not the custom in Sheffield, Knox, but it was the only way to avoid solicitous questioning, even at the cost of seeming to dramatize what he now thought of as his "disgrace." In the carefully matter-of-fact faces that he encountered at the drinking fountain, in the considerate but not unfriendly silence of his telephone, in the anxious smile of the old librarian, he could read sympathy for his predicament. Word of his unconventional behavior at George's party had spread like a prairie fire to the remotest corners of the firm. Timmy was a popular figure, except with one or two of the younger associates whom he might have driven too hard, but there was still the undeniable element of excitement in anyone's fall from an altitude. The crowd that had watched his slow climb with craned necks and staring eyes might be sorry to see the slip, the loss of foothold; they might gasp, raising their hands to their lips in horror, but it was too much to expect them to look away.

Now he contemplated with still seething anger the bitterness of his new resolve. It had been his premise since childhood that if one worked till one dropped—and this, indeed, seemed a condition of being, *his* being, anyway—there was still a recompense. Or at least a reason. One owed nothing and deferred to no one, murky God or visible man. They might be overseers of the task, but that was all. Oneself was free, and for such freedom any sacrifice was cheap enough. He had paid his world the compliment of taking it seriously, of assuming a degree of conviction behind its pompous premises. He had believed that *it* believed in the validity of the independent soul. And where did he find himself? An object of ridicule. Very well. He couldn't fight them both, Knox and Ann. They barred his way; they held out their hands imploringly and called him to come back. And couldn't he even detect in the scarcely articulate bray of their appeal, a note of entreaty, a plea to him not to shake the foundations of their world, a hint that neither might really quite survive his refusal to admit that he had been crazy? He laughed aloud, with a rather magnificent sneer, at this manifestation of the sand beneath their houses. He'd like to hear either of them say just one word against Sherry Dale in the future. Just one word!

When Larry, whom he had made his sole confidant, came in, he opened right up at him. "Do you want to know something?" he demanded. "Do you want to know how low a man can sink? Well, look at me! I'm going to apologize! I'm going to eat crow. I'm going to put on a hair shirt and stand outside Dale's gate in the snow, like that German emperor at Canossa. Except it won't be snow. It'll be mud. I'm going to roll in mud!" Larry's round young eyes were wide, a dumb Horatio to a soliloquizing Hamlet. "And what's more, you're going with me!"

"Me!" Larry protested. "Why do I have to apologize?"

"I don't want you to apologize. I want you to be a witness. I want you to be able to tell your father-in-law that I groveled. I want him to know how literally I've obeyed his orders!"

If he had asked Larry to be his best man, the latter couldn't have looked more honored. "Sure, Timmy. You can count on me, boy." He paused and shook his head ruefully. "But he won't make it easy for you. Not Dale."

Timmy gave a little mocking snort. "That's where you don't know him. He's going to make it all too easy. Easy as hell. We don't even have to go to Emlen's office. He's coming over here!"

When Dale's secretary called to say that Mr. Emlen had arrived, Timmy jumped up and hurried down to Dale's office, followed by Larry. In line with his prediction, Dale did not keep them waiting even a minute. He rested back in his chair as they came in and looked from one to the other with a dry, quizzical little smile. George was leaning against the window sill, smoking a cigarette, with a bored, embarrassed look. Larry, standing behind Timmy, was as stiff as a cadet.

"I've come to apologize, Mr. Dale," Timmy began immediately. "I've brought Mr. Duane because I want him to be able to tell Mr. Knox."

Dale dipped his great head as he bit his pipe. He sucked at the flame carefully for a few moments and then rolled one eye up at Timmy. "I think apologies are better when seated," he said in a level tone. "I suggest that you both sit down. And let's be specific. What exactly is it that you wish to apologize for?"

Timmy felt his breath short as he sat down, his hands on his knees. "I want to apologize to Mr. Emlen for speaking as I did the other night," he stated in clipped tones. "It was entirely inexcusable. I should quite understand if he never wanted me to work for him again." Here he turned formally to George. "I can promise you, however, Mr. Emlen, that nothing like that will ever happen again."

George flushed and turned around to face out the window. "It's all right, fella," he muttered. "Forget it. Too much has been made of the damn thing already."

Dale snapped open his lighter and applied the flame once more to the stubborn ashes in his pipe. Yet Timmy had no feeling that it was a gesture in any way connected with dramatic suspense. He might have done it, like anything else, in the same way alone. "If that's a promise, it's good enough for me," he said, shutting up his lighter again. "The practice of law can be confusing to a young man, I know. A lot of things look mighty raw until you grow up and discover it's a raw world."

"I appreciate that now, sir."

Dale shot him another of those penetrating glances, to be sure, perhaps, that he was sincere. "All right," he grunted. "I think now we may excuse Mr. Duane."

"I'll be running along, too, Uncle Sherry," George said hastily. "As far as I'm concerned, the whole thing's a dead duck. Next deal I get, I'll ask for Timmy. Okay, boy?"

"Thank you, George," Timmy said in the same flat voice. "That's very handsome of you."

There was an awkward pause until George, with a brief wave of his arm and a nod, left the room, followed by Larry. Timmy was about to follow, but Dale called him back. "I want to ask you something," he said and motioned him to close the door. "I want to know how you'd feel," he continued after hesitating for several rather ponderous moments, his hand on his jaw and his eyes fixed on Timmy, "about staying on and working in my department?"

"You mean you still want me in your department, sir?" Timmy asked, in some surprise. "After what's happened?"

Dale put down his pipe. "Look, Timmy," he said, folding his big hands on the blotter and giving him his level stare. "I'll be frank with you. There's a place for you with me. A big place. Of course, you're going to be made a partner in the firm. You know that." He held up his hand to silence any protests. "Obviously you know it, or you wouldn't have come here to apologize. But that's not the point. The point is, what sort of a partner? And the answer to that is where's your biggest chance? Let's leave out litigation and real estate. You don't want them. Now look at the number of partners who do corporate work and the number in my department. I have five to their ten, and who? Amory who's about to retire, Landon who was never worth the powder to blow him up with, Russell and Hyatt who are simply good, competent, average men. Some of the associates are all right, but they're young and don't have your experience. And think. We bring in forty per cent of the fees of the whole damn firm! The despised estates and trusts that *I* built out of nothing! One quarter of the partners and forty per cent of the income! Think that one over, Timothy Colt, before you go scampering back to Knox and his happy slaves."

Timmy was startled at the almost careless way that he spoke of the relative capabilities of his partners. "You'd want me to do estates work?"

"I'd want you to know how to do it," Dale said with a shrug. "I don't want to make a specialist of you. You're too much that way already. No, my idea, Tim, is that you'd be my right-hand man. Help me in everything. Help me with clients. Help me with policy. With planning. Don't worry about trust accountings and all the paperwork in this field. Hell, we've got a dozen associates already on that sort of thing. They'll probably be doing it when they die. I want a first-class man for the big stuff. And don't worry. You'll go places with me, boy. Further than you'll ever go with old Knox. What does *he* do for the men who work for him, do you think, besides give them ulcers? But I'd give you clients. Clients of your own! The minute you're a member of the firm I'd start turning them over to you. And they'd be your clients, too, boy. Don't fool yourself. Sherry Dale's no Indian giver. The proof is that I've got more than I can handle."

"It's certainly an interesting proposition, sir."

"It's more than interesting," Dale retorted. "It'll make you. And there's another thing. Between you and me and the lamppost Mr. Sheffield is going on eighty-eight and Mr. Stevens is hardly compos. All right. Suppose Henry Knox took it into his head to retire one of these days? All right. Just think it over, my boy. Just think it over."

"Thank you, Mr. Dale," Timmy answered, getting up. He was not so dazzled as to forget how to play his cards. With

Knox one couldn't lose by seeming overeager. With Dale it might be just the opposite. "I will certainly think it over. In the meanwhile, I take it, sir, you want me to finish up any loose ends on the Emlen deal?"

"Just as before, my boy." Dale waved the hand holding the pipe in a genial arch. "It's as if nothing at all had happened."

As Timmy retraced his steps down the corridor, he felt a conflict between excitement and anticlimax. Was *this* how it would come, the partnership for which he had waited so long? Not with Henry Knox glancing at him over his spectacles and then rising to clasp his hand, wringing it and murmuring with a catch in his throat: "My dear Timmy, you don't know how pleased I am," not with his slipping unobtrusively into the empty seat at the end of the table at the partners' Monday lunch, awed and self-consciously quiet at the prospect of his inclusion in such a circle, not with returning to an almost hysterical Ann and going out to drink champagne and toast the future. No, none of that. Simply with Dale tossing it over to him as if it was nothing but a visa, a form to be filled out, mechanical, a touch boring perhaps, but something that was required of all who took the grand tour under the auspices of Sherry Dale. He paused as he passed Knox's door, and a surge of bitterness swept over him. He found Knox alone, reading; the latter looked up and gave him a rather weary smile.

"Well, Timmy?"

Timmy walked up and stood before his desk. "I've done your job," he said shortly. "I've groveled. I've eaten crow. I hope you're satisfied."

"I'm proud of you, Tim," Knox said gravely. "If that means anything to you now. Which I assume it doesn't."

"Good! I get a gold star!" Timmy's tone was bitter. "Except I should have got it long ago. Maybe I'm stupid. On the other hand, maybe I was badly taught."

"In what?"

"In what the practice of law was meant to be." His voice, faintly mocking, rose in pitch. "You taught me that we were the men who greased the wheels of finance and business. That our contribution to the general welfare was direct and creative. That it was our glory to have worked out the relationship between government and industry! Oh, we were something!" His voice rose to a sneer. "We were the architects of society!"

"All this I've said," Knox agreed.

"It was a concept that excited me," Timmy continued, his voice tense with emotion. "All during the war I never wavered in my desire to come back and work for you. It didn't matter to me that society was disintegrating so long as *I* was not on the side of the disintegrators. So long as *I* was constructive. For several years you gave me that sense. Of having my own little smithy in a crazy world. It was all I needed."

"No matter how crazy the world?"

"Well, it wasn't *that* crazy," Timmy replied. "Or at least I thought it wasn't."

"I see," Knox nodded. "Go on."

"And then you assigned me to the lower regions. The *real* world." Timmy turned away to the window. "You watched my apprenticeship with equanimity."

"Yes."

"You wanted me to make my peace with the devil. Well, I've made it! You won't catch me making an ass of myself again. Now I'm with Dale, I'm staying with him!"

Knox thought of all the things that he could say that he had said before. The element of compromise, the impossibility, in any profession, of wholly dispensing with it. The danger, above all, of taking oneself too seriously in a complex world. But the words, limp and inert as his state of mind, refused to take articulate shape. For Timmy was logical and consistent as he had wanted to make him, as logical and consistent as he had once wanted to make himself. Timmy had actually *been* the lawyer that he had visualized himself as being. The lawyer who didn't really exist. Because he couldn't exist. Not in their firm. Or in their world. God only knew where and how far he would go now, but could he tell him that he was wrong?

"All right, Timmy," he said at last. "I accept your rebuke."

Timmy stood at the window, his back still turned, his very stillness irresolute. "Is that all, sir?"

"You wanted a scene perhaps?" Knox asked wearily. "You won't get one. You're quite right, you know. I *have* led you astray. Oh, there are things I could say in my defense, yes. But how to make you *see* them?"

Timmy turned around, almost pleading. "See what, sir?"

"That you're a damn fool," Knox said with a shrug. "To look to me. Even to look to Dale. To give a hoot in hell what anyone thinks but yourself. But, well—what's the use? We'll talk about it another time. Maybe. If either of us

95

should want to." He shrugged and turned his chair away. "But leave me be now. Thanks, Tim."

Timmy paused, undecided. When Knox, however, failed to speak to him, he turned and left. It was later that day, in the middle of the afternoon, that Miss Glenn, Knox's elderly secretary, finally found him in a corner of the library. She wore a rather distracted look on her thin grey features.

"Oh, Mr. Colt!" she exclaimed. "There you are. I've been trying to locate you for half an hour. He's gone home. I'm afraid he's not well."

"Not well?" Timmy stood up. "What's the matter?"

"I'm afraid it's his heart again." He could see that she was really concerned. Her eyes roamed from side to side. "I called Mrs. Knox, and she said to tell him to take a taxi. He promised me he would, but you know how he is. That's why I tried to get you. To see that he did. He's so proud, you know. And the men his age all cling to the subway. As if it was a proof of something!"

"That's all right, Miss Glenn. I'm sure he took a cab. Maybe it's not as bad as you think. He seemed fine this morning."

"Oh, I don't know, Mr. Colt, I don't know." There were tears in her eyes now, large, tremulous, anxious tears. "He looked so pale. And he's so stubborn, you know. One can't *make* him do anything. Not him. I'd have felt so much better if you'd been with him!"

"We'll call the house after a bit," he reassured her. "I'm sure he got there all right. Don't fret, Miss Glenn."

She nodded gratefully, happy to have someone to take over, to share, even in the smallest way, her anxiety, and Timmy, watching her go, discovered with an unpleasant surprise that he was actually angry with Knox for having already stolen his little scene.

12

HE SPENT an almost sleepless night after the day of his scene with Knox. He did not dare describe the scene to Ann at supper, knowing in his heart that she would only think it worse than he did; he had warded off her inquiries into his moodiness with monosyllabic rejections, letting her conclude, not unnaturally, that it was an after-effect of his apology to Dale. It was not until the early hours of the morning, as he lay beside her sleeping figure, staring up at the pale slant of refracted street light across the ceiling and thinking of his words to Knox, those bitter words, bumping gently against the plaster like foolish little red balloons, that his muscles relaxed, and he faced the simple fact that his state of mind was unbearable. He had been willing to pay dearly for his pride, but not a price like this. He would go to Knox in the morning and ask to be taken back to his old work. He would tell his story frankly and apologize frankly. And already he felt a glow in his chest at the prospect of hearing the half-checked rumbling cough and the dry, sharp: "You've learned that only idiots are consistent? Good. I was just about to give you up." They would be friends again, better friends, if anything, for the rift. It was idiotic, he told himself, not to realize how often clocks *could* be turned back. And he fell asleep at last, exhausted but resolved.

When he woke up he had to think for a moment what day it was. Ann was not there. "Ann!" he called. Walter appeared in the doorway. "What time is it?"

"Half past nine, Daddy."

"Past nine! Holy cats, why didn't someone wake me?"

"Because it's Saturday. Mummy said you were to sleep."

"Sleep!"

He hurried into the living room and sat down by the telephone. With one hand on the instrument and the other scratching his head, he slowly recalled the Knoxes' number. Then he dialed it.

The line was busy. This was not unusual, in their house, at any hour of the day or night; in fact, it was even reassuring, for hearing the sharp, insistently repeated tone, he knew they had not gone to the country. When he tried the number again, however, and then a third and fourth time, he began to fear it was out of order. It would seem about to ring, and then the busy signal would suddenly clash again in his ear, all the louder for his moment of anticipation. On a final try, however, the number answered immediately, as if someone was sitting right by the receiver. But it was not Mrs. Knox's voice. It was like hers, but higher, dryer, melancholy.

"Is this Mrs. Knox's house?" he asked.

"Yes. This is her sister, Mrs. Herbert."

"Oh. Could I speak with her? It's Timothy Colt." He would speak to her first, he decided, and find the opportune moment for his visit.

"I'm afraid she's not taking any calls." The voice was even sadder now, but ladylike, executive. "I'm sure you'll understand. Can I take the message?"

Timmy felt rebuffed and was about to say, no, there was no message, when a hideous fear suddenly broke in on him. "Has anything happened?"

"Oh, you hadn't heard?" The voice softened, prepared to discharge its message of sympathy. "My poor brother-in-law passed away last night. At home, just as he was sitting down to dinner. It was his heart, you know. Mercifully, it was all over very quickly. In a matter of minutes."

"Mr. Knox!"

"It's been a terrible shock, I needn't say. But my sister is wonderful. The children are all here. I'll give her your sympathy? Mr. Colt, is it?"

"Yes," Timmy murmured. "Yes, oh yes. Please do."

He dropped the receiver into its cradle, unable to ask for further details, unable, in his sudden weakness, to feel that it was anything but an imposition to hold her on the line. He got up and walked blindly across the room, collapsing at his desk, striking at the blotter with his fist and repeating again and again to himself: "Here is only me and the blotter and the desk, and not Knox, not Knox or death." Desperately, like a man trying to ward off a slashing blade, he dodged and turned in the dark cavity of his mind to escape the realization. But surging all around him, it engulfed him, and he could only wonder, dazed, how it was possible for anything to hurt so savagely that was only breath, communicated by a woman whom he didn't even know in a distant part of the city. He hadn't seen him dead, had he? And then slowly at first, soon faster, mocking his question, the pictures began to slide across his mind, pushing one after another like still photographs projected on a screen, large and light and oddly immobile, frozen vacation scenes and remembered attitudes: Knox after tennis, perspiring, calling loudly for a whiskey and water, Knox reading Leacock to his daughters by the lake in Vermont, Knox coming out of the Securities and Exchange Commission, a hand on Timmy's shoulder, laughing his regret at not having taken his advice. And he knew the ugly one at the bottom of the box, the last to come, and knew he couldn't stand it, must ward it off, that otherwise he would be sucked down forever in the mire of self-hate.

Ann came out of the kitchen and put the coffeepot on the table. "Who were you talking to?" When he failed to answer she turned around and took in his expression. "Timmy, what's happened?"

"He's dead."

"Who's dead?"

He looked up at her blankly. "Knox, of course."

She gave a little cry. "Oh, darling, no!"

"Oh, yes." He nodded. "His heart, you know." And he suddenly felt his shoulders trembling helplessly and knew that he was sobbing.

"Oh, my poor darling. I'm so sorry." She stood there, looking at him helplessly, miserably, and George and Walter appeared, very grave and curious, at the kitchen door to contemplate the phenomenon of a weeping father. It was Walter finally who went over and took him by the hand.

"Please, Daddy. Please don't."

And then George was crying, too. Timmy got up suddenly and walked towards his room. "I'll get dressed," he said in a muffled tone. "I've got to go out."

"Timmy, have some coffee!"

"I don't want to have anything," he said curtly. "I've got to be alone!"

Half an hour later, in the Knoxes' street, he walked covertly past the brownstone front of their house. As he did so the door opened, and two ladies whom he didn't know came out, talking in low voices. He turned away quickly, crossed the street and stopped to gaze at the house from the other side. It seemed to have an even bleaker, more somber look than its neighbors.

"Timmy boy!" He started and almost hurried off, but it was Larry. "Have you just been in? She's wonderful, isn't she?" Larry was radiantly grave with a new black tie.

"Yes, I mean no. I decided I wouldn't. There'd be too many people."

"Oh, come on, Tim." Larry put an arm around his shoulders. "You're one of the family. Nobody's going to miss him more than you."

"Later, Larry, later. I've got to go downtown now."

Larry looked at his tense, taut face and then nodded. "Right you are, boy. Come in later."

The reception hall at Sheffield, Knox seemed strangely muted. There was the same atmosphere of people moving about, less, of course, because it was Saturday, and the same high clear tones from the switchboard room across the way: "Mr. Stevens is busy, will you wait?" The autocall still bonged, but everyone knew what had happened, and if they spoke at all, and in normal voices, it was only because they didn't want to seem dramatic.

"Mr. Dale wants to see you right away," the receptionist told him. When he came into Dale's office, the latter rose and walked over to him. He even put a hand on his shoulder.

"I know what this must mean to you, Tim." Timmy only stared at him. "Sit down, my boy. Sit down. You've lost a great friend, and I've lost a great colleague. Henry Knox saved this firm. Nobody owes him more than I."

"I owe him everything," Timmy said in a dull voice. "Everything."

"Henry never liked me," Dale continued. "You know that as well as I do. There's no point pretending otherwise. But that's neither here nor there. I always admired him. He was a great lawyer."

"Yes."

"And we want his funeral to be everything it should be. A great tribute to a great man. That's where you come in, Tim. I don't mind getting right down to details because I know that occupation is the best thing for you now. I want you to act as a sort of liaison between the office and Mrs. Knox. I realize this is an unusual thing to ask of someone who's not yet a member of the firm, but you were closer to Henry than anyone in the office. I've thought it all out, and I know what I'm doing. I've got a draft of the obituary column now, and we can go over it, and then you can clear it with the family and the newspapers."

Timmy went home that day for lunch and found Ann subdued but anxious.

"I saw Mrs. Knox," she told him. "Just for a minute, of course. She was wonderful. Very sweet and grave and dry-eyed. She asked if everything was all right between us. Imagine her thinking of that at this time!"

"Dale wants me to help with the funeral," he said.

"It'll be small, of course. Mrs. Knox wouldn't want a big funeral."

"But Dale does."

"Dale! What does he have to do with it?"

"He simply happens to be the senior partner now," he said wearily. "A man like Knox doesn't belong only to his family. He's a public figure."

"You're talking like Dale already!" she cried. "Darling, don't!"

"Please, Ann," he said, rubbing his brow. "Can't you see I've been through enough?"

"Oh, Timmy, what is it?" She came over and sat beside him on the couch, putting a hand on his knee. "I've never seen you quite this way. So—so defeated. I know how you loved Mr. Knox, darling, but isn't there something else? Had you quarreled? What happened?"

He closed his eyes. "Ann, I beg of you. Leave me be."

"Darling, I can't!" There was a note almost of panic in her voice. "You had a fight?"

"Yes!" He jumped up to get away from her. "We had a fight!" he almost shouted. "I said brutal things! Horrible things! Are you satisfied?"

She shook her head sadly, looking down at the spot where he had been sitting. "He didn't mind, of course. But you'll never believe that. Not now. Never in a million years."

He went back to the office that afternoon and threw himself into the work that Dale had given him with a nervous fury, obliterating himself in details. Meeting with Larry and the other sons-in-law he went over the long obituary column for the newspapers. They found nothing to change. From there they progressed to the seating at the church, the arrangement of cars to the cemetery, the notices for the service, the telegrams to the older clients. Everyone deferred to him; almost embarrassingly, they acknowledged his special relationship. If he felt a fraud, if he heard Knox's quizzical, mocking laugh in his ears, he could turn to the file on his desk and tear at papers. For Knox was dead. He *had* to learn that. Behind the muted bustle of the funeral preparations he could sense already in the atmosphere of the firm the bewildered, shocked question: "Where do we go from here?" Dale, long organized for this moment, had taken over the running of things without arousing a protest. Small wonder, Timmy reflected with a dull but already unresenting bitterness, that he wanted a muffled Mark Antony to bury Caesar.

His worst moment was at the house with Mrs. Knox. It seemed full of her sisters, tall, large-boned women in black with misty eyes, rustlingly silent, being "wonderful." Mrs. Knox, the calmest of all, stood with him in a corner of the living room.

"He loved you, Timmy," she said. "You know that, don't you?" He could only hang his head, unable to bear those

101

still, clear eyes. "I hope everything is all right between you and Ann?"

"Oh, yes," he muttered. "Quite all right."

"Because all she wants is your best good," she continued, as if interceding. "You'll try to remember that, won't you?" He nodded. "You've been such a help about the arrangements. I don't think I'd have permitted a large funeral if you hadn't been there to help. You know we've all lost something, Timmy. I wonder if we won't be harder people without Harry."

"Please, Mrs. Knox," he murmured, and then someone else came up to speak to her.

Preparations seemed to overwhelm him right up to the moment of the service itself, on Monday afternoon, when he stood in a mourning coat by the doors of the grey somber church on Madison Avenue, its dark-wooded, empty-pewed atmosphere almost garish with banks of flowers, to act as one of sixteen ushers. And suddenly he wanted to stand alone in a corner of the church and watch the casket from a distance; he was suddenly anguished at the way his jumbled preoccupations had stood between him and the thoughts that he must think. But there was to be no pause even now; through the open doors and under the canvas awning the people were coming in, and the ushers, detaching themselves suddenly like fighter planes swooping, moved off down the nave followed by slow huddling little groups of mourners. Timmy waited until he was the last and then moved forward mechanically to escort an old lady who murmured in his ear how great was their loss. Walking back up the aisle with the organ's Bach thundering in his ears, past the black-veiled sisters of Mrs. Knox, with bent heads, past the rows of grey and bald heads of the Bar Association committees, the judges, the Orders and Societies, past the pews of awed young associates and their wives, past the family servants, the office elevator men, the aided of the Legal Aid, he wondered if the bitterness within him would not burst and release his aching soul to find his friend above the pungency of the flowers, above the peal of music, above the perfunctory sincerity of the hundreds of mournful eyes.

Someone was at his elbow. "Mrs. Knox and the girls are coming in in a second. I'm joining the partners in their pew now. I haven't seen Judge Lanahan, but if you spot him, for God's sake see he goes up front."

It was Dale, of course, turning away from him now, arranging his features for a hasty nod of sadness to old Miss

102

Sheffield who was hanging on Larry Duane's arm. Timmy turned abruptly off and went to the back of the church to stand by himself. He had to wait until his sudden tears had dried. Looking down over the back of all the heads at the coffin and its pall of red roses he wondered if in all his life he would ever get over the bitterness, the agonized bitterness of knowing what his last scene with Henry Knox had been. And burying his face suddenly in his hands he found himself trembling with a passionate anger that his guide and mentor should have so betrayed him, even by dying, so deserted him in his hour of need.

PART TWO

THE GREAT WORLD

1

One of the first acts of the reorganized firm of Sheffield, Dale & Stevens was to make Timmy a partner. At the same time he was given a large new office immediately adjoining Dale's and the best secretary from the stenographers' pool, a Miss Onderlin, nasal, efficient, smilingly impertinent. For Dale, as the new senior, was no longer in charge merely of estates and trusts; he was master of the firm now and meant to assert his control in unmistakable fashion. The entire office, he announced to his partners at a Monday lunch, was to be reorganized, and Timmy was to be his first lieutenant in carrying out the task.

"The trouble has always been that Henry Knox found administrative problems beneath him," he confided to Timmy afterwards in his slow, emphatic way. "He despised all that sort of thing. He used to describe us as a 'group of gentlemen loosely associated by a common enthusiasm for the practice of law.' Now that may have had an Old World charm, I concede, a flavor of Ephraim Tutt and the roll-top desk, but it just doesn't work when you get up to eighty-six lawyers with an overhead of a million a year. Then, like it or not, you're a big business, and you ought to act like one. That's what I want you to get across to the staff, Timmy. Cut out the waste. Every last penny of it. Squawks or no squawks. Don't worry, I'll back you up to the hilt!"

Timmy went at his new job with his customary dedication. He even retained a firm of business consultants to make a survey of the office to determine the exact amount of waste in each department. The outcry was immediate. Loud were the laments for the passing of the "great old days," the easy informality of the former regime, so vital, it was claimed, to the truly professional point of view. Shrill were the prognostications that this new reign of machinelike efficiency would obliterate the last vestiges of individual aptitude and daring.

But Timmy, wedded to his task, was ruthless. His test was efficiency, pure and simple. Was it necessary for the partners to receive so many hours of accountants' time for their family affairs? How many coffee breaks did a stenographer actually require? If the associates were averaging an hour and ten minutes for lunch, should it not be cut to an hour? He did it all well, too well, indeed, but the new severity of his manner reflected the paucity of his inward satisfaction. He had always, like Knox, regarded the office administrator as a goldsmith might have looked on a chimney sweep, and to find himself not only in the latter position but actually in charge of the goldsmiths, seemed curiously ironic, but, like so many other things in this new world of Dale's, a fact to be accepted. The only thing that he would not do was even to try to persuade himself that he was doing work on the same level as before. On the contrary, he went out of his way to exaggerate the sorry light in which each aspect of his new existence might have appeared to the sorrowing eyes of his late chief. In his determination to face the facts, he lowered the blind on other prospects.

The bitter resentment occasioned by the reorganization fell naturally on his head. The partners, reluctant to oppose Dale but unwilling to share the odium of his program, elected to take a detached, amused point of view, treating Timmy as if he were engaged in a form of manual labor beneath them. The associates, on the other hand, regarded him with sullen hostility as a turncoat, and Timmy, once so popular, became known in a shockingly brief period as Dale's hatchet man, a spy on idlers and a catcher of wasters. It was even rumored that he wanted every Lily cup to be used twice. Nor was the resentment confined to the lawyers. The older staff employees, once his staunchest friends, now faced his inroads into three decades of habit with angry protests tempered only by concern for their pensions. And Larry made matters worse. As Timmy's principal assistant he carried out instructions with the devotion of a young hound, delighted to have power even at the cost of popularity, rushing about the office with a zealous efficiency that aroused muttered comparisons to a Hitler youth guard. Dale, however, was gratified by such enthusiasm from a Knox son-in-law, and Larry's future in the firm, to the general surprise, was considered to have actually improved by the change of senior partners.

Timmy observed with a rather detached curiosity the rapidly widening circle of antagonism around him. Was this the old Timmy, people seemed to be asking, who was always so sympathetic to the younger men and never failed to see that the credit was shared? Was this the friend of Austin, the man who used to send flowers to the switchboard girls on their birthdays and always played in the spring baseball game with the office boys? No, he would answer grimly to himself, it was not. That Timmy had lived in a small sunny world under his own control. However hounded by his obsession with duty he had still been free; he could still brandish the finished product of his labors in the face of the gods and defy them to snatch away his liberty while his craftsmanship was what it was. But Knox had awakened him to the world, the real world. That was all, wasn't it? It was better, anyway, to see it that way than to have to admit the searing doubts of what he might have done to Knox. God! He would close his eyes and shake his head and pray, moving his lips desperately, for relief from the horror of that. Yes, better that Knox's death should have clanged shut the rattling iron gate on any such speculations, that he should be left alone in the dark that he had asked for.

He had little desire to share these new problems with Ann. She herself was too anxious; he felt in their evenings alone the full brooding weight of her preoccupation.

"I don't see how Mr. Dale can put you on a job like this," she told him. "What does it have to do with your experience? With your real abilities?"

"He wants me to learn, that's all," he answered gruffly. "He wants me to be practical. It's only temporary. As soon as I've got it licked he's going to start me on his own clients."

"You mean rich old ladies and their wills?"

"Well, what if it is? They pay, don't they? It's all part of the practice."

"You never used to think so."

"There are a lot of things I never used to think."

"Evidently." She turned away, shaking her head.

"I was only a hack before," he retorted. "A guy on a salary. Now I'm part of the firm. And with Dale I can become a bigger part. Much bigger."

"Darling, forgive me if I say something, will you?" He stirred irritably as she fixed her worried, questioning eyes on him. "Will you admit that you're impressionable?"

"What do you mean?"

"Well, when Mr. Knox was alive, you *did* rather model yourself on him, didn't you? Is that fair?" He simply shrugged in answer, impatient at her constant need for admissions.

"And you *were* like him, too, darling, that was the wonderful thing. But if you're going to model yourself on Mr. Dale, aren't you running the risk of becoming like him?"

"And what's wrong with Dale?"

"Oh, Timmy, if you're not going to be serious, we can't talk," she said with sudden sharpness, getting up and walking to the fireplace.

"I'm entirely serious."

"Maybe you are at that," she said, staring into the grate. "Maybe you really are. But I don't like it. I don't like it a bit. I don't seem to know what's happening to you these days. What is it, Timmy? Won't you tell me?"

"I've got a lot on my mind, that's all," he said sullenly. "Must something always be *happening* to people, Ann?"

In the silence that followed she picked up a book and sat down by the fireplace. "I suppose not," she said with an air of ending the discussion. "And I suppose George Emlen wasn't so bad, after all. Maybe the trouble's just in us. It's a good thing to know, anyway."

He began to wonder if she might not be right. He had moments of a remarkable lethargy when he could hardly answer questions at the office. He would know, when he had the perfect opportunity to utter the encouraging word, that he was not going to utter it, when he wanted to stop for a chat in Austin's office, that he was going to walk on, that in the evening when Ann was quietly knitting and waiting for him to tell her about his day, he was going to fix his eyes instead on a magazine that he would not be reading. Part of his existence took on a dreamlike quality, as if he were watching himself engage in dangerous activities, teetering on a precipice, diving from a high cliff, unable either to stop or to stop watching himself, so that the unhappy twins, the taker of risks and the compulsive onlooker, seemed locked forever in a helpless union. And then he would try to console himself with the thought that he need not really worry, that the whole thing was a product of his own self-pity, that if worse came to worst he could always beg Ann to forgive him and persuade Austin that their friendship was as strong as ever and reconcile the chief file clerk by buying her an enormous box of candy, as big as the Christmas turkey that Scrooge had bought for the Cratchetts. But could he? Could he still? In the middle of the night when he woke up and blinked at the darkness, he would have seizures of near panic at the idea that something more drastic was happening to him, something more out of his own control, that he was simply

110

turning outwardly into the creature he had always really been.

Amid such uncertainties he sought and found distraction in his new clients. For Dale had been good to his word and was already breaking him in with some of the choicest, starting with his own sister-in-law, Mrs. Emlen, mother of the very George to whom Timmy had so abjectly apologized. He had appointed Timmy as her co-trustee in one of the smaller Emlen trusts. Mrs. Emlen, with her husband's textile stock, was a widow of some importance in the financial world. To a lesser degree she and her sister, Mrs. Dale, also figured in it as members of the Bertrand family, owners for three generations of a famous jewelry store on Fifth Avenue. She prided herself on her business acumen and liked to feel that she never delegated her powers, even when her co-trustee bought and sold for her.

"There's one basic tip I'd like to give you," Dale coached him. "You'll have to give lip service to the widely spread fallacy that in this country it's the women who run things. Of course it's not. They could, perhaps, with the amount of money they control, but they don't. They may have the power, but it's we men who use it, even when we make them think otherwise. Just the opposite from the way it is in France. That's your job with Florence. Let her think she's running the show."

And so his visits started, on Friday afternoons, to the brownstone house on Sixty-fifth Street which wound its discreet way in back through an L-shaped gallery to the "east wing" which was actually another, smaller brownstone facing on Lexington Avenue. It was Timmy's first experience with the lack of ostentation of the very rich. He would never have suspected, behind that sober façade, the parquet floor of the exquisite Adam hall, the stifled luxuriant green of the small conservatory with its plopping fountain, the grey and gold paneled elegance of the French library. Neither did he suspect at first the sybarite behind the large, soft, rather crinkled whiteness of Mrs. Emlen, whose plump, pretty hands had a tendency to flutter over the papers that lay between them. She assumed, a bit comically, the executive pose; she pursed her small lips; she coughed; she tried to elongate her rounded figure in the Louis XV armchair by the desk, seeking, he was quick to feel, his approval. He found that as well as a lawyer he was expected to be a secretary; their conversation would veer from the trusts to her children, to infant grandchildren, to bills, to servants, to the summer place and, inevitably, to

111

taxes. He was fascinated by the reverence of such a woman for the smallest principles of tax avoidance.

"It's a pity I can't give anything more to my daughter Anita this year," she told him one afternoon with a sigh. "That husband of hers has been so improvident. My George used to say, Mr. Colt, that a beachcomber was really a bargain for a son-in-law. They cost so little. But one who has to be set up in business!" The hands fluttered to an unprecedented height. "And what does poor Anita get out of his wretched business? Nothing, poor lamb!"

"But you could let her have something," he suggested, thinking to be helpful. "You'll have a surplus this year. You could give her some of that."

"But Sheridan says absolutely not!" Her eyes were round and startled. "I've used up my exemption for the year. I have to wait till January. Surely you know that!"

"Yes, I know," Timmy conceded. "But you could still give her something over and above the exemption. There'd be a small gift tax, but that doesn't mean you can't make the gift."

"Oh, it's quite out of the question!" she cried, shocked. "Sheridan would never allow it."

He learned not to protest. There were principles in her world, iron-clad, and he had to pick his way carefully at first. He also learned not to minimize routine things which to her had a special dignity. One day when she had signed a paper that had to be notarized, he made the mistake of suggesting that she use the notary at her club or bank, or even one in the stationery store at the corner.

"But aren't you forgetting that this is no ordinary paper," she had reminded him, surprised. "This is a *document.* Hadn't we better use a *real* notary? One, say, from your office?"

Timmy knew enough now to suppress his smile and to bring up a notary from the firm the following day. When he told this to Ann, however, she did not laugh.

"But, Timmy, you're becoming an absolute sycophant!" she exclaimed. "I wouldn't have thought it possible. And in so short a time!"

"I'm only doing a job."

"I suppose I should have seen it," she went on, shaking her head gloomily. "That same perfectionism switched from companies to rich old ladies. Heaven help us! What will it do to you?"

Even when he felt uneasily that she might be right about his perfectionism, he still had his reservations about her own lack of curiosity. For was she not rather glorying in middle-class limitations? Was it so wrong to be amused? He was frankly fascinated by Mrs. Emlen and her younger, thinner, blonder sister, Mrs. Dale. He thought of them together because they were constantly together, the kind of women who found intimacy only in the easy sympathy, the unresented criticisms, the common presumptions of a sibling relationship. Their joint laps were complacently, indifferently available to the gifts of this world. That the witty should demonstrate their wit to them, the beautiful their beauty, the artist his most finished piece of work, they assumed with the unself-conscious complacency of Goya infantas. Yet this was not from any observed conceit. That anyone should have expected them to be amusing or beautiful or even artistic would have struck them as quite absurd. Nor did it seem to spring from any sense of class or money; Timmy could never make out that they saw any difference between the fortune that had been partly inherited by the late Mr. Emlen and the money earned by the self-made Dale. Such things were expected of men. It even occurred to him that they felt entitled to the world for the simple reason that they were women. If it was so, then Ann was just the opposite. She seemed to feel entitled to reject it for the same reason.

2

ANN WAS even more concerned about him than he thought. At first she had supposed that his remoteness was only a mood that would pass away with time, but when she began to identify it with his new line of work at the office, she became more alarmed. Without Mr. Knox to lead him back, could he be led at all? She even went so far as to discuss the problem with her mother-in-law—for she could hardly burden Mrs. Knox with the problems that her husband's death had brought to others—but Genevieve had been far from reassuring. "He's simply taking his place in the world, my dear," she had told her blandly. "It happens to everyone when they move up a peg. High time, too. You'll get used to it. As a matter of fact, you've been rather spoiled, you know. Timmy's never expected anything of you in his office life. Now it's going to be different. We'll all have to spruce up a bit." Ann was perfectly willing, even anxious, to concede all this, but it seemed hardly a necessary part of their new picture that Timmy should be so distant. She would dress up if she had to, go to the opera or polish her French or whatever it was he wanted; she would do anything in the world, God knew, if she could only feel they were doing it together. But this new abstracted Timmy, this silent, rather brooding Timmy, this Timmy who forgot a promise to take the boys to a ball game, who took it for granted, in their private conversations, that she actually cared about Mrs. Emlen's taxes, this Timmy who was even beginning to be fussy about his clothes, seemed to have changed as suddenly as girls used to change in her school days when they would turn with the passage of a single vacation from the love of Byron to the love of fingernails. She had not known that adults could change so, and when she taxed him with it, for, obsessively, she could not stay off the topic, he would only retort dryly that one couldn't stay in the baby's crib forever.

It was at the office Thanksgiving party that she first began to notice how different he was with other people. This was a cocktail affair for all the lawyers and their wives given by Mr. Sheffield in his old grey shabby Parisian house in the east fifties now surrounded by shops. In the atmosphere of rather tawdry splendor, amid faded tapestries and pale Nattier portraits, the young associates and their silent, clinging wives moved cautiously about in indissoluble pairs to greet the elaborately jovial partners. Timmy, on public view for the first time as one of the latter was so self-consciously good mannered that she left him in disgust and went over to talk to Austin.

"How does it feel to be a partner's wife?"

"Well, I'm beginning to feel it's a position you don't acquire simply by being a consort," she confessed. "You have to do it on your own. Timmy's made the grade, and it seems I haven't."

He smiled briefly. "You must put away childish things, Ann."

"That's what Timmy says."

"Timmy evidently has found it less difficult."

"Is that what they say in the office?" she asked, but he simply shrugged. "Is it, Austin?"

"Well, you know how it is, Ann. With the boys who haven't made it. I wouldn't worry. Those grapes are apt to be a bit sour."

"No, tell me, Austin," she insisted. "What *do* they say?"

He shrugged again. "Oh, simply that he has a very short memory. That's all."

"You mean that it's gone to his head?" She paused to reflect. "And yet it hasn't, fundamentally."

She could read in Austin's eyes his polite disagreement. But then Austin, she knew, for all his integrity, his decency, was devoid of subtlety. One *had* to be subtle, she thought unhappily, to understand these things. She turned from him now as she sensed a movement across the room and saw that Mrs. Knox, in heavy black, had just come in and that there was a respectful converging of older partners around the door. When Ann went over, Mrs. Knox drew her aside and kissed her.

"I'm so happy about Timmy," she murmured. "I only wish that Harry could have seen him a member of the firm."

Their conversation was continually interrupted by people who came up to speak to her. Each had the same air of muted solicitude; there were the same cautious inquiries, the same violent head shakings to signify accord with any response that the widow might make. Ann felt that it was awkward for Mrs. Knox to have to repeat herself so many times before the same witness, but she did not quite know how to break away or where to go if she should, and, besides, there was a certain defiance that made her want to show in public how strongly she still did and always would cling to this mourning symbol of the old regime.

"You're not meant to go to a party like that and sit like a bump on a log," Timmy reproved her as they walked down the street afterwards. "The partners' wives are meant to act as hostesses."

"I suppose I should have talked to your Mrs. Dale!" she retorted angrily. "I suppose I shouldn't have wasted all that valuable cocktail time with a poor old has-been like Mrs. Knox!"

"You weren't wasting *your* time," he pointed out dryly. "You were wasting hers. Presumably she doesn't go out to her first party since her husband's death in order to talk to you."

Ann was taken aback by this and said nothing. Reflecting on her conduct later she decided that he had been right, that

115

she had betrayed only egotism in her behavior. She even went so far as to wonder hopefully if she might not have exaggerated the extent of Timmy's change of heart, if it might not be her own prejudice against the Dales and Emlens that made her so quick to criticize his least tendency to admire them. She was only too happy to take the blame for their altercations and determined to be more co-operative when they went out in the future. It was unfortunate that the very next time should have been her first dinner party at Mrs. Emlen's.

Mrs. Emlen, it was true, was pleasant enough as she greeted her on the threshold of her Chinese drawing room, filled with glorious screens and black lacquered furniture, taking her by the arm, calling her "my dear" and introducing her with apparent solicitude to the people in her vicinity. Yet Ann had an immediate suspicion that this short, dumpy woman, so scarved and beaded with restless, watery dark eyes had no sense at all of her as a person, had not really seen her and was only seeking for a place, as if she were an awkward bundle, to set her down. When she had accomplished this, leaving her with her daughter, Mrs. Ferguson, a tall, angular, disagreeable-looking woman, she hurried away while the latter continued talking to her group about a decorator called "David" who was known, apparently, to everyone but Ann.

"He's shocked that I choose my pictures to go with my curtains," she was saying in a high mocking tone. "Isn't that lovely? Aren't you shocked, too, Mrs. Colt?" She paused to give Ann a brief stare. "Imagine, that I should choose my pictures according to my curtains! Fancy it! Doesn't it shock you all?" And she repeated her joke with an almost maniacal insistency, four or five times, exploding in little fits of gasping laughter. Ann was sure that it was best to say nothing, barely even to smile. It was to volunteer at such a juncture that made one look an ass. And happily the conversation went on as if she had not been there, nor was it even noticed when she got up and went over to where Timmy was standing.

"You'll see," she told him. "They may not talk to me, but they'll never let me talk to you. That's the one thing they can't abide." She was afraid that he might frown and be cold to her, but when he smiled faintly instead and touched her hand she could not repress an "Oh, Timmy, darling" though she knew he would resist the least show of sentiment at such a time. His hand withdrew, and both looked up as Mrs. Emlen bore down on them.

116

"Good heavens, my dear, you can't talk to your husband. That will never do." She saw the butler in the doorway and nodded. "Anyway, we're going in now."

At dinner, as she had feared, Ann found herself next to George Emlen. It made it easier, however, when she realized, as she did after only a few minutes of conversation, that the issue of his conduct to Timmy which had fluttered like a dark banner between them simply did not exist for him. That he should have changed Timmy's whole life and her own was evidently something that he had not even forgotten, that he had never quite realized. As she took this in, as she studied that dry eye, that half-turned plump cheek, that pouting, raised chin, she felt suddenly that it was good for her, good to know that Timmy's problem had nothing basically to do with these people, that it existed, if at all, for her and him alone. Down the table she could hear Timmy's voice, talking to George's mother. It pained her that it sounded forced, synthetic.

"What a beautiful house this is," she said to George, trying not to hear Timmy.

George shrugged. "You don't see the bills. I bet Mother's spent twice what it cost Father to build it."

"But it's amused her?"

"Amused her? Maybe. That's all she and Aunt Clarissa think of. Amusement."

"And that's so wrong?"

"*I* think it's wrong," he said flatly. "I believe in the English system. Where the widow retires with a becoming dignity to the dower house."

"In India they had a custom called 'suttee,'" she pointed out. "I understand that it disposed of the widow problem completely."

She was sorry as soon as she had said it, but it wasn't necessary. George hadn't even heard her. He was talking already to the lady on his other side. After dinner, when she heard the ominous talk of bridge, she managed to slip unnoticed into the empty library where she pulled out a huge illustrated volume of *The Idylls of the King* and allowed the hypnotic effect of the big, rich print to elbow her gently away from her apprehensions and set her on the dreamy road to Camelot. It must have been an hour later when she looked up with a start and saw Timmy watching her from the doorway.

"I must congratulate myself," he said. "With such a wife

117

there's no reason I shouldn't go to the very top of the social ladder!"

She shrugged impatiently and glanced about the room. "Is this where you and Mrs. Emlen work?" He nodded. "All alone up here? How she must love it, with you murmuring in her ear how clever she is!"

"She happens to be our hostess," he pointed out. "I think you owe her an apology for walking out on the party."

"No thank you! No more apologies to Emlens! We've seen what *that* leads to. Can we go home now?"

"There's certainly very little point in our staying."

"Oh, Timmy, don't *be* like that!" she retorted, jumping up. "The world's not going to come to an end because I've been reading Tennyson in the library. Do you think we have to say good night or can we just slip away?"

"Of course we have to say good night!"

She brushed past him and went down the stairs to the drawing room and up to the table where George's mother was playing bridge.

"Good night, Mrs. Emlen," she said firmly. "I've had a lovely time."

"Oh, there you are, my dear," her hostess murmured vaguely. "Well, I was so glad to have you. Dear me," she added, looking around the room and recalling now that she had not placed her at a table. "Where *have* you been all evening?"

"In the library," Ann replied. "Reading your beautiful edition of Tennyson. And having such a good time. I hope you'll let me come again and look at all those wonderful books!" She had meant at first to let the sarcasm come out, but when she actually heard her own words and saw the gathering dismay in her hostess's eyes, she remedied the situation instinctively by raising her tone to a pitch that was too high to be taken for anything but an eccentric sincerity. Mrs. Emlen gave her a weak little smile and turned back to her cards.

"I'm glad you liked them, my dear," she said with an amiable indifference. "I'm sure that we'd *all* do better to read more."

Timmy said nothing until they were in a taxi, and then asked her, in a tense, dry tone, staring straight ahead: "Did you *have* to speak that way to Mrs. Emlen?"

"What way?" But her conscience, for once, was bad.

"Did you have to make fun of her?"

"I wasn't making fun of her. I *did* enjoy seeing those books!"

"You know perfectly well you made her feel she'd neglected you. You wanted to rub it in. And, God, how you succeeded! But it might have occurred to you, if you hadn't been so dead set on making *me* pay for taking you there, that it's just as much your fault as hers. It takes more than the hostess to ruin a party!"

"Then why do you make me go to the foolish things?" she exclaimed angrily, truly stung at last. "Why can't I stay home? They only want you, anyway. They made *that* plain enough! Why don't you tell them I'm an invalid? It would make you so romantic, too. The faithful young husband, chained to a nagging cripple, slipping out to have a moment's consolation in the bright, gay world of the Emlens!"

"You'd love that, wouldn't you?"

"I?" She paused, surprised. "Love what?"

"If I went out without you."

"Well, just try it, why don't you?" she cried. "Just see if I don't. Do!"

Which, of course, was exactly what he proceeded to do. Only two weeks later he told her at breakfast, with a studied casualness and without looking up from his paper: "Oh, by the way, I have to be out tonight. I'm dining with Mrs. Emlen. She wanted you, of course, but I remembered our conversation and said you had a cold."

"I'm sure she was heartbroken."

"As a matter of fact, she told me how sensible you were not to go out with a cold."

"Wait till *you* have one, dear boy. She may change her mind."

With this small, wry interchange their discussion ended, nor would Ann have resumed it or asked him a single question about the dinner party for anything in the world. An invitation from Mrs. Ferguson was handled in the same fashion, and Ann, glum but still stubborn, knew in her heart that something serious was now happening to her marriage. There could be arguments by the thousand and silences, bitter, throbbing silences, but to have Timmy leave her twice alone while he went to parties was as different from anything that had gone before as Dale was different from Knox, as the new office from the old. One coasted along with a sense of small continuous bumps until suddenly one, seemingly no bigger than the others, jolted one from the tracks. But how or why remained a mystery. Ann knew that her own stubbornness was a factor, but even in the sudden panic that now gripped her she had the capacity to wonder if it might not be only through this stubbornness that she could find out, at long last, who the real Timmy was. At the lowest level of disillusionment there was still a surprising space for her reckless curiosity.

3

THERE WERE moments, of course, in the office when Timmy's nostalgia for the old days of his corporate work was almost unbearably keen. If he passed a conference room and saw Austin Cochran with a shirt-sleeved group, intent on printed proofs, he would feel like a sissy, a boy in a Sunday suit who watches his companions on the baseball diamond. But one thing that made this easier as time passed was the number of resignations among associates of his age that followed his own elevation to partnership. There was nothing personal about this; it was simply that he, of their class, had been selected. The others moved on. In less time than would have seemed possible only Austin was left of the old intimate circle who could still get through to hurt him. Timmy found himself almost wishing that Austin, too, had resigned; it was obvious that Dale had no use for him. One day, when they had finished discussing a new tax regulation, Austin hovered in the doorway.

"When you send for me next, Timmy," he said in an even tone, "you don't have to do it through Miss Onderlin. You can call me yourself. You haven't been a partner *that* long."

Timmy looked up and tried to smile. "Sorry, Austin. It's so easy, you know, with her right here. I forget."

Austin hesitated a moment and then came back to Timmy's desk. His dark eyes had a look of sudden concern that somehow bloodened his air of paleness. "Timmy, we've always been friends. Can I talk to you?"

"Sure."

"You and I used to laugh together at the way people behaved right after they'd made partner. How for a while they were even friendlier to the boys who hadn't. To show they weren't stuck-up. And then gradually, how it changed. They were embarrassed at finding themselves in charge of old cronies. They found they rather liked being 'sirred' by the younger men. They became distant. Do you remember all that, Tim?"

"Naturally." He was careful to sound just the least bit bored.

Austin stared down at him with a quizzical coldness. "Well, you certainly haven't made *that* mistake," he said with an emphatic snort. "Nobody could accuse *you* of hypocrisy. The day after you made the grade, you might have been a partner for ten years!"

"That was honest, wasn't it? Not to beat around the bush? Not to do what you and I used to laugh at?"

"Was it honest, Tim?" The concern came back into Austin's eyes. "Was that the way you always really felt? Could I have been *that* wrong about you?"

Timmy turned away uncomfortably.

"Dale's honest, too," Austin continued in a dryer tone. "If that's the kind of honesty you want. Do you know what he said to Mr. Hillyers when *he* made partner?"

"No," Timmy said impatiently. "And who the hell was Mr. Hillyers?"

"He was an old guy, a sort of retired special partner, who died before you and I came to work here. Apparently he was a sweet old gent, but garrulous, and used to come down to the office to open his mail and then buttonhole the younger men and bend their ears back with stories of the cases he'd won. But everyone loved him and put up with it. Except, of course, your Mr. Dale. Miss Glenn told me what happened the day *he* made the grade. She heard it herself. When old Hillyers waddled up to tell one of his usual stories, Dale fixed him with those cold black eyes and said: 'I don't have to listen to you now, Mr. Hillyers. I'm a member of the firm.' "

"Well, why not?" Timmy exclaimed irritably, hating the story, hating Austin for telling it. "Bores can be tyrants. Everyone knows that. Even nice old bores. Hillyers was pulling rank, wasn't he? Why didn't he pick on the older men?"

"You don't see anything wrong, then, in being mean to an old man like that?"

"Mean? Dale's not mean. He's simply businesslike."

"Maybe you're right," Austin continued in a more frigid tone. "Maybe mean is the wrong word. Maybe he's so warped that he really thinks we're all like him! That no one would ever stop for two minutes to listen to an old man unless he was a rung below him!"

"Is that warped? I wonder if it isn't pretty much the way the world is. Those who can dish it out and those who have to take it. Even dull stories. Getting ahead is a transfer from one class to the other, that's all. It's simply a case of telling the old man: 'Excuse me, hadn't you heard? I don't have to take it any more!'"

There was a heavy pause before Austin said: "Meaning you don't have to take it from me?"

"No, Austin," Timmy replied evenly. "I don't mean that. I hope you're my friend."

"Oh, Dale allows friends, does he?"

"Don't be an idiot."

"Tim, what's happened to you?" Austin demanded in a more heated tone. "Can't I help? Why have you become such a sourball?"

It was still there; the old pull to go back, but it was easier now to slam doors. Indeed, it was becoming a habit. "I'm not a sourball. I'm busy, that's all."

Austin ignored this. "Was it because of Knox's death?"

Timmy felt a sudden tremor in his shoulders. "I'm trying to do a job," he said sharply. "A job for Dale. It's not exactly a crime, is it, to save a hundred grand a year in office maintenance?"

"Who said it was?"

"Well, a lot of people seem to think it's that. Judging from the dirty looks I get. There's no point my trying to be popular. I've got a job to do, and I'm going to do it."

Austin stared for a moment and then nodded. "All right, Tim," he said softly as he turned to go. "Play it that way, if you like. I just wanted to help, that's all. If help was needed."

The effect of this episode was only to tighten Timmy's relations with Dale. Being identified with him he naturally sought to defend him, and defenses were not difficult to find. It was increasingly evident, for example, under the studies made, that the office *had* been extravagantly run in the Knox days. Dale's aim to reduce overhead annually by a hundred thousand was actually not unreasonable. And then, of course, the man was undeniably agreeable. He could be moody, casual, above all indifferent, in a shrugging, pipe-puffing way, but he never lost his temper. Nothing ever seemed to be quite worth that. He liked to take Timmy out to lunch and tell him stories of how he had handled such and such a great lady when everyone else had failed. It was beginning to seem that even he, the great collector of acquaintances, had need of at least one friend.

One day when Timmy came into his office he signaled him to close the door. "I'd like to put you in the way of making a little capital, Tim," he began gravely. "Your percentage will be raised next year, but I know junior partners can't save a dime, and it's a tragedy to miss this market. Now here's a real tip, if you'll keep it to yourself. Okay?" The brown eyes glared as Timmy automatically nodded. "Meredith Products is acquiring the Schultze plants. The contract will be signed in a week. Schultze will covenant not to compete in New Jersey, New York and Pennsylvania. There'll be a stock split in Meredith, and you should make an easy quarter of anything you put up now."

Timmy nodded slowly as he took it in. "A sure thing?"

"I got it from Stanley Field himself," Dale said with a sudden grin. "And keep *that* under your hat, my boy."

Timmy's lips formed in a silent whistle. Mr. Field was general counsel to Meredith. "But if I haven't anything to put up?"

"Which is what I want to talk about," Dale said promptly. "I think you and I are beginning to understand each other. When a man has earned praise, I think he ought to be praised, and I don't mind telling you, you've been doing a damn good job. Who knows? In ten years' time you may be head of this outfit. I won't live forever, don't worry." He smiled a rather hard smile. "Anyway I want you to live a little better, dress a little better. These things can be important, you know. And I'm loaning you seventy-five hundred to start a market account."

Timmy accepted the money almost automatically. He was in the habit now of obedience. He invested the whole sum in Meredith which went up even more than Dale had predicted. When he suggested to the latter that he sell out and repay the loan, Dale shook his head roughly.

"You can pay me back when you've got fifty thousand in the kitty," he snorted. "Not a penny before."

Timmy told Ann about his good fortune that night and suggested that they use the money to get an apartment uptown. Her reaction, however, was far from pleased.

"But why did this man, Field, give Dale the tip?" she wanted to know.

"How should I tell? And what business is it of mine, anyhow?"

"It seems to me it's very much your business," she retorted. "I'd certainly make it *my* business if Dale were my partner! If Field is handing out confidential information about his clients, mustn't there be a reason for it? A darned good reason?"

"Nonsense. That sort of thing goes on all the time."

"Without a reason?"

"Well, what would you suggest?" he asked irritably.

"I'd suggest that Dale was handing out the same sort of information about *his* clients!"

This was certainly a sharp thrust, and Timmy was shaken. He had not thought she would be so astute. He had, of course, considered the possibility and had already rejected it on the theory that he had no grounds for so slanderous a speculation. But the rejection had not left him entirely satisfied. "I see no reason to assume that," he said coldly. "I prefer to imagine that Mr. Field is simply a blabbermouth. There are enough of them downtown, Lord knows."

"Well, I think it's terrible!" she exclaimed, finishing, as she hardly ever did, her second drink. "Anyway, I don't want Dale's dirty money. And I certainly don't want to live in an apartment bought with it!" She reached for the whiskey bottle defiantly and poured herself a third.

"You're very particular about Dale all of a sudden. I can remember a time when you were less so."

"Oh, you mean that old apology," she said disgustedly, throwing up her hands. "There's no connection at all. Just because you apologize to a man doesn't mean you have to take his miserable tips."

"It seems to me it's one and the same thing."

"Timmy, have you gone entirely crazy?"

"You've said that before. I may be crazy, but I fully intend to get that apartment."

"Then you can live in it by yourself!"

He watched with concern as she started on her third drink. "May I remind you that we're going to the Dales' tonight?"

She looked up sullenly. "Not this girl."

"Oh, Ann," he protested in alarm, "you promised me! This isn't like an Emlen affair. Mrs. Dale is *expecting* you."

"It's not a dinner party, so I'll never be missed. I'm going to stay here and get drunk."

"Ann!"

"Well, suppose I go and fall on my face? How would you like that?"

"I'll have to risk it."

She got up suddenly and went over to him. Leaning down she pinned him against the back of his chair, a hand on each of his shoulders. "Timmy Colt," she said, staring down at him, "do you know something? You don't really *care* about any of this. That's the crazy part. You don't even care if I fall down at the Dales'. You might even like it! It's as if you *wanted* to ruin yourself! Darling, you love me still, don't you?"

For a moment he felt actually dizzy, as if the time for turning back had finally come. Then over her shoulder he suddenly saw the clock on the mantel. "For Pete's sake, Ann, we've got to dress!" he cried, jumping up. "Of course I love you, but look at the time!"

She stood alone in the middle of the room, looking more dejected than he had ever seen her. "What does it matter about the time?"

"What does anything matter? It matters as much as anything else."

"As *anything* else?" she demanded.

"Why not?"

"All right," she said in a duller voice, reaching down to pick up her glass. "Let's go to the damn party. I'm game."

4

NINE-O-ONE PARK AVENUE had been built in the middle twenties, that easy, spacious architectural era of high ceilings and wasted hall space. Sheridan Dale had bought into the building in 1934 at the bottom of the market collapse in co-operatives, which had given him a fitting abode to offer Mrs. Polhemus when she had consented to be his bride in the following year. It had worked out perfectly. Neither of them had the least interest in country life beyond weekend house parties, and the apartment, even with Dale's increasing prosperity, continued to be their sole residence. The hall, the living room and the library, chambers of noble dimensions, were made for entertaining, and entertain they did, crowds of people, in great heterogeneous parties, invited by Sheridan, tolerated by Clarissa, members of the legal and banking worlds, journalists, artists, denizens of the exotic, lacquered universe of fashion and design. Dale's secretary kept the lists at the office and evidently thought she had a system, for people were always being regrouped, transferred from the cocktail list to the dinner or after-dinner list, dropped or added, but what the system was and which, if any, were the "good" parties, not even the keenest eye could make out. Dale, however, seemed content with it, for whatever purpose it may have served. He stood serene in the midst of the changing crowd with which he had filled his life, indefatigably introducing, never forgetting a name, taking elbow after elbow and propelling guests from noisy to would-be-noisier corners. Clarissa, who never remembered a face outside of her own small group of bridge and Canasta friends, blandly accepted her husband's way of life and left the organization to him while she reigned over the card tables.

Dale's favorite arrangement was a more or less intimate dinner of twenty followed, at half past nine or ten, by a large reception. The new arrivals were fresh, he used to claim, and served to freshen up the dinner guests. It was on such an evening, in the lull between the end of dinner and the arrival of the first of the later guests, that Clarissa's daughter by her first marriage, Eileen Shallcross, sat playing backgammon with David Fairchild in a corner of the deserted living room. The men, from whom David had fled, were still in the library, the ladies in Clarissa's sitting room. Both Eileen and David appreciated the novel quiet of the long high room that the latter had decorated. Like all his work, it was a mixture of periods with a prevailing Italian motif; there were pale frescoes of robed women with urns on the two end walls and an enormous mirror, framed in gilt with antique panes above the great red sofa with the high back. Over the expanse of grey stone floor were eight brilliant Chinese rugs and little groups of carved wood chairs.

"It really isn't bad at all," David said complacently, looking about him as he rattled his dice, "now one can see it. What a pity I couldn't have done it for someone who didn't keep cluttering it up with riffraff."

"But you couldn't ask for better publicity," Eileen pointed out, "if it were put up in a window in Sloane's. I should think you'd be grateful."

"You forget I'm an artist."

"You forget it's my home."

There was perfection about Eileen. Perfection in her slim, diminutive figure, in her pale, lineless, heart-shaped face, in her large, blue, clear eyes and dark hair. She was dressed in light blue, matching her eyes, with one bracelet of opaque sapphires. But if there was sophistication in her simplicity, it was still simplicity. Her repose was not assumed. David, on the other hand, was nervous. His looks, like the red vest and bow tie that he wore with his dinner jacket, struck at one when he entered a room; he was a ballet dancer arriving on stage with a bound. Thick blond hair retreated in full waves from the triangle on his high forehead; his broad green eyes, small aquiline nose and high cheekbones made up the outlines of a handsomeness that one felt sure had frequently been photographed in *Vogue* and *Harper's Bazaar*. They were the looks, ideally, of a very young man, but David wore them well in his early thirties and would, one decided, wear them almost as well in his forties and even later until they suddenly wizened, perhaps in a single day, like dried skins cracking in the sun.

"We work and work, we artists," he continued, ignoring her last remark, "and who cares? Does your mother even *see* this room? Never. She takes it for granted, like everything else."

"I wonder if people ever enjoy the things they take for granted," she said, concentrating on her next move. She could never beat David, except as now, when he was indignant.

"They enjoy the appearance of them," he answered with a shrug. "Which is all Clarissa could understand, anyway. She lives in a world of externals. A literal world. It's difficult to imagine how things must *look* to Clarissa. Like those pictures, I suppose, of how the world looks to a bird."

Eileen's throw was just the six and a two that she had hoped for. "I'm sending them home," she observed, picking up two of his men, "for making remarks about their hostess. Not to mention the fact that she happens to be my mother."

"You'd never know it, for all the attention she pays you."

"She gives me a roof over my head," she retorted.

"You still cultivate the homely virtues, don't you, Eileen?" he asked, looking at her keenly as he threw his dice. "Good manners. Humility. Respectfulness. Perhaps it's what gives you your style."

"Four, not three," she corrected firmly, as he tried to bring a man out on the latter point. "Do you imply that I put them on? These manners?"

"On the contrary. True style must be sincere."

She shrugged, accepting his compliments as she did his strictures, without enthusiasm or reproach. She knew that what he said about her mother, however true, was mostly illuminating about himself. It was only natural that to envious eyes Clarissa should seem a monument of complacency. It was a fact that she had needed neither charm to gain husbands nor wit to win smiles; the world from her youth had been a too available pap at which she perfunctorily sucked. "I suppose it's something to be called stylish. Even today."

"It's something your mother needn't worry about."

Eileen put down her cup. "Now you're being abusive. And that's never fun."

"But I'm not, I'm quite serious," he protested, putting down his in turn. "She has no style. Where would she have acquired it? She was never old New York like your father. She got her money out of a jewelry store and looks it. And as for Lawyer Dale—well, they're a perfect match. What more can I say?"

"You might say a lot less."

He threw up his hands. "Really, Eileen, it's getting boring, this filial loyalty. What do they ever do for you, either of them, but beat their gums over your improvident marriage? Or rather your improvident divorce? And keep you strapped so you have to live here and help them with their ghastly parties?"

"What more should they do?" she demanded. "They gave me money, and Craig lost it. They don't owe me any more."

"Don't kid yourself," he retorted. "They owe you plenty. The only really snappy people who come to this house are your friends. Do you think it's to watch Clarissa gamble or to hear your stepfather name-drop? Not likely. It's your charm, my girl. Your old-fashioned Knickerbocker, Polhemus charm."

She picked up her cup and shook the dice. "Hardly one of the qualities that Sheridan admires," she pointed out. "If he's even aware of it. Is that why you resent him?"

"I don't resent him. That would flatter him."

"Oh, but you do, David," she insisted. "You resent him

128

terribly. You think he sneers at you. But that's where you're wrong. Sheridan admires any kind of success."

"Even a decorator's?"

"The 'even' is yours, David. Not mine."

It was his turn to throw, but he only sat and looked at her, with a small, suspicious smile. "Where do you get your tolerance from, Eileen?" he demanded. "That cool, chilly tolerance? You mustn't ever tolerate me, you know. I won't stand to be tolerated."

"What do you want tonight? Everything I say is wrong."

"You look too far into me," he answered with the same smile. "I guess I'm not used to being looked that far into."

"Don't you trust me?"

"I don't say that. But I never *have* trusted anyone."

His tone was serious, but she shrugged. "I have no wish to intrude."

"I know." He nodded. "Which is precisely the reason that you might be allowed to."

"But I'm not curious, David. It's simply that we're friends. I like you."

His smile became twisted. "Like a brother?"

"No, David," she answered in a level tone, returning his stare. "Like a human being."

He laughed almost pleasantly. "I never can trap you, can I?" he exclaimed. "No matter how I twist and turn. You always say the right thing. Maybe it's because you're genuine. The one true flower in a pasteboard world."

"Maybe it's because I don't fit into your preconception of what women are."

"They're all spiders to me, aren't they, Miss Freud?" he retorted immediately irritated again. "Tarantulas or lobsters with giant claws? Castrating claws?"

"Do you ever see them as disinterested?"

"What's more castrating than that!" he cried and then paused. "But you have a point," he continued, rolling his dice and moving two men to the same point, his long fingers sliding deftly across the board. "*You* are disinterested. It's why I could never have an affair with you."

"You out-David David tonight. Is that the ultimate compliment?"

"I wonder if it isn't," he mused. "I've had affairs with other women. You know that?"

"You've told me. With a rather schoolboy pride."

"Well, you needn't repeat it," he said with a laugh. "You might ruin my reputation. But the thing about those affairs was an excess of motivation. On the woman's part curiosity, a sort of feminine glee at conquering so notorious a faggot. An apotheosis into Venus herself. And on mine the desire to revenge an earlier slight or else the need to show myself the equal of some stupid husband, some Sheridan Dale, who had *my* success in the world downtown." As he paused and took in her expression of surprise, he suddenly burst out laughing. "Don't worry, Eileen. I'm not implying that your mother and I—"

"David!" she said sharply. "You can go too far!"

"So can you," he retorted with hauteur, "if such an idea ever so much as slipped through that agile mind of yours. Anyway. There are plenty of people who can enjoy affairs from motives. But I doubt if you're one of them. With you it's all or nothing. It's why we'll probably always be friends."

With her next throw she closed his home board. "There," she said. "Now I've got you. You can sit and be quiet while I throw off." She threw her dice rapidly several times in succession and moved her last men home as he gazed around the room. At the far end the ladies were just returning; some of the men had come out of the library to join them.

"Who's that young couple?" he asked.

"Where?"

"In the hall."

Through the great doorway, turning, she could see into the hall where the first of the after-dinner couples had appeared. The wife, in a plain brown evening dress, entered the room with a hesitant air. Her husband, behind her, seemed more detached. He had a pale, aloof countenance, and longish black hair. Eileen noted the nervous way in which his wife nodded as she greeted Clarissa and how she ran one hand over the back of a chair. "They must be the Colts," she observed. "He's a junior partner of Sheridan's. Supposed to be brilliant. Clarissa told me to keep an eye on them. They won't know a soul."

"So like your dear mother. It's a wonder she hasn't put you in the coat room in a black dress and apron. But wait. That will come."

"Mrs. Colt is obviously miserable," she continued, watching them. "I'll have to do something."

David's eye was appraising. "He's rather cute, don't you think?"

"I understand they're idyllically happy," she said dryly, "and have two nice little boys."

"Really, Eileen. Are you warning me off?"

"I don't want you to waste your time, dear."

"You mean you don't want me to get in your path?"

"What an absolutely foul mind you have."

"Dirty old David," he said mockingly. "That nasty habit of saying what everyone else is thinking."

"Two people simply walk into a room and you immediately leap to obscene conclusions!"

"Now just a minute," he retorted. "Let's be fair. I only said he was cute. What did you say? That he was brilliant and happily married. Who's leaping to conclusions?"

"But you know nothing in the world about him!"

"I wonder if that's quite true," he said, stroking his chin as he paused to observe Timmy across the room. "I think I know something about his marriage already. And I wonder very much if it's idyllically happy."

"That's what you think about every marriage."

"And I'm so often right."

"The next thing you'll be saying is that he's—"

"That he's like me!" he finished for her triumphantly. "All right. They so often are!"

"Oh, David!"

"Look, my dear. Listen to me for a minute and allow your prejudices to subside. Only temporarily, of course. I'll give them back. We have agreed that Mr. Colt is handsome?"

"But what does that signify?"

"He is, would you not say, more than averagely attractive to women?" He turned to make another appraisal of Timmy. "Oh, definitely more than averagely."

She shrugged. "I suppose."

"His wife, on the other hand, is an obvious frump. Can you deny it?"

"Certainly I can," she said, turning back to examine Mrs. Colt. "She's really quite pretty, if you'll only look at her. Except now she is obviously ill at ease and not at her best. You live too much in a blue-haired world, David."

"We won't debate the point. You will admit, at any rate, that she is the less attractive of the two?"

Eileen shrugged again, and rolled her dice.

"Very well," he concluded. "Tell me this. Why did he, a peacock, select for his mate this ill-at-ease brown hen? And don't tell me it was for her money or social position. My practiced eye can tell at a glance that she has neither."

"Maybe he loved her!" she exclaimed, looking up at him. "Maybe he's a man who looks for more in a woman than sophistication and poise!"

"A pretty opinion," he retorted, "but only your own. I suggest the contrary. I suggest he's a cake eater."

"A what?"

"One of those who practices the gentle art of possessing his cake while consuming it. I suggest that your stepfather's brilliant young partner is only another inhibited invert who has sought a disguise of masculinity in a sexually unaggressive wife."

With her next throw of the dice she took off the last of her men. "You're quite impossible tonight," she said, getting up, "and I'm not going to be drawn into it. Anyway, I've won the game. Now I'm going to bring Mrs. Colt over, and you're going to be absolutely charming to her."

He rolled his eyes to the ceiling. "I was right!" he exclaimed. "You *are* a spider!"

"And this is one web you're not going to get out of."

She went across the room to the Colts who had just been abandoned by Clarissa and were standing uneasily by themselves. "I'm Eileen Shallcross," she explained to Ann. "As the daughter in residence I'm allowed to strong-arm people. I want to take you over and introduce you to an absolutely charming man." She led her, bewildered, over to David who rose from the backgammon table and bowed as they approached. Then she returned to Timmy.

"I've heard so much about you from my stepfather, Mr. Colt," she began. "You'll have a lot to measure up to."

"You're Mrs. Dale's daughter?" he asked in surprise.

"Don't we look alike?"

"Oh, no. Not at all, really."

"Well, we needn't go into whether or not that's a compliment," she said lightly. "Shall we sit?"

He took a drink that was passed, and they sat on two chairs by a small table. He examined the slowly filling room with care. "Isn't that old lady Mrs. Wardell?" he asked. "The one talking to your stepfather?"

"If Sheridan is talking to her," she said without turning her head, "I'm sure it must be."

"Why do you say that?"

"Because she's a very important person. And would make a heavenly client. Am I too crude? Or don't you and Sheridan work that way?"

"I'm talking to you, aren't I? What good will that do me?"

"Ah, but you forget. I trapped you into it."

He looked quizzically around the room again. "Do you know most of these people?"

"I have to earn my keep. Mother can never remember names, so it's up to me."

"Your mother can't remember names?"

"Dear me," she said, noting his concentrated expression. "You do take one up on things, don't you? No, I'm afraid there's no division in Mother's mind between the different categories of people who come to her parties. They're all just guests. Lovely guests."

"But to you it's different," he pursued. "You've done your homework. That's how you know about me."

She gazed at him for a moment, with the smallest sense of disappointment. She wondered, after all, if she was going to like him. A classifier, a simplifier. Perhaps just a bit of a bore.

"Yes, I know about you," she said, nodding. "And I know about that nice old Mr. Sheffield who comes here sometimes." He burst out laughing. "Have I said something wrong?"

"Oh, no," he protested. "Not in the least. It's just that I see how constricted a life I've led. Perhaps that's what I need, to hear Mrs. Dale's daughter bracket me with Mr. Sheffield."

"You mean, I suppose, that I shouldn't have associated you with someone who's so old? And perhaps retired?"

"Oh, not that!" he cried, laughing again. "It's only that Mr. Sheffield is God and that I'm not even a cherub! And to walk into a party like this and hear a beautiful girl speak of us in the same breath—well, it gives me a sense of new worlds!"

Eileen felt slightly embarrassed, not so much at the compliment as at her immediate sense that it was not his normal way of speaking. "Thanks anyway for the 'beautiful', Mr. Colt," she said in a more reserved tone.

"My name is Timmy."

"And mine is Eileen."

"Oh, I didn't mean that," he said, confused.

"But aren't we members of the same office family?"

He seemed dubious. "Are we?"

"Well, how do I become one? Who's a member in good standing? Not Mother, I suppose."

He laughed again, as if such things were taken for granted. "Oh, even less than you," he replied. "I'll tell you who is. Mrs. Knox."

"I don't think I know her."

He threw his hands in the air. "Well, that *really* shows what different worlds we live in. When Mr. Knox was alive, and they used to give parties, probably half the guests were from the firm. Or clients. And whenever they went down to the country for the weekend they took one of the younger couples, sometimes two. It was simply the way they lived. The firm was more like a club to the Knoxes. And they assumed everyone felt the way they did. That was the charm of it."

Eileen noted the evident sincerity in his tone as he said this. He seemed for the moment detached, almost as if he had forgotten her. There was, she supposed, an implied criticism of herself, or at least of her family, in what he said, but she had to smile at the gravity with which he spoke of "younger couples," as though even the great could never be sufficiently reminded of the base on which the pyramid of a law firm rested. "And were they fun, Mrs. Knox's parties?"

He looked at her in surprise. "Oh, I don't suppose she ever thought of parties in those terms."

"Dear me," she said. "That does give me rather a picture. I suppose we're out of step here because Mother joined the office family so late. You'll have to help me to catch up."

"Now you're laughing at me."

"On the contrary," she insisted. "I want to learn to be a good office stepchild. Is it too late, do you think? Have I a chance?"

He laughed again suddenly, and his face cleared. The lawyer and the office man disappeared at once; as he rubbed his forehead and pushed back his hair, he had the charm of the boy whose existence she had already suspected behind his rather heavily assumed manhood. It was disarming, very disarming, but she was cautious. She had learned a good deal about boys from her husband.

"Why should you care about things like that?" he asked. "I'm the one who should be learning from you. You have all this." He indicated the room with a sweeping gesture. "You had it before your mother even married Sherry. What do you care about a lot of Babbitty lawyers and office parties?"

The plainness of his sincerity, the speed with which he swept clear the whole shelf of his preoccupations, was unsettling. "But you mustn't say that," she protested. "After all, what could I teach you? There isn't anything much to be learned at a party like this. Except maybe to be otherwise engaged when the Dales ask you again."

He looked about the room again with a rather devastating air of speculation and shook his head. "I disagree," he said. "I'm sure you could teach me a lot."

Eileen glanced involuntarily to where his wife was sitting with David. "Nonsense. Anyway, you have that sweet wife."

"Ann?" He laughed, but not unkindly. "She's a worse hick than I."

"Maybe you're both doing all right the way you are."

"Yes," he allowed, nodding, "there's always that point of view. If you talk to Ann you'll get it strongly. But what about you? Which is Mr. Shallcross? Is he here?"

"I'm afraid not. We're divorced."

"Oh. I'm sorry." There was an awkward pause. "My mistake."

"No, mine."

"I mean I'm sorry I asked," he said, now thoroughly confused.

"Don't be. Isn't it the sort of thing you expect of the non-office world?" But she should have known already that he was not one to make light of things.

"If you mean by that that I find you worldly or superficial, you're wrong," he said gravely. "I'm sure that whatever happened, it wasn't your fault."

She stared at him, her heart suddenly beating fast. She was almost inclined to say something sharp, to ask him if his drink was really that strong. "You sound like Sheridan," she said. "Must there be a fault?"

"Wasn't there?"

She turned away from him and watched her mother cross the room towards the library where the card tables were. Clarissa, spotting her, gave her the quick backward nod that indicated: Carry on here, will you? Eileen ignored it. "If there was any fault it was mine," she said slowly. "Mother and Sheridan warned me against Craig. But why should I have listened to them? *I* knew I shouldn't marry him. That was the important thing."

"And why did you?"

She was pleased now at his literalness. "Because I had to. Because I wouldn't have made any sense to myself if I hadn't. Can you see that?"

"Yes."

She decided that he could. "And those are the mistakes you never regret. The ones you make with your eyes wide open."

"I think I know the kind of mistake you mean," he said, with a slight frown. "I wonder if it's true that one never regrets them."

"Maybe that's the difference between us," she said, formal

135

again, and looked up as her stepfather came over. "I like your Mr. Colt, Sheridan. And I'm sure he's a good lawyer. You can't imagine how much he's got out of me."

"I've come to take him over to your Aunt Florence," Dale said with his usual abruptness. "She wants to talk to him."

Eileen got up, but turned back to smile at Timmy. "So you know Aunt Florence?" she asked. "Then you're a bit of a fraud, aren't you? What can we teach you? We're hicks compared to her!"

Timmy crossed the room with Dale to where Mrs. Emlen was sitting. "Your stepdaughter is charming," he told Dale. "I like her approach to things."

Dale paused and turned to face him. When he had a philosophic reflection to make, even his sister-in-law's impatience had to be protracted. "Timmy, she's the damndest girl I ever knew," he said, gravely. "The good Lord gave her looks, intelligence, money, breeding, and what does she do? Throw herself away on an oaf who could hardly sign his name. A member of one of those impoverished old Maryland families that prefer horses to men. And a brute, too, into the bargain. Never gave a damn about her. Went after her money and blew it all."

"Maybe she loved him."

Dale looked at him with the expression of one who wonders if he will ever come to an end of the irrational in his fellow beings. "Love?" he demanded. "She could have had love. All the love in the world. It wasn't as if her mother and I had been trying to force her to marry a man with money. We'd have been tickled pink if she'd married some young guy like yourself who could make his own way. But this man! And now look at her! Back at home, divorced and not a penny to her name. Who's going to want to take that on, I'd like to know? You can't expect her mother to set her up again. She did that once, and what does she have to show for it?"

Timmy agreed that it was all very difficult.

"But enough of that," Dale said dryly. "I haven't got all evening." He always had the trick, Timmy reflected, of making the other person feel that he had been doing all the talking and rather too much of it. "Florence has been shouting for you. You've done a first-class job keeping the old girl happy." Dale gripped his shoulder reassuringly. "Keep it up, boy. Keep it up. I meant what I said about turning things over to you. I can't run everything in the damn shop. Not forever, you know!"

136

To Timmy, walking across the room with his host's heavy hand on his shoulder towards the broad, already smiling face of Mrs. Emlen who was now nodding to him, the air of the party seemed to tremble with the gold dust of his new future. As he passed Ann, talking to Fairchild, he glanced apprehensively at her drink and then looked resolutely away. He could only take up one thing at a time.

David was surveying his companion with something less than enthusiasm. The after-dinner guests had now largely arrived, and it seemed hard, when he might have been securing the commission for old Mrs. Wardell's new house in Jamaica with a few bold jokes and compliments, that he had to be tied down to an unimportant young lawyer's wife who was noticeably intent on the darkest scotch and soda he had ever seen. Really, the things he did for Eileen!

"Do you live in the city?" he asked with a rather exasperated politeness.

"Yes, we do still. Do you?"

"Where else?"

"Well, with children it's more of a problem," she explained, still staring at her glass. "Particularly with little boys."

"I fail to see why," he retorted. "*I* was brought up in the city when I was a little boy."

"But it was different then. Now everyone's moving outside."

"And the husband is sacrificed to the early death of the commuter," he observed, "that one child may pick a dandelion. But I guess it's fair. The child grows up to do the same thing."

"You dislike the suburbs?"

"I don't even recognize them."

"You dislike uniformity, I suppose," she went on with a vague nod. "Yet, in a way, you owe it so much."

He stared. "I?"

"All the girls I know want their husbands to make more money so they can have a David Fairchild room."

He sat back and blinked. "Why, you've heard of me!"

"Of course I've heard of you," she said. "Aren't you famous?"

David was much mollified. He even decided that Eileen was right, that Mrs. Colt *was* rather pretty. Good skin, anyway. Or was it simply that he liked compliments, compliments from anyone? He smiled, remembering how Eileen had compared him to a trained seal catching fish. Any number

137

went down before you knew it. "Are you much interested in decorating?"

She smiled briefly and took a sip of her drink. "No. But my husband wants me to get a new apartment. He'll undoubtedly want you to do it."

David's air became the least bit stiffer. He was used to young couples, met at parties, who wanted cut rates. "We'll have to see," he hedged. "I should be delighted, of course, but I do get a bit swamped."

"But you don't understand!" she protested, turning on him suddenly. "We can't afford it. Not really. And even if we could, we're not—well, we're not that sort of people."

David raised his eyebrows suspiciously. "What sort of people?"

"The kind of people who can afford David Fairchild. Or maybe I mean the kind of people who can appreciate David Fairchild."

"You mean that you and Mr. Colt are too earthy?" he inquired coldly. "Too basic for my frills?" He saw that she was confused and noted the subsequent sip of her drink. "Is that it?" he pursued.

"Why do you fence with me?" she asked. "Can't you see what I mean? I wouldn't mind if Timmy really wanted you to do an apartment. Or even if he went broke paying for it. I mind his wanting it because it's the thing to want. Why, three months ago Timmy had never heard of you!"

"And was a purer man, no doubt."

She shook her head several times in succession. "I won't let you put me in a corner, Mr. Fairchild," she said stubbornly. "You know what I mean. You're too bright not to."

David was silenced. The prototype of philistia, the armed domestic female, had collapsed with the violence of her appeal into this poor creature. It was not agreeable to glimpse the egotism behind his own preconceptions of others. David felt ashamed, and immediately resented having been made to feel so. After all, wasn't she making rather a scene over her husband's small scrap of worldliness? "I suppose you mean he wants to get ahead," he said. "What's so wrong with that? The act of transition, I concede, is always unattractive, but once he gets to the top, he'll settle down and care less. I've seen too many of them. Take our host, for example."

"You take him."

He did not like the moody way in which she was staring at her drink. It might have been her first of the party, but it

138

was clearly not her first of the evening. "Maybe you have a point," he said in a kinder tone. "But don't worry. Your husband will never be like Dale."

She looked up defiantly. "Won't he? How do you know that, Mr. Fairchild?"

"Well, in the first place he's too good-looking."

This remark, intended to lighten the basis of their too serious discussion, had just the opposite effect. She seemed suddenly to crumple. "He is, isn't he?" she said in what threatened to become a wail. "And you saw him with that lovely girl. Weren't they a graceful couple? Didn't they seem made for each other? Say it, Mr. Fairchild!"

"Please, Mrs. Colt!" David exclaimed, now quite alarmed. "Don't go on that way. This is meant to be a party. We're supposed to be having fun!"

"Fun!"

Her very soul seemed to have jumped into those large, bewildered brown eyes to repudiate the word. And as he watched her, not knowing what to do, she suddenly jumped up and hurried from the room.

"I'll look after her, never mind," came a voice from behind him, and Eileen, ever watchful, had moved quickly after her. "Pretend nothing has happened!" she murmured over her shoulder.

In Clarissa's room, sitting on the broad, pink-covered bed with the Venetian bedstead, she found poor Ann looking dolefully at the mess she had made. Right in the middle of the pillow. "Poor Mrs. Colt," she said, closing the door behind her. "I hope you feel better. Is there anything I can get you?"

"Don't be sorry for me," Ann murmured sullenly. "Try not to be, anyway. I know I'm a horror. I shouldn't have come."

"Anyone can be sick."

"Have *you* ever been?" Ann was looking at her defiantly now. "No. And, if you thought you were going to be, you'd rather die than be seen. I know your type. I've envied it too much not to know."

Eileen looked at her quizzically. "I'll get your husband," she said calmly. "You'll probably want him to take you home."

Ann shook her head. "I'm sorry about the bed."

"It doesn't matter."

When Eileen, back in the living room, leaned down to whisper to Timmy, he stood up immediately. He felt little

139

enough surprise. It was as if he had known all along that he was getting beyond himself, as if there was almost kindness as well as inevitability in Ann's plucking him back. It had been her decision, had it not, from the beginning?

He said nothing, however, when he went to Mrs. Dale's bedroom. There was no need for it. He would allow her to bring the drama to a close in her own manner. If she chose not to speak to him, to go glumly to the hall, barely pausing as he put a coat about her shoulders, if she chose further to ignore the clucking of Mrs. Dale roused from her Canasta by a reporting maid, if she wanted to ring down the curtain with a masterpiece of bad manners, it was enough for him to watch, impassive. She was lucky indeed, he thought with a tug in his heart of the old affection and pity, that he did not say, "I told you so!"

Eileen, returning to her mother's room to be sure the bed was being changed, the guests' coats removed, heard running steps behind her and turned to face an elated David.

"Is it true what Clarissa told me?" he cried. "All over her bed!"

"Don't be disgusting, David."

"But is it? Tell me!"

"Yes, but shut up about it."

"It's poetry!" he exclaimed. "I tell you she's a great woman, that Mrs. Colt. Think how many hundreds, if not thousands, have been through these rooms, have attended these ghastly crushes. And, of them all, who besides that lonely, baffled creature has had the wisdom and the courage to express her soul by regurgitating in the very center, the neat, pink center of your mother's bed? I wonder if I'm not in love with her!"

Eileen smiled faintly as she continued down the corridor, thinking how angry she could make him by saying that it had taken one miracle to produce another. She thought of Timmy Colt's impassive paleness and wondered if he, like Craig, could be cruel.

5

THE FOLLOWING morning Timmy got up without waking Ann and prepared breakfast for himself and the boys. He told them to be quiet because Mummy was not feeling well, and when he had sent them off to school, brought her cup of coffee to the bedroom. She was sitting up now, staring despondently out the window.

"Thank you," she said in a toneless voice when he handed her the cup.

"I thought you wouldn't want to get up."

"That's right."

He paused, uncertain.

"Timmy," she said, as he turned to go, "would you mind sitting down? I think we should discuss what happened last night, don't you?"

"Not now, Ann. A lot of things are better left unsaid. Why hash it over?"

"That's so like you," she said in the same listless tone. "You can go for years without discussing things. But I can't. Timmy, we must have this out, once and for all."

"I only want to point out first," he said firmly, sitting down on a chair by the bed, "that I haven't said a word of reproach. And that I don't intend to."

"I know," she agreed, nodding. "You've been entirely correct. You didn't say a word in the cab. And that was a very pretty apology you made to Mrs. Dale."

"Oh, you heard it?"

"Certainly, I heard it. I wasn't that drunk."

"I suppose you'll admit," he said with a frown, "that an apology was in order?"

"No, I won't, Timmy," she said, shaking her head. "Not fundamentally. I think the Dales owe me an apology for what they've done to you. And for what they've done to our life."

"Ann!"

"I mean it. And, furthermore, for what they're turning you into."

"What is that?" he demanded, his throat beginning to tighten with irritation.

"We've been over it all before," she said wearily. "I see no point going into it again. You refuse to understand it. You've congealed, Timmy. I didn't know how much until last night. Why, you might have been a stiff English governess taking home a naughty child!"

"What did you want me to do? Fall down on my hands and knees and bless you for making us the most conspicuous couple at the party?"

"Yes!" she cried, sitting up in sudden excitement. "That's

just what I wanted! I'm not going to be ashamed of saying what I want! I wanted you to be on my side. I wanted everyone to know my husband was with me through thick and thin! That we had something together that made their whole party as unimportant as—well, as a mosquito!"

"Really, Ann, you're out of your mind."

"Oh, I didn't want you to *say* anything," she continued, sullen again. "Though I'd have gone on my hands and knees and blessed *you* if you had. I only wanted you to make me feel that it wasn't important. What I'd done. To us, anyway. I only wanted you not to sit like a ramrod in the cab all the way home, fretting about what I might have done to your career!"

"Well, if this isn't really and truly the limit!" Timmy was on his feet now, pacing the room. "*I'm* the one who should do the apologizing! Because I behaved myself at the party? Because I didn't get sick on Mrs. Dale's bed?"

"Even Mr. Fairchild, whom I'd only just met, was more considerate than you."

"And why not?" he demanded, turning on her. "Were you *his* wife? Were you making a fool of *him?* I bet he enjoyed the whole show!"

"Oh, Timmy, you're disgusting."

"And who made me disgusting?" he cried, trembling now with anger. "Who made me swallow my pride and crawl to George Emlen? Do you think I don't understand anything? Do you really think you can sit here with a pile of books in a little vacuum of untarnished ideals and send *me* out to roll in the mud? It's where you're wrong, then. We're in this thing together. And it was *your* choice!"

"So that's it," she said in a lower tone. "You're punishing me. Of course."

"I'm not punishing anyone," he retorted. "I'm simply being consistent. I was perfectly happy living the way we were. *You* were the one who wanted to change. Well, now we've changed, and we're going to go right on changing. Right on till we've reached the top! For if you think I'm going to be content to have sold my soul for a mere junior partnership, you're crazy!"

"I see," she said again, nodding slowly. "There's a sort of desperate logic to what you say. Yes, I can see it. But it brings me back to the thing we've got to discuss." She paused. "We can't go on this way, Timmy."

His jaw dropped. "What?"

"It will never work out. You'll be much better off without me."

"You're not serious!"

"Oh, but I am." She closed her eyes for a moment. "I've thought and thought about it. We don't seem to be able to communicate any more. Everything I do and say aggravates you—"

"What about what *I* do and say?"

"All right," she conceded, looking even paler. "If you want. That aggravates me, too. I don't know if that's the word, but never mind. The point is that something has snapped between us. Maybe we were never as close as we thought we were. Maybe these things never came out because I lived, as you say, in a vacuum. Because we both did. But whatever the reason, here we are."

Timmy felt the bitterness within him, like an icy tide, grip his whole being. He took in appraisingly her unjustified expression of reproach. "What is it that you propose?" he asked coldly.

"That we separate. For a while anyway. That you go to your mother's or a hotel. Coming here, of course, to see me and the boys whenever you wish. Till you've thought this through, Timmy." Her eyes appealed to him in desperation. "Till I've pulled myself together. Till we know where we are, darling, and where we're going."

"And where *are* we going, Ann?" he insisted in the same hard tone. "To Reno? Is that your idea?"

"Oh, Timmy, please." She suddenly dropped her head in her hands. "Don't make a drama of it. You know how I love you."

"I'm sorry. I'm not sure I know that at all. You pick a most unusual way to show it."

"Can't you see I'm at the end of my rope?" she cried suddenly. "Why do you think I did what I did last night? Have I ever done anything like that before? Can't you see that I want to save our marriage? We've *got* to know where we stand, Timmy! Go to the Dales, go to your parties, they'll be delighted to have an attractive extra man. See what it all means to you. You must, darling! For there are things going on inside of you that I simply don't understand. And I have this hellish fear that being with me only makes them worse!"

The sense of her suffering was too acute; he had to look down to avoid her desperate eyes. Yet why, he still asked himself bitterly, clenching his fists, were they even having such a scene? Had it been *his* idea? "All right, Ann," he said, turning away silently, weary suddenly of the very ambivalence in his feelings. "We'll try it your way. I'll go to the Stanford. The firm has rooms there now. How will you explain it to the boys?"

"I'll tell them you have to work," she said in a barely audible tone. "To work at night. That's one thing, poor children, they're sure to believe."

Timmy walked to the subway in a daze, but a daze that was still protecting him from what seemed the more real prospect of turning and hurrying back to tell her that she was crazy, that they loved each other, that a separation was impossible. This was the obvious thing to do, and the thing, it seemed to him, that, of course, he *would* do, to help his rather ordinary destiny achieve its rather ordinary end. But he was still able to observe, with a deep little tingling satisfaction in the heart of his bitter sadness, that every step was taking him further from that obvious solution, that had-to-be-done thing. If he crossed the next street, he would say, he was lost; no, if he passed the door of the corner drugstore, no, if he actually entered the subway. But as he hovered before the last he was shoved forward by a friendly grip on his shoulder and found himself descending the stairs with Larry.

"When are you pulling out of this dump?" Larry was asking. "When are you moving uptown where all good partners go?"

"I don't know. I'm not sure yet."

"I know a terrific real estate broker if you need one."

Larry was always helpful these days. Since his father-in-law's death and Timmy's elevation to partnership, he had clung to the latter even more fiercely. But Timmy cared less for motives now; he was hungrier for the uncritical forms of friendship.

"Ann's left me," he said flatly, as they stood on the platform waiting for the train. He had wondered how it would sound, this thing he had been going to tell nobody. "Or rather she's kicked me out."

"No kidding?"

"Would I kid about a thing like that?"

"You mean you've really split up?"

"So she tells me."

"Good!"

Timmy turned in shocked amazement to face the defiant congratulation in Larry's eyes. "What are you saying?"

"Only what I've been wanting to tell you for a long time! Only that it's made me sick and tired to see what she's been doing to you! Who the hell does she think she is, I'd like to know, dragging herself around with a face a mile long? She's jealous, that's all! Now that you're beginning to hit the big league, she wants to suffocate you in a steam bath of neuroses!"

"Larry, please!"

"I'm sorry," Larry went on recklessly, warming up to his theme. "I just happen to be your friend, that's all. You'll probably hate me for telling you this. But I've always picked you for a winner. Right from the very beginning, Timmy boy. I want to see you go to the top, and I'm dead set against anyone who's in your way! Even if it's Ann!"

The black train rattled along the platform, and Timmy got in without a word, standing beside Larry in the crowded center of the car. Glancing at the latter's set, half-averted countenance, he noted curiously that it was still handsome, despite the long cheeks, the oval, moled jaw, with the handsomeness of blond youth. But what he also saw was that this impression would barely survive the passing of youth; one could already make out the hardness, even the hint of brutality, in what the older man would be. Larry's boyishness and rather whiny charm had concealed not only his selfishness; they had concealed as well a greater shrewdness and ability than Timmy had suspected. Larry would see the practice of law in terms of people and how they could be handled; he would fit in well in a world of Dales. And Timmy who wanted now to reject and repudiate him, who wanted to cry defiantly: "But no! You could never understand my Ann! Never in a million years!" was silent, wondering if he was really man enough to stick to his chosen path.

6

EILEEN SHALLCROSS had grown up in the one small niche of serenity that she had managed to carve out of the ordered turbulance of her mother's life. Clarissa Dale and her sister, Florence Emlen, were always pursuing pleasure in noisy but organized forays; if amid the stamping of hooves and the blowing of trumpets the elusive creature got away, its escape was unnoticed by the riders who had come, after some speculation as to what they were after, to confuse the hunt with the capture, the shouts with the emotion that engendered them. Eileen's father, Theodore Polhemus, a reserved, gentle, affable man, of an honorable family on Brooklyn Heights, renowned, however, more for their stillness than for any sound or jarring note, had early been dropped from the picture. Only Eileen, it seemed, had really been conscious of his shedding, or rather of his return to the Heights; to her he was a consoling but ineffective ally, and whenever Clarissa forgot that Wednesdays were reserved for her visits to him, Eileen, normally a child of the evenest disposition, could scream and stamp and carry on alarmingly. Such occasions, however, were rare. It was her father, consumptive and dying, who taught her to make her peace with the Bertrands, who opened her eyes, without malevolence, to the curious fact that whatever her mother's family turned their hands to, they managed to do badly. He wanted her, like all parents but more particularly the moribund, to succeed where they had failed. He wanted her to do things well.

And she did. At a surprisingly early age she dressed well, talked well, rode expertly and developed a real card sense. She had not only the knack but the charming quality of making little of it; she would simply shrug off her talent and make the observer feel, whatever his modest endowments, that those, now *those* were something worth talking about. And in a literal world, at least in a Bertrand world, people were apt to take her at her own evaluation. Clarissa never for a moment suspected how exceptional a creature she had produced. Nor did Aunt Florence or her cousins, George or Anita. But other people did, and as a companion piece to their admiration, Eileen learned early to accept their resentment. She irritated them because she seemed so easy to pigeonhole, while in fact she would never fit. Seated at the bridge table it was tempting to classify her as a parlor lily with one small artificial aptitude. Then one saw her in a black riding habit, perfectly cut—all right, she was a dude. And then one watched her take a five-foot jump. Really! It was hardly fair. Nor did it make things any better that Eileen seemed to sense their confusion and half to apologize for having proved them wrong. She would have been wiser to have tossed them a fault and let them pin it on her. People would have liked her more had they thought her conceited, cocksure. They would even have welcomed a charge of insincerity or deceit. Nothing is more detested than perfection.

Eileen, however, was not perfect. She had one great vanity: the idea that nobody had a greater love to give. Such a love, of course, was not a commodity to be wasted, except for a few gentle drops here and there, on family or friends. It was a dripping beaker to be emptied, in one full flood, on the man of her choice, or rather, for Eileen was not a forward type, on the man who should choose her. It was not in her fantasies that he should have an equal or even a comparable love to bestow; having received so little from her own progenitors, she was no doubt unworthy. It was only important that *she* should love and love completely, and it was thus that she became the handmaiden of Craig Shall-cross.

He was a tall, knobbly gentleman farmer from Maryland whose silent ways only partially concealed a bad disposition and whose love of animals could never quite cover his aversion to humans. But he had the talent to assess Eileen correctly when they first met on a weekend house party in Baltimore. He was not dazzled by her capabilities, but he recognized them, and he saw what others failed to see, their availability. It was a new experience for Eileen to find herself taken for granted, without either envy or admiration; she promptly took his inability to be impressed for masculinity, his lack of imagination for strength. She gave herself over to the adoration of this new god because she had always told herself that she would; neither her mother, whom he bored, nor her stepfather whom he irritated, nor any of her friends, whom he antagonized, had the slightest effect on her. She married Craig a month after they had met, put her money in his hands and went blithely off to live on his Maryland farm.

When she thought later of the drab years of her married life, it seemed as though she had sold her heritage for glimpses: his swinging shoulders as he walked to the barn, the careless wave if he returned from the hunt in a good mood, the lazy smile after four drinks. She had shared him with animals, with bottles, for the stingy moments of an athlete's love; for these she had given up everything that he could not share, her reading, her music, her old friends, even her cards. She had sought his level in everything, and she had finally come to be resented, as deep down she had suspected to be inevitable, for her very compliance with the

147

stupidity of his way of life, for her own exhausting enthusiasm for everything in him that was least like the best in herself. She had even been able to appreciate the irony of a fate that had selected for her rival and successor a Baltimore girl of grotesque affectations who detested farm life and made no secret of it.

"I should have seen it from the beginning," she told Craig in her one moment of outspoken bitterness. "Every man wants a woman to be a bitch occasionally. Your mistake is that you've picked one who'll make it a full-time job. She'll use the barn for cocktail parties and have you hanging Japanese lanterns. And you'll like it, that's the killing part. You'll like it for maybe a whole year."

She came back, empty-handed, to a mother who was pleased enough to have her back, however often she underscored the obligation. For Eileen was more than decorative; she was soon almost indispensable. Clarissa could now spend all her time at the card table while her daughter was charming to Sheridan's friends and clients. It was little enough to expect, wasn't it, in return for her clothes and board? And to Eileen, after the years in Maryland, even her stepfather's parties seemed glittering.

She was, in fact, starved for everything that New York could offer, for music, pictures, friends. She was starved for elegance, even for artifice. And ever conscious of her inward wound, she now had a small, veiled defiance that she had not had before. She had loved and been rejected. Very well. Now she was on her own, with no further need of apology. If there were still people who were jealous of her blue eyes and her talents, that was simply too bad. They could envy themselves green, for all she cared. And it was just this attitude, of course, still perceptible behind the veil of her perfect manners, that gave her a new power over people, that made David Fairchild who had once found her "sticky" now delight in her company. It was no easy job for a single woman to carve out a place for herself in the social world, but it could be done, and Eileen accomplished it. With her ability to blend with any group, her ease and yet deference with older people, she could pass from the personality dissection of the fashion world to the stately give and take of Newport, the castellated grandeur of Mrs. Edwin Wardell herself. Dale, more observant than his wife or sister-in-law, was quick to see that Eileen was moving into circles not yet available to him, for all his marriage and his downtown success, and, in the guise of a kindly stepfather, began to suggest that she ask some of her own friends to his parties. And Eileen, understanding, but amused, was quite willing, so long as he was not too obvious in his attentions to his new guests, to act for the time being as his social retriever.

One thing, however, she had kept away from, and that was love. She associated it now with subjection, and Craig had given her enough of that to last her for a long time. She valued her new independence, at least her independence of men, and however disconcerting this may have been to the occasional bachelor who saw in so charming a divorcee the opportunity for an easy and unentangling affair, it could be as gratifying to older husbands, timid of temptation, as it was immediately endearing to their wives. All of which did not make, of course, a complete life, but it made a peaceful one, and anyone who had been through what she had been through could appreciate peace. It was consequently with very mixed emotions that she now contemplated her new preoccupation with Timmy Colt. She was startled by the bound of her heart, only three nights after the party, when her stepfather announced at dinner that his wife had left him.

"Left *him!*" Clarissa exclaimed. "I should have thought he'd have left her. Perfectly revolting, the way she behaved. Do you know, I think there's still an odor in my room. Or do you suppose that's just imagination?"

"Of course, I'm not sorry, for one," Dale continued, ignoring his wife. "Timmy's too good for her. It's the old story. The husband with the future and the wife who can't keep up. So she goes around feeling sorry for herself. Might as well chuck her now as later. The quicker it's done, the less it hurts."

"Poor Mrs. Colt," Eileen commented sadly. "Does she really have to be chucked? Couldn't there be a school for wives like that? I'm sure she could learn."

"She's a lame duck, Eileen. Don't go wasting your sympathy on lame ducks. They never learn."

"If she'd just learn not to do what *she* does in her hostess's bedroom," Clarissa said severely, "it would be an excellent first step."

Eileen did not suggest that they ask him to dinner, now that he must be lonely. She was only too sure that they would do this; she had a funny feeling that there was something fated in her relationship with Timmy, that she could afford to wait. And it was accordingly a shock one night, coming home from dinner, to find him in the hall

149

taking his leave of Sheridan. She had not really anticipated that she could miss him.

"But you're not going already!" she exclaimed before she knew it. "Just as I've arrived. It's *too* mean. Sheridan, you should have told me he was coming!"

"I didn't know you were friends," Dale said shortly, glancing from one to the other. Timmy, looking surprised but not unpleased, evidently didn't know it either.

"Oh, but we had the longest, most searching talk, didn't we?" she went on, taking refuge in her social manner. "Come on back and have a nightcap!"

"Look, Eileen, he's a working man," Dale said irritably. "He has to get up in the morning, not like the crowd you play with."

"I really should go," Timmy said doubtfully.

"Then come back to us," she said with a determined smile. "Come back to us soon."

She worried about this the following day. She was afraid she had seemed tinny and social, that he would have thought of her not as nervous, but as simply silly. For the first time since Maryland she felt the upsurging of her old need to apologize. She even went so far as to contemplate calling him up to tell him. But this turned out not to be necessary.

"I was sorry only to catch a glimpse of you the other night," he said in rather a rush, when he telephoned. "I was wondering if you'd like to have dinner with me. Tomorrow?" And before she could answer he added awkwardly: "I don't know how you say this, but Ann and I have separated. I guess I should have put that first."

"I heard," she said sympathetically. "Sheridan told me. I was so sorry. I hope it had nothing to do with what happened that night at the party."

"Oh, no. Well, not exactly."

"Maybe it can be worked out. In time. Don't you think?"

"Maybe." He sounded embarrassed. But what, under the circumstances, did she expect him to say? She could have bitten her nervous tongue off. "I mean, I don't know," he continued confusedly. "I rather doubt it. But what about tomorrow? I guess it's terribly short notice, and of course I don't really know you very well. But when you said the other night—"

"It is not short notice at all," she broke in firmly. "I'm free as air. Would you like to pick me up here or shall we meet somewhere?"

"I'll pick you up. At seven?"

Agreeing quickly, she hung up and sat by the telephone in a happy tense silence. Even the prospect of having to get out of her engagement with David to go to the opening of his brother's night club, which he, of course, had decorated, seemed less than terrifying.

"I'm wondering what your excuse will be," David said calmly in his shop when she told him that she could not go, his long, agile fingers wrapping a heavy piece of gold material. "You know how important tomorrow is to me. I'm hoping you will have made up a story worthy of both of us."

It would never have occurred to her not to tell David the truth. His powers of perception were too uncanny. But she did not deceive herself that he would be nice about it. Supreme as he considered the excuse of sex to justify himself for breaking in and out of engagements, she knew that he would not extend it to her. He depended on her, more than she on him; it was partial proof of his very need for that he hated the idea of their being rivals in the pursuit of his own sex. It was as if he knew that her victory was preordained, that it behooved him, in protection of his kind, to keep her behind the chaste walls of his cynically constructed shrine.

"I have a date with Timmy Colt."

He fixed his green eyes on her coldly. "Is that any reason for adopting his vulgar idioms?" he demanded. "I'm surprised at you, Eileen."

"All right," she said meekly. "I have an engagement."

"That's better." He nodded. "A subsequent engagement, I take it?"

"I'm afraid so."

"And this Timmy Colt. He is the lawyer with the wonderful wife who was sick on your mother's bed?"

"They've separated."

"Already?" David raised his eyebrows. "You're a fast worker, my dear."

"Oh, David, it's not that, you know, it's—"

"You fancy him?" She nodded. "I thought as much." He shrugged his shoulders with an air of weariness. "I could see it starting that night. You can't fool old David, you know."

"Do I try?"

"No. Not yet anyway. But you're a deep one. Well, run along and hold hands with your Timmy. I release you for tomorrow night. However, I question your taste."

"But you liked him yourself!" she protested. "You said so!"

David held up his hands with a pained expression. "It always amazes me how even the subtlest of your sex, and you are that, my dear, lack taste in matters of the heart. That was a very crude remark. However, you may bring him to the opening if you wish."

Eileen, however, did not wish it. When Timmy called for her the following evening, looking brushed and scrubbed and apprehensive, rather like a boy, in fact, she offered no demurrer to the expensive restaurant that he suggested. She had no wish to disconcert him even slightly with alternatives. He was a bit slow and careful with the ordering but she had determined not to be bright and helpful, with the attendant danger of seeming condescending. She ordered what he had ordered, with two slight changes to indicate that she was not simply following him (that, too, might have been condescension) and urged him to have a second cocktail while declining one for herself. And then at last she began to relax; however constrained he might be she had a whole evening to reassure him.

"You must have been going through a very difficult time," she told him. "I don't wish to pry, but I do want you to know I sympathize. With both you and your wife. As I think I told you, I've been through it myself."

"You're not prying," he assured her hastily. "I wanted to talk about it. I don't really seem to have anyone to talk about it with, except Mother. And she's no help because she's never really liked Ann. But I don't want to bore you."

"You won't. Everyone's interested in other people's marriages."

So he told her. He told her about Mr. Knox and the Emlen deal and about Ann's making him apologize to Sheridan. He told her about their old life and the one they had been leading more recently. He told her about Ann's bitterness and her decision to leave him. Eileen was at first fascinated, then appalled. She had never conceived of her cousin, George, or of her stepfather as they might have appeared to people like the Colts; not having been able to take her family quite seriously, she had never imagined their impact on dependents, employees. Now she found it shocking.

"I thought everyone knew that George was a horror," she said musingly. "It's taken for granted among all my friends. And to demand apologies! Fantastic!"

"But that's not the point," he continued, arguing more warmly as he proceeded. "I'm not worried about your cousin or whether or not he was justified. That's simply the way people like him are. I've made my peace with them. It's Ann who can't. She's so appallingly stubborn. She didn't like our old life, and she can't face the new."

"Isn't there some middle ground?" she asked dubiously.

"Well, you know how women are."

She looked at his large, grey indignant eyes and smiled. "Do I?"

"Oh, I don't mean women like you," he protested quickly. "That's what struck me about you immediately. You're different. You're more accepting. More philosophic."

"Not always to my advantage." She paused, reflecting how odd it seemed that two people could separate over the issues that he had presented. More uncomfortably, she wondered if he was not still in love with his wife. "I think that you and Ann are going to work this out," she made herself say. "With time."

"I don't know," he said moodily. "I don't know if I want it any more. You see, Eileen—" He paused and then laughed. It was the same shy laugh that she had noticed at the party, the one that stripped his face of almost too many years. "I want to learn about things, now I've started. All the things I've been too busy to care about. Concerts. Theatres. Art galleries. Attractive people." He laughed again. "I guess that sounds awfully hick."

She smiled. "Rather pleasantly hick."

"And here's the thing," he continued eagerly. "I thought maybe you'd help me." He looked down suddenly at the table, really embarrassed now. "You were kind enough to say you were sorry to have missed me the other night at your mother's. Or maybe that was just a bit of polish. Good manners."

"Oh, no. I meant it."

"Then maybe we could go to a couple of concerts together?" he asked, his face brightening. "Or plays? Maybe you'd take me in hand for a bit?"

"I think it's a charming idea," she said, laughing quickly as if to spill some of the emotion out of her head. She felt quite giddy. "Except that I need your tutoring quite as much as you do mine. It's a fifty-fifty proposition."

"What could I teach you?"

"Oh, so much!" she exclaimed earnestly. "You've taught me so much already. About my own family!" She paused as the waiter put down the bill. "Shall we go?" she asked, but seeing his face fall, added: "We might have a drink at the family's."

In the front hall they met her stepfather standing in the doorway to his study in a red evening jacket, a pipe between his teeth, and she had the odd sense of being a girl again, coming home late to a father who had waited up. Except, of course, that Sheridan had never waited up.

"Good evening, Sheridan!" Timmy said, a bit boisterously. "We've been out on the town!"

"Don't see how you do it," Dale answered with a grunt. "After a full day at the office, too. Of course, you're not exactly my age."

"Has Mummy gone to bed?" Eileen asked, trying still to retain her moment of nostalgia.

"Like all sensible people. Where I'm going." He nodded good night and ambled on down the corridor to his bedroom, implying with a shrug of his shoulders a most matter-of-fact curiosity, an attitude of: I don't know what the hell you two are up to, but you're on your own, and don't blame *me*. Timmy followed her into the great living room that seemed so strangely smaller as it showed its unwonted emptiness to the sudden light that she switched on. The Italian chairs, huddled in groups, were gauntly awake. She went over to open the black carved cabinet that was a bar and was placing ice in the glasses when he put his hand on her bare shoulders.

"Eileen," he murmured and kissed her on the cheek. When she made no movement to resist, he turned her around and kissed her on the lips. There was a stifled, smothered quality in his passion, a violence in his need that had to do too little with her and too much with his loneliness. Yet it might have been just this that so nearly overwhelmed her. She saw the black again after the candlelight years and with a sudden gasp pulled herself away from him.

"You're a nice boy, Timmy," she said in a flat voice. "You shouldn't go around kissing people."

"I don't," he retorted. "Since I married."

She finished mixing the drinks and put one in his hand. "Is that true?"

"I swear it."

"You don't have to swear to me," she said, going over to the sofa. "I'm not entitled to it. But you knew you were going to kiss me tonight, didn't you?"

"Didn't you?" He came over and sat opposite her.

154

"I could see you thinking about it all during dinner," she continued. "How you would do it. When you would do it. Obviously it was to be the symbol of something. Of your break with Ann, I suppose. Your new life."

"You're very analytical."

"Am I very wrong?"

"No, I don't suppose so." He thought for a moment. "But analyzing things doesn't make them less real."

"It doesn't make you any less real," she agreed, a bit dryly. "To me, anyway. That's what you haven't considered. What you might be doing to me. You've been full of yourself tonight, Timmy."

"I'm sorry," he said, taking a sip of his drink as he watched her. "It's your fault, really. For listening so well."

"Which makes me a kind of accessory, doesn't it?" she mused. "After the fact, or whatever you call it. I'm to help you prove something about yourself."

"Don't grudge me that, Eileen."

"Shouldn't I?" She became passive. "It isn't considered sportsmanlike, you know, to catch someone on quite such an obvious rebound. I should throw you back in the water. But I wonder if I can. I wonder who's caught whom."

"Don't underestimate yourself."

"I don't." She was more positive now. "I quite see my own rather conventional role in your picture. I don't exist, really. Just a sympathetic ear."

"Much more," he insisted. "You couldn't be just that."

"But if I'm anything more, I'm a homebreaker!" she cried.

"Of a broken home?"

"Oh, it's not broken," she said bitterly. "It's scratched, that's all."

He looked gloomily into his glass. "I'm not sure of that."

"And where does *that* leave me?" she continued. "What can I do now?"

"Go back to where we were at the restaurant," he said, looking up eagerly. "Back to the idea of your educating me. I'll be good. I promise."

Looking at his anxious eyes she wondered if he might not mean it. Around her, in the dark corners of the great room, she seemed to hear David's mocking laugh at the disappointment in her heart. But if he really meant it, she said defiantly, half to herself and half to David's shadow, was there any reason for not doing as he asked?

"Well, it's a large and lonely city," she said at last with a shrug, directed half angrily at her own skepticism. "I don't really see why two people who want to be can't be friends. As a matter of fact," she said, putting down her glass, "I don't really see why we don't start right now. Let's get our coats. It's not even midnight. I'm taking you to a night club opening. Don't worry," she added with just a suggestion of sarcasm, "it'll be part of the education. All the best people. Even Sheridan would approve!"

7

TIMMY was good to his word, and Eileen to hers. They were soon meeting twice, even three times a week, and on nights when she was otherwise engaged, she managed to make him feel that what she was doing was something terribly stupid. It was hard for him to tell if she meant this, for her manners were so uncannily good, but if manners were that good, he began to wonder, how much did sincerity matter? He had never known anyone remotely like her. She seemed, at first blush, to stand for everything in the world that he lacked and hence distrusted: ease, poise, cultivation; he didn't see, basically, that they had a single thing in common, yet it was impossible not to yield to those clear blue eyes when they appealed to him, whether the issue was a piece of modern sculpture or a salad dressing, as if his judgment must, of course, be superior to her own for the simple reason that he was a man. Lying awake at night in a truculent mood, he could even sneer at her cult of the external, call her mannered, meretricious, but when he saw her the following evening, smiling with such a seemingly unaffected pleasure as she spotted him in the lobby, the restaurant, wherever it was that they met, he faced anew the depth of his problem. For whatever Eileen was, she was *not* meretricious.

His own life at this period would have been quite impossible without her. The loneliness of an office without Knox and a hotel room without his family would have driven him back to Ann on any terms. As it was, he had a sense of unreality, of time suspended, of a void slowly and hypnotically filled with the perfume of Eileen. He had never imagined that a person like himself could possess anything as lovely as her, and the fact that he still did not, however frustrating, did not strike him as basically unreasonable. It even intensified his sense of playing a romantic part against a handsome backdrop that smelled only gently of paint, a sense, too, that was compatible with the postponement of other decisions. If Eileen seemed to ask for nothing but the opportunity to be agreeable to him, would it not have been churlish to refuse?

Her tact was such that he did not mind her educating him, even though he had asked her to. Her attitude seemed to be that if he had so much of the "real" world, a measureless superiority in things "downtown" that truly counted, he should not begrudge her the opportunity of a few small hints in the science of beautiful things. For beauty, he saw, was everything to Eileen, beauty in her surroundings, in painting and music, beauty in the wearing of a scarf, a jewel, beauty even in the arrangement of a cocktail party. Sometimes it occurred to him that she might be confusing beauty with elegance, that she was preferring the atmosphere of beautiful things to the things themselves, but it was never as simple as that. He always came back to this, that Eileen was not simple. When he watched her at one of the Fifty-seventh Street galleries which they visited on Saturday afternoons, her face so intently still as her eyes seemed to be establishing an almost personal relation with an abstract painting, he had to concede that it was more than the faddism which he had suspected to underlie the world of modern art. And once, looking himself at a strange crisscross of blue and grey lines called "Seaport," he had a sudden sense of the East River gleaming under its dark, dirty bridges. It was literally the first reaction of his life to a painting; he even wanted to buy it until she intervened.

"But why not?" he protested. "You're always saying the first test is to like something. To relax and like it. All right, I have relaxed, and I *do* like it."

"I never said to buy everything you like."

"So there!" he exclaimed. "It *is* snobbery, after all! We can like what we like, but we buy what others do. Is that it?"

"Not at all," she said, smiling at his indignation. "But you have no idea how fast your taste will change now. Wait for two weeks and then buy it if you still like it."

"But it may be gone!"

She glanced at the little canvas with an appraising eye. "I wonder."

And, of course, she had been right. Two weeks later the picture was still there and his enthusiasm was gone.

She began to take him to the houses of her friends. It took him a little time to grasp that she moved in more than one world, that her friends were literary, even political, as well as what he rather slightingly called "social." He had assumed that Eileen led the buzzing existence of a gilded insect at the top only of their vast cage; it had been rather humiliating to have to concede that her life was broader than his own. She had a remarkable tolerance of people which extended even to their prejudices, however narrow and whether to the right or left. The only thing in the world that she could not stand, she told him once, was cruelty, and cruelty she judged by the amount of pain that it caused, never by the alleged motive for which it was inflicted. But if her friends were varied they had in common an aptitude for accepting him easily which he suspected might be more a tribute to Eileen than to himself.

"That painter friend of yours, Max whatever-his-name-is, is certainly frank," he told her one night on their way home from a studio party. "He congratulated me on our affair." He glanced over to see her change of expression.

"Oh, I suppose so," she said quickly, caught, as she rarely was, by embarrassment. "He would, of course. Heaven only knows how many affairs he's attributed to me since my divorce."

"But that's just the point. He hasn't. He thinks I'm your first."

She gave him a brief, startled look and then shrugged again. "Oh, well, who cares?"

"Don't you?"

"Not in the least. Why should I?"

"Well, that's a new one," he confessed. "Most people don't mind the idea as much as the talk. You're just the opposite."

"I have no objection to—well, to those things as such." The subject was obviously distasteful to her. "But you and I, of course, have a special deal."

"Because of Ann?"

"I don't say only because of Ann," she said with a shadow of a smile. "You're very self-confident, my friend.

158

But we needn't go into it. Ann alone is a good and sufficient reason."

"Because you won't be the cause for my not going back?"

"Timmy, we've been through all this."

"I know," he said impatiently. "But do you think having an affair is the only way to keep a man from his wife?"

She became very grave. "No, I don't suppose it is," she murmured.

"There are millions of ways," he said with sudden roughness, "and you know them all. But what I'm trying to get you to realize is that they have no application here. You and Ann are two entirely different parts of me. Whatever happens between me and Ann will not be your doing. That I promise you."

"I've heard that," she said almost wistfully. "That men have watertight compartments in their hearts. It's inconceivable to me, but that doesn't mean it isn't so." She paused, looking down at the evening bag in her lap. "I think I'd like to believe it."

"Ask your friend David."

"Oh, David," she said with a shrug. "What does he know about the heart?"

When David Fairchild went out to dinner with them, as he occasionally did, he never seemed in the least aware that his presence might be anything but a pleasure to them. Timmy at first was disturbed, disapproving. He did not know quite what to make of this paradoxical and opinionated young man. But he was afraid of seeming provincial in Eileen's eyes by being put out of countenance by a homosexual, and this, combined with David's unflagging good spirits and his seeming determination to make Timmy like him, produced in the end something like a friendship. Timmy had to admit that it was flattering for a downtown lawyer to be cultivated, even if Eileen was the motive, by a man so esteemed in the world for his wit and taste. It was true that whenever he admired the wrong things or confessed his total ignorance of such a field as ballet, David would mock him as a philistine, but as he always included Eileen in the same category, it made Timmy feel unexpectedly closer to her. One night when they had dropped her at the Dales', David went up to Timmy's hotel room for a nightcap. He sat cross-legged on the bed and stared at Timmy in his intent way while the latter poured the drinks.

"Do you always leave Eileen home like that?" he demanded. "Don't you ever take her here?"

"Does it offend you?"

"Gracious no. But poor girl, it must be terribly frustrating for her."

Timmy laughed, surprised at his own ability to make light of it. "It's quite by her choice, I assure you."

"Is it? Then I must have been building false hopes. I was thinking that deep down you might be in my boat."

Timmy noted the glitter in his eyes as he handed him a drink. David was quite serious now. A month before he would have thrown him out for such an insinuation; now it was simply a part of his new world.

"Deep down I may be in anyone's boat, David," he said easily. "But as long as it's in the subconscious, it doesn't do you much good, does it? I guess we'll have to leave it there."

David threw back his head and laughed. "I like you, Tim," he said, apparently giving it up. "I've heard the way you are downtown. Hard and ruthless. A machine of efficiency. That's the way people ought to be. I can't stand slop."

"I do a job. That's all."

"Don't be modest. It bores me. I'd like to be a lawyer and tell people what to do. And it's the way into politics. I'd adore to be in politics."

"Maybe you will be."

"A decorator?" David sneered, looking about the room. "Fat chance. There'd have to be a revolution in sexual mores before *I* got the vote. But in the meantime," he continued with a shrug, "I suppose I can make myself useful. We must get you an apartment, and I'll fix it up. Don't worry. It will be entirely chaste and masculine."

"I can't afford it, David. I have a family to support."

But David raised a hand to quell opposition. "You can't go on in this rathole. That's for sure. My services will be free, and the material a bargain."

"But I can't just accept that, David, I—"

"I will only be doing it half for you, my dear Timmy," the other interrupted firmly. "The other half will be for Eileen. If you ever decide to put your relations with that poor child on a healthier basis, I want her to have an attractive place to go to. She cares so."

David was good to his word. In a week's time he had turned up a garden apartment in a rent-controlled building which was only twice as expensive as Timmy's hotel room. He and Eileen argued hotly about how to decorate it, without in the least consulting Timmy, but as she was able to save him money by loaning furniture from storage, her ideas generally prevailed, and David was forced to limit his plans to a black and gold screen and Empire brackets that Timmy regarded with the profoundest distrust. When he was settled, however, he had to concede the improvement over his former quarters and felt quite touched at all David had done. He was ashamed to admit to his helpful friends how expensive he had found the whole project.

"He's really a good guy," he told Eileen. "It's just that he's afraid to show it."

"Too afraid," she agreed. "That's why I worry about David. If you play at being mean too long, can you really believe you're not?"

He was learning to value her concern about whether or not people were mean. In fact, one of the most important parts of their relationship was the fact that she made him feel like a "nice" person again. It was hardly a feeling promoted by his weekly visits to Ann and the boys. For Ann, obviously wretched with their separation, would look at him with the same eyes of misty gloom that he attributed to the shade of Henry Knox. The boys, too, now fully aware of the situation between their parents, seemed to take their mother's side without ever having been asked to; they were less communicative with him and totally unconfiding. He assumed in his heart that he would ultimately go back to them; anything else was inconceivable even in the strangeness of his present mood, but ultimately was not now. Ann, after all, had been the one to ask for it, and there was a perverse satisfaction in making out his life as gayer than it was, in underlining, before her lengthening face, the fact that he was still not through with it. He even went to the extreme of mentioning Eileen to her as a person who was "fun to do things with."

"I remember her," Ann said in a flat voice. "She's very beautiful."

"She's a good deal more than beautiful," he said in an easy tone. "She's been able to hammer some modern art into my thick skull. And *that* takes something."

"I could have done that. But you never wanted to go to exhibitions."

"I guess I have more time now," he said uncomfortably.

"I see. I suppose you're in love with her."

"Oh, it's nothing like that." He did all he could to keep his tone light. "That husband of hers gave her a terrible time. Eileen's through with love."

"A sabbatical, no doubt," she retorted. "Which can be interrupted at any time. Oh, Timmy," she cried suddenly, "you don't *know* anything about people like that! You take them at face value!"

"I haven't got *your* social experience, in other words?"

"It's not that," she said, relapsing into flatness. "It's that they don't make up to *me*."

After this conversation he could not endure the prospect of an evening alone. Particularly as it had been followed by a day in the office again ringing with the shrill protests of the outraged chief file clerk over the Dale reorganization. He hurried uptown to find Eileen in the small French drawing room that her mother allotted to her, looking up from a book and murmuring:

"Why, you poor thing, you look exhausted. Let's not go out. Let's stay here and listen to records."

And sitting with a drink while she put on Monteverdi and Bach, he told of his frenetic day and she of her more quiet one, and he felt the peace of it, the temporary, almost euphoric peace, as if he was in the bosom of a loving family with Eileen's sympathy forever to be counted upon, as if Clarissa popping in and out, just conscious of his existence, and Dale, passing in the corridor with a cigar, an accepting nod, were the approving but tactful parents, sentimental, concerned, trying at once to keep out of the way and still to know what was going on. If it was only a fantasy world, it was a surprisingly robust one.

8

DAVID FAIRCHILD's "shop," as he called it, consisted of the lower two stories of a brownstone on East Sixty-third Street, just off Madison. The old stoop had been removed, and a freshly painted red door with a huge knocker peered out from under a blue and white striped awning with the woven legend "David S. Fairchild, III." In the back was a chaste white office with a black lacquer table where David went to be alone with his ideas. In the front was pandemonium. Coffee was served at all hours of the working day, and the ladies who came in periodically to perch on the edge of David's chair were known as the best-informed ladies in the city.

Anita Ferguson had pushed her way one morning into the privacy of David's back study. This was typical of Anita. Like her brother, George Emlen, she had no sense of when she wasn't wanted, of enough being enough. Her easily hurt, hostile, darting eyes seemed the only co-ordinating elements in her big, slope-shouldered, ungainly form.

"The curtains haven't come for the dining room," she began. "Neither has that blue rug. What's happened, David?"

"You know perfectly well what's happened," he said coolly. "I wasn't joking the other day. As a matter of fact, despite what people say, I never joke."

"But you know my credit is good!"

"I know you haven't paid a bill in six months. To me or anyone else."

"But I will. It's just that Hank needs all he can get for his business." Anita seemed honestly outraged. "Everyone knows they'll get paid eventually!"

"You mean when your mother dies?" he asked with a thin smile. "She'll bury you, Anita. It's common knowledge that Hank has lost every penny you've given him. Do you think I don't know that you're living on an allowance from your mother right now?"

"You think you know everything, don't you?" she sneered. "But you don't know that one of our trusts falls in when Lolita is thirty-five. Next month. Then I'll pay. Ask your friend Timmy!"

David shrugged. "I will. And I'll ask him at the same time what the chances are of Hank getting his hot little hands on it before your creditors."

Anita was peering at herself in a looking glass, screwing her lips up to check on her make-up. David surveyed her with scorn. She preferred, however condescendingly, the company of homosexuals where she could feel rejected because of their tastes rather than her own plainness, where she could pretend that she was more than a poor creature who had been married for money that was already spent.

"Aren't you taking a rather high stand?" she asked, taking out her lipstick and applying it to her lips. "I know you're cock of the walk and all that, but Mama still counts for something around New York." She turned to him suddenly. "Or didn't you know?"

"I think I can count on your mother in any showdown between us, Anita," he retorted. "Children begin to lose some of their appeal when they get cross and middle-aged."

"I wonder how much *you* can count on Mama," Anita suggested, thoroughly angry now. "When she finds that you've been promoting an affair between her niece and her ducky boy lawyer!"

"She knows all about that. Obviously we couldn't wait until she heard *your* version. And what's more, she thoroughly approves. You're jealous of Eileen, Anita. You always have been. Because she's sweet and good-tempered and everyone loves her."

"I wonder if I'm the one who's really jealous of Eileen," she said venomously. "Jealous of what she's got, that is. Wasn't he rather *your* friend, her precious Timmy?"

"Really, Anita, you're too cheap to be borne," he said disgustedly. "Clear out, will you? I'm busy."

Anita left with a high, sneering laugh, and he sat quickly down at his desk, determined not to have his day ruined. He had won, hadn't he? She would never get those curtains now. Unless, of course, she paid. He closed his eyes and tried to visualize the foyer of the hotel in Cleveland that he was doing; it rose suddenly in bold colors with a fresco that he hadn't fully seen before. Quickly he made notes. It was at such moments between telephone calls and fantasies, with closed eyes, that his best ideas came. And relaxing, his thoughts shifted to Timmy and Eileen and his own obsession with their love. The door opened, and one of his girls came in.

"A Mrs. Colt to see you, David."

"*Mrs.* Colt?"

He went to the door and saw Ann. She was standing alone, gazing with a troubled air at the group of coffee drinkers in the corner. "Have you changed your mind?" he asked, stepping up to her. "Have you decided on a David Fairchild room?"

She started. "Oh, Mr. Fairchild, could I see you alone? Please."

He gazed at her quizzically, shrugged and led her back to his office.

"I want you to tell me about Timmy and Mrs. Shallcross," she began as soon as he had closed the door.

164

"Why *me?*"

"Because I know you see them all the time. And because I liked you when I met you at Mrs. Dale's," she said anxiously. "I thought you were sympathetic. And nice."

Half touched, exasperated, he looked away from her worried stare. "I'm *not* nice," he said firmly. "It's perfectly outrageous how the most respectable people today go about insisting that one is nice." But no, David, he had to tell himself; it was bad Oscar Wilde.

"And besides, you're the only person I know who can tell me."

"What is it precisely that you wish to know?"

"Well is he—is he seeing a good deal of her?"

"You mean are they having an affair?"

She looked down dejectedly. "I don't know. I don't speak that language. All right," she continued with an air of almost childish resolution, looking up at him. *"Are* they?"

The limpid misery in her eyes held him uncomfortably. "I assume so," he said impatiently. "Isn't it rather a waste of time otherwise?"

"I see," she said in a low voice. "You'd be on her side, of course."

"But it's not a question of sides," he retorted, thoroughly, unreasonably angry. "It's a question of sex. Honestly, you married women are the limit! You catch a handsome boy young and want to keep him in a box for the rest of his life. You have the home, the children, the respectability, the social approval, even the money, but no, it's not enough. You must have undeviating fidelity as well. You think your world is coming to an end because Timmy sleeps with Eileen. You don't know what trouble is!"

"But it's not only me!" she exclaimed, as worked up now as he. "It's Timmy's whole life I'm worried about. You remember how we discussed it at the Dales'?"

Remember! My God, he thought, the egotism that lay behind humility! How could *he* remember? "I'm afraid not."

"I told you how he was beginning to care about all the wrong things," she continued breathlessly. "Appearances and who was what and so forth. And this Mrs. Shallcross. Will *she* help that?"

"Eileen is one of the finest people I've ever known," he retorted stuffily.

Ann's features were vivid with disbelief. "But the world she lives in. It's not good for him, is it?"

165

"My world?"

"Oh, but, Mr. Fairchild, you can handle it. You know all its tricks and turns. But my Timmy never will! He's so literal. So stubbornly consistent!"

"And what am I to do about that, pray?"

She faltered before his stare. "Couldn't you sort of—keep an eye on him?" she begged.

"Because I'm 'nice'?"

"Exactly!"

"Really," he burst out, "it's too much! You come into my shop on a hectic business morning and make me behave like a complete heel, telling you a lot of nonsense about Timmy and Eileen. And then, having calmly made me reveal my bad temper as well as my bad taste, you have the nerve to tell me I'm 'nice.' And the unkindness to believe it!"

"If I only knew someone was keeping an eye on him," she protested, "someone I could occasionally see, it would make such a difference!"

Looking at her in perplexity for a long moment, he finally gave up. "I tell you what I'll do, my dear. I'll give you a tip. An invaluable tip. A tip that *could* save your marriage."

"Oh, Mr. Fairchild!"

He raised a hand to keep her quiet, a teacher lecturing to a child, the other behind his back as though hiding the rewarding candy. "The trouble with you wives is that you feel *entitled* to your husbands. And the moment you feel entitled to a thing, you can't be bothered to fight for it. You howl instead for justice."

"But I don't feel entitled to Timmy," Ann protested. "On the contrary. I never felt good enough for him."

"Don't give me that," he warned her. "That mock humility. It's only a smoke screen to fool yourself. It doesn't fool anyone else. Right this minute you're throbbing with the outrage of Timmy's unfaithfulness. Not the pain of it, mind you. The *outrage!*"

"All right," she murmured, faltering before his hard stare. "What should I do?"

"Be nice to him!" he exclaimed. "Just as nice as you can be. It's as simple as that. Oh, don't be whimperingly nice. Don't be slobbily, self-pityingly nice. Don't affect sad airs and say: 'Go your way. I only want your happiness.' Be a sport. Pull yourself together and be what you naturally are. The healthy, hearty type."

"But how can I compete with *her?*"

166

"Oh, she's not so hard. Don't worry. Men always wind up resenting Eileen. I wouldn't be surprised if Timmy hasn't started to already."

"But *why?*"

"Because she's a goddess!" he exclaimed. "And mortals don't really like goddesses. With reason, too. Read your mythology. They always play it rough. Turning us into tree trunks and things."

"A goddess," she said slowly. "You really *are* on her side, aren't you?"

"In my devious way, perhaps. But you can trust me. You see, I want to turn *her* into a tree trunk. A pretty Dresden tree trunk."

"So you can have her for yourself?"

"All right. If you *will* have your sentiment. So I can have her for myself."

"Thank you, Mr. Fairchild," she said, picking up her purse. "I think you've really tried to help me. And I'm going to try the impossible. I'm going to take your advice."

David thought about this odd visit all that day. He thought about it through the afternoon and evening, and even that night, when he lay in bed, on the coverlet of squirrel furs that he had not bothered to remove, he thought of Ann's brooding eyes and that foolish brown hat with the absurd feather. What business, really, did such a creature have to come barging into his life with her luminous reproach, making him feel the very throb of her wounds? Was she a woman hurt as he had wanted women to be hurt and did he take the guilt of his wishes on himself? Was that what a psychiatrist would say? Or was he really, in some wild, perverted fashion, falling in love with her? And then he sat up abruptly at the sudden picture that flooded his mind of Eileen, with her alabaster skin, lying inertly in Timmy's arms, neither in the least aware of him, obliterating him in their act. Him maybe, he thought, trembling with fury, but not Ann! *She* would give them something to worry about, coached by himself! And feverishly he pictured Eileen's dumb misery and Ann's subservient gratefulness; he saw the latter coming into his shop to give him some humble, tasteless present, begging him to accept it as a token of her and her children's feeling. Oh, you great, brave creature, he cried aloud in his disgust, falling back on the bed, you gaudy peacock with the heart of gold!

9

TIMOTHY was gradually becoming used to his new life. It had a quality of unexpected serenity. As long as he continued to regard it, as Ann had authorized him to, as a recess in their marriage, a period of stock-taking, there was nothing that had to be done about it. If his marriage was eventually to be resumed, and he continued, however evasively, to take this for granted, it began to assume the aspect of a heavenly reward to a light believer, a solace, but only to be contemplated in moments of anxiety. The immediate prospect, now that he was less apt to work at night, of an evening planned by Eileen was more absorbing. Even his office life had improved. People were beginning to accept the reorganization. He had only been unpopular, in fact, for the contrast to his former self; once that was forgotten, which took only a few months, there was nothing really for people to dislike. The downtown world, a masculine world, was notoriously easy to please.

But best of all was the change in Ann. She had put away her expression of reproach and talked quite pleasantly now on his visits. The old nervousness, of course, was still there, underneath, and she did make him feel a bit like an elderly, formidable relative to whom she had been told to be polite, but it was better than the way she had been. The apartment, moreover, was astonishingly improved. The electric train had been removed, and the broken crystal on the mantelpiece clock changed. The books were all placed in order on the shelves, and the rug had been cleaned. It gave him a pang to see how light and worn it looked; he was shocked at the degree to which Eileen had heightened his perceptions.

"I've never seen the old place looking so well," he told Ann. "I guess I must have been the messy one."

"No, it was me all right," she replied with a rather determined cheerfulness. "But people *can* change. How's your place?"

"Oh, fine," he said evasively. "And speaking of apartments, I really don't want you and the boys to go on living down here. I can afford something better now. Something uptown. I think we ought to consider putting the boys in a private school, too, don't you?"

To his surprise, she seemed to accept this. "All right. But don't you want them to finish out the year where they are?"

"Oh, sure, I guess."

"Good." She nodded briskly. "That'll give me plenty of time to look into schools. Mrs. Knox will help me, I'm sure."

He felt obscurely deflated. "Well, that's dandy," he said after a pause. "I don't know why, but I thought we'd have a scene about it. I had an idea you'd cling to the old place."

"Oh, now it's only memories," she said quickly. "I don't have any real friends here except Sally Duane. And they're moving uptown. I think it's hard on you to have to pay for two apartments, but I'll have time. I should be able to get a bargain. And there are some courses I want to take at Columbia."

He looked down at the rug, making out the slight shadow where the old inkstain had been. "Then the present arrangement—I mean about you and me—is all right? For the time being anyway? I take it you don't want a divorce? Or a legal separation?"

"Oh, no!" Glancing up, he saw that she had paled. "Why would I?"

"Well, about money, and things like that."

"Oh, but I know you'll always take care of me and the boys," she protested, and then hesitated. "But maybe *you* want a divorce?"

He looked at her sharply. "Why do you say that? Because of Eileen?"

She nodded, avoiding his eyes. "There's no reason you shouldn't see her."

"You don't mind?"

"Of course I mind." She looked back at him more boldly now. "But I have no right to mind, that's the point. That's what happens to wives who are foolish enough to leave their husbands."

"Oh? You admit it was foolish?"

"I admit it was idiotic."

"And now you want me back?"

"Of course I want you back." It was his turn to avoid her

169

frank, searching stare. "There's never been anyone but you for me and never will be. I'm one of *those* girls. The sticky type. I just lost my head when I said we'd separate. That's all. But nonetheless I lost it. That's what *I* have to face. Along with the possibility that you may never think it worth your while to come back."

He got up abruptly and started pacing the room. "Ann, you've got to give me time. You've *got* to give me time!"

"I don't have to give it to you. It's yours already. To do with as you please."

"I may not need much. I may only need a few weeks, months. I don't know. But I can't come back yet." He stopped pacing and turned on her almost passionately. "I can't come back yet!" he exclaimed in a louder voice. "Can you see that?"

There was a long pause. "Yes, Timmy," she said calmly. "I can see it."

"You're an extraordinary girl," he said, again deflated. "The most extraordinary girl I've ever known."

"Perhaps not quite," she answered with a small smile, and he changed the subject abruptly. When he left her, after half an hour of constrained talk about the boys, his only thought was that he didn't want to think. That he couldn't afford to. He decided in the taxi to go straight to a party that Eileen was giving. He wasn't dressed, but they would have finished dinner, and, anyway, he was wearing a dark suit. Hell, he didn't care. He felt suddenly the need to defy Eileen.

It was not at all, he could tell immediately, as he entered the big living room, with the exception of David, a Dale evening. Eileen was careful, unless it was going to be a perfect blend, not to mix her groups. Too careful, he reflected a bit sourly as he looked around. Tonight there was none of the brittle chatter of the fashion magazine world; in fact, there was no chatter at all. There was a respectful half-circle around Sheldon Pratt, a smooth, long, already greying gentleman not more than ten years older than himself, who had already been an assistant secretary of state and was now a partner in a law firm similar in size to Sheffield, Dale but of a more conservative tone, a firm, for example, where Dale himself would have been unthinkable. Pratt was politely if somewhat pedagogically answering questions as to the state of the world. It was a habit of Eileen's, picked up from political hostesses, to feature one guest, and she could be very firm about it. She had just smiled to him when he came in;

now she was gazing at Mr. Pratt, one elbow on her knee, her chin resting lightly on fingers.

"You mean, Sheldon," she asked, "if the government woke up tomorrow and found that Red China somehow *had* been recognized, that it was a *fait accompli,* in other words, deep down they might be just a bit relieved?"

"Oh, I think quite a bit, not just a bit," Pratt answered easily, looking around the room. "I won't be quoted, will I? The Republicans would have my scalp. All I mean is, the problem would be solved."

Timmy began to be irritated. It had never been his habit to think very deeply on international subjects; his preoccupation with immediate legal problems had interfered. When he did, however, he was inclined to be isolationist, a right-of-center Republican, not a McCarthyite. He knew what this group was, Eileen's favorite, a handful of highly tailored, highly mannered, highly serious but surprisingly young and good-looking women married to older, abler husbands of inherited means and Democratic persuasions. He was uneasy with them because they were so distinctly nice. They gave him the benefit of too many doubts. It was taken for granted that any friend of Eileen's would believe in all the "right" things, a strong military, high taxes and federal aid to almost everything. He glanced around at Dale, but the latter was impassive. Obviously, it was Eileen's party, and there was to be no interference. Timmy got up and walked, not on tiptoe, into the dining room to pour himself a drink.

"That was all I needed, an example," he heard David's voice behind him. "Why didn't *I* walk out?" David poured a great deal of whiskey into a large glass. "When will that little group learn that liberalism is *vieux jeu?* They're so drearily nineteen-thirty."

"And Eileen swallows it all," Timmy agreed. "That's what gets me. She wears a liberal opinion as if it was a new hat."

"So you've found that out? Already?"

Timmy glanced at him suspiciously. "Found out what?"

"That to Eileen appearance is everything. Taste is God. That hers is the profoundest kind of superficiality. She must dress well, walk well, eat well, think well, pray well. Not to the eyes of others, but to her own. It makes for a wearing life. Because she's an exacting judge."

"I suppose it's all a substitute for something," Timmy said uneasily.

"Don't be too sure! You think she'd give it all up for you?

Not on your life, man. If you were starving, she wouldn't let you make a thirteenth at table."

"Unless I was an assistant secretary of state," Timmy retorted bitterly and went back into the living room. He saw Eileen turn her head to gaze at him quizzically for a moment. Then she looked again at Mr. Pratt. He felt a flicker of pride beneath his irritation that he was enough a part of her to make her sense his moods. "I wonder if I might ask you something, Mr. Pratt," he said suddenly and felt the eyes of the half-circle turn on him.

"By all means."

"Well, I may be wrong, but I seem to detect a feeling in the room that we all have to be led by the nose by a few enlightened internationalists. As if we were children being persuaded to get our feet wet. Now isn't it possible, just possible, mind you, that the majority could sometimes be right? This Red China issue, for example. Why should we recognize a bunch of bandits?"

Mr. Pratt became painfully polite. "Well, it seems to me, Mr. Colt, you've really asked several questions in one. In the first place, let me say I quite agree about the bunch of bandits—"

And they were off, on a long and rather tangled discussion of relations with China, with others intermittently joining, the general temper growing gradually warm. Timmy knew that his question had been aggressively phrased, that he had no real point to make, only a prejudice and that by sticking argumentatively to it instead of really listening to Mr. Pratt, he was making a dismal impression on the room. Eileen for all her self-possession was manifestly uncomfortable; she even tried to come to his rescue a couple of times with such remarks as: "I think what Timmy really means is—" or, "I wonder if we're not really all agreed that—" But he wouldn't be helped. Stubborn, recalcitrant, he even managed to deepen the isolationism of his point of view before the evening was over. And when the Pratts finally rose to go, followed in quick succession by the rest of the party, he stayed on, sitting morosely with a drink before the yawning Dales and a rather ominously silent Eileen.

"You're quite an arguer, aren't you, Timmy?" Clarissa asked. "I don't think I've ever heard you say half as much as you said tonight."

He almost laughed at the realization that Mrs. Dale, of course, was the only person in the room that night who might have meant this as a compliment.

172

"Rather too much, if you ask me," Dale said dryly. "Not that I didn't agree with you, Tim. I did. I can't abide these pinko rich boys who dabble in appointive politics because they know they couldn't get elected dogcatcher. But you let him put it all over you tonight."

"Oh, Sheridan," Eileen protested warmly, "you can't call Sheldon Pratt a pinko!"

"I can't?" Dale said, rising and winking at Timmy. "In my own house? I'd like to know why not. But anyway it's too late to argue. I'm going to bed. Will you turn out the lights, Eileen, if you're going to sit up?"

"I think I'll go, too, Sheridan. I'm tired."

"No!" Timmy said suddenly. "You're coming out for a drink with me, Eileen."

All three stared at him.

"Well, thank you, Timmy," she said uncertainly. "But I'm tired."

He suddenly had the feeling that his mood of rather childish pique had given him a new stature. The big room with its filled ashtrays and empty glasses had ceased to be formidable. Dale himself, yawning, was just another stout, tired lawyer and his wife, haggard under the eyes, under the foolish gloss of her golden hair, another weary hostess.

"All right," Eileen said quickly. "I'll get my coat."

In the elevator she said nothing, only shaking her head when he started to speak, with the briefest glance at the elevator man's back. Evidently she distrusted his mood. He wondered resentfully if there could be any grosser violation of her code than a betrayal of emotion to a subordinate. He, at least, he thanked Providence, had not been brought up that way. Not to discuss religion at table because one's maids were Catholic or money in the car unless the partition window was up. In his world anyone could hear anything. Why not?

"One drink," she said as they came out of the building. "One drink and home. There's that bar on Lexington."

He stopped a taxi and opened the door, placing a hand firmly under her elbow. "We're not going to any crummy bar. We're going to my place."

"Aren't we masterful tonight?" she murmured, and got in.

"I've been led around by the nose long enough," he said as they drove off. "The ring's beginning to hurt."

"Who put it there? Who came asking for lessons?"

"When I go to school, I still expect vacations."

173

"Why? If attendance is voluntary?"

"Anyway, I think your friend Pratt's an ass."

"Timmy!"

He laughed aloud as she pointed, frowning, to the driver's back, and they finished the trip in silence. In his apartment he went straight to the bar table while she seated herself on the small sofa, rather primly, he thought, spreading her red pleated skirt uninvitingly on either side.

"You were ashamed of me tonight, weren't you?" he demanded, turning to give her a glass.

She looked at him calmly as she took it from him. "I'm never ashamed of you, Timmy. I thought you were persistent, that's all."

"And it's vulgar to be persistent, isn't it? Common?"

"They're your labels. Not mine."

"Of course they're yours," he retorted angrily. "You may be too well bred to mention them, but you're thinking them! It's in your whole demeanor. All you care about, Eileen, is what things *look* like!"

"I know that theory," she said. "I've heard it all my life. Maybe some day I'll be convinced of it."

"If you admitted it, you might be able to correct it."

"Do you want me to change, Timmy?" she asked in a graver tone. "How would you like me to change?"

He sat leaning forward, his hands clasped between his knees, once more deflated. "Only to be less perfect," he said mildly. "Maybe I'd feel you were more accessible then."

"It seems to me I've been fairly accessible. Let me tell *you* something now. Don't believe everything David says. He's very clever, but fundamentally he's always wrong. He doesn't really see people. He sees his bright little images of them. The images seem more exciting, but only temporarily. In the long run it's the people themselves who count."

He looked up at her. "How do you know what he says about you?"

"I can imagine. Because he's selfish. A dog in the manger. He wants me all to himself."

"But he's not interested, is he?" he asked staring. "I mean, *that* way?"

"That's just the reason."

He felt his heart beating faster as he watched her, so white, so extraordinarily still. "There's one thing he's not wrong about," he blurted out. "And that is we're kidding ourselves."

She looked up intently. "How?"

"About our being just friends."

"I'm not kidding myself," she said, glancing down again, "I haven't from the beginning."

"Then why do you keep me off?"

"Oh, you know, Timmy. You *know!*" She suddenly closed her eyes and raised her hands to her cheeks. "You may think I'm all glass and hard, but some things take effort. *That* took effort!"

He stood up suddenly, his throat very dry. "I've told you about Ann," he said roughly. "She has nothing to do with us."

Her eyes, open again, pleaded with him. "But that's false, Timmy. It's false!"

"Look." He took a step nearer her. "I promised myself that if you came up here tonight—well, that we'd cease to be just friends."

There was a silence, and then she seemed suddenly to collapse. "Don't you think I knew that?"

In a moment he was beside her on the sofa, his arms around her, his lips hard on hers. And she who had been so still, so seemingly passive, came suddenly to life; her fingers were in his hair, her body pressed against his. There was an urgency to her that took him by surprise; it was as if to hide her from herself that he reached finally behind her to switch off the light. And he discovered in the hour that followed, bewildered in the very violence of his gratification, that Eileen's need for beauty was not confined to what she saw and heard. She was an artist in the act of giving herself.

10

DALE DREW little squares on his office pad while he listened to George Emlen. They represented houses on a city street in his mind; with a more sweeping motion of his pencil he now surrounded them with walls and more walls and then a moat. Then he started on another city.

"Anita and Lolly want the readily marketable securities," George was saying. He had been talking for several minutes about the distribution of one of the Emlen trusts, speaking in the rapid, rather excited tone that he used for such discussions. "It's only natural. They want to sell them and give their husbands the money. Crazy, I grant you, but that's their funeral. They don't want the Fibre stock. It might take months, even years to get its true value in cash. So that's my proposition. *I* take the Fibre stock as my third, and they get the rest."

"Have you had the stock appraised?"

"When Father died. It's about sixty. But calling it sixty and getting sixty for it are two very different things."

"What do Anita and Lolly say to this?"

"Oh, they're all for it."

"No doubt." Dale finished the moat on the last town. "Women have a liking for ready cash. Very few of them know how to wait. For the larger rewards."

"Of course, I'd be taking my chances, too," George pointed out. "I can't be sure Holcombe will want the Fibre stock. Obviously it's not the kind of thing they can put in writing. But I'm pretty sure they'll come in with me in the dextron process—"

"I'm not interested," Dale interrupted roughly. "I'm not in the least interested in your relations with Holcombe Textiles. Can't you get that through your head, George? You and Lolly and Anita are free, white and substantially over twenty-one. If you want to divide this trust among yourselves in some particular way that is mutually agreeable, all you have to do is tell me. I'll see that it's done."

"Sure, I know." George did not seem in the least rebuffed by his tone. "I was only wondering about Timmy, that's all. I never did quite approve of your putting him in as trustee after that scene at my club. He's too volatile."

"Now, George, we've been over this a dozen times before. Timmy is *my* responsibility."

"All right. All right." George raised both hands to moderate his uncle's irritation. "So long as you know what you're doing, I'm perfectly satisfied. So long as everything works out. And, by the way, I might just mention in passing that at the last board meeting at Holcombe I brought up the question of your acting as general counsel. It was *very* favorably received. I think you could even shoot for a directorship."

"How you run on, George," Dale said dryly, shaking his head. "How you do run on."

He continued to the end of the interview to treat George as a rather irrepressible child, but when he walked out to the reception hall with him afterwards he guided him slowly by the elbow in avuncular fashion. As every passing stenographer knew, few clients were similarly honored.

Again in his office, Dale settled back in his chair with a cigar to contemplate the textile future. He was well satisfied with his interview with George. The only trouble had been in keeping him from saying too much. George had no delicacy; like so many businessmen he had to underscore things. He had done well, it was true, with his inherited money; his small ventures had made their mark in the textile world, but none knew better than his closely watching uncle how heavily his position depended on Holcombe Textiles. George had succeeded his late father to Holcombe's board, and the Emlen trusts had considerable Holcombe stock, but the company was far too big to be influenced in any such fashion as this. Now little George was going to have something that Holcombe wanted and wanted badly, and he would never have had it, either, if his uncle hadn't pushed it under his very nose. It was all most satisfactory. After years of doing the bulk of Holcombe's legal work while the main fees went to its sleepy and venerable general counsel in Boston, the situation would now be altered. Dale saw another puzzle solved, every piece in its place, the whole a shiny, seemingly indestructible solid. It was remarkable, he was even able to reflect, after the passage of so many years, with so many successes, how definite and heart filling the satisfaction still could be.

After some moments of closer thought he rang the buzzer for Miss Schulze and dictated a memorandum to Timmy.

I talked today with George Jr. about the Emlen No. 6 trust that falls in on Lolita's thirty-fifth birthday. As you know, he and his sisters take the principal in equal thirds. It is my understanding that the trust owns all the stock of Emlen Fibre, a family company that does a small but steady business in leasing textile patents. This stock, being closely held, is hard to value, but the Treasury accepted sixty for estate tax purposes in George's father's estate. George, being in the textile business himself and having some sentiment about family holdings, wants to keep the Fibre Company under his own control. The idea is that he will take all of its stock

177

as his third, and the girls will divide the cash and marketable securities. This may give them a bulge over him on market values, but he doesn't mind and will sign the necessary papers. The girls, of course, are delighted. I told him that you and his mother, as the trustees, would make the final decision, but that I was sure you would go along with the idea. Basically, as I see it, it's the property of the Emlen children to do with as they wish.

Timmy found this memorandum on his desk on a Friday evening as he was about to leave the office. When he called Dale he found that the latter had already left for Andover where his son, Eileen's half-brother and the only child of Dale's marriage to Clarissa, was playing in a football game. He studied the memorandum again thoughtfully. It troubled him. This particular trust was his first, and although it was not one of the big Emlen trusts, he had worked hard to justify the confidence reposed in so youthful a fiduciary. He had planned to make an even split in each holding, so that neither George nor his sisters could ever complain of unequal treatment. Now Dale was proposing that he do just the opposite. Even if he was covered, as he would be, by the family's releases, he still did not like it. Why did George want the Fibre Company? It was quite true that he was in the textile business, but it was certainly not true that he entertained any "sentiment" for family holdings. George had sentiment about nothing. After a restless hour alone, he called Larry and asked him to come in the following day for a piece of file research.

"I'm sorry," he told his rather grumpy junior. "It's probably a lot of nonsense, but I just don't feel right about the thing. I'll tell you about it in the morning."

That night he canceled his engagement with Eileen and went to a movie alone. He concentrated, however, very little on the screen; it served only as the backdrop that he had meant it to be for his analysis of Emlen facts. Taking as his basic premise that someone had to be unfairly benefited by the transfer of the Fibre stock, who was it? The girls? Clearly not. Their relations with their uncle were largely of a business nature; Timmy had heard Dale's complaints on the subject of their extravagance and bad temper. Surely, even if Dale was involved, he would not have lent himself to any plan that favored them. George, on the other hand, was close to his uncle; they had worked together with mutual sympathy on

178

many deals. George, if anyone, was obviously the person to be benefited, which could only mean that the Fibre stock was more of an asset than the girls, now so ready to give it up, possibly conceived. Yet how? He knew the company, as controlling trustee, backwards and forwards; it had not paid a dividend in two years and he had retained it only because a satisfactory price had not been available. Its benefit to George, if benefit there was, had to stem from some peculiarity in George's business position, some hidden need or opportunity. And what was his position? Well, of course, he was involved in many things, but the textile business was certainly the common denominator, and surely the biggest feather in George's cap was his directorship in Holcombe? Holcombe, Timmy mused. The Holcombe that was always remodeling and replanning, that everyone in the textile world admired for its philosophy of incessant modernization. The Holcombe that swallowed small, tired family companies. Did Holcombe want Emlen Fibre?

"It's a question of putting ourselves in George Emlen's shoes," he explained to Larry the following morning when they met in the file room. "This is really detective work. I think it's safe to assume that he knows or should know any information that we have in our files. The Fibre Company's in his family, and he's on the board of Holcombe."

All that day they worked on a systematic search through the files. It was dreary and unrewarding work, and Larry was obviously discouraged. He kept muttering under his breath about needles in haystacks. They thumbed through months of correspondence and glanced over contracts; they even scanned decrees in litigations and arbitration settlements. Timmy concentrated on Holcombe's last registration statement, a mine of information, comparing it carefully with the Fibre Company's inventory of patents, but without the least illumination. Towards evening he was beginning to think that he had been unjustly suspicious when Larry, who had been in another corner of the room checking the unfiled correspondence, came hurrying over to his desk waving a memorandum.

"Get a load of this!" he cried. "Holcombe's memo of new business!"

"Where did you find it?"

"I was going through the unfiled confidential. On the off chance."

Timmy scanned the brief memorandum. It dealt with a proposed increase in the production of a new kind of washa-

179

ble summer suit. Turning the last page he came to a list of patents to be acquired for the process, with penciled check marks by those whose acquisition was in negotiation. With the elation of one who sees to the end of his puzzle and disdains to fill in the final squares, he tossed it back to Larry.

"How many on that list are owned by Emlen Fibre?"

Larry cross-checked the list with the one on Timmy's desk. "Thirty-two, sixty-seven and seventy."

"Are they marked?"

"No."

"So there we are." He sat back wearily in his chair. "Georgie really *has* something, after all. Or will have. When the trustees have turned it over to him."

"I bet he really sticks Holcombe for those patents!"

"Oh, no." Timmy shook his head judiciously. "He's much too smart for that. If he was paid too well, the girls might find out and start screeching. He'll turn over the patents to Holcombe for a reasonable sum. And then you'll find that Holcombe will suddenly become a very good customer of George's mill in South Carolina. Oh, there are ways and means, Larry. The possibilities are limitless. What I'm wondering is, does Dale know?"

Larry stared at him, open-mouthed. "Are you kidding?"

"No. Why should he know? George wouldn't have to tell him."

"He wouldn't, but he would. They're two of a kind. I'm just wondering what Dale's cut is."

Timmy almost laughed at Larry's expression of worldly wisdom. His assistant varied between hero worship and cynicism, pirouetting between the enticing extremes of total loyalty and total contempt.

"Well, I'll see him on Monday. Perhaps we'll find out."

"Be sensible now, Tim. Don't expect him to come right out with it. Steal up on him."

Timmy made a little bow. "I shall be ruled by you in all things."

"You laugh at me," Larry said, hurt. "But you'll see."

Timmy found Dale in a rather beaming mood when he went to his office the following Monday. His son's team had won the game, and with a paternal pride that he rarely displayed, he showed Timmy a picture of "Junior," a squat, heavy boy with rather slanting eyes. Timmy had some difficulty introducing his subject.

"I've been thinking a good deal over the weekend about the Emlen trust," he managed to get in at last. "Frankly, I

180

don't like it. I'd rather make a distribution across the board, one third of each holding to each. Why should I ask Mrs. Emlen to take the risk that the Fibre stock is worth a third of the trust?"

"You don't have to ask her. I've told you what she wants." Dale's tone was a touch dry. He was always very careful not to treat Timmy like a dummy trustee, but the care was discernible. "It's the children's money; that's the way I look at it. Why not let them divvy up as they choose?"

"Why can't they divvy up later?" Timmy returned. "*After* I've made an even split?"

Dale puffed at his pipe for a moment in silence. Timmy knew that this was his method of controlling his temper. "Because that involves putting three good clients to a lot of unnecessary trouble," he said with a touch of asperity. "Which is not the way I like to do business. And, furthermore, it might get them into a serious gift tax problem. People in their bracket can't just go around swapping securities, you know."

"But supposing we had reason to believe that one of these good clients was putting something over on the others?"

Dale looked up immediately. His eyes were stern. "Which one?"

"George."

"Do we know this, or are we just supposing?"

"We know it."

"Explain yourself."

Timmy told him in as few words as possible about the memorandum of new business and the list of patents. Dale stared down at his blotter, carefully moving his silver paper cutter from one side of the desk to the other. His reaction, however, when Timmy had finished, was unexpected. He uttered a long, low whistle.

"Well, I'll be damned!" he exclaimed. "That George is a clever little bugger, isn't he? Cleverer than I thought."

Timmy stared down at him. "Of course, the deal's off now," he said brusquely. "As a trustee I'm on notice."

"Now let's just wait a second," Dale cautioned him in an easier tone, settling back in his chair. "Just a second. You go snooping about on your own, like a good little Sherlock Holmes, investigating a deal that fundamentally doesn't concern you. I say fundamentally, because even though you're a trustee, this is a matter between three adults who are willing to give you a complete release." Dale waved his hand grandly in the air to indicate the totality of Timmy's exoneration.

"But the release isn't enough for you. You want to dig deeper. And so, in your diggings, you stumble upon the fact that one of the three may—and I repeat, *may*—have a slightly better deal than the others. Because he's a bright boy and is willing to take a long gamble, while his sisters are shrieking for ready cash. I wonder if it's entirely fair, by anybody's standards, for the trustee to step in, like a solemn governess, and mess up his little game?"

"But if the trustee's on notice, Sheridan!" Timmy cried. "I'll do anything the family wants. *After* I've told the girls."

Dale dropped his speculative, almost storytelling tone. "Is it your opinion that this changes the book value of the Fibre stock?"

"To Holcombe it does. Vitally."

"I'm talking about book value," Dale retorted. "Has Holcombe made any offer for the patents?"

"Why should it? If it gets them for nothing?"

"But it hasn't. Let's stick to the facts. Has anyone else made an offer?"

"No."

"There's no secret about the patents, is there?" Dale's voice had risen to a command. "Can't anyone who's interested find out what Emlen Fibre has?"

"Yes. But their true value is only in connection with what Holcombe proposes!" Timmy became so excited that he almost forgot that Dale, of course, might know. "Don't you see, Sheridan? They'll never have to *pay* George for the patents. I mean, pay him more than book value. There'll be other ways of helping him."

"And that's so undesirable? You're against George?"

Timmy stared. "I guess Anita might think it undesirable!" he exclaimed. "And Lolita. If they find their brother's getting stock which they could sell to Holcombe for three times the value of what they're getting!"

"Wait a minute!" Dale held up his hand abruptly. His face seemed even rounder and darker; it had a more stonelike appearance than Timmy had ever seen. "How do you know that? How do you know that Holcombe would buy the patents from them? How do you know that Holcombe would buy them from *anyone?*"

"I don't. But it stands to reason, doesn't it, that Holcombe—"

"It does *not* stand to reason!" Dale exclaimed sharply. "I thought I had broken you of that habit of irrelevant speculation. Has it ever occurred to you, Timmy, that you have an

182

actual prejudice against clients? Against George anyway? How do you know that Anita and her sister haven't got inside information about some of the securities that *they're* getting? Something that'll make George look green when he hears about it?"

"I don't know, of course."

"Well, more power to them if they have, I say!" Dale continued triumphantly. "You haven't heard Anita complaining about the deal, have you?"

"Quite the reverse. But then she doesn't *know*."

"Doesn't *know!*" Dale mimicked him. "And *you* don't know. And I don't know. And nobody *knows* what Holcombe wants to do about the Fibre patents! And I say it's none of our damn business!"

"None of yours, maybe," Timmy said in a low, stubborn tone. "But you're not the trustee."

Dale sat back in his chair again with a look of weary patience and turned to the window. His lips were shaped as if he were about to whistle again, but no sound emerged. "That's true," he said, suddenly indifferent. "I'm not the trustee, am I?" He leaned forward and reached in a concluding manner for a letter on his blotter. "And the trustee, obviously, must make the decision."

Timmy stood uncertainly while Dale appeared to be absorbed in his correspondence. "That's all the advice you have to give me?"

"It's all the advice I can give you, Tim," Dale said in a detached tone, looking up. "I won't deny I'm troubled that you have to go chasing after gossamer moral issues every time you find yourself up against a simple, matter-of-fact problem. It makes me wonder about your future. It honestly does. *I* don't mind telling you that I had hoped to make you number two on the Holcombe account. With the idea that you'd eventually take over the client. I can't run everything around here, you know. But, frankly, Timmy, if you're not going to live in this world, if you're going to leap about from cloud to cloud—"

"Tell me, Sheridan," Tim interrupted in a muffled tone. "Do you think I shouldn't tell Anita about the patents? Do you say that?"

"I don't say anything, my dear boy," Dale returned blandly, ringing the buzzer for his secretary. "I don't say a blessed thing. As you point out, you're the trustee. You must do as you see fit."

183

"Yes," Timmy said heavily, turning to the door. "I must do as I see fit."

Back in his office Timmy sat perfectly still, staring at the closed door. The telephone rang, but he made no move to answer it. "This is it, Tim," a voice kept repeating over and over in his brain. "This is the world. *Your* world!" It was as if Dale's proposition was the challenge that he had known all along must be lurking, the dark hirsute thing behind the green leaves of his new prosperity. Rapidly, mechanically, he reviewed his expenses, that of his new apartment and of the one he was getting for Ann, the private schools for Walter and George, the whole business of amusing himself and Eileen. He thought of collecting pictures and of driving long, low, noisy foreign cars, of out-Daviding David. And yet in all his oddly perfunctory cataloguing what really held him so tensely still was a curious bleak awareness that he was gathering motives for something that he was going to do anyway, that he was seeking the concocted excuses of Ann's needs or of Eileen's imagined extravagance, of pictures and cars that he had never had, to explain the quixoticism of his deepening involvement with Dale. Oh, true, he had his pressures, plenty of them; he wanted money and promotion, but did he want them that much? In fact, now that he made himself think of it, did he really want them at all? Wasn't it rather that he was sitting alone in a darkened projection room, watching the unreeling of his own life, inextricably bound up in its logic? For it was because of this logic, because of this only consistency, that he oddly enough felt himself bound to sacrifice everything. He had made decisions, had he not, crossed Rubicons? Was it seemly now, even feasible, to turn his steed and go galloping back pell-mell before astonished spectators on the road he had so defiantly taken the day before?

The door opened, and Larry entered conspiratorially, closing it behind him. "Well, did he?"

Timmy stared. "Did he what?"

"Did he *know?*"

Timmy realized with a sudden shock what it was he was asking. He had quite forgot that Larry knew. "He didn't know a thing," he snapped. "We were barking up a wrong tree. Forget it."

Larry stood in front of him, smiling now. "Oh, I see," he said softly. "We're going to play it that way, are we? He didn't know a thing. Well, fine!"

"Haven't you any work to do, Larry?"

"Sure, sure." Larry was still smiling. "Don't get huffy. I can be smart. I know when the party line changes."

"Oh, go soak your head."

As Larry left, the telephone rang again, and this time he answered it. It was Eileen.

"I know you hate to be bothered, but it's about Mrs. Wardell's," she said apologetically. "Can you or can't you? I do have to know."

"Tonight?" He reflected irritably how she *cared* about such things. Her stepfather, at least, cared about Mrs. Wardell because she was the widow of New York's largest owner of railroad securities. But Eileen cared because she was old, because she was a remnant of a vanishing era, because her house was eighteenth century, because she was a collector's item. "All right, why not?" he said rather brusquely. "I'll pick you up for dinner first. At eight?" He would have time first, he reflected quickly, to call on Mrs. Emlen, and hanging up, he immediately dialed her number.

11

FLORENCE EMLEN waited at the desk in the library for the visit from her young co-trustee. She wanted him to surprise her at her work and was wearing over an expanse of floating grey hair her "think bonnet," a loose velvet hood that gave what she hoped was the effect of an eighteenth century lady at home to her friends of learning. There was a whiskey decanter on a silver tray if Mr. Colt cared for a drink, but no tea. Tea was not for working hours. Tea would never have gone with the paraphernalia of business set out so neatly on the broad surface of the desk: the seal, the sealing wax, the great steel stapler, the wheel for stamps, for scotch tape, the penholder, the clean, crisp yellow pad and the daily dozen of long, sharpened pencils. Only in an atmosphere of order and organization could she hope properly to orient her thoughts on the great affairs to which she had daily to give her attention.

Mr. Colt was really a great find. She had to concede that her brother-in-law had a way of finding people. The young man was serious, yet always lucid, and his manners were charming. Of course, there was that unfortunate story about what he had said to George at the club, but then—well, it was no secret to George's mother how provoking George could be. It was also true that she had thought him a bit young to be trustee of even one of the small trusts, but then she had to admit that he was learning as fast as Sherry had predicted. Of course, he did not have *her* experience. How could he? It had not been *his* fate to be left a widow and crushed with unsought responsibilities. And a widow, too, whose natural bent had been for the arts, who had asked nothing better out of life than the chance to paint flowers and poke around the galleries in Fifty-seventh Street and who instead—with what an agony of discipline!—had had to run a veritable little empire of stocks and bonds and mortgages, of bits and pieces of businesses, of demanding charities and huge demanding summer cottages, to preside, a brave little queen-mother, the inspiration of a handful of loyal servitors, over her and the children's domain. And she had known better, too, she reflected wryly, than to have expected thanks from those children. How dry and sharp they were; how like Emlens! Ah, to be dry, she thought, to lack imagination, not to feel things as she did, *that* was the way to get through the life. She did allow herself to hope, however, that George would not prove too dry to marry. She had not quite forsaken the naughty little vision of having her house to herself, free of that critical, economizing presence as oppressive as his late father's. Had he not bored her half to death with lectures when he discovered the tiny Renoir that dear David had *made* her get for the drawing room? And what on earth would he do when he found that she was planning a whole new house on Long Island, a "folie" as David so delightfully called it! But she didn't have to cross *that* bridge till she came to it. After all, as David always reminded her, whose money *was* it?

The door opened, and she saw with a little pleased flutter that it was Mr. Colt. Looking even paler and more serious in a blue suit that she hadn't seen him in before.

"Oh, Mr. Colt, how nice!" she exclaimed. Should she call him Timmy, she wondered. He was younger, after all, than her own children. "Thank heavens we're going to get rid of that old children's trust at last. Everytime one of them falls in, I feel that much weight off my shoulders. And it's been a heavy weight, Mr. Colt. For a heavy number of years, I don't mind telling you."

But for some reason Mr. Colt did not seem disposed to listen to her with his usual respectful attention that afternoon. He sat rather broodingly staring at the papers on the desk.

"Have you given any thought to the Fibre Company?"

"You mean the one George wants?" She was rather taken aback by his abruptness. "Certainly I have. I always give thought to my duties as a trustee."

"May I ask what you've decided?"

"Well, I suppose he should have it," she said a bit uncertainly. It was not in this clipped way that they usually did business. "He's badgered me enough about it, heaven knows. And, after all, he *is* the business man in the family."

"What about your daughters?"

"But you know what they're like, Mr. Colt! They simply sell anything that they can lay their hands on. For those husbands of theirs." She wondered if she should tell him frankly how low an opinion she had of Anita's husband. Both her daughters, she thought with a little quiver of distaste, were not only richer but bigger than their husbands, yet still afraid of them. "They're always looking to me for more money. 'Queen Lear,' I call myself!"

"What they'd do with the company is not really our concern, I suppose."

"Not our concern!"

"As trustees, I mean. We should only consider what they're entitled to."

"But a trustee isn't meant to be completely blind! Surely we're meant to use *some* common sense?"

"That's rather a moot point, isn't it?"

"Do you mean to sit there and tell me, Mr. Colt," she demanded indignantly, "that in dividing up property in my husband's trust—*his* property, mind you, of which he made *me* trustee—I am not to consider what is in the best interests of each child?"

"But I *do* tell you so," he insisted stubbornly. "I must. As a lawyer. You and I are not Santa Clauses handing out presents, Mrs. Emlen. We're trustees!"

Florence drew herself up. She had never thought she would have this kind of trouble with Mr. Colt. He was even verging on the impertinent. She remembered the story of his rudeness to George and wondered if he might not be a secret

187

drinker. "I think I've been a trustee for a good many more years than you, Mr. Colt," she said crushingly. "I learned the nature of my duties from Mr. Sheffield himself. I think you might not be making too great an error to consider my views in the matter."

"But I *am* considering your views, Mrs. Emlen," he protested. "I'm simply pointing out that the trust instrument instructs us, on your younger daughter's thirty-fifth birthday, to divide the principal equally among your children. The word 'equally' means just that. Even in the law."

She blinked, uncomprehending. "But we *are* going to divide it equally."

He threw up his hands. "Then, of course, there's no problem."

"It's simply that George gets the company for his share. Which he wants and which he knows about—"

"Do *we* know about it?"

"Well, after all, Mr. Colt," she said in exasperation, "neither you nor I are businessmen."

"Exactly."

"What do you mean, exactly?"

"How do we know that the company isn't worth more than his third?"

"But it's not!" she exclaimed. "We know what it's worth. It's right there in all those papers. Something called 'book value.' Besides, George runs the company, and he *told* me all about it. He says that he may actually be getting a worse deal than Anita or Lolly."

"*He* says."

"What are you implying, Mr. Colt?"

"Well, he's the one who's getting the stock, isn't he? I'm sorry, Mrs. Emlen, but trustees are bound to be suspicious."

Florence stared at him in sudden fascination and fear. One lived surrounded by the dark, dry wall of masculinity, of counselors, lawyers, trustees. One heard and tried to make sense of their incessant financial chatter. They criticized one's simplest expenditure as extravagance. They predicted bad times in good and worse times in bad. They despised and threatened a gentle butterfly like David and made as if to drag him from one's very feet as if they were Scottish barons and he, poor dear, a Rizzio. But that they were honest, that they were on one's side was never in doubt. Wasn't it the keystone, actually, of one's world? It was *too* bad of her one new friend to challenge principles as fixed and immutable as the tides, to talk about what one *should* do, as if he would recklessly tear down the enveloping wall and let in a whole blaring hell of personal decision. She put her hands to her ears.

"Suspicious?" she gasped. "Of *George?*"

"Of everyone!"

"But do you mean that George might not have been telling me the *truth?*"

"He could have made a mistake, couldn't he? People can. Particularly when it's in their interest to do so."

"But George is *never* careless!"

"Very well, then." He nodded grimly. "We've eliminated the element of mistake."

A faint muffled beat reverberated in Florence's mind as she continued to stare at him. It was like a drum, or the suggestion, anyway, of something martial, the phrasing of a nebulous but imperious question, the shaping of the dim concept, terrifying but even strangely fascinating, that instead of the seals, the staplers, the paper clips, instead of the pretty, rounded signature so impressive at the end of blue-backed documents, instead of the form and the flattery, the endless reassurance, there might even be the reality of Florence Emlen.

"You think George could really do such a thing?" she faltered. There was a footfall on the stairs outside. "That may be he now!" she cried in sudden, desperate relief and hurried from her chair as he entered. "Oh, George, I'm so glad you're here, dear!" She put her arms around him. "Mr. Colt's been upsetting me so! He's full of the wildest ideas! That you might have something to gain out of the Fibre Company and haven't been telling me everything! Tell him it's all right, will you, dear?"

George turned to Timmy with an ominous blankness of countenance. "What's the idea, Colt?"

Timmy had had time to reflect, in the brief moments between the sound of George's step in the corridor and his now blunt question, that his little game was up. There was to be no more evasion, no further chance of skirting his problem by the too simple expedient of frightening Mrs. Emlen with vague insinuations. If he was still to defeat George's scheme, it could only be now by showing all his cards, by exposing him to his mother and sisters, and the price of this, in terms of his own future, was not in doubt.

"I was just being a boring trustee, George," he said casually. "Telling your mother how careful we have to be. I wasn't speaking personally, of course."

"But women *take* things personally. I don't want you to confuse Mother."

"Confuse me!" Mrs. Emlen protested. "Really, George! I'll thank you to remember I'm your trustee!"

George still ignored her. "I'll thank *you* to remember," he continued severely to Timmy, "that I've gone to a lot of trouble to make the whole trust picture clear to Mother. It's very well for you to be a conscientious trustee. I know all about your conscientiousness. I've had to deal with it in the past, God knows. You may remember what I had to say about your habit of flying into the wild blue yonder. But you don't have to upset the whole apple cart, do you? Just for conscientiousness? If Anita and Lolly and I are happy about what's being done, what business is it of yours?"

"Don't worry about it, George. As I say, I was just being a boring trustee."

"Well, don't be too boring, fella," George said, looking at him fixedly. "Don't be too boring, that's all I ask."

When Timmy left them, he wondered grimly if he might not end by slipping between two stools, detested by everybody including himself. For what had he accomplished but to antagonize Mrs. Emlen as well as her son? Later that night, sitting with Eileen at their customary restaurant, his mood was biting. He wanted to feel committed by his talk with the Emlens, to feel the decision behind him, to make the wretched distribution. Sullen, he saw everything as tawdry, the Toulouse-Lautrec reproductions, the bad French of the Hungarian waiters, the huge purple handwriting of the menus.

"Now I suppose they'll come over," he snapped, as Eileen nodded to a couple across the room. "You know how I feel about table hoppers. Why can't we go some place where you don't know anybody? If there *is* such a place."

Her blue eyes gazed at him mildly. "They won't come over. And if they did, it would be only for a minute."

"A minute!" he retorted. "But our life is made up of these minutes! Sometimes I think you believe we only exist to waste time gracefully."

Her gaze was still on him. "What's wrong, darling? A bad day at the office?"

"No, no." He stared at the menu. "It's just that I sometimes think you're too urban, Eileen."

"You forget I lived on a farm with animals. For five years."

"Yes, and I bet you even did that elegantly." He knew

190

from the uncomfortable silence that followed that he had gone too far.

"Are you implying that's how I lost him?"

"Lost whom?"

"Craig."

"Good God, no. Don't take me up like that!"

"If you think my life is stupid and trivial, Timmy, I wish you'd say so."

"You don't understand," he protested, twisting now to get out of it. "It's not that at all. It's just that I take things more in my stride than you do. Probably because I'm coarser."

"What sort of things?"

"Things that coarse people don't mind. Crassness. Bad taste. Vulgarity. Things that you and David fight away from, but which you really know very little about. Why, I bet you even look upon Sheridan as a boor. Yet he's a man of cultivation to most people."

"Not to anyone he hasn't fooled."

"But he doesn't have to fool them. He's *one* of them, don't you see? He's not a special person, like you."

"Why am I so special?"

"I meant it as a compliment," he insisted. "But of course you won't see it. I think of you as rare. Do you know that you've never met my mother?" he demanded suddenly. "And do you know why?"

She looked startled. "I assumed she disapproved of you and me."

"On the contrary. She'd be tickled silly to meet you. I'm the one who's prevented it. And why? Because I'm ashamed of her! That's the long and short of it. I'm ashamed to have you meet her!"

She was embarrassed by his violence and glanced quickly towards the table on her right. "It doesn't have to be the end of the world, you know. Plenty of people are ashamed of their mothers. As a matter of fact, I'm rather ashamed of mine."

"But that's different," he said stubbornly. "You're ashamed of your mother because you think she's silly, and she *is* silly. But I'm ashamed of mine because she's dull and dreary and lower middle class. And that's contemptible!"

"Oh, Timmy."

"It is, Eileen! After all, I'm just like her. I'm all thumbs at the parties you take me to. And I'm tickled pink when some old woman like Mrs. Wardell makes a fuss over me. Or when

David wants to be friends. And you, oh, most of all, you! I've been terrified of your finding out what a crumb I was."

"A crumb? You, Timmy?"

"Me, Timmy!" There was no stopping him now in the catalogue of his crimes. "All the art you've shown me, all the music you've taken me to: do you think I've really liked it? No. I've liked having you as a guide. But fundamentally, I don't really trust art. I haven't any need of it."

"Of course you do. Everyone does."

"*You* do," he said emphatically. "You have to be surrounded by beautiful things. And you should be. They can't damn you."

"What a funny thing to say," she observed softly. "Can they damn you?"

"Perhaps."

"You're not being dramatic?"

"I'm always being asked that!"

"Not by me."

"No, dear." He took her hand apologetically. "Not by you. But we met too late to have shared all our moments of crisis."

"I wasn't being jealous, I was being factual. How can they damn you?"

He looked at her for several moments before deciding to tell. When he did so it was because he could no longer bear to have her on so different a plane; he was too alone with his guiltiness. Slowly, painstakingly, with a spoon to represent each of the Emlen trusts, he explained. She followed intently, without comment, until he had finished.

"Well, is that so bad?" she asked, after a pause. "Or have I missed something? It seems to me that George *should* have the company."

He felt suddenly ashamed. It was so greedy to take her out to dinner and bore her with legal details stacked in his favor, to gain a release from her lips that had no validity even in the court of his own depreciated conscience. It was cowardly not to risk her disapproval, to rig facts before an unqualified judge.

"Maybe. Maybe you're right. Oh, look, your friends *are* coming over."

He turned with relief to the couple who were approaching, glad to drop the subject while she was still reassuring. Yet he noticed, when they had gone, that she did not revert to it. It might, of course, have slipped her mind. It might. But it was also possible, was it not, that she, too, wished to avoid a subject which, explored too deeply, might defy even *her* powers of reassurance?

He had been to many houses with Eileen, but never to one like Mrs. Wardell's. It was like a great London eighteenth century house, with a high, bare marble stairway with niches for classical sculptures and an oblong Georgian parlor with tall, dark dusty portraits by Lely and Kneller. He knew almost no one at the party, but the very size of the room gave him a rather restful feeling of anonymity as he stood silently by Eileen while she greeted people. He could tell now when she really loved a house, and she really loved this one. She was even quieter than usual, smiling less frequently, and he caught her eyes almost surreptitiously taking in the great crystal chandelier, the scarlet and green of the mammoth Turkish rug.

"I suppose they're not really good," he murmured to her. "The pictures, I mean. Aren't they anybody's ancestors from any English home?"

She looked a bit surprised, as if she had to concentrate a moment. But she would concentrate, that was the thing about Eileen. Even when he thought she was farthest away, she had a quality of coming back to him. "Oh, but, of course they're bad," she agreed. "They should be, to have style. Pictures in the eighteenth century were things you inherited. Things you had. Isn't there something rather vulgar about little jewels of masterpieces with tiny spotlights beamed from the ceiling?"

He laughed, giving it up. Eileen was devoid of preconceptions. She gave herself to each new atmosphere with a completeness that might have alarmed him, had it not mildly irritated. She had quite put out of her mind the penthouse they had seen the week before with the Chinese screens and the Gauguins, which had excited her so. There were seven whole days of impressions between her and it.

"Well, well! If you two don't look as bored as a married couple!"

They both turned to face Eileen's cousin, Anita Ferguson, alert and bright-eyed in a gold dress that would have done wonders for anyone else. Nothing, however, could quite conceal her ungainliness, quite confer grace upon her nervous motions. She seemed helplessly aware, too, of her own compulsion to say the wrong thing; she had drawn her head back like a bird, and her round startled eyes seemed to chirp, at once defiantly and apologetically: There! I suppose I've done it again!

"As bored as you and Hank?" Eileen asked gently. And it *was* gently, Timmy reflected with admiration. It was another of the annihilating things about Eileen that she could retort kindly and almost mean it kindly.

"How is my trustee?" Anita had turned abruptly to him. "Not busting his head about my silly accounts tonight, I see."

"You think I should be?"

"Oh, don't be so literal!" she cried and faced Eileen again. "You know, dear, I'm really suspicious of your Timmy. He's closeted all the time with Mama, and you know about widows and handsome young lawyers. I'm sure I shall be totally disinherited."

"Oh, I think 'my' Timmy is harmless enough," Eileen said, smiling. "He wouldn't think of the things you and I might think of, Anita. You see, he has to earn his living."

"Well!" Anita's mouth fell open. "I never know what you mean, Eileen. And I know better than to ask. But if you could hear Mama go on about him, I think even you might be jealous."

"I shouldn't dream of competing with Auntie Flo," Eileen said turning to go off. "I'd be sure to lose."

Timmy was about to follow her when Anita grabbed his arm. "I want to speak to you," she said. "Wait."

It was the tone of the woman of property. Anita, defeated in her efforts to be witty, to be charming, even to be kind, always fell back like a spoiled child on more solid points of advantage.

"Certainly," he said, inclining his head.

"When are we going to get our money from that trust?" she demanded. "What's holding it up?" Her tone became sharper with the sense that even she had of the total inappropriateness of time and place. "Is George going to welsh on taking the Fibre Company?"

He controlled his surprise. "Not that I've heard of."

"Because if he is," she continued heatedly, "there are one or two things you should know. It's only *fair* that he take that stock. What does he need cash for? He's a selfish old bachelor without a care in the world, living off Mother. Why, she even pays his laundry bills!"

"But these are hardly considerations that should affect a trustee."

"Well, I don't see why not," she retorted. "A trustee shouldn't be a complete ostrich. George is rolling. Do you know that Daddy set up an extra trust for him over what he

194

did for us girls? And that he got two parts of Grandma Emlen's estate when we each got one!"

"Well, if he's rolling," he pointed out as lightly as he could, coughing to cover the slight tremor in his tone, "isn't it all the more reason that you and your sister should get your full due?"

"Exactly! Exactly what I mean!"

"And shouldn't your trustees take extra pains to be sure that you're not missing out by taking the securities instead of your share of the Fibre Company?"

"But that's all been settled!" she exclaimed. "Is *that* what's holding it up?"

He hesitated for just a second. Then he nodded.

"Well, I think that's taking too much on yourself!" she cried angrily. "Hank has looked into the Fibre Company, and so has Lolly's husband, and we want the securities. Now what concern is it of yours what we do with our own!"

"I'd hate to see anyone gypped," he murmured.

"Well, I think you might let us handle that. We're not children, you know. Hank and I want that money, and we want it now. I could give you my reasons, but I don't see that you're entitled to them."

Timmy wondered if a sharp face and cross eyes had ever seemed lovely to him before. Through the great open doors he heard the strain of a waltz, and he felt his heart leap. Was he not now exonerated? Suddenly he wanted to dance with Eileen. "There's no reason you should give me your reasons, Anita," he assured her. "And I don't see why we shouldn't wind up distribution of the trust next week."

"Oh," she said, taken aback. "Well, that's very nice." She paused. "Perhaps I spoke a bit hastily just now. You didn't mind, I hope?"

"I didn't mind in the least."

She took in the obvious sincerity of his smile. "Well, you're rather good-natured, I must say," she said with a shrug. "I don't know what it is about me. I get excited, and then I say the wrong thing. It's very trying."

"You should relax, Anita. We all should relax!"

As he walked away from her to the ballroom, he felt the beauty in everything, the portraits, the great dusky mirrors, even in Anita's gold dress. Was this, he asked himself happily, why Eileen came to parties? Because she always felt this way? He went over to the long table where the champagne was being served.

"I feel sardonic tonight," he heard David's voice in his ear.

195

"It comes from dancing with rich, elderly women and reflecting on the inequitable distribution of goods in our society. Why aren't you, too, sardonic? You should be. Like a young hero in Balzac out of the provinces to watch the splendors of Paris. And ending up harder than the hardest."

"Except I'm not from the provinces," Timmy pointed out. "I'm probably one of the few native New Yorkers in this room."

"How true," David conceded with a shrug. "Things are quite the reverse in this town. Odd as it may seem, our hostess is the provincial, though no one remembers that now. One can see it, of course, in this house."

"Do you think so? To me it has a rather easy, aristocratic air."

"Oh, does Eileen say that? Of course, she would. But you have to watch Eileen. She sees things through the haze of a rather perfervid imagination. She sees this house, I'm sure, as it ought to be and Mrs. Wardell as a sort of Gainsborough duchess. She won't see the show-off. The bad proportions of the hall. The excess of glass in the chandelier."

"And should she?"

"Well, that's a question, isn't it?" David held out his empty glass to the elderly waiter. "Is it better to live in one's imagination if one's imagination is a finer, cleaner place? I suppose if anyone should do it, Eileen should. It gives her the capacity to move through a rather vulgar world without the least contamination. But make no mistake, Timmy. It's a singular gift. Not everyone can do it."

"Are you warning me?"

David's eyes had still their mocking expression, but his tone was serious.

"You might call it that," he said, shrugging. "Do you feel you need a warning?"

"Not in the least. Even if I'm an ass to say it."

Leaving David abruptly, he made his way to the dance floor and cut in on Eileen before the brief euphoria of his mood could quite collapse. "I'm happy again," he whispered desperately in her ear. "I like everything now! I'm sorry I was such a stick."

"What changed you?"

"There's nothing like a little talk with Anita to buck a man up."

"Haven't I always said," she asked, smiling up at him, "that Anita was not a woman to be underestimated?"

"You know, I still don't quite believe in you, Eileen. What

have I done to deserve you? Why should you happen to *me?*"

"Oh, I've 'happened' to quite a few people," she assured him. "Or tried to, anyway. I'm not such an uncommon event."

"Can we really go on like this, dancing in fantastic ballrooms? Laughing at friends of yours in whose existence I don't really believe?" He felt her grip tighten on his shoulder.

"Please, darling," she murmured, "don't. Don't spoil it."

She made no objection when he suggested that they leave and go to his apartment. The ease with which she blended into the atmosphere of the party, her very relevance to such surroundings made it all the more necessary for him to possess her in a place that was more his own. It was as if only thus could he preserve any part of the mean little ego which he insisted, however arbitrarily, that she threatened, as if otherwise, a conquered Peter Ibbetson, he might be lost altogether in the spacious elegance of her dreams. Yet she had been everything to him that he had asked her to be; she had been open and generous with her life. Deep down he was uneasily aware that what he was trying to do was to brand her generosity as possessiveness. To have faced it frankly would have involved facing as well the stinginess with which he held back the one thing she wanted. And what was that but his love?

12

EILEEN, as it happened, was neither as indifferent nor as undiscerning in matters of the conscience as Timmy might have hoped. It was quite true that, even more than most women, she had a tendency to minimize the moral aspects of what men did "downtown"; shrewdness and aggression seemed merely other aspects of their masculinity, and the border line between this and dishonesty was a shadow land where a woman's mind had little need to penetrate. But her intelligence was very clear, and when it focused on such a problem as Timmy had focused it, it took in the final subtleties. Even so she might not, under normal circumstances, have been too much concerned. Hers was the gift of living in the moment;

she saw no sense in having a pleasure spoiled by the long, meddlesome, dirty fingers of the future. But people, she had been made to recognize, could never let one be, could never endure the idea of a futureless pleasure. The moment they spotted content on a face or satisfaction in a general air, they came rushing and whooping, a motley, noisy mob, with boxes and sticks and nets, to catch the butterfly of happiness and nail it to the cardboard of their senseless classifications. Who cared if the butterfly was killed in the process? And recently, it seemed, everyone around her had taken upon themselves, unurged, the obligation of discussing her future with Timmy. Even her mother.

Clarissa had summoned her to her bedroom to discuss it. She was about to take the train for Andover to watch young Sheridan play in another football game, one of the few maternal duties that Dale insisted on, and she was unusually sour.

"I'm not one to interfere, you know," she began, seated at a long dressing table and tugging with a comb at her crisply set golden hair. "It's just that I like to make my plans. One wants to know a little ahead of time."

Eileen, puffing a cigarette on the chaise longue, looked pensively at her exhaled smoke. "What sort of plans do you have to make?"

"Well, I happen to run a rather large apartment," her mother retorted, "in which you occupy three rooms. If you're thinking of leaving, it would be convenient to know."

"Are you thinking of asking me to?"

"Oh, Eileen, don't be tiresome!" Clarissa turned on her irritably, comb in hand. "Isn't it perfectly natural for a mother to be interested when her daughter is seeing as much of somebody as you are of Timmy?"

"Natural, yes."

"Well, are you going to marry him or aren't you?"

"Oh, I thought you knew. He's already married."

"I didn't ask you in here to make fun of me," Clarissa said tartly. "Of course, I know that. But he's left her, hasn't he?"

"Yes. For the moment."

"For the moment! Well, I should hope so! And I'll thank you to make it clear to people like Aunt Florence that your friendship started *after* his separation. You're entirely too casual, Eileen. I know you travel with a very smart set, but you'd better remember that there are still people who don't relish girls who break up homes."

"Is there any difference between keeping a man away from his home and taking him away? I don't want to persuade people I'm anything I'm not."

"There's all the difference in the world!" Clarissa cried. "Really, child, you are impossible. I've made a point of telling all my friends that Timmy had to leave his wife because she was an alcoholic. *Before* he met you."

"What!" Elieen exclaimed, sitting up. "Mummy, you can't have done such a thing! It's monstrous!"

"Monstrous! When she was sick all over this very bedroom! Maybe that doesn't count for anything in your world, but let me tell you, my girl, it counts for plenty in mine!"

Eileen lay back in the chaise longue, suddenly faint. She could imagine only too vividly how Timmy would react to this. "Please, Mummy," she murmured, "*Must* you say such things?"

"Oh, I know," Clarissa continued sulkily. "It's poor taste of me even to mention that she was sick. You've always had a horror of ugly facts, Eileen. But occasionally we *do* have to face them. I'm assuming your Timmy, if he has any sense in that handsome head of his, won't let that woman ruin his career. Divorce is the only answer. Even Sheridan thinks so."

Eileen opened her eyes. "Does he?"

"Well, yes." Clarissa appeared to reflect, for even she was a bit hesitant about misquoting a man as definite as her husband. "I think he's torn between his desire to have Timmy for a son-in-law and his fear that you'll spoil him."

"Spoil him?"

"Oh, you know." Clarissa shrugged and turned back to her mirror. "Take him to too many of your silly parties."

"And what about Sheridan's parties? They're not silly, I suppose?"

Clarissa turned to give her daughter a quick look, one of their rare women's moments of communication. "Of course not. They're business. Anyway, I have to catch that damn train. Darling, do you remember who little Sherry's team is playing? The *things* I'm expected to know!"

"Exeter." Eileen got up to leave. Clarissa, anyway, was safely distracted. Really, she thought later, as she went out to her shopping, could one never be allowed even the illusion of a carefree moment? It was what was wrong with the world, really, its inability to accept bounty. Or at least to watch others accept it. But she knew, catching a glimpse of her own eyes, evasive, preoccupied, in the mirror at her hairdresser's, that she was only trying to obscure her fear of what was really happening to Timmy. For it *did* seem to her, in that sudden grim moment, hiding it from her own image behind a copy of *Harper's Bazaar*, that it was a shabby thing that he was doing to Anita and Lolly. She did not think the less of him, for she never judged him as a lawyer or trustee. Such things had no relevance to herself or to their relationship. But she did face the fact of her own involvement; she *had* to know if she was contributing, however subtly, to the moral disintegration of the man who seemed to be becoming her whole life. Action would then be required, and action was distasteful, but if one's airy castle was bound in any event to be leveled by the envious, wasn't it better to emerge over the drawbridge in full armor than to perish in the smoke of the citadel? At least it seemed so. If everything was lost, she thought hopelessly, picking up the telephone by her chair, there was the last hollow refuge of the becoming gesture.

"It's about tonight," she said when Timmy came on the wire. "Are you coming? To Aunt Florence's?" He would never know, she reflected, what skill it took to hold such invitations open for him as long as she managed to.

"Oh, I'm sorry, I should have called you earlier. I can't, Eileen. I've got to work. Is it terribly inconvenient?"

"Of course not. I just had to know, that's all."

"You don't mind? Really?"

"Really."

And she didn't. It was as if she had been given a reprieve. Going to a dinner party in a new dress and thinking of Timmy while she was there could, under the circumstances, be almost preferable to having him with her. Decisions, actions were for the time in abeyance; people could be counted on, in theory anyway, to talk nicely about nice things. In her aunt's Chinese drawing room that night, when David came up smiling, to hand her a cocktail, she wondered why so much store was placed on sincerity.

"You don't think you're giving Timmy rather a dose of it?" She looked up as if he had struck her. "A dose of what?"

"Oh, you know." He shrugged. "Your life."

"I suppose you think, like Sheridan, that I'll corrupt him. I never knew before, David, that you and Sheridan were so alike."

His eyes widened with mock reproach. "Dear me, aren't we snappish tonight?"

"It's only that I'm beginning to wonder if it isn't my patience with people that gets me into jams."

"All right, all right." He raised his hands as if to keep her away from him. "I only wanted to drop a gentle warning. He hasn't exactly your background, you know."

"Background," she retorted. "All people can talk about is background. As if we were figures in a landscape. Does it require so very much imagination to see that we're all basically the same?"

"But we're not. Anyway, I'm not."

"That's true," she said, turning away from him. "You're God's own snob."

She avoided David and the subject of Timmy during dinner, but afterwards, among the ladies, while she was sitting alone in a love seat her cousin Anita came up to break into her solitude.

"What luck to catch you alone, Eileen!" Anita settled herself, with many nervous tugs and pulls at her dress, glancing about for an ashtray, a place to put her drink, in the other half of the love seat. "You know, I simply can't understand why Mother should ask David to the house when I'm here. Can you? Everyone's talking about our row. Wouldn't you think she'd know better? I mean it's so embarrassing for both of us."

Anita had the Bertrand "crossness" to the point of seeming a parody of her mother and aunt. Yet being an Emlen, with at least the reputation of money, was enough to make people who searched, often sincerely, for an excuse for having taken her up find eccentricity in her bad manners and novelty in her humorlessness.

"I don't suppose David minds."

"I don't suppose he does," Anita retorted. "He's too brash. As a matter of fact, I think it's rather disloyal of you to be so chummy with him after the way he's treated me."

Eileen laughed aloud. "But I can't cut everyone you cut, Anita!" she protested. "I should have no friends at all."

"I can't imagine why you should want to be friends with him, anyway," Anita continued with a sniff. "It doesn't do a girl any good to be seen around with a pansy. First thing you know, people begin to say she's queer herself."

"I note that didn't stop you before you quarreled with him!" Eileen exclaimed. But Anita was not worthy of her fire; Anita was too pathetic. And feeling suddenly warmly towards her cousin, she wondered why she too shouldn't be serious at parties. "Why are you hostile to me, Anita?" she asked in a different tone. "Why do you grudge me my friendship with David? I've always cared for you."

Anita, staring, seemed paralyzed. Then the corners of her small mouth turned down, and Eileen thought for an awkward moment that she was going to cry.

"I'm not hostile to you," she said in a low wail. "I've always thought you were wonderful, really. You had all the things I wanted. Even when you were only ten or eleven, and I was practically coming out, Mummy used to tell me to behave like you. I envied you, Eileen. I still do!"

"Then you've never stopped to consider our respective situations," Eileen said firmly. "It's rather egocentric of you, really. You have a husband and two lovely children and plenty of money, even if you do find yourself strapped now and then. And I, what have I got?"

Anita looked at her dubiously. "You have lots of friends."

"Well, I don't make them by antagonizing people."

Anita gave another little wail. "Have I antagonized you, too, Eileen?"

"Well, of course not!" Eileen felt almost cheerful. So this was action! This was coming out of the shell and talking back! "Anyway, we're family. One can't antagonize family. I can *prove* I've nothing against you, Anita."

"Prove it? How?"

"By giving you a little tip. But you must first promise you'll never let anyone know I told you. Or *what* I told you!" She almost laughed at Anita's air of bafflement. Her heart was beating fast, but she thought she saw her way. How could Timmy do anything wrong if there was nothing wrong to do? And as for the future, well, *she* would handle the future. "I won't tell you a thing," she warned, "unless you promise!"

"I promise."

"On your honest-to-goodness word of honor?"

"On my honest-to-goodness word of honor."

"Very well." Eileen paused to choose her words. "There's some sort of a Fibre Company in one of your trusts, isn't there? That George is going to get?"

Anita's eyes immediately narrowed. "Go on."

"Well, take your share. You and Lolly. Don't let him get it all."

There was a pause while Anita, motionless, continued to stare at her, and Eileen had a sudden sensation of panic.

"Why do you say that?" Anita asked in a slow, suspicious tone. "Is the company worth more than they let on? Who told *you?*"

"A little bird."

"A little bird called Timmy Colt? Or Uncle Sherry?"

"That's not your affair. Just be quiet about it, as you promised, and take your third."

"But I can't!" Anita almost shouted. "The distribution's been made. George got all his shares this morning!"

Eileen felt the rush of black panic to her head. She raised her hands to her temples. "Then forget all about it, will you? It was only a joke, anyway!"

"A joke!" Anita laughed harshly. "You don't joke about things like that. If you won't tell me who told you, I'll make it my business to find out!"

"But, Anita," Eileen gasped in horror, "you *promised!*"

"Promised!" Anita seemed outraged at the very suggestion. "Of course I promised! But you never told me it was about money!"

Aunt Florence was already standing over them with instructions to join the gentlemen. Eileen, dazed, followed the others into the living room and felt only gratitude when David joined her.

"Are you in a better mood?" he asked.

"I'm in no mood at all," she answered bleakly. "I thought I was good at evasive tactics, but now I'm beginning to doubt myself. What do you do when there's something too painful to be thought about?"

"Well, there's liquor, of course. But you're not really the type. And besides, your aunt is surprisingly stuffy about that. I would suggest playing cards for rather more than you can afford. It's distracting, whether you win or lose."

"That's it." She nodded slowly. "Can you make up a table of bridge?"

"With pleasure." He bowed his head. "But not as your partner, dear. Not tonight."

13

SHERIDAN DALE sat humped in his chair, staring at the grey spotless blotter before him. He could feel, like distant thunder, the rumblings of his incipient wrath; he could sense, too, the sudden white flicker of his panic. But there was no time for anger or fear. They were luxuries; they impeded thought, and thought was more essential than ever, with the soft, insinuating Georgia drawl of Hank Ferguson still echoing in his ear. It was little help, in his desperate search for clarity, that he had detested Ferguson, more acutely than he usually allowed himself to detest people, from the very beginning of their relationship. Hank had always managed to insinuate at family gatherings, with a sly wink or even a shove, that he and "Uncle Sherree" were united, not so much by the bond of having married into the same family as of having married into it for the same reason. It had been all Dale could do to keep his temper every time that Hank, going over family accounts of which he was trustee, with a frank, smiling skepticism, would glance first at any others present and then at him, before saying: "Now Ah'm sure no one's goin' to mind if Ah just ask Uncle Sherree here a couple of rooteeen questions." Dale suddenly struck the surface of his desk with his full heavy palm at the idea that this wretched man's suspicions might even threaten his own directorship at Holcombe! It was intolerable, indecent, lewd—but no. He forced himself to take a deep breath. This had to be thought through. Hank had to be bluffed. And then maybe settled with.

"Mr. Emlen, sir," he heard his secretary's voice, and George came in, the door closing behind him.

"Sit down, George," he said gruffly. "We can talk in the cab, but I'd like to find out a few things first."

"Where are we going?"

"To my apartment. Your mother and the Fergusons are meeting us there at six. Tell me, have you still got those patents?"

George's long oval jaw dropped. "Of course not! I transferred them to Holcombe last week. The purchase was authorized by the board."

"I see." Dale's face reflected nothing. "I thought I had suggested that you wait a while."

"But what was the point?" George had ceased immediately to be the nephew; his dry, sharp tone was already that of the dissatisfied client. "Everything was arranged. What I want to find out is who tipped off that poor white trash of a brother-in-law of mine. I figure it came from this office. Have you asked Timmy?"

"He's uptown today. I can't reach him."

"You will remember I was never sure of him," George said dryly. "I never really trusted him after that time he insulted me at the club. This is on your head, Sheridan."

Dale's impatient head shake gave no hint to George that his distrust might be shared. "I'll vouch for Timmy. Don't you worry. My only concern is how to settle the damn thing. Of course, if you had the patents we could rescind the whole deal. This way it's tougher. You may have to pay something, George. Something rather stiff."

"Well, if it turns out that Timmy *was* responsible," George said in an even dryer tone, "I shall expect to be compensated by free legal services. To the *full* extent of that something rather stiff."

"We'll see," Dale said noncommittally as he rose from his desk. "We may be worrying unduly. Let's go uptown. And remember, George. *I* do the talking."

When they walked into Dale's study in his apartment half an hour later they found Mrs. Emlen and the Fergusons already waiting. The former had a reproachful, afflicted look; she gazed out the window, occasionally raising a handkerchief to her lips with an air of: *This* is what I get; *this* is my thanks. She had no understanding of what Hank and Anita were complaining about; it was enough for her that she was a trustee and that they were, in fact, complaining. Anita was tense and fidgety; her husband, who looked deceptively young with his bad complexion and long messy blond hair, smiled tolerantly at everyone.

"Ah'm sorry to bring you gentlemen uptown," he began. "But Ah knew we all wouldn't wish to make Mrs. Emlen go down." He paused to look around the room complacently. "Well, Ah suppose Ah may as well start the ball rollin'. It's like what Ah said to you on the phone, Uncle Sherree. Mah spies tell me that old George here has been transferrin' patents as fast as his hot little hands can move 'em."

Dale remained impassive. "Well?"

"A pretty quick turnover, wouldn't you call it?"

"Do you imply that the patents were not George's to do with as he wished?"

"Oh, no." Hank's smile broadened. "They were his, all right. Old George saw to that."

"Anything that slipped by your snout must have been invisible," George retorted.

"Just about, George," Hank replied amiably. "Just about invisible. That's mah point."

205

"You imply then," Dale continued, "that these patents were of greater value than was represented to your wife?"

"That's sort of what Ah'm implyin'. Ah won't deny it, suh."

"Then George, I presume, received a great price for them?"

"Oh, Ah don't say yes to that." Hank put his head to one side and smiled at him foxily. "Ah don't say for sure he received a great price. They's more ways than one to skin a cat."

"There are all sorts of ways a big company like that can pay off!" Anita broke in excitedly. "Tell them, Hank. The way you told me! About all the business they could steer George's way!"

"Honey, will ya let me tell it mah own way?" Hank asked softly. "Will ya please?"

"What's all this about, Sheridan?" Mrs. Emlen demanded suddenly, turning indignantly to her brother-in-law. "What's Anita saying? Why is it that everyone keeps interfering with my business things?" She turned resentfully on her daughter. "I don't know what makes you think, Anita, that you're qualified to speak on matters in which your uncle and I are so much more experienced."

"I may not be an expert in textiles," Anita retorted, "but if George is doing me out of my inheritance, I want to know!"

"Will ya leave it to me, honey?" Hank repeated, more ominously now. "Please?"

"George isn't doing anyone out of anything," Dale broke in with an angry rumble. "And I'm afraid we're not going to leave this matter to you, Ferguson. It's all very well for Anita to let you handle her business affairs if she wants. That's her own choice, whatever the family may think of it. But when it comes to accusing her own relatives of improper conduct, I think she'll have to speak for herself."

"Not if she wants me to speak for her!" Hank exclaimed.

Dale did not even deign to look at him. "If I can't talk to my wife's niece in my own home, I shall conclude this interview," he said sternly. "How about it, Anita?"

"There, Anita!" her mother cried. "Listen to him!"

"Hank thought something might be wrong," Anita said, faltering as she glanced at her husband. "He said his lawyer thought it looked funny, too."

"What?" Dale's voice became a sudden bark. "What do you mean, his lawyer! We've never had other lawyers on family accountings! You will be good enough to tell Hank we have no need of his counsel. We can handle this thing in the family."

"I'll do no such thing!"

"That's it, honey. Tell 'em!"

"Anita!" her mother exclaimed.

"What does he think Hank's lawyers will find out?" Anita demanded, reckless now. "Something about his precious Timmy?"

"You're being ridiculous, Anita," Dale said in a calmer, condescending tone. "I'm not in the least concerned about Timmy or any vicious slander that you may care to spread about him or me. We can survive that. What I *am* concerned about is the spectacle of your mother's name being dragged through courts and newspapers. You seem to forget that she's also a trustee."

"Well, of course!" Mrs. Emlen exploded, turning wrathfully on her daughter. *"Now* will you see? Or do you want to treat the public to a sordid family row?"

"But, Ma," Anita protested, shocked, "no one will think *you* did anything. All you did is sign things."

"Sign things!" Mrs. Emlen drew herself up. "Is *that* all you think I do for you children? Poring over papers and statistics and documents, afternoon after afternoon. And you say I just sign things!"

"Really, Anita," Dale said sternly, "I think you might do your mother the favor of not chasing lawyers after her."

Anita wavered, looking from her mother's powdered anxiety to her uncle's dark reproach. It was a moment, actually, of supreme crisis in her life. For Anita's mind had always been a tumult of imagined slights. If a friend failed to speak to her on the street or to send her a Christmas card, if a bank teller asked proof of her identity or a store clerk checked on her charge account, it was always another manifestation of the human conspiracy to humiliate Anita Ferguson. In her universe no allowance was made for shortsightedness, for lapses of memory, for natural bungling; everything was smoothly and efficiently organized in a fabric of malicious planning against which she had no defense save her own alertness and bad temper. Yet no such fantasy could be quite complete. Even Anita had her momentary suspicions that coincidence was still a fact, that indifference could be as prevalent as malice and that on occasion her batteries might be opened up on persons who didn't even know of her existence. Even she could not live entirely in the spontaneous combustion of her anger. Her crisis now was that this suspicion had suddenly become a desperate hope; she actually *wanted* her uncle and Timmy to have been honest with her. It might be almost too terrifying, mightn't it, to find that one had all along been right? That there was, in fact, a conspiracy?

"Very well!" she cried, jumping up. "But on one condition! If Timmy will come in here and tell me that everything's on the up and up! If he'll look me straight in the eye and tell me on his word of honor that I've gotten all I'm entitled to! Will he do *that*, Uncle Sheridan?"

"Of course Timmy will do that," Dale said dryly.

"Then let him!"

"As soon as I can get hold of him. He was out of the office this afternoon."

"But he's right here!" Anita cried, her eyes popping with renewed suspicion. "Right in your own living room, having a drink with Eileen! I saw them!"

Dale hesitated, but he did not flinch. A series of ugly possibilities flashed through his mind, but he would have to risk them. "Will you get him, please, George?"

When Timmy, following George into the study, saw who were assembled there, he felt, even with the quickening of his pulse, a sensation of curious relief. So this was it. Ever since the final distribution of the trusts he had lived in a state of suspended animation, going about his tasks and his pleasures with a purely mechanical skill, unable to participate because he was unable any longer to identify sympathetically with the central character of his own drama. Those two weeks had been like a film when the sound track was broken; now, even with the sudden jar of the resumed noise, it was not altogether misery to know that his story was again moving forward. Recognizing the tension in the room, he greeted nobody, waiting for the question to be put.

"Anita has something she wants to ask you, Tim," Dale said gravely. "The reassurance that she's looking for is rather peculiar. However, I trust you'll make allowances. She wants to know—"

"I'll ask it, Uncle Sheridan!" Anita cried suddenly. "I want to know, Timmy, when you turned over our trusts, if you had any idea that George's share was worth more than Lolita's and mine!"

Timmy stared, fascinated, at those small, squinting black eyes. For a moment he was speechless. He only knew what he could not do; he could not break the sound track again. "Mrs. Ferguson," he said in a distant tone, "I cannot see that I'm under any obligation to answer that. And what is more, I cannot see what good an answer would do you. There's no point having any discussion with a trustee whom you don't trust. If you're not satisfied with me, I must advise you to retain your own counsel."

Anita's eyes moved nervously from side to side. She glanced at Dale.

"Aren't you being a little hasty, Tim?" Dale asked, smiling, in a tone of labored good nature. "We don't have to be too lawyeresque with Anita. I know her question's out of order, and I've told her so. She has no business asking it at all. But you know how it is. Women hear all kinds of things at dinner parties that they don't know how to evaluate. They haven't our training. Now I tell you what. You tell Anita that everything's on the up and up, as you and I know it is, and I'll see that she apologizes to you. Is that fair?"

"But you see that's exactly what I won't do," Timmy answered sharply. "She's asking me to deny that I've been dishonest. Such a denial would be worthless to her and degrading to me. Get a lawyer, Mrs. Ferguson," he continued, turning back to Anita. "It's the only way."

"Look, Timmy," Anita exclaimed, going over to him and shaking her finger. "There's something you don't understand. My information came from a source that I couldn't possibly ignore. No woman would have. You're a partner of Uncle Sheridan's and Mummy's lawyer. Don't you think you owe me a denial?"

"I've given you my answer."

Anita stamped her foot. "It was Eileen who told me!"

For a moment he was too stunned to speak. Then everything fitted. "All the more reason that you should get a lawyer," he said quietly and turning on his heel, walked out of the room.

"I will!" she cried after him, in a raucous tone. "You'll see I will!"

"Fact is, we already have one," he heard Hank's voice, and then the door slammed. But there were heavy footsteps behind him.

"Timmy!" Dale's hand on his shoulder stopped him. "Come in here." He felt himself propelled into the dining room and heard another door closed. "What the devil do you think you're up to?"

"Why should I put up with her impertinence?"

Dale's breath sounded heavily in the dark room. "She's a bitch, of course," he said with a rough wave of his hand towards the study. "Everyone knows that. But what the hell? She can make trouble. Plenty of trouble."

"I'll handle it, Sheridan. Don't worry. After all, I'm the trustee."

"But she'll go to court, man!"

"Let her. What can she prove?"

"Damn the proof!" Dale cried. "What about the publicity?"

"I don't care about the publicity."

There was a pause in which Dale's breathing sounded even louder. "You don't care, in other words," he said in a lower, sterner tone, "that Mrs. Emlen may be dragged into court to answer baseless charges? You don't stop to think how happy the press will be? You don't bother to consider Mrs. Emlen either as a client or an elderly, proud woman? Why, a thing like this could kill her!"

"Oh, I fancy she'll survive it," Timmy said with a shrug. "Better, at any rate, than I."

"Than you!" Dale exclaimed. "What harm can it possibly do you? You will simply take the position that you had no knowledge of any deal between George and Holcombe!"

"Will I?"

Dale stared, half confounded. "You will unless you wish to perjure yourself! You will because you *had* no knowledge of any such deal!"

Timmy was now smiling. "I didn't, did I, Sheridan? You know that because you saw to it that I didn't. That I was never told."

There was a long pause at the end of which Dale nodded abruptly. "Very well," he said. "I see you're going to handle it your own way. Obviously, I can't stop you. But I'll give you a warning, my boy. If you lose this case, you'll stand alone. If it's proved in court that you in any way abused your trust—in *any* way, mind you—I shall immediately request your resignation from the firm."

Timmy inclined his head. "I would assume that."

"As you know," Dale continued heavily, "I advised you from the beginning that the responsibility was yours. If you would do as I say now, I would stand behind you. But if you want to play it your way, that's your gamble."

"Fair enough, Sheridan."

Opening the door, Timmy left the dining room and went down the long corridor to Eileen's little sitting room, a green eighteenth-century room with reproductions of Fragonard panels. She jumped up as he came in.

"What's going on, Timmy. Why are the Emlens here?"

"You know, don't you?"

He wondered if he had ever seen her more beautiful as she paled.

"You mean it's—it's what I told Anita?"

"So you did tell her."

She put her hands on his arms, but he didn't move. "Oh, darling, what's going to happen?"

"Do you care?" He shrugged his shoulders. "A law suit, I suppose. A mess. Not a big mess. Not big enough to amuse David and the rest of the crowd."

She stepped back as if he had pushed her. "What do you mean by that?"

"Well, that's all you're really after, isn't it?" he asked savagely. "A topic that will amuse them? Is there anything in the world you wouldn't sacrifice for the right story or the right laugh? Or just the right way of coming into a room?"

She sat down again, staring dazedly at the floor, shaking her head. "Timmy, you can't mean that. You can't really."

"Why can't I?" There was a desperate satisfaction now in striking at her. "It's not a criticism, really. It's your world, after all. Those are its standards. I'm the one who's intruding. I'm the silly ass who can't seem to tell when something's crooked and when it's simply amusing. The rest of you have a formula, God knows what it is. But as I've said before, I'm a hick. I just don't seem to know how to play the game." He paused, waiting for her to answer, even wanting her to. But Eileen would not even look up at him. Of course! He was being vulgar, wasn't he? As such he had ceased already to exist for her. "When I first met you," he continued bitterly, "I thought that you and Sheridan were the most different people in the universe. I was wrong. Basically you both belong to the same world. With the same mores. It's why you're able to live under the same roof. And why you'll both be a good deal better off without me."

Walking down the corridor to the front hall past the murky green of the tapestries and the gleam of Spanish cutlasses, leaving her without another word, without even waiting to see if she would look up, he wondered if he had yet come to the end of the dusty road that had started with Knox's death. It was like a nightmare in which he was an actor, declaiming and gesturing with passion, yet somehow wrongly, as if his heroic denunciation had found its way into a situation of comic relief, as if his bombast was ridiculous and his own awareness of it only made it more so. But at least he was declaiming again; at least he was performing. Somehow, at whatever agony to himself and others, there would be an end to it.

14

THERE WAS no question in his mind as to where he was going. It was so obvious to him that he had to be reminded by the cab driver to give the address. For the idea of a permanent rift with Ann had never been quite real to him. Like an angry child running away from home, he had always suspected, deep in his heart, from the very vagueness of his future plans, that return might be inevitable. Smarting now with the hurt of Eileen's disloyalty, he was eager for Ann's consolation, impatient to be soothed in the totality of her unfailing concern. Never had her virtues seemed finer, her devotion more indispensable. He must have been mad indeed to have left her to be tossed again on the horns of Dale's terrible family-in-law. Ann had seen through them all from the very start! She had warned him that he would never understand people like Eileen. That he was too literal. And how right she was!

It was George who opened the apartment door. Walter was standing behind him, peering curiously out. Neither smiled.

"Mummy's across the hall at Mrs. McLane's," George said. "She'll be back in a moment. Do you want me to get her?"

"No, I'll wait." He went in and took off his coat. As he hung it up in the closet, staring into the darkness, he thought for a moment. "Look, boys," he said, turning around suddenly to find them still watching him. "I want to come back. For good this time. Do you think Mummy will have me?" They exchanged glances. "It's up to all of you, you know. You don't have to if you don't want to."

"Have you been bad?" George's tone was curious.

"I've been seeing a lot of stupid people and not paying attention to you and Mummy. I have no excuse, really. Except that maybe when you're older, you'll understand."

"But you promised you'd *never* say that!" George protested. "Grownups are always saying that."

"So I did." Timmy smiled ruefully. "All right, maybe you can understand now. I sort of went off my rocker for a bit. But I'm all right again."

Walter's eyes bulged. "Did they put you in jail?"

"Of course not," George snapped at him.

"I wasn't *that* crazy," Timmy explained. "And I'll be okay from now on. I promise."

"You won't go away again?" George demanded.

"No."

"Really and truly?"

"Really and truly."

Walter came up silently and put his hand in his father's. It was difficult not to pick him up and hug him, but Timmy resisted the impulse. He knew better than to let him steal the scene from George and kept his eyes fixed on the older boy. "How about it? Will you help me sell it to Mummy?"

George nodded, businesslike. "I'll see what I can do."

They heard the key in the front door, and all turned as Ann came in. Closing it behind her, she looked from one to the other. "But, Timmy, I didn't expect you today!"

Walter let go of Timmy's hand and ran over to his mother. "Daddy's coming home to stay. He's promised! If you'll let him. You will, won't you? Please, Mummy!"

Timmy was surprised that his predominant feeling should be one of admiration. Ann was so remarkably calm. She looked thoughtfully at Walter for a moment and then turned to her older son. "What about it, George?" Her tone was modulated to be serious, without making too much of it. "Walter seems sold."

"I'm for it. He's promised to be okay."

"Did he?" Her eyes lingered on Timmy for just a moment. "But you must remember, boys, if he comes back, he'll be Daddy again. Just because he promised doesn't mean you can hold that over him. You'll have to mind him and respect him, just as before. Is that understood?" They both nodded. "All right, then I tell you what. You both go down to Mrs. McLane's and play with Billy for half an hour while Daddy and I talk this out."

"But you'll be nice to him?" Walter protested.

"Oh, darling. I'm always nice to Daddy. You know that."

When they had gone she looked at him hard for a moment and then sighed, as if suddenly exhausted. She sat down abruptly on the sofa, her hands on her knees. "Tell me what's happened," she said quickly, closing her eyes. "Tell me."

Sitting down opposite her, he told, as she stared at the rug, the whole story of the Fibre Company and Eileen. "The thing's been a nightmare," he concluded. "From the very beginning. The whole crazy world I've been playing with."

"Was *she* a nightmare?"

"But the essence of it!"

She smiled a bit sardonically. "I wish I could believe it. It would make my role easier if I had to deal only with fantasies. Unfortunately there are people behind them." She looked up, as if to change the subject. "I went to your apartment the other day. Did you know that?"

"No. But I gave you the key. It was quite all right."

"I wanted to see what it was like," she continued, nodding as if to confirm an impression. "I had to, in fact. I looked at everything. Inspected everything. The glass. The line. That little surrealist seascape that I'm sure she gave you."

"Did you like it?"

"Oh, yes, I liked it," she said, turning away. "I liked the whole apartment, I suppose."

He smiled. "Almost as much as you hated it?"

"That's it." She shrugged. "Because it's not all her. That I wouldn't have minded. Some of it's you. Some of the neatness and the austerity. It made me see that the messiness really *had* been all mine."

"But I liked the messiness." He moved over beside her on the sofa. "I rather miss it now," he said, looking around the room. "Everything's so spic and span. Do you suppose we could ever go back to the old way?"

"Oh, Timmy." She turned around suddenly and put her head on his shoulder. "It wouldn't have to be that way again. I *can* improve, you know. I can learn that it's not necessarily trivial to be feminine. I can never be like Mrs. Shallcross, of course, but I can at least be orderly."

"Poor Ann. You've taken so much. How can you still want me back?"

"I told you years ago. I'm a clinger. I warned you."

"Even after this thing of Anita's? It's a dirty business, you know."

"But you're going to fight it!" she exclaimed, sitting up suddenly. "You're going to fight it and win!"

He almost laughed at the immediate energy of her partisanship. "What makes you so sure?"

"Because you're not that Timmy Colt any more!"

"What Timmy Colt?"

"The society lawyer!" she cried. "The trouble shooter for Dale." She stood up now and stared down at him. "The slick man of the world!"

He stared back, astonished at her violence. "Was *that* how you saw me?"

"Wasn't it how you wanted to be seen?"

"Why?"

"Because a Timmy like that could be ruined, couldn't he? A Timmy like that could be destroyed?"

He raised his eyebrows. "By conspiring with Dale?"

She paused. "No. By getting caught."

His expression was faintly mocking now. "You mean I did it subconsciously?"

"On the contrary. It was entirely conscious. I bet you had to *make* yourself give that Fibre Company to George!"

"And if I did? What do you deduce? Why should I have?"

"To punish yourself." She paused again, as she scrutinized him carefully. "For killing Mr. Knox."

In the silence that followed, his expression did not change. "But I didn't kill Mr. Knox," he said quietly.

"Only in your fantasy." She turned away from him. "Which I suppose is the realest place to kill people. If you have to kill them at all."

"It isn't a nice thing to do, is it?"

"It isn't a nice thing to think. But we can't *help* what we think. That's the point." There was a brief silence.

"Why do you bother about me, Ann? I'm not worth it, you know. Mental murderer or true thief."

"Because you're the only thing I have to bother about!" she exclaimed, turning back and seizing him by the shoulders. "The only thing I want to bother about! I let you go once, like an idiot, because I didn't know how to handle you. But I won't let you go again. Not even back to that apartment to get your things. I'll get them myself in the morning."

"What a firebrand you are."

"We're going to *fight* this Ferguson woman!" she went on,

agitated. "You must talk to Larry about it. He knows all the office gossip. *Now,* darling. He's in now. I was just talking to Sally on the phone."

"It's just what I'll do," he said, as the value of the idea struck him. "Just exactly what I'll do."

Two hours later, at a side table at a Third Avenue bar, he and Larry were still drinking beer, immersed in plans. The latter was flushed and enthusiastic.

"It's a lead pipe cinch!" he kept exclaiming. "Everyone's *got* to be on our side. Mrs. Emlen because she's a co-trustee. Georgie-Porgie because he's scared to death of what Holcombe may do to him if he's found out. Dale because he can't afford a scandal in the firm. Everyone except Mrs. Ferguson. *That* bitch. Will I ever strip her in court! Oh, boy, oh, baby, what a case to fight! Timmy, you're my pal!"

Timmy, with a small fixed glitter in his eyes, waited for some of Larry's excitement to abate. "They'll put George on the stand," he continued. "They'll ask him what he got for the patents. The price will disappoint them, of course. Then they'll go on a fishing expedition to see what else he got. But they'll never drag it out of the boys at Holcombe. Never in a million years. It was probably only an oral promise, anyway. Known, maybe, to only one officer. The point is that if you and I couldn't prove it, how the hell can Anita?"

"Exactly. And after all, you and I don't really know it, do we? It was all a speculation from the beginning. A speculation in *your* mind!"

"And how did I behave when this speculation came to me?" Timmy continued eagerly. "What did I do?"

"You told your doubts to Mrs. Emlen. And to Mrs. Ferguson herself. Oh, man, we'll destroy her!"

"It fits like a glove," Timmy went on, shaking his head to indicate that Larry's voice was too loud. "Look. I'm faced with a proposed family arrangement. Everyone's over twenty-one and in favor of it. I distrust it. I say so. I am overruled. George then proceeds to sell his patents at a price that substantiates his own version of the company's small worth. And Anita, hearing a bit of loose gossip from a cousin—even *that's* good, you see? I've been so worried I've even talked to her cousin about it—becomes hysterical. Hell's bells, man, suppose she *proved* a deal between George and Holcombe, could she prove *I* knew of it?"

"Never! Because you didn't."

216

Timmy took a long drink of his beer and wiped the foam from his lips. "I've got to think it through, though," he said more guardedly. "I don't want to hurt anyone. I want to put things back as neatly as I found them. That's all. The case may prove humiliating to Anita, but that I can't help. She brought it on herself. And George may lose the fruits of his dirty deal; on the theory that whoever his pals in Holcombe are, they won't dare pay off now. But that I can't worry about. What about you, Larry? If you act as my lawyer, will Dale ever forgive you?"

"Of course!" Larry cried eagerly. "That's just the point! Dale can't afford to have this case lost. It'll be the making of me. And I need it, too. As you know, the memory of my late lamented father-in-law isn't the asset around the shop that *he* was."

Timmy felt a sudden dizzying pain at the thought of Knox hearing their conversation. He closed his lips tightly and looked down into his beer. "I guess I won't be much of an asset around the shop, either," he said after a moment. "Win, lose or draw. Dale will never forgive me for letting the cat out of the bag. Not that I care. Not that I honestly and truly give a damn."

"But you're wrong again!" Larry protested. "Well, maybe not about his forgiving you, but about your not being an asset. He's going to be scared to death of you. You *know* him, don't forget. All you have to do now is transfer back to corporate work, which is what you like anyway. Everything will be just as it was."

Well, supposing it was, Timmy thought defiantly to himself. Was it too presumptuous to expect it? Was there a moral obligation always to expect the worst from the universe? To insist on punishment or penance? Wasn't it better to be reborn and reborn joyfully, to go back to the family he loved and support them doing the work he loved? Did it *help* matters to be gloomy? "Larry, we're going to win this case!" he exclaimed. "They'll find they've bit off more than they can chew!" And the dusty clouds that had hung over his sky since the telephone call had revealed Knox's death began to roll off on all sides, and a shaft of light, as in a drawing by Gustave Doré, seemed to illuminate the little group of his wife and sons. Well, all right, he thought defiantly, suppose his visions were corny, were they any the less his? If *he* liked them, did anything else matter?

217

15

WHEN ANITA'S lawyer filed her petition in court for a compulsory accounting in the Emlen Trust, alleging that her release was invalid as fraudulently obtained, it created a sensation within the firm of Sheffield, Dale, but little commotion on the outside. The legal world was too used to the routine tautological insults of pleading to do more than shrug. Another hysterical woman with a shyster lawyer—what counsel for trustees had not run across *her* path? Most men professed, if anything, a perfunctory sympathy for Timmy; there were friendly grips on his shoulder at the lunch club, and he was careful to smile at the jocular: "I hear you're a crook, old man." But the uneasy surprise, the suppressed consternation that existed among his partners at so savage an attack by Clarissa Dale's own niece began to seep its way into more public channels when Lolita joined forces with her sister under the respectable auspices of Tyson & Grimes. Everyone knew that Charlie Tyson was not a man to be careless with the word "fraud," particularly when dealing with a partner of Cyrus Sheffield's, and now the case began to be picked up by gossip columnists. The ultimate bombshell, however, was when Mrs. Emlen herself, in a sudden frightened flurry of sails, a panicky, elderly Cleopatra at Actium, discharged the firm that had represented her for forty years and fled from the churning waters under the neutral banner of Helving, Loftus & Bissell. Their answer to Anita's petition, eschewing sides, set forth in a silvery cascade of hand-washing the sorry fact, so long obscured by Mrs. Emlen's own boasting, that she had never read the account or any account; that she had signed it blind; that, in short, she knew nothing whatever of business affairs and that Timmy alone was the responsible trustee. Timmy smiled grimly as he read this, remembering the long sessions in her library where, as she had liked to put it, he had been "instructed in his duties" by his senior trustee.

His position in the firm was now that of a man on probation. Dale, although he made no statement to the effect, would obviously have nothing to do with him until the case was decided. Even his room had been changed, to make less frequent the inevitably embarrassing meetings with the senior partner. And he found that, as he wished to be, he was left to himself. It was not that people consciously avoided him, but it was only natural, with the vague odor of "trouble" hovering around his now inhospitably closed door, that they should not lightly push it open.

Larry, of course, thoroughly enjoyed the whole thing. He enjoyed anything with drama in it. If it was power, even unpopular power, it could still be fun; he had loved inspecting the files and the library under Dale's reorganization, like a reviewing officer, taut and smart. Now he could enjoy his new reputation in the office for self-sacrifice, for identifying himself with the cause of a man so obviously out of the good graces of the senior partner. He could play Eros, escaping the sorrow of Anthony's death by falling on his chief's sword. He would shake his head gravely when people asked him about the case, intimating that it was a dangerous, almost unbeatable frame-up. After so gloomy a prognostication he would only emerge the more brilliant in ultimate victory. He became inscrutable, secretive; Timmy even began to suspect that he might be conferring with Dale on less open but possibly surer methods of winning the case.

"I want to know everything you're doing," Timmy would tell him sharply. *"Everything.* I've got to be sure no one's going to be hurt."

"Nobody's going to be hurt, Tim," Larry would reassure him, as if he were a nervous client who couldn't be told all. "Don't *worry.* Take my word for it. Everything's okay."

It was soothing, anyway, to be home with Ann and the boys. He had the feeling of having returned to the reassuring normalcy of a base camp after an exotic but dangerous safari into a green and yellow tropical land. It would have been more tactful to have been silent about what he had seen and learned there, but half the fun of doing things had always been in telling Ann about them. He would check himself when he saw the hurt flicker in her patiently attentive eyes, but, as she pointed out herself, it was her own fault for being so curious a listener. He even took her to a French restaurant to show how competently he could order and to an art gallery to show off his new taste. He was a bit disappointed in the gallery to discover how much more she knew than he. But with the boys there were no such unexpected moments of superiority. His pleasure with them was unadulterated. It was only when he thought of the case that he had moments of panic.

"Seeing them makes me sick about the idea of things going wrong," he told Ann one night. "Really wrong, I mean."

"But they won't, darling. They can't."

"One's never sure in a lawsuit. It could ruin me, you know. Disbar me, even. Then how would we live?"

"I'm not in the least worried about that," Ann said firmly. "Having you back is the big thing. We'll always make out. I sometimes think you forget how poor we were when we met."

"Yes. But there wasn't any George or Walter then."

When the trial actually started, however, he found that his predominant emotion was the last that he might have anticipated. It was boredom. It seemed only grimly appropriate that the issue of his fiduciary misconduct should be decided in the Hall of Records, a flourishing Victorian misconception of what a Loire château might have looked like, a great dark sanctity of wills and trusts where the voice of the dead was daily heard. In the somber paneled courtroom, with its never-used pink terra-cotta Renaissance fireplaces and its flaring globe lights in ornamented brackets, he tried to think of the proceeding as Larry might be thinking of it, in operatic terms, with himself as Radamès, submitting with a haughty impatience to the cumbersome deliberation of high priests. He picked Radamès, he reflected sardonically, because Radamès had in fact been guilty. But it was no good. Everything seemed unreal, monotonous. Looking around the almost empty chamber, he felt tensity in every face but his own. Ann, sitting in the back, pale and still, intently following the testimony, had given him only a single scared nod. Anita, bolt upright beside her husband in the front row, flashed her little black eyes back and forth between the witness and examining counsel. Mrs. Emlen, behind her, with a black veil, sniffed occasionally. The Dales were conspicuously absent.

The case was proceeding exactly as he and Larry had anticipated. In the morning George Emlen was examined at length by Mr. Floyd, the tall, spare, dry member of Tyson & Grimes who had supplanted Anita's less reputable lawyer, on the subject of what Holcombe Textiles had paid him for the patents. George was laconic, faintly shoulder-shrugging; he tried to convey the impression that what he was undergoing was the kind of treatment that any conscientious brother of such sisters had to expect. His head shook wearily. No, he had been paid nothing more for the patents. No, there had been no concealed advantages. No, he had received no secret promises. Mr. Floyd, for all his subtlety was unable to shake or perturb him, unable, apparently, even to interest him. On cross-examination Larry, after warning him with the utmost solemnity that he was under oath, asked him only a single question. Had he ever discussed the patents with Mr. Colt? George replied emphatically that he had not. He even implied that it would have been none of Mr. Colt's business. The officers of Holcombe who followed him to the stand were equally definite, but more indignant. They scouted the very idea that it was possible to do business in the manner suggested by Mr. Floyd and indicated that it was an imposition to be summoned to court to deny it. Would the plaintiffs, they seemed to imply, be responsible for the cost of their time in being subjected to this miserable fishing expedition?

At the noon recess Larry was jubilant. "They're desperate," he told Timmy over a cafeteria sandwich. "I hear they're even going to put poor old Mrs. Emlen on the stand. Well, I'm ready for her!"

Which, indeed, they proceeded to do when the court reconvened. Mr. Floyd himself assisted her slowly and deferentially to the witness chair, as though to make plain to the impassive surrogate, whose long brown face flickered momentarily with impatience, that this distinguished lady was only by legal necessity a co-defendant and would be treated in every possible way as an ally. She settled herself in the chair with nervous little wriggles in her plump frame and a faint gasping in her throat and reluctantly raised her veil with small, fat, black-gloved hands to uncover eyes that roved the courtroom as if looking for the rack.

Mr. Floyd examined her gently and gently admonished her to raise her voice so that the surrogate could hear her half-whispered answers. She sniffed and sighed and kept raising a silk handkerchief to her small, running nose. Oh, no, she knew nothing about the Emlen companies. Certainly not, she *never* interfered in business things. Why, naturally, she left all that to her son, George, and to her brother-in-law and more recently—here she sighed again—to Mr. Colt whom she had *trusted* so. When Mr. Floyd had finished, Timmy felt Larry spring from the seat beside him.

"You say you never discussed business matters with Mr. Colt, Mrs. Emlen," he began softly enough, as she turned, in a shock of surprise, to this unknown and unannounced young man. "Are you quite sure that you never discussed the transfer of the Emlen Fibre Company to your son?"

"Well, I'm not sure," she faltered. "There were naturally so many things to be discussed."

"May I remind you that you're under oath?" Larry snapped.

Mr. Helving, her lawyer, jumped to his feet. "Your Honor, is there any reason that Mrs. Emlen should be insulted? She is perfectly well aware that she is under oath."

"My client's reputation may be at stake!" Larry exclaimed. "That's at least as important as Mrs. Emlen's sensitivity!"

"Proceed, Mr. Duane," the surrogate said dryly. "The witness has been amply reminded of her oath. If there was any need, in the first place." ·

Larry turned back to Mrs. Emlen. "I suggest that you and Mr. Colt had a full discussion of the question of giving the Fibre Company stock to your son."

"Well, I don't know if it was a 'full' discussion," she said with attempted dignity. "We discussed it, of course."

"I suggest further that Mr. Colt was concerned about the value of the stock."

"Well, he should have been!"

"Should he have? Should he, indeed?" Larry became very dry. "I suggest, then, that you were not in the least concerned. That you told Mr. Colt that George knew what he was doing. That you and your children resented Mr. Colt's implication that there might be anything in the least wrong with what George proposed. That you told Mr. Colt, in short, to mind his own business!"

"But you exaggerate so—"

"Answer me this, Mrs. Emlen," Larry cut in. "Did you or did you not give Mr. Colt to understand, when he brought up the subject of the value of that stock, that it was a matter on which you wanted no further discussion?"

"Well, I suppose I may have given some such impression—"

"Did you or didn't you?"

There was a pause. "Very well then. If you badger me so." She sniffed again. "I suppose I did."

"Thank you, Mrs. Emlen."

As she stepped from the witness stand, pulling down her veil with one hand while she pressed a handkerchief to her nose with the other, Timmy froze to hear Mr. Floyd call: "Mrs. Shallcross." He turned desperately to Larry as the latter returned to his seat. "You didn't tell me they were going to call Eileen!"

"Don't worry, Tim," Larry said, grasping his elbow. "Don't worry, I tell you. It's going to be *all right*."

"You mean you know what she's going to say? You've talked to her? *When?*"

Larry raised his finger to his lips. "Leave it to old Larry, will you? Look, here she comes."

Timmy turned in anguish as Eileen brushed past them to the stand. She must have been sitting directly behind as he had not seen her. She was wearing a smart black suit and a tiny black beret; she walked with a swift, ordered self-possession to the witness chair and took her oath in a low, serious voice. When she was seated, she looked either at Mr. Floyd or down at her feet, never at the courtroom.

"Mrs. Shallcross," Mr. Floyd began politely enough, "you are a cousin, I believe, of Mrs. Anita Ferguson?"

"Yes. A first cousin."

"Do you remember that you had a conversation with her last February at the apartment of your aunt, Mrs. Emlen?"

"I do."

"Did you advise her at that time not to consent to the transfer of the Emlen Fibre Company to her brother?"

"Not in so many words."

"What did you advise her?"

"I told her that I had heard about the proposed transfer to George."

"From whom had you heard this?"

"From Mr. Colt."

"Mr. Colt is a friend of yours?"

"Oh, yes." She gave her examiner a small, friendly smile. "Mr. Colt is practically a member of the family. He's a partner of my stepfather's."

Mr. Floyd paused a moment, as if to swallow. Damn his hide! Timmy thought savagely. "Is Mr. Colt in the habit of discussing with you the trusts of which he's a fiduciary?"

"Certainly not," she retorted, instantly reacting to his hostile note. "But these trusts were different. They were family matters. Mr. Colt was afraid that if he gave Mrs. Ferguson what she wanted, she might not be getting her full share."

"That is not relevant," Mr. Floyd snapped. "That is for the court to determine. I must ask you to confine your answers to the questions asked."

"I was trying to," Eileen replied with spirit. "But you were implying that he was indiscreet. He wasn't!"

"Very well, very well. What exactly *did* you tell Mrs. Ferguson?"

"I told her not to give up the Fibre stock. I told her to keep her third."

Mr. Floyd pounced on it. "Did you have any reason to believe it had greater value than Mrs. Ferguson knew?"

"No. But how could one tell? It was a family company."

"Exactly. A family company. And why were you so anxious that Mrs. Ferguson should keep her shares of a family company?"

"Because Anita—Mrs. Ferguson, I mean—has never shown any responsibility about family things." Eileen had assumed a grave, almost maternal tone. "I wanted her to keep her share and take an interest in it. Not just grab the other stocks and bonds and sell them to raise money for her husband."

There was an immediate stir from Anita's corner, and Timmy could see that Hank was trying to keep his furious wife from interrupting the proceedings.

"Let me ask you something else, Mrs. Shallcross," Mr. Floyd continued with a brief, apprehensive glance in the direction of his clients. "Wasn't this a rather unusual conversation for two ladies to be having at a party?"

"In *my* family?" Eileen smiled again. "Not in the least, I'm afraid. We're very serious about money matters."

"Even at parties?"

"Even at parties. It's only at parties that we get together."

"Thank you, Mrs. Shallcross. No more questions."

Larry rose immediately to say that he would not re-examine. As he sat down Timmy plucked his arm furiously. "You made her do that!" he whispered hoarsely. "You made her perjure herself!"

"Will you shut up?" Larry hissed.

"You did!"

"Pull yourself together, will you? I didn't do any such thing. If you must know, she came to me herself. She didn't want you to know, but—"

"She came to *you!*"

"She wanted to help you. What the hell? Can you blame her for that?"

"Mr. Colt!" Mr. Floyd called.

"Take hold of yourself, kid," Larry murmured, squeezing his elbow. "Go to it now. It's in the bag!"

Timmy walked in a daze to the witness chair and mechanically took the oath. He looked over to where Eileen had been sitting, but she had already left the courtroom. He looked at Ann, at Mrs. Emlen, at Anita, but they seemed figures in a play. Even Ann. There was nothing real for the moment but what Larry had said.

"As a member of your firm, Mr. Colt," Mr. Floyd began, coming straight to the point, "you had at least a working idea of the setup at Holcombe Textiles?"

"Yes." He concentrated, blinking, on what this strange man said. "I frequently worked on their matters."

"And as a trustee of the Emlen trust, I assume you were familiar with the affairs of the Emlen Fibre Company?"

"That is correct."

"And you had access, either as counsel to Holcombe or as a trustee under the Emlen will, to the files of both companies?"

"I did," Timmy replied, nodding.

"Would it be going too far, Mr. Colt, to say that you were in a unique position to determine whether or not the Fibre Company possessed any assets of particular value to Holcombe?"

"I was certainly in a position to make such a determination."

Mr. Floyd paused, studying him carefully. "Now tell me this, Mr. Colt. When you proposed to make a distribution of the Emlen trust, giving shares of one company to one beneficiary and those of another to another, instead of dividing each kind of stock equally, was it not your special duty to see that each beneficiary got an equal portion of the whole?"

"It was."

"And dealing with closely held stock like that of the Fibre Company, whose value was, to say the least, uncertain, was it not your duty to make a careful investigation of its assets and liabilities?"

"It was."

"And did you make such an investigation?"

"I did."

"Did you investigate its list of patents?"

"I did."

"And did you not know," Mr. Floyd demanded, now in a rising tone, "that three of these patents were substantially indispensable to a particular project of Holcombe's? A favorite project?"

"I did."

There was an immediate rustle through the courtroom. Timmy found himself staring at the veil-muffled face of his

225

fellow trustee. She was raising a handkerchief again sniffingly to her nose. Even Mrs. Emlen, not understanding, could sense catastrophe. Then he looked back at Mr. Floyd who stood silent, his eyes fixed on him, manifestly taken aback for all his courtroom poise. Moving gingerly, incredulously, fearing a trap, he pressed cautiously on.

"And did you not also know that George Emlen, to whom you planned to distribute the Fibre stock, was involved in business relations with Holcombe?"

"I knew it."

"Is it possible," Mr. Floyd exclaimed, pushing forward in his excitement now, reckless of traps, "that it did not occur to you there was a special advantage to George Emlen in your proposed distribution of the trust?"

Timmy had a sudden picture in his mind of the guns of his old destroyer, raised and trained, of planes coming in low over a yellow sea, of the endless moment before the order to fire. He hesitated.

"Yes, it occurred to me," he heard himself say in the same level tone. "I can't say that I didn't think of it."

"And did you convey your suspicions to your co-trustee? Or to the plaintiffs?"

"In general terms, yes."

"Did you see fit to tell them about the patents?"

"No. I did not."

Mr. Floyd turned around and walked one or two steps away from the witness chair. The rising elation in his countenance had faded already; his half-shrug conveyed a faint disgust. It was all very well to win; it was what the game was about, in fact, but not if one's opponent wouldn't play. Who enjoyed a suicide?

"Would you mind telling the court," he asked in a suddenly soft, weary tone, turning back to Timmy, "why you failed to act on your intuition? Why you deliberately proceeded, without proper warning to your co-trustee or the plaintiffs, to distribute the Fibre stock to the one beneficiary who was in the best position to know of its unique value to Holcombe?"

Timmy turned now to face Ann and her intent, staring eyes. "Because I was more interested in the welfare of Holcombe," he said in a clear voice. "Because I neglected my trust."

In the buzz that followed, he saw Ann cover her face with her hands. Mr. Floyd hurried over to the table to consult his fellow counsel. While they whispered excitedly, the Surrogate turned to Timmy. "Do you mean to tell this court, Mr.

226

Colt," he asked incredulously, "that you *deliberately* made an unequal distribution of trust assets?"

"I'm under oath, Your Honor."

"Yes, I see." The Surrogate coughed and looked down at his papers. "Your candor, no doubt, does you credit. But I shall still have to refer the matter to the Grievance Committee. Have you nothing to say in extenuation?"

"Nothing, Your Honor."

"I don't know what more there is to be said, Mr. Floyd," the Surrogate continued dryly. "The case is unprecedented in my experience. Do you wish to cross-examine, Mr. Duane?"

"No questions, Your Honor," Larry said sullenly.

"We may as well proceed with the question of how far the co-trustee is responsible for this," the Surrogate was saying as Timmy left the stand. "And I shall want to examine Mr. Emlen myself on the question of the patent profits. Even if there weren't any, as he states, it is manifest that the trustees gave him a more valuable asset than they gave his sisters. For this they must stand responsible."

Outside the courtroom Timmy heard a step behind him and turned. It was Larry, and there were tears in his eyes.

"I'm sorry," Timmy murmured.

"I hope you enjoyed your scene!" Larry cried scathingly. "Of course you never thought what this might mean to me, did you?"

"I know. Dale counted on you."

"I hope they disbar you, you son of a bitch!" Larry shouted. "I hope they do!" he almost screamed as Timmy turned and walked away.

16

FLORENCE EMLEN was opening her new house on Long Island with a supper dance. It was a small octagonal Georgian white brick building with two greenhouses as wings and an oblong garden pool in back around which small tables and rented gilt chairs were tastefully arranged. Beyond was a marquee with a red canvas cover under which the guests were dancing. Japanese lanterns abounded. It had not been, of course, that Florence had really needed a new house. She had, in addition to her city brownstone, a dark weather-beaten pile of shingle on the Southampton dunes and a Spanish convent in Palm Beach. But David had persuaded her to look on these as drafty barns out of keeping with the times. Her real need, he had pointed out, was for a "folie," a "Trianon," that could be used for weekends and run on a shoestring. And led along tightly in the noose of his irresistible arguments, she had proceeded to construct a fourth house on the ostensible grounds of economy.

"I could always retire here if I couldn't run the house in town," she told Eileen for perhaps the dozenth time. "That's the point I make to George. He's been so nasty about it. Do you know he wouldn't even come tonight?" They were standing away from the guests by the buffet. Eileen, in lavender and white, with no jewelry looked taller and pale beside her short aunt. "How do you think the party's going?"

She looked over the lawn at the white coats and white shoulders in the dim glare of the lanterns and the heads, old heads so many of them, gold, purple, silver, orange. Beyond lay the damp, cricket-sounding woods. She wondered if there would ever be an end of parties for her. "All right," she said.

"Really all right?"

"Yes, really."

"Oh, good." Florence sighed in relief. "It makes me feel that everything's back to normal again. After all that wicked young man did to us."

"Please, Aunt Florence," Eileen closed her eyes for a moment. "You know I don't think he's a wicked young man."

"After what he did to *me?* Do you know Anita wants me surcharged? My own daughter! My own flesh and blood!"

"Oh, Anita." Eileen shrugged.

"And what about poor Sheridan? Whom he's practically driven into a nervous breakdown. And what about yourself, my dear? I suppose you think he's used *you* well?"

"That's my affair," Eileen said bleakly. She saw David, immaculate in a white coat and red tie, coming across the lawn to greet them. She had almost given him up, for it was well after midnight. He moved swiftly, in his graceful, feline, defiant way, as if aware of the threat of concealed attack.

228

"Dear Florence," he said to her aunt in his mocking tone, "it's a temple of beauty. Eileen, my dear, you look a vision."

"You're late," Florence reproved him. "Shockingly late. Your punishment is to dance with me."

Eileen saw in the flicker of his eye towards her that he had a message, but her aunt led him off to the marquee. Going back to the house to be alone, thinking she might even escape to her room, she encountered her stepfather in the empty parlor. He was highly agitated.

"He's here!" he cried when he saw her. "He's actually here at this party!"

"Who?"

"Colt! Did you bring him?"

"No." She reflected, suddenly breathless. "David must have. It would be like David."

"Well, of all the God damn nerve! That little fairy! I'm going to speak to Florence and have them both thrown out!"

"Interfere between Aunt Florence and her favorite decorator?" Eileen, thinking rapidly, even managed a smile. "You're a braver man than I thought, Sheridan."

Dale stared at her, his breath coming in pants. "Maybe you're right. Maybe I'd better not speak to her. But I'm certainly leaving myself. This very minute."

"With Mummy?"

"You know she won't ever leave a party. I asked her, but she won't. 'You always make mountains out of molehills,' she said. Mountains out of molehills! My God, Eileen, after what I've been through!"

"Parties have always come first with Mummy," she said with a shrug. "Surely this is nothing new?"

"I know." He sighed, turning away from her. "God knows, I know. I should be resigned to it by now. But life catches up with us, Eileen. When I married your mother, I thought I understood all about that side of her and that I'd never mind it. Well, I did understand, but I *do* mind. We've been married eighteen years. Eighteen bloody years, and she won't give up one miserable party if I ask her."

"She's wholly consistent. She always has been."

Walking away down the hall back to the party, she felt no pity for him. It was not, any more than with others who had wronged her, that she condemned him, even for destroying Timmy. This she accepted as the unsurprising act of an unsurprising stepfather. But it was too late to go along with his belated greed for sympathy, for kindness, for all the things he had turned a lifetime's back on. It was unfair to her, but worse, it was unfair to himself. He could finish his game out as he had started it; that, at least, would not degrade them. Crossing the lawn to the marquee, she walked slowly around it, staring through the crowd to find Timmy. There was a defiant, a rather reckless satisfaction in making no effort to conceal her preoccupation. She entertained sudden, irresponsible fantasies; that Ann had left him, that he had come back to her, that they would flee together into the night and make a new wonderful life far from Emlens and Dales. Her heart seemed to stop when she found him at last, standing alone on the other side of the lawn, a drink in hand, looking oddly young and solemn in his dinner jacket. He came up immediately when he saw her.

"I quite understand if you don't want to speak to me," he said abruptly. "But would you listen? Please? Just for a moment?"

She stared. "When have I not?"

"I crashed the party."

Even at that moment she could smile. He was as belligerent as a small angry boy. "Aunt Florence will be so flattered. No one ever crashes her parties. I must tell her."

He caught her hand roughly. "I had to talk to you. I *had* to. When David said he was coming tonight, I made him take me. He let me out halfway up the drive, and I came in through the back."

"That wasn't necessary," she said, gently disengaging her hand. "Where is Ann? Did you bring her, too?"

"I haven't seen her since the trial."

Her heart jumped. "You mean she's left you?"

"Oh, no, she's called me every day. I've been staying with David. She's begged me to come back. But I couldn't see her, Eileen!" He stamped his foot. "Can you understand that? I couldn't see her!"

"Because she wouldn't understand?"

"Because she *would* understand!" he cried. "Because she's always understood. Because she'd forgive me again. Even after what I've done to her and the boys!"

Her hope sank. "Is it so terrible to be forgiven?"

"Yes! Before one's ready. I hope you despise me, Eileen. As I despise myself!"

"Despise you? Why?"

"For letting you hold the bag that day in court. Didn't you?"

"No." She reflected for a moment. "I thought it was rather beautiful, as a matter of fact. Your sitting there and telling the truth. When nothing else in the world could have lost your case. I'm sure the judge was impressed."

"But I didn't do it for the judge!" he exclaimed violently. "Judges aren't interested in that kind of truth. They expect people to be truthful about what they've done. Not *why* they've done it. I deserve anything I get."

"Oh, poor boy, what will it be?"

"That doesn't matter now. What matters is my reason."

"Oh? And what was your reason?"

"That I couldn't stand it. Your telling lies for me."

"Oh, Timmy, it wasn't *that* hard!" She turned away to hide her disappointment. "You don't know about women!"

"I know about *you*."

She shook her head quickly. "There was Anita, don't forget. And my pleasure at getting back at her."

"That meant nothing to you!" he insisted heatedly. "You *despised* what I did about that Fibre Company. From the very first moment I told you! You pretended not to, but you did. And then you got involved in the whole dirty deal because you wanted to save me. You got up in court and lied for me. You violated every natural sensitivity you had. And why? Because you loved me!"

So this was to be it. His talk of love. Her love. At Aunt Florence's "Trianon" with the party under the marquee looking small and bunched up from across the lawn, a tight, rather desperate circle of color and muted sound. She turned away as she felt her tears. "You can't have only learned from that that I love you."

"No. I think I understood you the night we first met. And I think I understand you now. But in my fantasy you had to be heartless, superficial, worldly. You *had* to be!"

"Why do you tell me this?"

"Because I owe it to you."

"You owe me nothing!" she cried in sudden pain. "If you can't tell me that you love me, why tell me anything at all? That's all I want. You know it's all I want!"

He looked away, embarrassed. "You're well rid of me," he muttered. "I shan't be bothering you again. Even as a gate crasher."

"Oh, Timmy." She raised her hands to her eyes. "Why couldn't I have met you first? Why couldn't you have come to tutor me instead of the Knox girls? Why couldn't I have been the girl who couldn't learn economics? Oh, but that's it, isn't it? I never needed to be tutored in anything! And, of course, you love Ann. That's the whole thing." He plunged his hands in his pockets and stared at the grass. "I know I'm behaving badly," she continued bitterly, "but I can't help it. You may have to leave me, but I won't make it easy for you. I love you, Timmy. You'll have to live with that." Putting her hands suddenly on his shoulders she kissed him on the lips. "There! I hope Aunt Florence saw me. Now go home to Ann. Good-by, darling. I'll be good from now on. Don't worry."

"Eileen," he said desperately. "Eileen, listen to me—"

"No, no, that's enough. Do you want me to bawl?"

"But I can't bear to have you think—"

"Am I intruding?" David demanded cheerfully, appearing from nowhere. "I've brought Timmy a scotch."

"I'll take it," she said quickly. "Timmy can get another."

"You?" David's eyes were wide with mock surprise. "Something must have happened if you've turned to whiskey."

"You always pigeonhole people, David," she said impatiently, taking the glass. "I have my whiskey nights."

"David, can we see you a bit later?" Timmy asked irritably. "We were having a personal talk."

"My dear boy, don't put it that way. 'Personal' is so illbred. Say: 'Will you excuse me? There's something I've got to say to Eileen.'"

"There's something he *has* just said to Eileen," she interrupted firmly. "Something that Eileen has answered, too. We've finished our 'personal' talk, David. You can stay."

"Eileen!" Timmy protested. "You know we haven't finished!"

"Oh, but we have, dear. It's just what we have done. Why don't you get yourself a drink? I'm afraid I've taken yours."

"Won't you even hear me out?"

"Please, Timmy!" She raised a hand again to her eyes. "I'm too tired. I honestly and truly am. I'm going to bed. But don't feel you have to go out the back way. I'll square it with Aunt Florence. And stay as long as you like."

He looked at her for a heavy moment and then turned abruptly on his heel and strode off to the bar.

"Bravo!" David applauded. "Quite a little scene."

"Oh, David, shut up," she retorted. "And find us a table. I've got to sit down." By the end of the pool they found two deserted chairs. "My Grandmother Polhemus always told me that ladies never intrude where they're not welcome," she said sadly. "That ladies let go gracefully. I certainly have not been much of a lady tonight."

"But you sent him away. I heard you."

"Yes, I sent him away." She nodded mournfully. "But I did it bitchily. Tearfully. I made him feel as badly as I could. Oh, if I'd been a lady, I'd have made it so easy for him. I'd have seen his desire to go and tactfully dismissed him. I'd even have made believe that I was just the tiniest bit bored. That I was too wedded to all of this;" here she made a sweeping gesture to take in the pool, the marquee; "to give it up for a man in disgrace. A man with no money."

David's smile, maintained throughout, had become slightly stale. "You don't think you might be? The tiniest bit?"

She took a long sip of her drink and placed the glass carefully on the ground at her feet. He could bear anything but the assumption in another that a feeling had been experienced. "You mean he was right," she said dryly. "That I only want him with parties."

"Well, you don't have to put it quite that way," he demurred, warned, perhaps, by the glint in her eye. "But do you really think he'd be as much fun if he wasn't a refreshing change at your Aunt Florence's? Let's face it, dear. You and I both adore Timmy, but we can still admit he's a dull boy."

So even David thought she minded dullness. Even he judged her as Timmy had once judged her. As she had made them both judge her. And maybe they were right. Maybe everyone was right. It was impossible to know everything about oneself. But against the very idea of it her whole being now revolted. There had to be limits to self-analysis, to rationalism, to toleration of David's pretended perception of herself. It might be indecent to despise oneself, to tear down the last shred of natural vanity. There had to be an end somewhere to her passivity, her amiability to a world whose professed admiration of her was so full of hostility.

"Who do you think you are, David?" she asked coldly. "Some little Roman Emperor, all in purple, sitting up in the imperial box and watching the gladiators fight?"

"The idea has charm, I confess."

"You've affected unkindness too long," she continued. "Now you've become unkind. You've played at being cynical and heartless. You fancied it rather becoming. You're like the child in the nursery tale who was making faces when the wind changed. Now you're stuck with it."

He smiled again his brightest smile, but there was noticeable effort in it. "At least it was a role that became me," he said dryly. "I think I should warn you, you're not the type."

"It doesn't matter," she said, getting up. "With the amount of instruction I've had, I should excel."

She went into the house and up the stairs, past couples talking on the steps, past the door where two ladies, sitting on a big bed, were talking with passionate earnestness, to her own room. Closing the door she sank into the chair before her triple mirror and surveyed the blank resignation of her own pale countenance. Mechanically, she took off an earring.

"Eileen! Are you there?"

Before she could even answer the door had opened and her mother was upon her. "Darling, I've got to talk to you!"

"Mummy, I'm dead. Can we talk in the morning?"

"That's no way to treat your mother," Clarissa reproved her, sitting down, uninvited, on her bed. "Besides, you couldn't sleep anyway with that noise outside."

Eileen looked helplessly at Clarissa's troubled reflection in the glass before her. "What is it, then?"

"It's about Sheridan," her mother started immediately. "He's just made the most appalling scene. My dear, you can't imagine. He blustered about loyalty and parties and Timmy Colt and God knows what. He *demanded* that I leave right now! What do you suppose has got into him? Has he been drinking? He never behaved that way in his life!"

"You haven't known him all his life," Eileen pointed out, brushing her hair. "I'd go if I were you."

"But I *like* this party!" Clarissa declared petulantly. "And it's my own sister's housewarming. Why did Timmy have to come anyway? He couldn't have been invited, could he? And he must *know* how Sheridan hates to see him!"

"I suppose it's just possible he doesn't care."

"Doesn't care! He must be very bold, that young man!"

"Really, Mother, you're fantastic," Eileen retorted, turning around. "Do you honestly think, after the way Sheridan fired him out of the firm, that Timmy should still care if he spoils a party for him?"

Clarissa stared in perplexity at her incomprehensible child. "Well, we can't go on this way," she said decisively. "It's too much of you to expect. It's too hard on Sheridan. You'll have to give him up! That's all there is to it!"

Eileen stopped her brushing. "Sheridan?"

"Don't be absurd! Timmy. If he's not enough of a gentleman to avoid embarrassing Sheridan on social occasions, then this thing between you and him must stop."

234

Eileen turned around, intrigued, to watch her mother's expression of attempted firmness. "And if I don't agree?"

"Well, I don't very well see how you *can* disagree while you're living in my home. After all, it isn't as if I ever asked you to give up things. I think you'll agree I've been a most undemanding parent."

"All you ask is a lover!" Eileen started to laugh at first gently, then almost uncontrollably. "All you ask in return for the loan of your purse is that I give up a lover! You wouldn't ask me to give up a dinner or a weekend or even a good game of Canasta, would you? Oh, no! Because you're not a demanding parent, are you? But a lover! How could I be so selfish as not to give up one poor lover?"

Clarissa glanced nervously to see if the door was safely closed. Her lips were pursed in distaste. "You're being very crude, Eileen. I must say, it's not like you."

"Well, I won't give him up!" Eileen exclaimed defiantly. "Whether or not he's mine to give, I won't. Not for Sheridan, anyway. Or for you. And if you think I owe you anything more than I've given you, I'll be glad to move out of your house! I've lived up to my bargain. Ask Sheridan!"

Clarissa's face was a mask of horrified surprise. "How will you live?"

"I don't care! As long as I'm honest!"

There was a moment's pause, as she faced her mother down, and then the latter broke. Never before had Clarissa been so questioned and badgered; it was as if all the shiny faucets that continually poured hot consoling water into the bathtub of her complacency had turned suddenly into writhing, scalding hoses, uncontrolled.

"I don't know what I've done to deserve this," she sobbed, her head in her hands. "Your carrying on with a man who wants to destroy Sheridan. And threatening to leave me into the bargain!" She looked up, almost in panic. "Oh, Eileen, you don't know what my life has been since this business about Florence's trust. You can't imagine how it has hit Sheridan. He suspects everyone of suspecting him. He can't sleep at night. Do you know what he told me just now? That he'd *leave* me if I didn't come home! Me! After all I've done for him! The position I've given him! Oh, Eileen, if you desert me now, I don't know *what* will happen!"

Eileen shook her head sadly as she watched that weeping figure. Victory had come too quickly not to be defeat. David, Clarissa, even Sheridan, they were cardboard figures who fell over at the first push. If only she had done it in the days gone by when they could have fallen on someone besides herself. Going over to her mother now, she put an arm around her shoulders and sat beside her in silent commiseration. But it was mostly commiseration for herself. For she would stay on with Clarissa and Sheridan now; that was inevitable by the very scene she had forced. There would be more parties and more weekends; she closed her eyes before the vista of people, thousands of them, holding drinks and laughing. Laughing perfunctory laughs. And somewhere, maybe, if she waited patiently, in that large Italian room, she would see at the door another pale face and dark eyes that would flicker away and then back to meet hers and a man who at last would not draw away resentfully from everything that she reached out her arms to give him.

Timmy stayed on at the party until long after daybreak. Nobody seemed to care that he was there, and as David refused to leave, he was marooned. He drank what seemed to him a very large quantity and talked to all sorts of people he had never met before, but it never seemed to him that he was getting any drunker, even when he failed to recognize someone with whom he had been exchanging the most intimate confidence fifteen minutes before on the dance floor. At six o'clock, when there was only a rather frayed little group left of the party, Mrs. Emlen having gone to bed, David, who himself looked a bit crumpled, suggested that they return to town.

"I think I'll go and see Ann," Timmy said.

"Ann? Is she down here?"

"At Mrs. Knox's." Timmy waved vaguely.

"Do you think they'll be particularly pleased to see you at this hour?" David surveyed him quizzically. "Maybe they will, at that. Maybe it would be rather romantic, your stumbling in on them, the world in ashes. Redeemed."

"But you think I should go back to her, don't you, David?" he insisted. "Really? Haven't you always?"

"I?" David turned away, impatiently. "Certainly not."

"You think it's better than Eileen?"

"I think it's better than Eileen, yes," he retorted. "Better than the Dales and your silly law firm and all those ridiculous parties and clients. I don't think it's better than life. Better than the whole world. Why don't we take a year off, Timmy? You're out of a job, anyway. I have some money. Why don't we damn it all and cruise in the Greek Islands and go to India and paint in Indo China? I mean it. We live all our lives and see nothing. Feel nothing. How about it, Timmy? Shall we explore the universe? You're the one friend I could do it with. You have no preconceptions."

"Sure, I'll explore the universe with you, David. But on one condition. That I can leave myself behind."

David reached in his pocket and took out the keys to his car. "Take it," he said brusquely. "And go see your Ann. I'll catch a ride back with one of the others. I'm sick of my own involvement. With all of you."

Timmy, speeding down the empty highway in David's red Jaguar, felt light headed as never before. When he turned in the drive of the former Knox place where the widow now occupied the renovated superintendent's cottage, he had a giddy sense of fleets of boats burning behind him. He met Mrs. Knox in her dressing gown, silently, rather grimly questioning, behind the screen door. She must have seen him drive in and park.

"I'll get Ann," she said briefly, when she had determined that he was not drunk. "You can sit out in the garden."

Ann was dressed when she came down. She looked very grave and frightened. She said nothing at first, and he followed her out to a wooden bench behind the house.

"You've been to a party?" she asked.

"So it would appear."

"With Eileen?"

"She was there." He shrugged. "I wasn't with her."

"Was it a nice party?"

He almost laughed at her nervous show of good manners. "I'm not drunk, Ann. I should be, but I'm not. Really."

"Is that what you came to tell me?"

"No."

"What then?"

"I came to tell you something quite different."

"That you want to marry Eileen!" Her eyes were wide with a sudden, almost shocking panic. He looked at her for a moment, startled.

"Why no," he said finally, in a mild, rather reasonable tone, as if to a question not hitherto considered. "I don't think my qualifications as a son-in-law to the Dales have been exactly enhanced by recent events. Do you?"

"Would *she* care?"

"She'd never admit it. Even to herself." He paused to reflect and then nodded. "But, yes," he lied. "She'd care."

"Too much?"

"Enough." He shrugged.

"Timmy, what is it then?" she begged him. "What have you come to tell me?"

"I came to tell you that I'd thought it out," he said carefully. "That I was free of myself. That we could have a new life together. That's what I *came* to tell you."

"Oh." She was barely audible now. "And now we can't?"

"I thought I had played my little scene in court of my own free will," he said with rising bitterness. "That it was *my* decision. As a sort of reparation to Eileen. I thought *if* it was that, I would not be ashamed to come back to you. But if it was self-destruction, self-indulgence, the thing we talked about once, if I had ruined myself and you and the boys for my own selfishness, then I didn't know how to face you."

"But it wasn't that!" she cried. "I know it wasn't!"

He stared. "How?"

"Because I saw the expression on your face," she said slowly, as if searching in her mind to bring it back. "The way you looked at me from the witness chair. I can't describe it, but it wasn't defiance. That I'm sure of. It couldn't have been defiance. Oh, Timmy," she said, clutching his hands, "I'm glad!"

"It makes that much difference? To *you?*"

"No, of course not. Women don't care about those things the way men do. It's you I care about. But I'm not so far gone that I can't be proud of a husband who'll throw up a career rather than perjure himself."

"Like little George Washington and the cherry tree?"

"Timmy!" Her eyes were indignant now. "I won't let you talk that way! You've done something that only one in a thousand would have the guts to do. I won't have you belittle it!"

"How can a motive make all that difference, Ann? The same act and two motives?"

"You know how!"

"I wonder if I do." He felt deflated. The damp chill of the early morning was wearing off; it was going to be a hot day. Rubbing his cheek, he realized that he needed a shave. "What an incredible couple we are," he continued in a more reflective tone. "Who would believe in us, really? It takes a kind of genius to mess up two lives the way we have, when you come to think of it. I guess we must get a kind of bang out of it. Putting on our own tragedy and rushing for front row seats."

"If there's a bang to it," she demurred, "I know I've never felt it."

"David was right," he went on. "He knew I thought it would be dramatic to come back to you like this. Breaking away at dawn from a brilliant party, half intoxicated, ruined. The thought was elating. But I don't feel that way now. I feel sober. Realistic. I'm wondering how I'm going to support you and the boys."

"Oh, darling. Will they disbar you?"

"Probably not. Because I wasn't paid anything to turn that company over to George. Or even promised anything. I'm told the committee may regard it as a quixotic breach of trust and only censure me. But it's not going to make it any easier to get a job."

"Timmy." She leaned down to hide her tears. "Timmy, I don't mind anything if you can believe in yourself. If you can give yourself credit for what you did."

"Aren't you asking rather a lot? To know one's own motives? Oh, I thought I did. Sure. I was even drunk with it. But now, in the early morning, with the future as clear and grey as it is—"

"Only this once!" she begged him. "Just believe it this once. Of course, we're complicated, and our motives aren't clear. But there are still moments, Timmy. Moments above the damn subconscious. Like the moment when you told that judge the truth!"

"I was sentimental, Ann," he said brusquely. "How do we know it wasn't ecstasy? The top of my jag!"

"Because I won't let it be!" she exclaimed. "You've got to hang on to something. And that was truth!"

He shrugged. "A kind of truth. A *willed* truth."

"I don't care!" she said defiantly. "It's something we can build on!"

"*You* can build on it," he said. "You can build on anything if you have to. Most women can. Perhaps it's their strength. Not to be afraid of wishful thinking."

"Can't you build on it, too?"

"I've told you before. That doesn't really matter. If you can, it's enough for both of us." He took out his handkerchief, wrapped it neatly around his forefinger and dried away the tears carefully from under her eyes. "I'll see it your way, Ann. Fundamentally, I always have."

"But if you can face yourself, or yourself as you choose to see it, in the worst light," she protested desperately, "maybe I should, too. What about me? When I made you apologize to George Emlen, mightn't it have been to destroy you? How do I know that I haven't always hated you? For the way I

239

knew I'd suffer if you ever left me? Oh, Timmy!" She leaned forward and put her hands on his shoulders to stare wildly into his eyes. "We know each other so little! How do I know I haven't always resented your good looks and your charm and your brains? And the contrast that you've offered to me!"

But in answering her stare he suddenly laughed, and she fell forward, again in tears, on his shoulder just as George and Walter, having heard his voice, came rushing happily from the house to greet him. They wanted to know all about the picture that they had seen of him in the newspapers, coming out of a courthouse, under the mysterious black headline: "Trust Revelations."